S.A. Hogan

The
Death
Tax

Addison & Highsmith

Addison & Highsmith Publishers

Las Vegas ◊ Chicago ◊ Palm Beach

Published in the United States of America by
Histria Books
7181 N. Hualapai Way, Ste. 130-86
Las Vegas, NV 89166 USA
HistriaBooks.com

Addison & Highsmith is an imprint of Histria Books. Titles published under the imprints of Histria Books are distributed worldwide.

This work of fiction contains graphic language, violence, gore, brutality, and sexual violence, including racial epithets used in historical context.

Library of Congress Control Number: 2021953421

ISBN 978-1-59211-141-1 (hardcover)
ISBN 978-1-59211-286-9 (softbound)
ISBN 978-1-59211-290-6 (eBook)

The
Death
Tax

"Few are guilty but all are responsible. Indifference to evil is more insidious than evil itself."

— Rabbi Abraham Heschel

"There are a thousand hacking at the branches of evil to one who is striking at the root."

— Henry David Thoreau

"You may choose to look the other way but you can never say again that you did not know."

— William Wilberforce

"I believe that unarmed truth and unconditional love will have the final word in reality. This is why right, temporarily defeated, is stronger than evil triumphant."

— Dr. Martin Luther King, Jr.

"All it takes for the triumph of evil is for good men to stand by and do nothing"

— Edmund Burke

To eight-year-old Maelys de Araujo, whose body was found six months after she was abducted from a wedding reception in Pont-de-Beauvoisin, France. Having prayed for this little angel's safe return to no avail, I feel as if I have lost my daughter, joining her family in grieving her loss.

To my mother and fellow author Judith Ann Hogan ('*Shrooms*; *The Shade*), whose first book inspired mine.

In loving memory of Donald R. Schuster of Richmond Heights MO, my Replacement Dad.

Chapter I

Wanda Smith smiled as she gazed at the hummingbird feeding outside her window. She was an early riser and, though the sun had yet to rise, the bird's plumage — red or green depending on how the light caught it — added a splash of color to a watery backdrop indistinguishable from the sky this time of day. Watching the hummingbirds feed was a comforting ritual, strange given what had happened eight years ago. Despite the violent jostling of as many as half a dozen of them, watching them feed was a chance to confront these creatures and somehow be at peace with them; indeed, it was part of the healing process. Nowadays, she was able to convince herself that what had happened was a fluke, courtesy of the global warming phenomenon nearly everyone was saying was turning the laws of nature on their collective ear.

Another hummingbird entered the scene, and even through the glass she could hear the buzzing of their wings. Lots of people fed the hummingbirds at Lake Tanaka, her neighbors marveling that her feeder should get so much more traffic than theirs, to the point she was filling it every night. The reason was simple enough: While they did the usual four-parts-water-to-one-part-sugar, her ratio was two-to-one. While hummingbirds needed insects for protein, it was nectar (including in manmade form) that gave them the carbs necessary to maintain a metabolism so voracious as to make starvation seem imminent. Thus, the ferocious battles that raged around the feeder, she supposed. She thought about getting more than one feeder, but more than one made it a commitment. It owned you, just as Thoreau had warned about the plight of too many possessions in *Walden Pond*. She also preferred a single feeder for purely selfish reasons: It made for better entertainment as she watched the show in her robe and slippers, drinking coffee mixed with chocolate malt powder.

A third hummingbird entered the scene, dive-bombing the first one as a smudge of pink smeared the horizon. Many told her she had the best view on the lake, and she couldn't disagree. Her house faced slightly southwest, affording her glimpses of both the sunrise and sunset from her window, a near-panorama from her deck. Then there was the swimming platform forty yards out, crawling with kids in the summer, with an unimpeded view of the dam and the crowns of trees peeking above it. Given the right attitude, mornings like these gave her a pleasant feeling of solitude. The day's first precious half-hour: before the machinations of breakfast and preparations for her half-days at the used clothing store on Mondays, Wednesdays, and Fridays. Not that she needed the money. Between Social Security and her pension from the care center and Roy's railroad pension, she had plenty. Rather, it was the sense of purpose that so many of her retired friends lacked. As much as anything, the job was a way to escape their griping, the disproportionate significance medical problems had taken on in their lives — as if living had become an endurance race, with an absurd measure of pride taken in surviving the blows it dished out.

When she didn't have the right attitude, such mornings were tinged with melancholy and regret, usually involving memories of her husband. Roy going past in the boat with his buddy Ambrose, cheerfully shrugging his shoulders and shouting that once again they'd caught more beers than fish on this hundred-acre lake. Roy chugging up the hill with the mower only to swing it around and go back down; "When I need a ridin' mower for this little yard it's time to pack it in," he'd say, smiling and waving as she watched from the window, she miming with raised eyebrows and a finger pointed at her glass and he, ever macho, shushing her with his raised hand. He'd be through soon enough, and then beer would be his beverage of choice. Roy sitting on the big, smooth log by the lake, playing with the tomcat that was so much like him until a coyote — the first anyone had ever seen on the lake, and this, too, they blamed on global warming — dispatched him one night with a terrible squalling. That was three years ago, and it hurt her almost as much as losing Roy. Both of them had loved that cat; losing him was like severing the last physical connection to her husband. The bridge she had built to his memory was becoming ever more rickety. More and more she could see only his back as he pushed the mower down the hill, his body lost in the shimmer of the late afternoon sun on the water. God, how she missed him! How desperate and hopeless and suffocating her longing, like trying to reach back into a past she could never retrieve! That was another benefit of this job: it gave her less time to think about

Roy. In some ways a full-time job would have been ideal. Everyone at the shop loved her and, the wages being as low as they were — certainly not enough to support herself, even in a small Missouri town an hour south of St. Louis — it was conceivable she could have worked full-time. She tried working half-time, adding Tuesdays and Thursdays to the mix, but even then it was too much. She found herself needing a recovery day in between. Sometimes it alarmed her how much stamina she'd lost since her nursing days.

The day was gaining momentum, the pink smudge on the horizon turning to orange, then a flaming red that turned the underside of the clouds into rumpled cloth soaked with blood.

Red sky at morning..., she thought.

This morning she saw blood in the clouds. Drawn as irresistibly as her tongue to a loose tooth, her mind went back eight years.

Anniversaries were like this; she knew it well from her work at the care center, for older people especially. They became more agitated, more depressed, and all it took was a glimpse at their charts to see why. Then, the mental health people would be called in, a little extra TLC doled out, and it would pass... until the next anniversary. Funny how acutely aware people were of their anniversaries when they were so out of it in so many other ways. Something instinctive about them. The Anniversary Clock, it seemed, kept on ticking on long after most others had stopped.

As if to prove this to herself, she glanced at the calendar. It was a hummingbird calendar (what else?) her daughter had given her. She marveled at the skill it must have taken to capture one hummingbird after another in mid-flight. Depending on the effect the photographer was after, sometimes the wings were frozen, sometimes blurred. Always the birds had a jewel-like quality that couldn't help but elicit a smile of admiration for God's handiwork. The circled dates, the filled-in boxes of birthdays and get-togethers, the Special Event that seemed to occur every month or so, distracted her as she turned the pages, for the moment forgetting why she had picked it up. She smiled as she remembered, turning the calendar to the current month. The date was not hard to find because this was the month: April. Today was the 14th, and it had happened on the 15th.

A shudder went through her as she remembered this date eight years ago. It had happened, right here, as Roy was getting out of his car. She was making a salad, the potatoes already scrubbed and a couple of steaks tenderized and smeared with fresh garlic and ready for the grill. It was Friday, and dinner was an Event on Friday: the day of the week they made love, both of them surprised by how good it still felt, with no need for those little blue pills; Friday, that glorious day of transition from week to weekend. That day she had lost two of her favorite patients, with the social worker attending a conference and one patient's family in the building at the time. Everything was agitated that day. Hummingbirds filled the sky in an iridescent roar that pulsated red and green and blue depending on which way they moved, and that was mainly down. Raining down like a hail of darts as Roy emerged from his car, babbling to the neighbors about how a man down at the shop, a neighbor of his from the lake, was killed by hummingbirds, coming from nowhere, seemingly without reason, six miles from here. He was just stepping into the carport, his body divided between light and shadow, when a hundred hummingbirds came surging up the hill.

"Ah!" he cried as they went for his eyes, despite the fact he was wearing glasses.

She still had his glasses, wondering why she'd bothered to save them; another way to keep his memory alive, perhaps? Their shattered left lens with missing shards of glass, bloody cracks long faded to brown. The coroner had said this was the fatal blow, that the bird had gone through the lens and, at the cost of shredding its own body, plunged through his eye and into his brain. Only its rear legs and tail feathers emerged, and the ER staff shook their collective heads at something they had never seen before.

Two birds went for his right eye, and soon Roy was no longer yelling, he was lying on his back convulsing as the neighbors retreated to their house and peered from the safety of their window. For a long time, Wanda had hated them for that. She did not think, she only reacted. Storming out the door. Swatting at the birds with a broom. They converged upon her, and she nearly stumbled over the threshold as she backed into the house, shielding her eyes with her forearm.

One of them got into the house, and she raged after it. Closing one door, then another, the bird panicking as the playing field shrank.

Too bad, you little bastard! This is for Roy! her mind cried.

She smashed a lamp, broke old china, and knocked half a dozen pictures off the wall before she connected, slamming the bird against the wall. Bringing the part of the broom where the bristles met the handle down on its eggshell head. Her heart was thudding, hot tears streaming down her face. Rage made her fearless, ready to go outside and have at them, no longer caring what happened to her as long as she could take out as many of them as she could. Not bothering to look, she burst outside, the world flushed by her anger — only to find them gone.

Roy lay across the grate that separated the carport from the driveway, some of the blood that bubbled out of him soaking into the gravel, looking as if he had died of *lingchi*, or death by a thousand cuts. No area of exposed skin was untouched, with many new areas created through the tears in his flannel shirt and his denim coveralls. His eyes were reduced to bloody holes, his glasses lying nearby. But the thing she could never forget was his mouth. The same laughing mouth that could spin one yarn after another, tell dirty jokes with the best of them, yet still kiss her with a softness that belied his gruff exterior. A mouth that was reduced to that of a badly carved pumpkin, his teeth visible in spite of it being closed. Giving him the appearance of laughing even as he was dying…

Whomp!

A hummingbird hit the window, hard enough to jolt her from her reverie and form a bloody spider web in the glass. Not being the world's brightest creatures, birds tended to fly into windows, sometimes hard enough to break their necks. The fact her kitchen window lined up with the picture window that overlooked her deck gave the illusion of clear sailing. Every couple of months, a bird hit the window, but never a hummingbird and never like this. She watched as it peeled off the glass in a splash of red and green that seemed a cheerful irony to its death.

The sun was up now, red giving way to purple ranks of clouds that streamed across a pale, blue sky. Six birds were buzzing around the feeder now, with them the notion her morning ritual was about to change. What had just happened brought back a memory of Roy that wasn't content to remain in the past, a memory that was actively reaching for her in the present.

Drink up, you little bastards. Tonight this feeder comes down… and stays down!

The rest of the day passed without incident, as most of her days did. True, it did make the time go faster, but that was how she wanted it. Since Roy's death, it seemed she was only marking time, just wanting her life to pass as comfortably as possible. Sometimes she was afraid a sort of living rigor mortis was creeping into her and that she might be clinically depressed.

I'll cross that bridge when I can no longer will myself out of bed in the morning, she decided, secretly detesting all the smiling mental health cheeseballs she'd been forced to deal with in her days as a charge nurse.

That night she dreamed, a variation of the dream she'd been having for ten years now. It was a curious dream because the visual — hummingbirds at a feeder — never matched the aural: a man talking to a girl. She'd once shared the dream with Roy, and damned if he could make any sense of it:

"Come, join me on the couch, love," the man said. "Our show is on."

"I cannot," the girl said, in an accent that sounded French. "I have a paper due tomorrow, and I have not even started."

"What is the paper about?"

"Hummingbirds."

"Surely there is plenty of information about hummingbirds on the 'Net," the man said. "Come, spend some time with me, and I'll run something off for you first thing in the morning."

"But that would be cheating," the girl said. "My English is not so good. The teacher will know I cheated."

"You will not get in trouble, I assure you. Come."

"But…"

"Come! There, that's better. How about you sit on Papa's lap, and we watch some TV together?"

"I am still sore. Can we not just cuddle?"

"I miss my girl. She looks so pretty tonight! I want to be close to her."

"Well, OK."

"Slip off your panties. Lift up your nightie. Lower yourself; I'll help you. Don't worry, I'm lubed. He'll go right in. Ah, there we go. Nice and easy. Just ease yourself down. That's my good girl, my pretty girl. I'll be gentle, I promise. See, isn't that nice?"

"It hurts a little."

"It will be OK. Now relax, and let's watch the show."

"Ow, it hurts! I am not ready!"

"It will be OK, love. We've done this before. Just relax."

"Ow!"

"There we go. See, it's not so bad. I'm all the way in. Now just move up and down. Pretend you're on a merry-go-round. I'll help you. Up and down. Slow and gentle. Doesn't that feel good?"

"Ow, it hurts! It feels like I am on fire!"

"It will get better, my dear. I promise."

"No, it hurts! I want to get off!"

"You will get off when I say so! Don't forget whose house this is! Don't forget I can send you to the best college in the country or send you back home to grow potatoes with your family! I'm sorry, love. I don't mean to get upset. I just want to be close to my girl, that's all."

Sound of whimpering.

"Relax, love. Ah, we're almost there! Ah! Ah! Ah! Oh yes, love! Yes! Oh, yes!"

"Ughhhh!"

"Shh, it's OK. Here, let me help you off. You can go work on your paper now. Oh, are you bleeding? I'm sorry."

Sound of sniffling. "I told you I was sore."

"I'm sorry, love. Really, I am. Tell you what, this Saturday we'll buy that dress we were talking about and a pair of shoes to go with it. And maybe even a necklace. Then we'll have a nice dinner. You pick the place. OK?"

"OK."

"That's my girl."

Chapter II

Things move too fast at a big city newspaper, so fast that the stories that seem insignificant go whizzing by without a second thought.

So thought Paul Mahr, editor of The Harper Gazette. A pattern was emerging, one he wondered if anyone else saw. Every April 15th for the last ten years, other than taxes being due. That was the problem: Taxes overshadowed everything else, including big things that sometimes lurked in the shadows.

He rubbed his eyes. God, but running a newspaper, even a biweekly, was hard on the eyes! Although he had heard the horror stories about laser surgery, having peered through glasses with lenses thick as furniture coasters for many years now, he decided he had little to lose. The surgery was no less than a godsend, his euphoria lasting an entire year.

20/20 vision at last! No more being tied to big, clunky glasses draped over your nose like saddlebags on Sancho Panza's donkey!

While his eyes were more light-sensitive than before and he never drove in the daytime without sunglasses, what a joy it was to watch a baseball game with his own eyes! Ever married to his job — his eyes (tiny, shrewish, and somehow alien behind those lenses) providing a further hurdle to his social life — Mahr experienced a sudden spike in popularity. For the first time, women noticed his eyes, and, by golly, they were the same, luminous shade as Paul Newman's, even if he lacked the face to go with them. He compensated by growing his hair, giving him a slightly dangerous Bohemian look. Before he knew it, he was a pseudo-chick magnet at forty-five.

But that was a year ago, before the novelty had worn off. The fact of the matter was he was good at his job; few people seemed to realize editing was nearly as important as writing, making sense of the slop writers passed off as a "story," and he loved what he was doing except for the fact it was killing his eyes. Although he discounted the previous eye exam to simple fatigue, his second and most recent exam after a good night's sleep indicated a slippage in his vision to 20/40. Still good enough to drive, good enough to watch a ballgame, but slipping, and he knew it could only get worse. He looked at one of the old eye exercise books he'd once deluded himself into thinking was a cure… that is, if you were willing to avoid sugar and TV and wearing glasses as much as possible; if you were willing to work each eye more than the other by wearing an eye patch in your spare time; if you were able to make yourself relax in a biz where there was no such thing ("relaxation is all-important," the books invariably said); if you were willing to dedicate your whole fricking life to eye health! He looked at the book and resumed doing a couple of exercises that had given him some relief: "sunning" to rest and stimulate the eyes; "palming" as an emergency balm for eyestrain. The latter involved propping your elbows on a large book (a St. Louis phone directory was perfect) and cupping your hands around your closed eyes until they felt warm and moist, all the while breathing deeply and trying to relax. The rub was being able to do this at work when you most needed to. Always a well-meaning coworker asking if you were OK, in the process shattering any peace you had achieved. It was no use. Nothing but sleep and eye drops — a chemical crutch to the eyes' natural production of tears that ultimately wasn't good for them — could erase the burning sensation. It didn't help when his ophthalmologist smiled and mentioned the need for "periodic adjustments."

"Laser surgery may fix bad vision," he said, "but it doesn't make the eyes any stronger or fix bad habits."

Like staring into a computer screen, Mahr thought dejectedly.

It was early Friday evening, his eyes already burning from a day at the word processor, and the petering out of a six-month relationship which had at least temporarily made women seem loathsome, and here he was, staring into the screen. Unable to put to rest the pattern he saw taking shape over the last ten years on April 15th. It was easy to see because it was happening only twelve miles away, on Lake Tanaka, just outside of Benson. Although the couple of hundred families who lived on the lake were comprised of everyone from retirees to working professionals to future retirees on a weekend sabbatical from the city, every year on this date there were deaths, and they weren't limited to a specific group. Not the usual someone getting drunk and drowning or getting drunk and running his car into a tree — the lake being notorious for alcohol consumption — but dying strangely.

In ways that involved hummingbirds.

The first year it was Ed Mawley, napping in his hammock while his wife was in town running errands. She returned to find his face purple, his eyes bulging out of their sockets, his hands dangling lifelessly at his sides. There was a tiny feather in his teeth, and when they pried open his mouth they found five hummingbirds lodged in his throat.

Last year it was ten people, two families who had tied their pontoon boats together for one of those water picnics that invariably involved drinking and swimming. Except alcohol wasn't the problem, or a drowning. It was the hummingbirds. Every year at this time, there were suddenly a lot of them congregating in the trees beyond the dam. The day was unseasonably warm. Many boats were out, their owners availing themselves of that rare warm day in mid-April. Then, as eye-witnesses described it, the birds rose en masse — thousands of them, buzzing and flashing red and green against the sky like a swarm of monster hornets — and descended upon the lake, upon the families and their boats as they were cleaning up after the Sunrise Breakfast Cruise that had become a ritual for a farm family and a military family, the kids invariably daring each other to get in the water: three people in one boat; four in the other; three kids in the chilly water.

They went for the kids first, pecking the tops of their heads when they came up for air, followed by their eyes, followed by a kamikaze plunge into their shrieking mouths, forever pecking with beaks that were more like sewing machine needles. Pecking and pecking and pecking until three bodies in bright swimsuits were bobbing in the water like blood-diffusing teabags, all the while their families were waling at the birds with shouts, towels, and oars. One man pulled a gun.

"You might hit the children!" his wife said.

"The children are dead!"

"You don't know that!"

It was a moot point because soon enough the attackers were under attack. The birds descended upon the boats, ripping their canopies to shreds. Going for the eyes first — take out the eyes and the rest would soon follow — and if the eyes were shielded, then the ears, the arteries in the neck, the bluish veins of sun-starved legs; everything a hole in the gas tank that would make the car bleed out, leaving it bug-eyed and broken down along the road. Sunglasses flew off as they went for the secondary sites, and then it was back to the eyes. They were too fast, and there were too many of them, and they seemed enraged. Yet no one had done anything to provoke them, anything they could think of. The hummingbirds would not be denied. Human eyes reduced to seven sets of ravaged pits, blood and vitreous fluid streaming into their mouths. Little geysers of blood spouting from their legs. A bird with its head embedded in an ear, blood trickling onto the lobe and down the neck. Pecking, always pecking. Liberating death as if it were trapped in human flesh.

One by one, the bodies toppled onto the decks or into the water. One weekend captain got his foot hooked on a bench as he fell, dangling in the no-man's-land between boat and water, his Hawaiian shirt pulled up to reveal a pale, bloated belly. The birds took his belly button for a target, sinking their ice picks into him as its owner mustered a dazed shriek. The belly button opened into a wound, their claws coming into play as they surged outward, the stomach opening like a gruesome flower in time-lapse photography. Pecking, always pecking, at the murky membrane with the dark suggestion of organs beneath. Fatty innards heaving against a thin wall. A single peck and gravity sent it all spilling into the water, the flapping purple liver and the full bag of the stomach and the sausage coil of the intestines all smearing their way past the fat chin with the screaming mouth. The captain's body would be found still dangling, the last of the ten to die that day. April 15th, a year ago, and the lake was still buzzing about it as April 15th approached once again.

A pattern was emerging, unlikely as it was grim: one death ten years ago; ten deaths one year ago. But why? Why on April 15th? Why hummingbirds?

Mahr's eyes were smarting. A glance at the big clock told him it was almost seven, the growl in his stomach a further reminder of the time.

Mexican tonight! he cheered himself with the thought. Kicked off by a nice, big margarita — rocks, no salt; why on earth did anyone salt these puppies, anyway? Half of the salt only ends up in the bottom of the frickin' glass. With some fresh guacamole made tableside and a warm, salted basket of chips! But not yet!

You gotta earn it, baby!

On a hunch, he went back twelve years, a year before the first death, looking for signs of anything curious happening at the lake. There was nothing, no deaths, as he scrolled through the next issue of the Gazette and its two major competitors, the Herald and the Messenger.

His eyes were flaming balls. So intent was he on what he was reading he caught himself staring again. His newspaperman side vied with his human side, and the former was winning. Another glance at the clock.

Seven-twenty! Hit the road, Jack! No, one more paper, and I'm outta here... promise!

He began his perusal of the April 17th edition of the Countian, another bigger biweekly, silently thanking God that back issues were now available online, as opposed to inhabiting dusty stacks in newspaper backrooms or clunky microfiches at the junior college library. Nothing, nothing, nothing. Then, in a small box on the "Have You Seen Me?" portion of the next-to-last page, something: a single paragraph with a girl's photo, her name and age underneath. The next thing that struck him was her beauty. At thirteen, Millicent "Millie" Fremont had the large-eyed, intelligent beauty of a woman several years older. Even in a small black and white photo with a pensive look on her face, it was unmistakable. Such beauty at such a young age was undoubtedly both a boon and a curse, opening doors both good and bad. After graduation he had done some subbing in area schools, augmenting this gig with stringing for three local papers before landing a full-time reporting job here. The prettiest girls were always the shiest, the strangest. Somehow you always had the feeling they'd been... messed with. He had that vibe as he read the copy that accompanied the photo:

"Millicent 'Millie' Fremont, 13, an exchange student from Nantes, France, has been reported missing from Lake Tanaka near Benson since the night of April 15th. She had been staying with John Galvin, COO of Crystal Glass in Harper, who reported her missing to Benson police on April 16th. At his request, the woods around the lake

were searched, though no trace of her was found. A couple of her classmates at Benson Middle School described her as being depressed. Galvin speculated that she was homesick, adding that he was planning to send her home when she disappeared."

Enough!

Finally, he willed himself to turn off the computer, rubbing his protesting eyes. Dutifully he dragged the St. Louis phone book over and put his elbows on it, cupping his hands over his eyes. Uninterrupted by his colleagues, the sting abated, giving way to a warm glow that made them feel as if they were melting in their sockets. He couldn't help but marvel that, like sex, such a simple act could be so transformative. It was the best his eyes had felt all day. Disengaged from the distraction of burning eyes, his mind was free to roam.

John Galvin. A moneyed guy from back East — Philly? Why the hell would he move to some Podunk town an hour south of St. Louis? I remember when he came here, that something about him didn't feel right. People who made this sort of move were trying to escape something, maybe even trying to hide something. Maybe it was as simple as a need for greater privacy, maybe something more. What could it have been? He was a big fish in a big pond; they don't get much bigger than Philly. Why come here to be a big fish in a small pond, even St. Louis, where he originally had a house (if memory serves) in the Central West End? I thought his place on the lake was supposed to be a weekend retreat, but he ended up making it his full-time residence, and it sure as hell wasn't because he needed to cut corners. Nor was it about convenience. Benson is still a dozen miles from Harper; there are plenty of nice houses here, with views of the Mississippi. Sure, there is something soothing about living on a lake, but the communities around them tend to be clannish, worse than small towns. Not the best place to "get away from it all," despite the amenities. At the same time, Galvin has never struck me as a "community" sort of guy. Of course, he gives money, lots of it, to the point they named the new cancer wing at Harper Memorial after him. But there's something clean about giving away large sums of money. A generous donation excuses the donor from further involvement in a project, the polar opposite of rolling up your sleeves and spending the sort of time "community" is all about. Galvin smiles for the camera as he's handing someone an oversized check, tall and ruggedly handsome but somehow distant, and he's outta there. My God, he has a crushing handshake! He led some sort of special scuba diving team in the Navy. I attended a party at his lake house once. Big house like something Frank Lloyd Wright might have designed, spilling down the hillside, a circular living room with a big picture window, stone deck running all the way around the front, with not just a yappy family dog to warn of intruders, but the biggest damn Rottweiler I've ever seen and none too happy about being penned up for the evening, to actively tear them apart. A city house in the country.

Mahr's thoughts swam full circle. *What was it? What the hell brought him here, anyway?*

He opened his eyes. "Goddamnit!" he said, flipping the computer back on as he glanced up at the clock.

Seven-thirty! Eight o'clock, I'm fuckin' outta here!

"John Galvin… John Galvin… Why the fuck did you come here? Something to do with women, if I recall. Here we go," he said when the computer was booted up and he found the site he was looking for. "Your wife left you… your only wife… and so did your daughter, your only child. Your wife remarried a couple of years later and is living on the Oregon Coast. She refuses to speak about the marriage, probably because she took you to the cleaners and signed a non-disclosure. Nobody knows where the daughter is; I'm guessing she, too, has been paid to keep quiet."

The clock hit eight.

"Shee-it! OK, eight-thirty at the latest," he said, shaking his head with a resigned smile.

The burning sensation was back — *blink, you son of a bitch, blink!* — but he couldn't shut down his reporter side, especially when he felt he was on the verge of a breakthrough. Determining when Galvin came to the area, he went to the website for Philly's largest daily, combing it for articles that would have occurred before his arrival at the lake. On a hunch, he chose a date three months before, coming up with nothing.

"Fuck! Wait a minute! Think! Remember, genius, he didn't come straight here! He went to St. Louis first!"

He went back two years and came up with a headline on Page 2:

"SHAKEUP PLANNED AT MAGNUM; GALVIN COULD BE OUT"

Finally, a frickin' break at eight-fifteen! Thank you, Lord!

Something had happened to make Galvin persona non grata in Philly. Evidently, his skills as an administrator were legendary. More than once, he had taken a floundering company and, in a matter of a year or two, pushed it solidly into the black. Having accomplished this, he made himself available to the various suitors who invariably tried to lure him away. He allowed them to — for top dollar, with the cushiest of fringe benefits. Then, his mission having been accomplished, he would blow the smoke off his gun and ride to the next town for an even bigger payoff. He got his first penthouse apartment this way, during what he called his "three-year sabbatical" in New York, followed by his yacht: small by corporate standards, but a yacht nonetheless. He still owned it when he headed for the Midwest — save for Chicago, farther off the corporate radar, certainly, than either the West or the Southwest — and once thought about bringing it to the lake. Dissuaded when he noted the size of the lake and the rinky-dink pontoon boats the locals were tooling around in, with limits even on speed and motor size; all of which was good for the comparative quiet he seemed to crave, Mahr supposed. He already had the largest house, its owner who had built it in the sixties not as entrenched as he thought when Galvin offered him triple its worth, no doubt sealing the deal with a handshake that left you flexing your fingers.

No need to stand out any more than I have to, Galvin must have thought.

Yet John Galvin was the sort of man who couldn't help but stand out.

Corporate expertise was one thing, image another — and a poor image could sabotage the most successful execs. It was all about how people saw you; even if the product you were selling was good, they wouldn't buy it if something wasn't right about you. Mahr suspected that was why John Galvin had worn out his welcome at Magnum and, by association, the Philly corporate world.

Now that he was where he wanted to be, he skimmed the next dozen issues, looking for updates on what appeared to be a major local story. Another headline came up:

"MAGNUM BUYS OUT GALVIN'S CONTRACT FOR UNDISCLOSED SUM"

For probably the first time in a long time, John Galvin wasn't the one calling the shots. One of his suitors had dumped him before he'd even had a chance to work his corporate wizardry. Instinct told Mahr it related to his divorce. His wife and daughter, who were paid not to talk. They had gotten what they wanted, after all: no more of him and plenty of his money.

Another glance at the clock: *8:35 — damn! OK, nine o'clock! I think the restaurant part closes at ten — and I do feel like Mexican! I deserve Mexican tonight!*

Hunches were a precious commodity in the newspaper biz, and he found himself in a fugue state. Hunches led to scoops and, if a scoop was big enough, it could lead to a Pulitzer. *If you were on publishing's radar and worked for a major daily, that is,* he thought with a knowing smile. Still, good reporting was its own reward. Something satisfying about a story well told, regardless of its exposure. Instinct told him to keep riding this hunch while the trail was hot.

Who died at the lake? When did they die? Was there a pattern to their deaths? How could there be a pattern where hummingbirds are involved? he peppered himself with questions.

He called a friend at the courthouse, a fellow workaholic he knew would still be grinding away, no doubt trying to dispatch the week's paperwork in order to take some of the heat off Monday. A fellow workaholic in Benson, a place that didn't have a great Mexican restaurant to compromise his diligence.

"Hey Bob, this is Paul at the Gazette. Yeah, tell me about it; I can't get away from my desk, either. So much for 'Cazh Fridays,' eh? Say, can you do me a favor? I'm doing an article on the hummingbird deaths at Lake Tanaka. Could you send me a list of every property owner at the lake, including their addresses and when they moved in? Five minutes? No kidding? You're a prince — or at least a marquis."

Bob laughed.

"No, not that marquis! Hey, I owe you a nice Mexican meal — here, where we have a decent restaurant! Adios!"

He used the time to collate a list of who was killed and when. He was nearly finished when Bob emailed him the list in four minutes. The first name his bleary eye went to was John Galvin. He combed the rest of the list Bob sent him, matching the names with the ones on his list. His mouth went round and his eyes got big when he saw yet another pattern emerge: All of the deaths were long-time residents. No one who had moved to the lake more than a year after Galvin's arrival had been killed.

He felt like he was getting somewhere. Secretly he felt he was wasting his investigative talents on this small-town rag. He realized the breakthrough this could turn out to be could truly launch his career, starting with the big city daily just up the road, the two bigger ones in Chicago. They were bigger, but were they better? He had always felt a loyalty to his community, a satisfaction with his job in spite of the havoc it wreaked on his eyes. For the first time this week, he felt satisfied as he finally turned off his computer.

I need to interview some people at the lake, he thought, *but not tomorrow morning.*

It always happened on the 15th, and here he let superstition — or was it common sense? — overrule his reporter's instinct. Besides, he had already put in a full week, too full to be working all day Saturday for a biweekly. Ready for a much-needed sleep-in.

He looked at the clock and smiled. *8:57: three minutes early! They don't call me "PM" for nothin'! Viva la Margarita, my favorite señorita!*

Chapter III

Dr. Kevin Cousey, a retired ear, nose, and throat man, was out on his deck cooking burgers under clouds tinged purple-brown by the last streaks of daylight. As was his ritual whenever he barbecued, he got a quart of potato salad from the deli of the town's only supermarket, gussied it up with some bacon and onions, a hard-boiled egg or two and some mustard, and made a Caesar salad with homemade dressing to go with it. Much as he enjoyed cooking, he was damned if he was going to spend his time boiling potatoes when he could buy a decent potato salad for a couple of bucks and upgrade it into something as good as his own. He'd get this all done by the time the sun began its descent, then repair to his lovingly restored Gilikson lawn chair by the stump for a couple of beers: Two were enough if they were microbrews and well chilled, as he usually had a couple more with his meal. The medical side of him that had once been the only side of him told him four beers a day flirted with alcoholism. Society's take on alcoholism, that is. Highly subjective, hardly a hard science with cut-and-dried rules, though the practical side of him smiled and realized he was bullshitting himself. The fact of the matter was he had always enjoyed beer. It gave him something to look forward to, goddamnit, what with his career and then his marriage going down the shitter through no fault of his own. No fault of his own, save for instinct.

That was twenty years ago when he was in his mid-forties and all but taking the medical world by storm. He was good, God he was good, and his response was to smile and shuffle his feet in "Aw, shucks!" fashion when they told him he was cut out for bigger things than Harper Memorial. The headhunters pursued him. Barnes-Jewish, the biggest hospital in the city and among the country's best, seemed inevitable, and there was even talk of Mayo and Hopkins. Sandy was radiant then, an archetype of redheaded beauty with her blood-red hair and creamy skin and "come hither" look in her cat-green eyes: Nancy Drew, all grown up and ready for a roll in the hay. And roll in the hay they did, their union producing two beautiful children: a boy who grew up and never looked back and a girl who grew up and still kept in touch, albeit on her terms, both with families of their own.

And then it happened, with the seemingly random cruelty life can spring things on the unsuspecting. Two days before the Fourth of July, someone at the lake — to this day he never knew who — threw a firecracker big enough to be illegal through the passenger-side window of his car as he was headed down North Lakeview Way at the posted fifteen-mile-an-hour speed limit. It hissed like an elephant beetle, and instinct told him to get it the hell out.

How many times he had replayed those fateful moments, ever with the benefit of hindsight that showed everything in slo-mo and freeze-frame, mapping out with maddening clarity what he should have done. But life didn't work that way. Life rarely gave you time to react, let alone think, and this was how mistakes were made. Mistakes that could impact the rest of your life. Like not realizing the firecracker you were about to handle was a mini-stick of dynamite powerful enough to blow your hand off. Hindsight told him he should have hit the brakes, turned his back to shield himself from the explosion, closed his eyes, and covered his ears. Hindsight told him that he should have been defensive rather than proactive. This was hindsight, speaking a language only hindsight could understand.

Meanwhile, there was reality, and reality screamed, "Get that thing the hell outta here!" That was what he tried to do, except by that time it was exploding, rupturing his right eardrum and mangling his right hand, his professional hand, into a stinging ball of raw hamburger, the three digits that remained intact dangling from their tendons like gruesome little puppets. God only knew how he had the presence of mind to make it home — hindsight told him he was in shock — clean and dress his hand, then ask a neighbor, with the calmness of his profession, ever downplaying so as not to alarm, to drive him to the hospital. Thank God his kids were at soccer practice and the debate team, and Sandy was still at work. They would find out soon enough when the worst of the shock was past. They would help him through this because that's what families did.

Sandy was the key, and to her credit, she tried. For a full year she tried. But if the changes in his life were too daunting for him to accept — the hand had to come off, the best prosthetic device a good insurance policy could buy a poor substitute for God's handiwork, with it the loss of his career — in the end, they were likewise too daunting for her. Their marriage unraveled when he touched her in bed one night with his prosthetic hand and felt her cringe. He already saw himself as a freak, her shrinking away only confirming the fact she saw him as one, too.

"I'm sorry," she said, but it was too late. Her body had already spoken for her. Any excitement he had ever felt for her was gone, and it stayed gone.

At the time, he couldn't help but see her reaction, honest and understandable though it was — he could now see in hindsight — as a betrayal. A year later, his Perfect Wife was asking for a divorce, and, suspecting she was already getting her "needs" met elsewhere, he gave her one without a fight. It occurred to him only later — in hindsight — that she wanted his forgiveness, wanted him to want her again, to fight for their marriage, the kids she'd certainly be taking with her. As it was, he helped her pack, kept things amicable, even waved with his good hand and forced a smile as they pulled out of the driveway and — in the case of his wife and son — out of his life forever, holding back the tears that had long built up like water behind a creaky, earthen dam. As far as he was concerned, his life was over. He had bought a good bottle of Scotch and a .38. A lot of guys did target shooting in the woods; there was nothing unusual about owning a gun here, and tonight he would use them both. As he turned to go into the house, one he had resolved never to leave again, his eye caught the wings of the life-sized St. Michael the Archangel in his backyard, early evening sunlight glittering on the watery backdrop that framed it like the brushwork of a Monet. The statue came from a church in South St. Louis they were tearing down. He'd bought it at a church "yard sale," his biggest fear being the wings would break off in transport, though miraculously Michael had survived the trip intact. That night he decided it was the most beautiful thing he had ever seen and that, despite it being blurred by tears, no less than God Himself wanted him to see it. He went inside for the Scotch — in a brown paper bag to hide it, a red glass to disguise it: always the neighbors to consider — but not for the gun. For the first time, he realized the stump would work as a table, and he pulled up a lawn chair, the statue, swimming platform, and setting sun all lining up. He sat there and did something he hadn't done since the end of his residency: polish off a fifth of hard liquor in one sitting. It wasn't hard if you took

your time, and the good stuff didn't bludgeon you with the hangover the lesser
stuff did, like the single malt he could easily afford on the combo of SSI, a hospital
pension, and an insurance settlement that had him set for life. Because as he drank
and cried and remembered how life used to be, watching as the sunshine transformed the arcs of Michael's wings into flaming curves of hope, he knew there
would be a hangover, knew there would be a next day. Even as the grief spilled out
of him like blood, he decided he was going to keep living. No matter what...

His burgers were ready, and he marveled at how good even the simplest meats
tasted when cooked over charcoal. Tonight the sunset was an incendiary marvel,
an exclamation mark on a day that felt complete — and yet it seemed nothing at
the lake would ever be complete. It was April 14th, and as much as people tried to
pretend nothing would happen tomorrow, deep down they knew it would and
that it could no longer be written off to global warming.

More than anyone on the lake, Cousey had a sense of what was going on, even
if his grasp of the specifics remained elusive. Something was askew. Something was
fundamentally wrong, and he had sensed it ever since Ed Mawley's death over ten
years ago. The lake had a secret, a secret that had something to do with hummingbirds, and until it was discovered and resolved, he sensed April 15th would always
be significant here, and not just for taxes.

A feeling of foreboding seemed to inhabit the chill that swept across the lake
as night encroached. In the distance, he could hear a rustling coming from the area
behind the dam, and he knew there was more to it than leaves blowing in the wind.
Windblown pine needles made a hushing sound, and only the few dead leaves that
remained on the trees rustled, and there were not enough of them to rustle like
that. The rustling he heard wasn't leaves, and he damn well knew what it was.

Keeping busy wasn't the problem he had initially expected forced retirement
to foist upon him. Really, as long as you had Wi-Fi, a juco with the county's best
library a couple of miles away, and major bookstores in St. Louis, there was never
an excuse to be bored. Only people utterly lacking in imagination got bored. He
kept at his research and writing, once getting an article published in a medical
journal — "off-Broadway" as opposed to AMA — that had once published him
before he made it big, and he was determined to keep at it; harboring the notion

of remaining an expert in his field, despite his removal from the day-to-day that had once seen him ever in demand. Speaking engagements. Invitations to big dinners in the city like before. Hey, there had to be something more than marking out what could be another twenty years of life. No one in his family who had died of natural causes lived less than eighty years.

Unwilling to jettison the vocation that had once been his life, he kept himself ready, making sure there were fresh batteries in his penlight and that his equipment was clean and his license current — just in case. Occasionally it paid off, never in money — since his retirement, he never charged for his services — but always with the feeling he still had something to contribute.

There was the guy who returned from a deer hunting trip with something moving inside his ear.

Easy enough! Cousey thought, having the man sit with his head tilted as he squirted warm water into his ear. Dislodging a tick that was engorging itself with blood.

"Come back when the eggs hatch," Cousey said, much to the man's dismay. "Just kidding. That was a male. I've dealt with a few ticks in my time," he said, laughing.

Then there was the man who brought his ten-year-old son.

"Hi, I'm Dr. Cousey. What's your name?" he asked the boy.

"Josh."

"What seems to be the problem, Josh?"

"I can't breathe through my nose."

"All of it or part of it?"

"On this side," Josh said, pointing to his right nostril.

"How long has it been like this?"

"Hmm… a coupla weeks."

"What do you think caused it?"

"All I know is I was eating popcorn and my friends made me laugh."

Cousey smiled. "I think I know what the problem is."

He withdrew something from a plastic wrapper that looked like a soda straw except thinner and more flexible.

"This might be a little uncomfortable. It might make your nose bleed. I'll try to be gentle, OK?"

Josh looked apprehensive. "OK."

"Just pretend you were playing football and the ball got stuck up your nose."

Josh managed a nervous laugh. Cousey pulled up a chair, had him tilt his head back, and gently inserted the tube into his nostril. Feeling an obstruction, he tapped against it, and the tube went all the way through to his mouth before he withdrew it.

"Blah!"

"You're doing fine."

"There's… something in my mouth!"

"I'll bet we can guess what it is. Spit it into your hand and let's have a look."

Out came a single, unpopped kernel of popcorn coated with bloody mucus.

"Can I save it, Dad?"

"Only if you promise not to show it to your mother."

"I promise."

"Better now?" Cousey asked.

"Better," Josh said, smiling with relief.

"I don't know how to thank you, Doc. I know you won't take any money," Josh's father said.

"Say, aren't you Sam Tucker?"

"That's me."

"The handsome, hard-working owner of Benson Hardware but, just as importantly, the faithful husband of one Debbie Tucker, she of those famous cherry pies with the impossibly flaky crust?"

Tucker smiled. "I get your drift."

"Only if she feels like it. I bought one of them at the last bake sale, and I've been dreaming of another one ever since."

Then there was the time a woman brought her three-year-old daughter, the child wide-eyed and making whistling sounds when she breathed.

Cousey smiled at the child. "Sounds like something got stuck in the plumbing. I'm Dr. Cousey. What's your name, honey?"

"Amanda," her mother said.

"Amanda, love, have a seat and we'll have a look. What do you think it was?" he asked her mother.

"I think she swallowed a chicken bone."

Cousey pulled out his penlight. "OK, sweetie pie, open your mouth real wide. Just like that. That's a good girl! Aha, I see the little rascal! It's small and gray like a bone, and it's pretty far down there," he said to the mother.

He went to the cupboard and got out a large plastic bowl.

"Here, hold this under her chin," he told the mother.

Amanda's eyes widened further, puzzled as to what was going on and unused to all the attention.

"Now open up for me, honey. That's it. Nice and wide."

Cousey inserted his finger down her throat and made her throw up. Now she was crying.

"Good girl!" Cousey said. "You did real good, honey! Let's see if we got it."

He inspected the vomit. A piece of bone that resembled a gray snowflake was floating in it.

"Open your mouth for me, honey."

The child squirmed, the tears returning in force. "Amanda, sit still!" her mother said.

"Open your mouth for me, sweetie pie," Cousey said, inspecting her throat: no sign of the bone. "Breathe for me, sweetie pie. Give me a couple of nice, deep breaths. That's it. Good girl!"

The whistling sound was gone.

Cousey smiled. "We got it! That was easier than I thought."

He went to the sink, came back with a warm, wet cloth, and handed it to the mother, who proceeded to clean the child's face.

"What do we owe you, Dr. Cousey?"

"You've got it all wrong, my dear. I'm the one who owes you — for reminding me who I am and what I do. I wish I had a sucker for her; I used to keep them in my office."

Amanda had stopped crying. Cousey caressed her soft hair, finally getting a smile.

"That's OK; she gets enough candy."

They left quickly, for which Cousey was grateful. No sooner were they gone than he peered into his medical bag as if he were gazing into the past and cried...

Yes, he admitted he drank too much, and even though it was only beer, he was aware of the potential for trouble and tried to compensate in other ways. Like keeping a healthy discipline, working on the flower beds around the house where he grew yuccas, tiger lilies, and hydrangeas, and the vegetable patch by the lake where he grew watermelons and green beans, half a dozen stalks of corn — an experiment that worked! — and what consensus held to be the best tomatoes on the lake. A few times a week, if the weather were nice, he would take his hiking stick (i.e., dog deterrent) and walk the three-mile loop around the lake, all of it paved save for the grass that ran along the top of the dam. He'd gotten to the point he could walk it in less than an hour, even when he stopped to talk with the occasional neighbor who was out. These walks were the best therapy of all, the oxygenated air lending clarity to his thoughts. He always slept great after his walks. Except for the nightmares.

Though they'd never been upbeat, loss being their common denominator, his dreams had changed over the years. Ten years ago, he was still dreaming about the firecracker, symbolized by an overexposed flash that had swallowed his career and his marriage and very nearly his life. Then the girl came (Mildred Somebody? It was a French name), or, more accurately, the girl went, and everything changed. He dreamed of her, and, as much as he tried to censor his subconscious (good luck with that one, Doc!), his dreams were invariably sexual, yet never involving him and strangely unpleasant. How could they not be? She was what, thirteen? Sex wasn't supposed to be part of the equation at thirteen. OK, kids were doing everything earlier these days, from tattoos to menstruation. Maybe out of curiosity — with a boy her age or a little older — but certainly not with an adult. Certainly not with the adult he suspected with growing certainty.

Other than being tall, dark blond and, most would say, ruggedly handsome, John Galvin had nothing outwardly sexual about him. Nothing to indicate, say, a perversion. At the same time, there was a sense of determination about him, a sense that he would not be denied anything he wanted. With growing suspicion, Cousey suspected it was the French girl. Something about her reserved nature, her downcast eyes whenever he saw them together. The mental distance between them was palpable, born, he suspected, of a dysfunctional home life. Dangerously so, as evidenced by the telltale signs of abuse he as a medical professional had been trained to be on the lookout for: a blackened eye and cheek; a puffy lip; bruises on her upper arms that were unmistakable on her smooth, olive skin.

While his profession of necessity increased his awareness of the human body, proactivity had always been central to his nature. The first time he saw a mark on the girl that looked suspicious, he reported it to the authorities only to be told Galvin had already reported it. Seeing as how Cousey was a medical professional, he was often privy to what Galvin had told them. It seems his "adopted daughter" was distracted by laughter when she was out riding bikes with friends and didn't see the branch hanging over the road; thank God she didn't lose an eye! The first set of bruises on her arms was from a football game with the boys that had gotten "a little rambunctious." There was no corroborating the "facts" of her injuries with her friends because no one seemed to know who they were. He had, in fact, never seen her with kids her own age. In any event, the girl wasn't talking, the girl never spoke to anyone apart from Galvin, and maybe that was how Galvin wanted it. Cousey shook his head when he considered the dynamics of what he suspected was a classic case of enabling; the abused fueling her own abuse by, A. thinking she must deserve it, or B. seeing the advantages of tolerating it.

Other than a growing suspicion about Galvin, all his reporting of the man's alleged abuses accomplished was his unbridled ire. Suddenly, the hospital where he had worked for twelve years, ten as the head of his department, wanted nothing more to do with him. Even his former colleagues seemed anxious to leave his presence. Sometimes the consequences were more direct. One night Galvin met him on the lake road and revved his black military-issued Humvee to three times the speed limit, driving him perilously into the ditch. This, too, Cousey dutifully reported to the police. The incident was never repeated, but from then on Galvin would shoot him a chilling glance (accompanied by Fritz the Rottweiler snarling and crashing into the fence like a hockey player) whenever Cousey was walking past and Galvin was in the yard, leading Cousey to wonder if he could fend this dog off even with a stout stick. Still, he was determined to keep Galvin honest, even when the results were unnerving.

Even when the nightmares kept coming. They started even before the girl disappeared, and he began to see them as a portent. It was easy to hear things on the lake, especially late at night when, save for a weekend party, there was little going on. Sometimes he heard a girl's screams, and since the French girl was often screaming in his dreams, he could never be sure if they were real. Sometimes he would even burst outside, standing there shivering in his underwear as he listened intently, but by that time the screaming had stopped.

The following April 15th, Ed Mawley was killed in his hammock, followed by two people, Sam and Terri Middleton, as they power-walked their way around the lake in their "his 'n' her" sweats the next year. Each of their deaths involved hummingbirds, and, crazy as it seemed, a pattern was forming in his mind, though he was uninclined to share it with anyone. Then, the third year, when Roy Smith and two others got killed, he tried an experiment. There was a pattern to how the hummingbirds congregated: first in the trees behind the dam the night before; second on and above the swimming platform the next morning; finally, as if by a signal only the birds knew, a communal flight to every point around the lake, rising and swirling and folding upon itself like a tornado gone haywire, shimmering with a kaleidoscope of color depending on how the sun caught it; and by this time it was an "it," a lethal mass that killed whoever it bore down on. Cousey was still at that point of recovery — from life, not alcohol — that he needed a drink or three to soften the blow of another day. Even before breakfast, as the sun illuminated the sky like one mercury vapor light after another snapping on, he was at his usual place by the stump, St. Michael forming a line with the swimming platform and the dam and the trees behind it. A few boats were already out, early risers who savored the still, pristine beauty of the lake at this time of day. He noticed whose boats they were, waved at their "captains" whenever one of them came close to shore. He sat there and drank his whiskey, always in a paper bag, always from the red glass, ever the need to keep up appearances even though everyone in this close-knit community knew everyone else's business, and watched and waited. Promptly at seven o'clock, there was a sudden rustle of activity, a raucous assemblage on the swimming platform — as many hummingbirds as would fit, with plenty of jostling — that went on for a good fifteen minutes. What followed was a birdlike scream that echoed from one end of the lake to the other, chilling the blood. Then, promptly at seven-fifteen, there followed a vast and sudden exodus into the sky, a shimmering mass of color accompanied by a near-deafening buzz that wheeled over the lake only to branch off into lethal fingers and come streaming back down. At some boats, but not others. At some but not all of the early-morning joggers. At some of the people getting into their cars. At times there appeared to be a moment of hesitation, as if the birds were deliberating on who to attack.

That day three people were killed, including the guy who waved as he passed in his boat. The birds were all around Kevin Cousey: darting, hovering, surveying, but not attacking. Not this year and not the following year, when four more people would die. Or the year after that, when five would die. After that first time, he made a point of being out there; from then on, without the whiskey. It was getting increasingly hard to get wasted before breakfast with Michael there to encourage him every April 15th. Every year the birds came no nearer than ten feet of him, avoiding the statue and even the nectar-filled feeder. As far as the hummingbirds were concerned, he was OK, prompting him to wonder why — until he thought about Galvin and the girl.

Because I'm trying to do something about it? he thought. Even then, the thought made him uneasy about the sheer deliberation of their attacks.

But still the nightmares, and they were getting worse. There seemed an urgency about them, a message they were trying to convey, a hazy but sharpening connection between Galvin and the girl — and hummingbirds.

Why hummingbirds? The question spun through his mind on an endless loop.

And then, even as time was filling the bottom of the hourglass, if the present pattern continued, eleven more people would be dead tomorrow. New pieces, or at least the pieces his subconscious mind had been unable to fit together, were falling into place. Tonight's dream was a steady visual of what he had always perceived as a constant, the seemingly inconsequential thing that occupied the middle ground between the important things in the foreground — the whiskey; the statue — and the background — the dam; the crowns of the trees looming behind it; another sunset rioting across the sky: the swimming platform. A nondescript assemblage of boards originally painted blue but weathered gray, eight feet square. Big enough for a couple of sunbathers to stretch out, floating on thick blocks of Styrofoam, recessed to protect them from the boats, with a cable or chain anchoring it to the bottom. How deep? Fifty feet, maybe, though God only knew what lurked in the murky depths: probably not a rusty car, but maybe a rusty boat.

God only knew.

Something about the platform. The platform was the calm before the storm, the Before of the Before and After. The platform was the final shot in *Deliverance* after the credits had rolled: a shot of the surface of the lake. A lake from which the viewer had previously seen the nightmare vision of a pale, waxy hand emerge. A secret, unburied.

A secret that is killing people, he thought, even within the dream.

The soundtrack part of the dream kicked in. At first, it was the subdued cawing of early-morning birds, the gentle lapping of water against the shore before the first boats made their rounds.

A tone of protest in a girl's voice.

"No, and I don't care what happens!"

"Yes, my dear!"

A man's voice. Sounds of a struggle punctuated by slapping, screams, and a thudding sound.

Then silence.

"Oh my God! Oh my God!"

The man's voice. The thump of something being loaded into a boat. The sound of oars meeting water, rush of water as the boat leaves the shore. Night sounds on the lake. A secretive passage, no motor, just the sound of the oars dipped into water, the boat arriving somewhere. Splash of something entering the water, then something else. Sound of bubbles, then nothing. Then, minutes later, the sound of bubbles again. Sound of activity in the boat, the oars hitting the water again.

Just as the dream was ending, as audio was returning to video, the camera of his mind that had been zoomed in on the swimming platform pulled back. Michael was in the picture, and something was wrong. Two horizontal lines, thick and black like an "equal" sign, on the back of his head. Puzzled, Cousey pictured himself rising from his chair and, most unsteadily, with a mind clouded enough by alcohol to make him doubt the reality of what he was about to see, he walked around the statue.

St. Michael was wearing a scuba diving mask.

He awoke with a shudder, and when it passed, he shuddered again. It was five o'clock and still dark on April 15th. If normally chaotic nature were uncharacteristically true to form, eleven more people would die today as he sat with his coffee and watched it all unfold and continued to ask himself why. Not knowing the answer gave him a maddening feeling of impotence. At the same time, though it would be too late to save anyone today, he felt he was nearing a breakthrough. Like solving the first word in a crossword puzzle, one that would lead to others and ultimately the solution of the puzzle as the words fell like dominoes. Hopefully, a pivotal piece of information would present itself. Hopefully, he would finally see a way to stop it.

Something about the scuba diving mask, with it a sudden compulsion to start a scuba club, even though he hadn't scuba-dived since a summer camp counselor threw an oxygen tank into the deep end of the pool and he and two friends experienced the novelty of breathing underwater.

Chapter IV

The smallest things took on greater significance for those with little to fill their days. Such was the case with Wanda Smith on Tuesday, a much-needed day off after a crazy morning at the shop the day before, and the pleasant domestic ritual of getting the mail. Yesterday Pastor Eustace Baxter's wife Thelma, leader of a church group called Women Aflame, and Benson's self-appointed moral conscience, had given voice to the hysteria that always pervaded the town of Benson this time of year. Thelma had no "off" button, all the worse if you disagreed with her and she got her hackles up, her voice rising to the fevered pitch of the self-righteous. Things were almost as bad if you agreed with her, feeding the flames of an impromptu sermon that could go on for thirty minutes or more, leaving you feeling as if you'd been beaten about the head and shoulders with a wooden spoon.

"I guess you all know what day it is tomorrow. Don't fool yourself: There's evil on that lake," Thelma said. "Last night we had us a prayer meetin' at the horseshow grounds, so big we needed a circus tent to hold it. The church wasn't big enough. You should have seen my Eustace: full of the spirit, he was! Doin' what he could to stop the evil!"

A chubby young woman in spandex pants, shopping with her two small children, wasn't buying it.

"Ms. Baxter, every year about this time, you and your husband hold an all-night prayer meetin', and every year the situation out there only gets worse. How do you figure?"

"Well, now, aren't we the impudent one! Blamin' the fireman for tryin' to put out the fire! The devil's fire!" Thelma said.

"That's not what I'm sayin'. What I'm sayin' is the pastor is creatin' a whole lot of excitement, but it ain't solvin' nothin'."

"What would you have him do, my dear? You're obviously an oracle, put on this earth to enlighten the rest of us."

The young woman was taken aback, her mouth moving like a fish as her daughter gauped up at her.

"Why, Ms. Baxter, I don't think there's anything he can do. The earth has gone crazy with all this global warmin'. Maybe it finally got pissed off at everything we've been doin' to it."

"Miss, you need to watch your tongue! I'm a lady, and there are two young ones present!"

The young woman was in no mood to acquiesce. "These are my kids, and they've heard worse. Besides, a lady wouldn't talk to me the way you have."

"How dare you!" Thelma cried.

Wanda had been watching it all from the register with raised eyebrows. It was time to intervene.

"Thelma, it looks like everyone's getting upset here. Maybe it's time for a break. Why don't you have some coffee with me? I made a coffee cake last night, and I'd be honored to get your opinion. Helen, can you watch the register?" she asked her colleague.

It was just the out Thelma Baxter needed.

"Trailer trash," she muttered, under her breath but loud enough to be heard as she followed Wanda to the break room.

"We got off easy this time," Helen said to the young woman.

It wasn't the morning's only event. A large woman who evidently was used to having her own way, and God bless her husband — why was it always the women? The men were so much more laid-back about these things — came through the door with an armload of clothes and no receipt demanding a refund, despite the sign above the register that shouted: "ALL SALES ARE FINAL."

"Little Jimmy won't wear this, says the buttons are on the wrong side and it's a girl's shirt. These pants won't fit my husband; I keep forgettin' how much weight he's put on since the accident. And these shoes! There isn't anything in my wardrobe they match." And on and on.

Wanda listened calmly, her smile turning sympathetic as she pointed to the sign.

"I'm sorry, ma'am," she said.

The woman's mouth fell open, her face flushing with color.

"So why are you just standin' there, lettin' me carry on, and all this time you weren't gonna do nothin'? Some people! Unbelievable!"

Wanda smiled, reminded of her dealings with nursing home families.

"Ma'am, you came in here like a house afire. I couldn't get a word in edgewise."

"I'll show you 'edgewise'! Here's what you can do with 'edgewise'!"

One shoe pinwheeled across the room, then the other, just missing the big front window. The woman proceeded to scatter every article of clothing every which way, shaggy hair flying, heavy bracelets dancing on her wrists. By the time she stormed out, angering herself further by being unable to slam a door that featured a closer, items of clothing littered the floor, were draped over racks of pants and shirts or, in the case of a rhinestone T-shirt with a paint splotch on the sleeve, dangled from a light fixture.

"I'd better get that one," Helen said, reaching for the broom. "That one's gonna cook up there." She got it down and smiled. "It takes all kinds, doesn't it? I guess that's why they call them 'Mondays.'"

That's what Wanda loved about Helen. Helen, who always knew what to say and when to say it. Helen, who lived within walking distance of the store, ever the beacon of common sense.

Helen, who would cry the loudest at her funeral.

She puzzled at the thought. *Now, why on earth would I think something like that?*

As was her habit on April 15th, Wanda made a conscious decision to stay indoors, preparing for this by getting as much done outdoors as possible the day before — amazing how therapeutic an afternoon of weeding was after a hectic morning at work — so she wouldn't feel like such a coward for not going out.

Discretion is the better part... she reminded herself. *It's better to be a live chicken...*

There was nothing cowardly about wanting to stay alive, nothing illogical about self-preservation, especially when it didn't hurt anyone else. She thought of Roy lying in the driveway with his eyes pecked out, his blood soaking into the gravel, dripping from the grate that formed a bloody checkerboard on his back. She thought of Roy, and her mouth tightened for even thinking in terms of cowardice.

Lord knows I've suffered! Lord knows I've paid my dues!

That was eight years ago. Eight years ago, and people were still dying. Someone obviously hadn't paid his dues, whatever they might be. She noted the empty feeder.

How could something so tiny and adorable, so utterly fascinating to watch, be so deadly? she thought.

Then again, they never ate on...

She nipped the thought at the roots, shifting her attention to the music that filled her cozy two-bedroom house and reminded her of nature: Saint-Saens's *Organ Symphony*. That's what they called it here, but the French called it by its correct name; Symphony with Organ, since only two of its four movements were accompanied by an organ.

She had to smile. *People are always screwing things up. Somebody at the lake must have really screwed up*, she thought, the connection between the hummingbirds at the lake and what someone had done occurring to her for the first time. There was a connection, all right, and it had something to do with vengeance.

Her house was never more a sanctuary than today. Nothing must invade her sanctuary, including the screams she knew she would hear if the music weren't on. Screams she could do nothing about, anyway, until it was all over for another year, and it was time to comfort friends and bury the dead and regroup as a community. Sometimes her own oblivion was vexing to her, for in it she saw guilt. Survivor's guilt. This she tried to see as a coping mechanism. Surely other people felt this way. Most importantly, it kept her alive.

Still, she couldn't help but glance at the clock more than usual. She made a point of not wearing her watch on at-home days — watches were only reminders of the hamster wheel the working world put you on — but that didn't stop her from looking at the clock. Word was the birds "started" shortly after seven, and now it was after eleven.

The mail will be here soon. I wonder if those books will come today. They said it would be last Friday, she thought.

Trying to suppress the thought that the birds had had four hours to get their "business" done. The thought that people were already dead or dying, all of which seemed incredible with this beautiful music playing. A symphony brimming with emotion composed, quite ironically, by a composer who said he didn't believe in it. Her favorite symphony, played on a good sound system. Roy knew something about electronics and had put it together years ago, and it was still purring along. OK, maybe it was time for a new needle, though nowadays the CD player had made the turntable an afterthought

God, but I'll be glad when this day is over! she thought, gazing up the driveway through her kitchen window at a mailbox bathed in sunlight like expectation itself.

Bracing herself against the sink: old porcelain, just like the one in the bathroom. Thick, substantial handles labeled "HOT" and "COLD." No nonsense; nothing fancy. Made to last forever. Solid. Everything in this house had a solid feel about it, and there was something comforting, something timeless about solidity. The house was no less than her rock, the physical underpinning of her life.

She stood at the kitchen sink, barely aware of the thunderous finale that typically brought tears to her eyes — when she was listening, that is. A numbness had overtaken her, masking an amalgam of pain and fear that tingled like the nerve endings the shot couldn't reach. Pain when she thought about Roy; it was an anniversary, after all. Fear because it was April 15th, and they might still be out there, doing what they always did on April 15th. By the time the next disc came on — some Chopin preludes — the music had receded into the murky backwoods of her consciousness. Gazing at the shimmering interplay of sunlight and wind and leaves outside her window, she allowed her mind to wander. The occasional hummingbird she saw seemed an abstraction as it darted, hovered, and swept past.

How could anything bad happen on a day like this? she thought, still pleasantly full from breakfast, her house in order, everything in her life as ordered as it could be… without Roy.

She smiled when the familiar vehicle with the blue eagle on the side rolled up to her mailbox. She glanced at the clock, surprised to see it was nearly 1:00 PM.

I must have spaced out. Almost six hours now, she couldn't help but think. *He's never this late.*

The mailman reached through his window, and she thought nothing of it when three hummingbirds hovered nearby. She thought nothing of it because they did nothing, watching him with seeming curiosity and nothing else.

Maybe it's finally over for another year, she thought absently.

The mailman slapped the lid up and brought the flag down, attaching a package to the clasp with a thick rubber band before moving on.

My books! she thought.

She opened the house's only upstairs door and stepped outside, the rectangle of sunlit scenery before her looking overexposed from the shade of the carport. She climbed the driveway, intoxicated by the fragrant, warmish-cool air that was peculiar to early spring. Satisfying crunch of gravel as she climbed the driveway, the package clearly in view.

The bright sunlight made her sneeze, and at this a hummingbird appeared. She flinched as it swept down and hovered before her eyes, so close she could feel its wings fanning her face, see eyes as brown and blank as polished stones, the long, black thorn of its beak.

First time I've seen one act like that, she thought.

The hummingbird chirped and two more appeared.

Only three of them, she thought, reassured.

Still, a creeping unease. One that made her want to collect her mail and get back down to her house as soon as possible, to luxuriate over her books with a cup of coffee. To be done with the day's only reason for being outside.

Suddenly the first hummingbird lunged at her, its body blurring into a reddish-green splotch as it drove its beak into her left eye.

"Ah!" she cried, and when she did another hummingbird opened one of the veins under her tongue.

Her jaw closed involuntarily, severing its head with a frantic squawk that reverberated inside her mouth. Soon blood was spilling… from her eye, her tongue, the hummingbird. There were still only two of them, she could see them with her good eye, but they seemed enraged as she yelled and flailed her arms. She was no match for their agility, however, and one of them took out her other eye, her world suddenly going dark and frantic as the peck-peck-pecking began, like needles all over her body except thicker, deeper. A hummingbird opened one of the two main arteries in her neck, and now the blood was flowing freely. She was getting lightheaded, her world turning dreamy. Everything getting farther and farther away as the pecking went on in an endless cadence. Finally, a largely painless fall ended with the sensation of coarse gravel against her skin, warmed by the sun and wet with the blood that was coming out of her in earnest. Absently she realized that if this were the movies, her blood would be coursing down the driveway in a bright red tendril, joining Roy's blood in a visual metaphor of oneness that would have done Hitchcock proud. Instead, her blood soaked into the gravel around her, an effect that was anything but cinematic. Just as the injection was never as bad as that initial stick, bleeding out was never as gruesome as it appeared. Make a small hole in the bottom of a jug, and by the time the liquid all runs out…

Darkness encroached, edged with a strange, golden light, morphing into Roy lying in a round bed wearing only his pajama top. The covers were pulled back, and he was reaching for her, his manhood big and warm and ready to do the hokey pokey with her for all of eternity. Service with a smile! The darkness morphed into the silk bedclothes of a Bangkok brothel, the golden light into flames lapping all around the bed. With a sudden and utter clarity, she knew where the bed was going, knew it as sure as the screams she pretended not to hear echoing across the lake on that long-ago night of April 15th. Knew it as sure as the bruises on the girl's face and arms she tried not to see in spite of being trained to see them, any intervention she might have made on the girl's behalf checked by the crocodile smile of a man that warned her to look no farther, the same man whose name graced the new wing at the hospital. Kevin Cousey did look farther, and look at what happened to him. She suspected they would find his body floating in the lake someday.

Because people who minded their own business lived longer than people who didn't.

The mailman was just past the neighbor's box when he saw the scene unfold in his rearview mirror and screeched to a stop. Saw it only; what the hell else could he do? There were only two of them, but he had seen many more of them on the way in, seen what they had done all around the lake, his progress delayed by the presence of EMTs for the living and festoons of yellow crime scene tape for the dead. That's what he could do. He could let them know there was another body at #258 North Lakeview Way.

***

His reporter side ultimately triumphing over his desire to sleep in, Paul Mahr was already on the scene, having risen early in spite of one margarita too many. As far as anyone knew, it was over. Wanda Smith was the day's ninth and final victim. Feeders hung untouched. The swarm was gone. Not one hummingbird was left on the lake.

Mahr mentally scratched his head. Ten last year, nine this year. Something wasn't adding up.

Then he smiled as he remembered a similar dynamic four years ago. Four people were killed at the lake, two less than the year before. Then the obituaries came in from out of town. Obits were like homing devices, telegraphing their message from any place in the world to the folks back home. For some reason, people were interested in where you came from, made a point of letting the people living there know if anything happened to you. Sure enough, that year a family of three — former residents of the lake — died on a hike near Telluride, Colorado: attacked by hummingbirds… on April 15th. Bringing that year's total to seven. Maintaining the pattern. With a grim certainty, he realized a couple more fatalities would be added to this year's total. Even with Bob's help at the courthouse, it was too time-intensive to keep up with all the comings and goings of two hundred lake households. All he had to do was wait for the homing pigeons to return to their dovecote.

A chill went down his spine when he realized that not only could these hummingbirds count, not only could they choose specific people to attack, but they could… find people. People who had moved far beyond the lake.

***

The lake had a bad vibe for Jim and Jenny Spencer. Rather, it was the final straw in a series of events that had seen the sabotaging of Jim's promising IT career in St. Louis. He had come flying out of the chute after an undergrad degree at a prestigious university, so gifted that he forewent the Master's that was the norm for his profession. But a lost contract, a boss who found a convenient scapegoat in a young upstart, and it all unraveled from there. On top of it all, Jenny was expecting, and suddenly working in St. Louis and living on Lake Tanaka — an easy commute with a new highway that created the best of both worlds, they thought at the time — was no longer the golden scenario they had once envisioned.

Ever ambitious, Jim and his headhunter never stopped hunting, long tapped as he was into the exodus of jobs into the Southwest, and found him a peach gig in San Antonio. Jim had never been to San Antone, but an interview trip featuring lunch on the San Antonio River and the best Mexican food he'd ever eaten was enough to sell him on the idea. They put their home on the market the next day, and in two weeks they were gone.

In those two weeks, something else went down, something that compounded the bad vibe at the lake. The occasional glimpses of the pretty young girl; everybody at the lake knew her, or at least of her, looking bruised and subdued at the store, followed by those chilling screams coming from her house one night a few doors down that were not unlike the screams of a cornered animal.

Enough to jolt Jim out of a sound sleep.

"I need to check this out!" he said.

"My husband, the action stud," Jen said with a knowing smile. "Probably just some kid having a nightmare. Kids have been known to have them, you know."

"Honey, that's pretty intense even for a nightmare, don'tcha think?"

"We could call the police."

Jim sighed. "Then they'd ask me who I am, and I'd be right in the middle of it. I'd look like an idiot if it turned out to be like you say, just a kid having a nightmare."

Besides, they were new at the lake. What business did they have playing police or even involving the police? Mind your own damn knitting already. It was probably nothing.

"Methinks thou hast resolveth the issue," Jen said. "Now allow thy sexy wife to knock her hubby's socks off if he thinketh he might haveth trouble achieving sleep."

He laughed, and she did, and the next day a teenage girl was reported missing at the lake.

Oh shit! they thought, though still not convinced enough to contact the police. Besides, there was so much else going on. A few days later, it was all forgotten when they made the move to San Antonio…

It seemed so far behind them now, eleven years ago, as they sat on the veranda of a restaurant with blue-painted adobe walls on the San Antonio River; she eating the best tamales, and he eating the best bowl of chili they'd ever had. She wouldn't have thought about it at all had it not been for the significance of April 15th: Tax Day — the same day the girl at the lake had disappeared. Jim was entrenched in his career, with the luxury of being able to decline overtures from larger markets because the place had grown on him so. Its Mexican aura the ultimate fringe benefit, San Antonio was remarkably stress-free for being the seventh-largest city in the country. Even their ten-year-old daughter Janet was thriving here. He'd remembered what it was like starting at a new school, and he was determined not to put her through that.

At least finish high school before you consider another move, he told himself.

For the first time in their lives they felt settled, truly at home.

Janet was at her friend's for the weekend, having gone home with her after school on Friday, a favor Jim and Jen would repay when they hosted Janet's friend next Saturday. How nice it was to make love without fear of being overheard! After a leisurely lunch, they debated between a stroll along the river followed by a cruise, with some sunset margaritas forming a segue to dinner, or a quick trip home for a long, slow siesta not entirely spent resting. Jim and Jenny still had the fire for each other, lacking only the ability to carve out enough time to realize it in the course of their successful careers. At the same time, they were gratified that they still felt like it, having seen the relationships of so many friends go belly up. Since they were already here and traffic in a big city being what it was, the walk and the cruise and the margaritas won out in what amounted to a no-lose decision. There was always a leisurely Sunday morning followed by that great Mexican brunch just down the road to look forward to the next day.

As they walked hand in hand, their faces warmed by the early afternoon sun as they savored the simple bliss of each other's company, they became aware of a buzzing sound.

"Jim, look!" Jenny said, pointing to a swirling mass above the trees. "Locusts? In downtown San Antone?"

"No, hummingbirds!" Jim said as a few of them drew near.

A faint chill of recognition as he recalled an incident involving hummingbirds at the lake some years ago, so unusual that it made the local papers.

Goddamned global warming, he thought. *What the fuck are we doing to this planet?*

"Hey!" he said as a bird swooped at him, knocking his favorite hat — a mesh-sided safari number that perched like an irony on his pale, pudgy head — into the river.

As he stooped to fish it out, another bird jabbed him in the back, causing him to windmill his arms and make the world's most unseemly dive into the water.

"Shit!" he said, spitting river murk. "So much for my smartphone and maybe my watch."

Jenny was laughing. "Your watch is water-resistant, remember? I bought it for your birthday."

"My dear, water-resistant ain't the same as waterproof. Trust me, this puppy is toast."

"Ah!" Jenny cried as a hummingbird buried its claws into her cheek and pecked at her.

She lost her balance when she whirled and swatted at it, soon joining her husband in the water.

"Holy shit!" Jim said. "What has gotten into these guys?"

"Ugh! My cheek stings!" Jenny said.

"God, honey, he really laid you open! Geez, I wonder what brought that on?"

"My perfume? A certain color? Mating season? I don't know — ah!" Jenny said as another bird swooped down, then another. "Oh, God!" she cried as a bird caught her in the eye, watching the blood jet from it with her other eye.

Jenny opened her mouth, and river water that was more pleasant to look at than drink came in, followed by two more birds. They were everywhere, attacking the veins under her tongue when she lifted it to scream, one of the big arteries in her neck, everything taking on a dreamy, other-worldly brightness as the blood flowed out of her. Moments later, she was floating face-down, a red halo emanating from her head.

Jim thrashed his way toward her. "Honey! Honey! Oh my God!"

Even as he was reaching for her, a pair of hummingbirds converged on him. One of them opened a vein on the back of his hand while another opened a vein on his inner wrist. Soon his hand was spurting blood, and he grew lightheaded, as much from shock as anything. It was every man for himself as he thrashed his way to the riverbank, ten feet away. Alas, the river was designed for boating, not swimming, its walls slimed with algae. The only thing he could grab hold of was a bollard sitting atop the bank. As he leaped for it with his good hand, struggling to pull himself up with arms that hadn't seen a pushup in more than a decade, the two hummingbirds opened three more veins, transforming both hands into mini-geysers of blood, Jim's desperate thrashing only speeding up the process of bleeding himself out on a carefree, sunny day with his wife in a city nine hundred miles away from Lake Tanaka. The screams from an approaching tour boat melded with the screams of the girl he heard that fateful night on the lake as his mind finally connected the dots in its last, dying thought. Soon husband and wife were bobbing face-down in the water, dying as they had lived: side by side.

***

Paul Mahr had to wait a couple of weeks before he could put a bow on this year's total, but put a gruesome little bow on it he did when two more homing pigeons arrived at the lake. James and Jennifer Spencer, attacked by hummingbirds in downtown San Antonio (of all places), survived by ten-year-old daughter Janet, had brought the year's total to eleven. Just as he knew it would

Chapter V

A couple of things about Millicent "Millie" Fremont: As early as age eight, she had sought to escape men — and she loved hummingbirds.

At age three, she was incredibly cute, and at six, she was dangerously cute, with big, sweet eyes and long, slender arms and legs, and smooth olive skin that invited touching. Every male relative wanted to sit her on his lap. Away from the scrutiny of her mother and other would-be protectors, more than one of them caressed her legs, a seemingly harmless clap on the knee often morphing into a sneaky trip up the inner thigh, sometimes venturing as far as the forbidden territory of her panties. But these were uncles and cousins, family and friends of the family. All of them were familiar, and her child's mind equated familiar with good, so she grew up thinking such attention was normal. She felt a growing discomfort, though, when she was alone with them, usually in a babysitting capacity while Mama was away. Then their hands went beyond forbidden territory to the Special Place Mama told her to keep covered when boys were around. Something about "modesty" and "being ladylike." All girls had this Special Place, so only when girls were around was it OK not to keep it covered.

There was the time she was eight, sitting on the couch watching TV with Uncle Rene. Half of him was belly, and his belly looked like a big cushion when, dressed only in his bathrobe, he invited her to sit on his lap. She was in her nightie, her body warm and fragrant from her bath, and he lifted her nightie as he hoisted her aboard. The next thing she knew, something warm and stiff was nudging against her Special Place.

She smiled nervously. "Uncle Rene, what are you doing?"

He responded with a sleepy smile. "Ah, ma chérie, I am tickling you. Do you like to be tickled?" he asked as he moved her to and fro on the head of his manhood.

It was a strange sensation, not entirely unpleasant. It did sort of tickle. Then, as she felt him going into her, it began to hurt.

"Ow! Uncle Rene, it does not tickle! It hurts! I want to go to bed now."

Uncle Rene reddened, quickly lifting her off of him. "OK, love, to bed with you. How about I come in and we say prayers, and I read you a bedtime story?"

Her family rarely told her bedtime stories, especially during the harvest.

"Yes, I would like that."

"Good! Wash your face and brush your teeth, and I will come."

And so he did.

"Uncle Rene, can you read me my favorite book? It is right here."

"Ma chérie is too special for books. Uncle Rene wants to tell you a story — one he made just for you!"

"OK."

"There was once a small, white mouse…"

"Yuck! I do not like a mouse!"

"But this was a special mouse, very small and very cute. He never bit anyone… he never got into anybody's food… he never made a mess."

"Oh."

"Can you feel him crawling?" he asked, his fingers fluttering up Millie's leg and arm to her nose, then down them again.

Millie laughed.

"But this was a sad mouse. He missed his family, this little mouse, but he was locked outside his house, and his family did not recognize him; they thought a cat was trying to get in. The night was cold and rainy, and the little mouse was shivering outside. He wanted to go inside where it was nice and warm and sit by the fire."

With this, he slipped his hand under Millie's nightgown, where it skittered mouselike up her leg. If it had been light enough to see, she would have been alarmed by the look in his eye, the way he licked his lips. As it was, she merely felt him, crawling up her leg. All the way to her Special Place: He seemed to like it there.

"He knocked on the door, but he did so quietly. He did not want to scare them," he said, gently caressing the sensitive space between her legs. This time it really did tickle, but it also hurt a little.

"Let me in! Let me in!" he cried. "It is me, Antoine!"

Gently he wiggled his index finger — thick and rough — into her, up to the first digit.

"Oh, chérie! He is so cute! Will you let him in?"

Alarm bells were sounding in her young mind. "No! It hurts! I will not let him in!"

Uncle Rene lost his erection.

"OK, love, you get some sleep now. No word about our story time, our watching TV together, to Papa or Mama, eh? Promise me it will be our little secret, OK?"

Millie gazed somberly at his darkened figure. "OK. I promise."

"Good girl! Maybe we will go to the zoo this weekend. Good night, chérie."

***

Millie made good on her promise while making sure her uncle never bothered her again.

"Mama," she said in the kitchen the next morning, "I do not want Uncle Rene to be my babysitter any more. He is mean, and his breath stinks."

"He will be sad to hear that, chérie."

"I do not care. Let him be sad."

A month later, Uncle Rene's feelings would be a moot point. A month later, his body would be found banging against the embankment of the Loire River. He had been drinking, the orbits where his eyes used to be like tunnels of shredded meat, an artery in his neck laid open, with tiny wounds all over his body. The authorities attributed these injuries to the repeated scrapings of his body against the wall and the broken cognac bottle they found on the riverbank. They figured he was so out of it he'd slashed his own throat when he tried to drink from a broken bottle, the wound being too ragged to be caused by a knife. The only curious thing was the two hummingbird feathers embedded in one of his eye sockets. But they also found some vegetation, a small fragment of plastic in the other eye, figuring the river had washed it there.

***

Millie Fremont was finally penetrated at age ten when fifteen-year-old cousin Maxim came to spend the night. He was a big, dark farm boy who smiled and told her he enjoyed wringing chicken's necks. This was on her mind when Maxim came into her bedroom that night with a loud "Shhh!" put what must have been saliva on the head of his member, and took her from behind as she lay on her side, all the while covering her mouth and threatening to break her neck if she made any noise. It hurt as he moved inside her, as nothing but her own, curious finger had ever been inside her Special Place before. It was *her* Special Place, after all. What right did anyone else have being in there? His big, rough hand muffled her cries, followed by him trying to silence his own cries as what he was doing apparently excited him. Afterward, she was alarmed to feel moisture coming out of her. When she turned on the light, she saw a creamy substance mixed with blood. She was so sore the next day it was painful to walk. It stung when she washed herself or urinated, and she continued to bleed intermittently.

Mama saw Millie's undies in the laundry and asked if she was having her first period.

"Yes," Millie said, knowing vaguely about periods and not knowing what else to say.

"You girls are starting earlier all the time. I did not have my first period until I was thirteen."

Millie was not happy. One day when she was feeding her favorite hummingbird, Pierre, and a few of the others, she confided in them what she dared not tell anyone else. Pierre gazed at her with his tiny eyes, tilting his shimmering red head as if he understood. Chirping to the others as if he were telling them something. Of course, he was telling them something; she just did not know what.

A week later, Maxim was cut in half when he was helping direct his father's tractor to the hay wain and got caught between them. Distracted by the swarm of hummingbirds that converged on him. Led by a hummingbird with a shimmering red head.

Then, when she was twelve, and her breasts were budding, and she'd had her first period, her father came home drunk one night and entered her room. He slipped off his pants — the sound of his belt with its big, round buckle and its crooked tooth clanking to the floor — and his underpants and slipped into bed behind her. His breath stank of alcohol, and his whiskers were scratching against her cheek. Evidently, he was so drunk he thought she was Mama.

"Papa?" she said as he lifted her nightie and her leg and fumbled for her Special Place, a place she knew all about now. A place men were strangely attracted to.

He tried to go into her, big and warm and stiff, but she wasn't ready. There was no way for her to be ready.

"Ow, Papa!" she cried when he succeeded, every inch of him an ordeal.

"Shhh!" he said.

He did not have to cover her mouth; she was already afraid of him. She whimpered as she endured his invasion, every movement a bright flash of pain. Shuddering when she realized it was not an accident, meaning it could happen again.

When he finished, he said, "You will say nothing of this to Mama. You will say nothing of this to anyone. Do you understand?"

Millie sniffled. "Yes, Papa."

He put on his underwear and felt for his pants, the buckle of his belt glinting from the bar of light that came from under the door as he fastened his pants and stumbled out.

She sat up in bed, hugging her knees to her small chest, crying softly. Bleeding. Again. It felt like more this time.

Mama yelled at her when she saw the sheet the next morning.

"Millie, did I not teach you how to use a tampon?"

Millie eyed her mother grimly, caught between an inability to tell her the truth and an unwillingness to keep lying. Dreading the endless harassment she could see unfolding before her.

Her response, then, was in a sort of code. "Mama, I am not having my period."

Whatever it was, Mama seemed to understand. Her mouth went round. Suddenly she knew, hastening to brush away the fear disguised as denial of something too big to acknowledge. Something the consequences of which carried an uncertain future, no less than the end of life as they knew it — the possible loss of everything.

"You will say nothing of this to anyone, do you understand?" Mama said, as sternly as Papa had the night before.

"Yes, Mama."

"Now strip your bed and get ready for school."

Millie went to school and, since she was not having her period, she did not bring a tampon. When she was doing jumping jacks in gym class, she started bleeding again, a thin line of blood running down her leg and staining the top of her white tube sock.

The gym teacher took Millie aside. "My dear, are you having your period?"

Millie looked her in the eye. "No, ma'am."

"Oh my! We had better get you in to see Nurse Claudine."

The nurse was a kindly older woman who reminded Millie of her Aunt Brigitte. She did not feel self-conscious about taking off her panties, letting the woman examine her.

Nurse Claudine frowned. "Millie, I am seeing signs of trauma here."

"Madame, what is 'trauma'?"

"Trauma occurs when something has been injured. There is some swelling and bruising; one of your… lips has a slight tear. Did someone… do this to you?"

Millie avoided her gaze, shrinking at the thought of betraying her father.

"No one did this to me. I… I was touching myself," she said, too quickly.

Nurse Claudine took Millie gently by the shoulders, gazing into her eyes with a pained smile.

"My dear, it is normal for girls your age to be… curious about their bodies, to… want to touch and explore their private places. However, it is not normal for girls to injure themselves. I am afraid I must report this."

Millie's face turned white as a sheet of notebook paper. "No, Madame! Please, no!"

"My dear, the law tells me I must. Please, I must take some pictures," she said, withdrawing a small digital camera.

"No!"

"Please, Millie! Do not worry; I will not photograph your face. Here, put your leg up on the stool. Good! Now open yourself, just like that. Good! A few more. Good! We are finished."

***

That night Papa came home from the fields before nightfall. He had not been drinking, and his gaze was icy as it fell upon Millie at the dinner table.

"Mama got a call from your school principal today. He said you were bleeding in gym class, and that the nurse examined you and took some pictures. He wants us to come in tomorrow morning and talk to him."

"Me, too?" Millie asked, her appetite displaced by a hollow feeling in her stomach.

"No, just us."

Papa's voice was like venom, his eyes like darts. "We are in the middle of the harvest. I will miss half a day of work because of this. What did you say to the nurse?"

Millie looked at him, her mouth quivering, her eyes tearing up.

"Answer me!"

"I told her… I told her I was touching myself."

"Are you sure that is all you told her?"

"Yes, Papa."

"Well, you had better not be lying."

"I am not lying, Papa."

That night she heard yelling in her parents' room after they thought she was asleep, escalating to the point it would have awakened her, anyway. Papa's voice was gruff, Mama's increasingly shrill. Finally, there was a slap and a shriek, followed by Papa shouting "Enough!" and Mama crying softly.

Breakfast was even more uncomfortable than dinner, Papa looking like a farmer impersonating a banker in his mismatched tie and rumpled suit. A cup of black coffee sat in front of him, and he glared at her with his arms folded across his barrel of a chest. His stomach rumbled, and to her mind it was his whole being.

Mama smiled at her, but it was a sad smile. Her right eye and the cheek beneath it were puffy. They looked pasty, as if she were trying to cover something with makeup.

"Did you sleep well, dear?" Mama asked in a futile attempt to break the tension.

Millie forced a smile, looking wan in spite of her white teeth, high cheekbones, and olive skin.

"Yes, Mama," she lied.

These were the only words exchanged during breakfast. The drive was silent in the family's only road vehicle, her father's pickup, meticulously scrubbed and polished as if to excuse its very existence, every strand of hay and clod of dirt removed from its bed. Indeed, she had never seen it so clean, and this alone unnerved her. Mama sat between Millie and Papa, her father scowling at an arrangement that wasn't normal.

They arrived to the sight of a police car parked in front of the school. A gendarme was inside, his elbow angling from the window. Papa felt a chill when he saw the car. More chills as they were led to the principal's office, and he saw another gendarme sitting there, the school nurse in a chair across from him, and the principal behind his desk.

"Would anyone like some coffee?" the principal asked.

"No, we are fine," Papa said.

"Yes, I would like some, please," Mama said, only to be met by Papa's glare.

Contradicting Papa: It just wasn't done.

As she was going to her next class, Millie shuddered when she heard her name over the intercom, telling her to report to the principal's office.

The two friends she was with ogled her and laughed. "Oooohhh, someone is in big trouble!"

Millie smiled, but she was petrified. She entered the principal's office to find there was no place to sit. Instead, her parents sat on one side of a tight horseshoe of chairs, the nurse and a gendarme — *A gendarme!* she thought, his dark, crisp uniform registering "serious" in her mind — on the other side, with the principal's desk connecting the two sides.

"Millie, thank you for joining us," the principal said. "As you are probably aware, this is about you. Nurse Claudine has reported evidence of physical abuse as per her examination of you yesterday."

He gestured to the half-dozen photos fanned across his desk. Millie flushing crimson when she realized her Special Place was on display.

"I have one question for you, and then you may go back to class. Please, think carefully before you answer. Millie, it is wrong, very wrong, for adults to do this sort of thing to kids. Adults who do this sort of thing to kids go to prison, where even their fellow prisoners hate them."

Millie's eyes met Papa's. He looked away, but the unspoken dialogue of their body language was unmistakable, and everyone in the room saw it.

The principal cleared his throat and continued. "Millie, if we do not stop adults from doing this sort of thing, they will only do it to other kids — and those kids will have… issues… problems later in life. You do not want other kids to be hurt, do you, Millie?"

"No, monsieur."

"OK, I will ask you the question, and I want you to answer carefully: Did anyone do this to you?"

Another glance at Papa, another incriminating glance that everyone saw.

"No, monsieur. As I told Nurse Claudine, I was touching myself. Maybe I touched myself too hard."

Nurse Claudine sighed and shook her head.

The principal raised his eyebrows. "Very well. You may be excused."

Instead of returning directly to class, she lingered in the anteroom, empty save for two chairs and a coffee table scattered with magazines. Adult voices rose in the room behind her, the principal's foremost among them.

"Officer, she denies it! We have no choice!" Then, to Papa, in a tone calmed by menace, "Today you are a lucky man, monsieur. Tomorrow you will not be so lucky. One more incident, and I promise you the gendarmes will take you away! Do I make myself clear?"

Papa said nothing, glaring at him sullenly.

The principal's bald head was red as a balloon, his eyes on fire.

"We will be watching this matter closely, monsieur! I am warning you: one more incident!" he cried.

Millie hurried out of the anteroom, her heart thudding. Part of her was glad the truth was out, in spite of her best efforts to conceal it. But were they? It occurred to her the look she gave him in the office might have been seen as accusatory, even if it were involuntary. The truthful gaze of innocence.

Part of her dreaded the reception she would get at home. If she feared Papa before, she truly feared him now. Now she was afraid even to speak to him, even to meet his gaze for fear of being cuffed across the mouth. Or worse.

That night she was grateful Papa didn't come home for dinner. A shudder swept through her as she realized he was probably out drinking, and when he came home he would be loud and hit people and things. Still, only the most tepid of interactions between her and Mama at dinner, Papa's absence the trumpeting elephant in the room that couldn't be ignored.

A prolonged fumbling of keys accompanied by muttering and a loud crash as the front door thwacked open was enough to wake her from the shallowest of sleep. She sat bolt upright in bed, wide-eyed and hugging her knees to her chest. She was doing this more often lately — something about it made her feel safer — all the while ready to lower her head between her knees like a turtle retreating into its shell. She held her breath, betraying her wakefulness by whimpering softly when heavy footsteps stopped in front of her door, two pools of darkness breaking up the bar of light that shone beneath it. She listened intently as the knob moved slightly, her heart racing, but the door did not open. It was as if he were toying with her. The footsteps clumped on to Mama's room, accompanied by muttering.

"You are warning me, you bitch?"

"Shhh!" Mama said. "You will wake her up!"

"Oh, I will wake her up, all right! The trouble that little whore has caused me!"

"Do not call our daughter that!"

"Shut up! I will call her whatever I want to!"

Millie's heart was a trip hammer. Then a miracle happened. Roughly he closed the door to the room he shared with Mama and turned in for the evening.

For the next three weeks it went on. Far from abating, his anger seemed to fuel itself, despite her avoiding interacting with him as much as possible. Despite her making a point of staying the hell out of his way. An anger that saw her hugging her knees so hard every night that she was putting her legs to sleep. Falling eventually into a fitful slumber that saw him storming through her nightmares, always shouting, always coming after her with a weapon: the hatchet he used on chickens; the ax he used to chop wood; the saw he used to remove branches; the rifle he used to hunt pheasants and roe deer. Once, she dreamed of him coming after her with his member, marbled with veins like a blood-engorged serpent, bloody with her blood and poised to strike again. Sometimes she screamed herself awake, and thank God it was Mama who came. Sweet, soothing Mama, a balm in human form. No one in the house was sleeping well; Millie's pale golden skin was becoming ashen and anemic-looking, with brown semicircles forming under her eyes. Her friends noticed the difference. Everyone noticed what was happening to the seventh grade's smartest, prettiest girl. The principal was ready to call the police, lacking only the decisive piece of evidence.

One day Mama overheard Millie talking to her hummingbirds out by the feeders, particularly the red-headed one she called Pierre. There was an edge to her daughter's voice that troubled her.

"No, Pierre! I said no! He is my father! This will pass! And that goes for you, too, Jerome!" she said to the green-headed one.

The exchange chilled her as she remembered how Maxim and Rene had met their demise, hummingbirds being a factor in both deaths.

Could it be? she thought.

Immediately, she dismissed the thought as ludicrous, surprised that she should even think it.

One night it all came to a head. One night her father stumbled in, and this time, he did not stop at her doorway. Instead, the knob turned, and her bedroom door slammed against the wall, hard enough to put a knob-sized hole in the plaster. She had just gotten to sleep, and it jolted her awake like a nightmare become reality. She opened her eyes to see his hulking silhouette in the dim light of the doorway, swaying from drink. Whisking sound as his belt passed through the loops, its buckle catching the light as he removed it. Millie watched him come, hugging her knees so tightly that her arms hurt, her eyes huge with fear.

He was holding the belt not by its buckle, but by its strap.

Frantically the turtle's head went into its shell, bracing itself for the onslaught.

"Bitch whore!" he cried as the belt came down on her. Again and again it came down, wrapping around her arms and legs and sides like a bullwhip. Lacing her body with thick, red welts.

Mama flew up behind him, screaming, and Papa turned and sent her flying against the wall.

"God, Papa, please stop! Oh, God!" Millie cried.

His response was to grab the leather end of the belt and use the buckle, turning a whip into a bludgeon. The buckle came down with a clang, bruising her whenever its crooked tooth wasn't gouging and drawing blood. Again and again it tore into her, causing injury with every blow.

Then, all of a sudden, he stopped, his body shaking with sobs.

"Oh, my Millie! Dear God! What have I done to my Millie?!" he cried.

He tried to embrace her, but she screamed as if she were still under attack. She screamed, and her hands were claws, one of them finding his hairy forearm as she pushed him away with all the strength she could muster. He stumbled out of the room and closed the door of the room he shared with Mama, whom she could still see on the floor as she heard her father's sobs through the wall.

Her body was one giant ache as gingerly she got herself out of bed and turned on the light and went to her mother.

"My dear, sweet Millie! I am so sorry!" her mother said. "Oh my God, you are bleeding! Come to the bathroom, and we shall get you cleaned up. Oh!" she cried when Millie helped her to her feet.

"Please, I cannot be with him tonight. Let me sleep with you," her mother said when they were finished.

Somehow Millie slept, and when she awoke, Mama was gone and the house was quiet. Blessedly quiet. What had happened the night before seemed like a bad dream, worse than any of the others. As she surveyed her surroundings, she saw the mounting evidence that it wasn't a dream. Her bed was splattered with blood. There were deep, nasty little wounds all over her arms and legs, some of them crusted over, some of them oozing. Her head was throbbing, and when she touched it, she felt blood crusted in her hair. Her legs stung when she touched or even moved them, angry purple welts crisscrossing them like a busy intersection.

Strangely comforting to see Mama, the only constant in her life along with the hummingbirds, standing like a sentry at her usual morning post in the kitchen.

"Mama, are you OK?"

"Yes, my dear," Mama said, managing a smile over the pan she was stirring. "I have a pretty good lump on the back of my head, and my back is pretty sore, but I'm good enough to get to the stove and make us some breakfast."

Soon they were at the kitchen table having breakfast.

"Millie, your mama has something to say to you," Mama said, putting her hand on her daughter's arm. "I just want to say I am sorry. This never needed to happen, and it was my fault for not reporting your father's abuse sooner. I suppose

I was afraid — of him, of what getting him in trouble would do to our lives — but a life spent living in fear is no life at all. This never needed to happen, and I promise you it will never happen again. Today, I am not going to your principal, I am going directly to the police. No more of this. This ends today."

***

There was no other choice but to keep working until the harvest was in. Papa was accustomed to beginning his days with a hangover, though, albeit more stubborn than the morning fog, it usually burned off by noon. It did not stop him. He could not allow anything to stop him. He was out in the field on a tractor laden with onions when he saw a police car turn off the main road onto the gravel road that ran past the field. Even before the two gendarmes emerged, instinct told him what was up. They would not take him easily, these two city cops with their soft hands, not on his land, in front of his men. Using the tractor as a visual barrier, he eased himself down the far side and made a break for the river. Marked by rows of cypress and poplar, it was less than a kilometer away.

Once I make it to the river, let those city boys try to find this country boy! he thought.

The gendarmes were pale-skinned, more familiar with office than fieldwork, if you could call sitting in your car most of the time fieldwork. Seldom had they fired their weapons in the line of duty, shooting instead at targets they imagined as men. Millie's father knew it was hard to shoot a real man, not realizing video games made it easier than it used to be. Besides, the senior officer wasn't willing to age gracefully, the junior officer fresh enough from the academy to still be in reasonably good shape. They had also recently been to the firing range. Soon they circumvented the tractor and had a clear shot at the broad-shouldered man in a green flannel shirt they were not about to run down, for the simple fact they did not need to. Each of them stopped, took a knee, and steadied his aim.

"Police! Stop!" the senior officer shouted what he was compelled to, a gesture designed to be perfunctory and nothing more. Then, to the junior officer, "Aim low."

Two shots rang out. One of them raised a puff of dirt behind the man's right foot, causing him to zigzag and run faster. The other shot missed badly. Both shots having served their purpose of gauging the distance of a moving target, they shot again. One shot was a near miss; the other caused the figure to jerk and grab his leg as he went down.

The senior officer smiled. *Always better to take them alive*, he thought, speaking into his shoulder radio.

"Officer Du Maurier requesting an ambulance to the Fremont farm, five miles west of Nantes, north field, just off the old Doucette Highway. We are parked near the road. Lights are on."

Chapter VI

The hummingbird bug first bit her, hummingbirds not being much larger than bugs, when she was three years old and watching them feed at Grandmama's house.

"They live on nectar, red nectar," Grandmama had told her. "You make it with sugar, water, and red food coloring."

Millie didn't have the heart to tell Grandmama that she and the ninety percent of people who still believed this were wrong. She found out because as soon as she was old enough to read, she read up on hummingbirds. While the red feeders were an attractant, the red food coloring was unnecessary and even potentially harmful, differing from the clear nectar of the plants they pollinated. And, while hummingbirds needed the nectar for carbs, they also needed bugs for protein. She learned these things, and she just smiled and let Grandmama believe whatever she wanted to because she was old, and it was too late to change her, anyway. It was fun to know things other people didn't and have it be a secret. Like hummingbirds being the second most common bird species, with nearly 340 varieties, though only ten of those varieties could be found in Europe. Or hummingbirds being at least 22 million years old or able to live at 17,000 feet. Or that hummingbirds were twice as fast as Peregrine falcons, the world's fastest bird, for their size, their tiny wings able to fly five hundred miles without stopping.

Mainly, though, hummingbirds were cute and wonderful little birds, tiny jewels of life that bobbed and hovered, flicking hollow tongues designed to suck up nectar. My, how they chirped and dived at each other with those pointy little beaks, their wings buzzing like propellers! My, how she wouldn't want to get one of them mad at her, buzzing all around her like a huge, angry hornet, poking her in the eye with that sharp little beak!

Of course, such fears were unfounded. So used to her were the hummingbirds that by the time she was six, she would pour a little nectar into her hand. "Red, or they will never come!" Grandmama cried, and the bird would surprise Grand-mama by perching on Millie's fingers with its little scratchy feet and feed right from her hand. Sometimes it was fun to shut Grandmama up without saying a word! The adults were incredulous. Soon she was naming the birds, introducing them to her family.

"The one with the red head is Pierre: He is my favorite, but do not tell the others! The small, brown one is Madeleine: She is very shy. That is her over there. She will not come if there are strangers around. The one with the green head is Jerome. I think he is jealous of Pierre. They fight a lot!"

This from a six-year-old. Mama was only too happy to let her raise humming-birds. Considering she had six feeders, going all the way around the back porch and filled dutifully every night, "raise" was the right word.

One evening several years later, Mama was shocked to see two hummingbirds fighting at the feeder both of them seemed to favor — no doubt because the other one did — and her daughter intervene.

"Pierre... Jerome... stop! Jerome, you come over here, now!"

And Jerome did.

"Sacre bleu!" Mama said, her hand to her chest. "St. Milburg!"

With it, a renewed suspicion of how Rene and Maxim had died.

Millie studied hummingbirds and captured them on paper: with crayons and finger paint — Mama, of course, preferred crayons — when she was three, with watercolors when she was eight, and with Conte crayons and oil paints from then on. More than one teacher proudly displayed her work in class. So pretty and smart and sweet was Millie that no one begrudged her the attention. She was The Hum-mingbird Girl and, when she and her friends were sneaking off to the tattoo parlor at age twelve to engage in one of the rights of passage to adulthood, Millie traded the tattoo artist an oil painting of Pierre for a tiny tattoo of his likeness on her right ankle. No one but her closest friends knew about it, and every morning she smiled as she covered what amounted to a symbol of deliverance from her father with a sock. He was in prison, more than once asking Mama to see her, but the thought of ever seeing him again gave her pause. As far as she was concerned, he started dying the night he raped her and was dead and buried the night he nearly beat her to death. Pierre was her chief protector, and it occurred to her the beating never would have happened if she had allowed him and Jerome to have their way. In the meantime, having Pierre on her ankle was her good luck charm. For keeping men away.

Now that she was about to turn thirteen, she noticed men looking at her more often, even staring, the faraway look in their eyes softening into benign smiles when she met their gaze. But there was no disguising what lurked in their minds, free to roam where their bodies dared not venture. She saw their eyes, saw herself the way they saw her: with her panties off and her training bra down, riding up and down on the stiffness between their legs their wives could never satisfy. Maybe it was because their wives were adults, people who insisted on being treated as equals. People who could not be controlled the way a child could. Control: There must be something sexy about it, though, for the life of her, she couldn't understand what.

She was the top student in her class, the feminine radiance she exuded better suited to an eighteen-year-old. The sort of beauty that had always made her a target was beginning to pay off.

Almost a year to the day of that fateful meeting with her parents, the principal called her into his office. A squat woman with dark, curly hair smiled at her from a nearby chair.

"Millie, this is Madame Diaz. She is with an exchange student program in the United States."

"Pleased to meet you, my dear," Madame Diaz said.

"Pleased to meet you, Madame Diaz."

"Millie, how would you like to spend eighth grade in America?" the principal asked. "Madame Diaz has arranged for you to stay with a nice family in St. Louis, Missouri. Would you like that?"

"I do not know St. Louis, Missouri," Millie said.

"St. Louis is the name of the city, and Missouri is the name of the state it is in. States are kind of like countries. Some of them are very big. For example, the State of Texas is about the size of France."

"I have heard of Texas," Millie said.

"St. Louis was named after your king, Louis IX. There is a big statue of him in Forest Park, where the 1904 World's Fair took place. Where the hot dog and the ice cream cone were invented," Madame Diaz said.

"Really? Wow!" Millie said.

"St. Louis is in the middle of the country, about three hundred miles south of a much larger city called Chicago."

"I have heard of Chicago," Millie said.

"I am not surprised. Your principal tells me you are a very smart girl. St. Louis has a famous monument called The Gateway Arch, and its zoo and botanical garden are both very nice."

"What is a 'botanical' garden?" Millie asked.

"A botanical garden has plants from all over the world. Some of them are rare plants that scientists like to study," Madame Diaz said.

"I see."

"It also has a baseball team and a hockey team and is known for making beer. I am sure you will learn many things about this city."

"It all sounds very nice. This family I will be staying with, do they have kids?"

"Yes, they have a daughter about your age," Madame Diaz said. "They were hoping you could teach her some French."

"I would be happy to do that."

"If everything works out, maybe you could even stay longer than a year. And, if you do well in high school — what they call secondary school — you could earn a scholarship and stay there for college," the principal said. "Millie, this is a rare opportunity. Are you interested?"

"Do they have hummingbirds in St. Louis?"

Madame Diaz laughed. "My dear, I knew you would ask, so I did some research. There are more varieties of hummingbirds in St. Louis than there are here. Why, at certain times of the year, the trees are full of them."

"Wow! Yes, I am interested!"

"Good," the principal said. "Their school year is like our school year, meaning it is almost over, there is the summer break, and it starts up again in the fall. Early September, Madame Diaz?"

"Yes, monsieur, just after a holiday called Labor Day."

"So we will have the summer to make the arrangements, and you will have the summer to prepare for the trip and say your goodbyes. Does that sound good?" the principal asked.

"It sounds like a dream!" Millie said. "Thank you both so much!"

The principal smiled. It was nice to see him smile after being so angry at Papa.

"Millie, you can thank us by doing well — and teaching your new sister some French!"

***

The summer flew by like a hummingbird. Before she knew it, she was on the train to Paris, Mama looking sad as she watched the last remnant of her family disappear, then the train to the airport, neither of which she had ever been to. She was by turns excited, disoriented, and scared. She had heard it called "culture shock," and she was surprised to feel it in her own country, including when she boarded a plane for the first time, a plane with two levels of seats that held more than five hundred people. Still more culture shock as she looked out her window when the plane was landing and saw the spiky skyline of New York City. Arriving at last in a place she had only dreamed of. She wanted to see the Statue of Liberty she had pictured so vividly, disappointed when a flight attendant pointed out a small bluish-green blotch at the end of the island. Alas, her connecting flight to St. Louis left in three hours, not enough time for a closer look.

But this was no time to be disappointed, certainly no time to be disoriented. The airport was even bigger than the one in Paris. She was determined to stay with the herd of passengers who had disembarked with her, keeping a close eye on her passport and wallet. Although Mama had never flown, Auntie had, and Auntie had told her about the low-lifes that hung around bus stations and train stations and airports looking for people who looked confused, especially foreigners.

"They would take advantage of someone from another country?" Millie asked.

"I am afraid so, my dear," Auntie said. "That is why it is important to always look like you know what you are doing, even when you do not."

Millie shone, her skin glowing with summer color. People noticed her like they always did, though at least not for her passport or wallet. She smiled with would-be confidence, stayed with her fellow passengers, knowing they would lead her to Immigration and Baggage and Customs — "I Bring Cheerfulness," she remembered the phrase she had come up with to remember them in that order.

After Immigration, she followed the herd to Baggage, waiting for her luggage at one of several large carousels, under an electronic sign with her flight number on it. She was in the right place, she was sure, but a growing apprehension came over her when most of her fellow passengers collected their bags and left — for Customs, no doubt — while there remained no sign of hers. Moment of panic when there were just a few bags left on a carousel that resembled a giant thrift store bracelet with most of its "gems" missing, none of them hers, and no more bags came down the chute, and the flight number on the sign changed.

Oh my God! she thought. *Has somebody stolen my bags?*

There she stood, feeling like the last person on earth, looking utterly forlorn as the tears came.

A kindly older woman in a navy-blue coat with wings over the pocket came up to her.

"What seems to be the problem, my dear?"

"My suitcases! They do not come! I think somebody has stolen them!"

"Hmm. May I see your ticket?" the woman asked.

The woman looked official enough. Millie handed it to her.

Immediately the woman smiled. "Love, your bags are on the plane for St. Louis. You will find them when the plane lands there."

"Oh, thank you, Madame!" Millie cried, kissing the woman on the cheek.

The woman was pleasantly taken aback. "There, there, now. Let us see about getting you on that plane," she said, showing Millie to her gate.

Thanking the woman profusely when they had arrived, Millie celebrated with some fruit juice, bought at the nearest shop with the dollars Auntie said she should carry.

My first purchase in America! she thought, the fear of her most recent ordeal abating. Travel was more complicated than she thought, and first times were always the hardest

She sat in a row of chairs in front of a huge window, alternating her gaze between the planes going by and a monitor that showed the news in English. She understood some of it, thinking it odd that it should be in English and also have English subtitles.

For deaf people, she realized.

The words "St. Louis" and "flight" over the intercom broke through her reverie, and soon she was bouncing down a carpeted metal tunnel to her plane.

St. Louis looked hot and dusty and rather bleak in the late afternoon sun, much smaller than New York. There were three tall buildings — that was all — a couple of stadiums, and that was it. No, wait! There was that big, curvy thing in the middle, the one she'd been reading about: The Gateway Arch! Two hundred meters tall, and you could take a little train all the way to the top and see the view! Maybe this would make up for the Statue of Liberty! She was also looking forward to Forest Park and the zoo. True, it wasn't New York, but it sounded like there were still some pretty cool things to do here.

She tingled with anticipation as she disembarked, once again reminding herself to go through Immigration, Baggage, and Customs in that order. Before this trip, Madame Diaz was the only American she had ever met, and for some reason she thought she would be meeting her at the airport. Then she remembered it would be her host family, the Talbots, and how important first impressions were, especially with their daughter she'd be spending so much time with. Frantically she tried to remember their names. Actually, there was only one name she needed to remember: Their daughter's name was "Jessie"; no, it was "Justy," short for "Justine"! Her parents' names were easy enough: just call them "Mr. and Ms. Talbot," not "monsieur and madame." While they might find it "quaint" — a word she had learned Americans like to use when describing other cultures — it would be inappropriate. They might even laugh at her, a notion that uneased her.

Immigration was no problem, easier than New York — for her, at least. She noticed dark-skinned people, some of them wearing turbans, being taken aside by men in uniforms and animated discussions ensuing, passports being leafed through, etc.

Baggage was no problem. It seemed she was the only one traveling with a new set of mauve-colored luggage.

Ditto Customs — for her, anyway. Whenever there was a commotion, she turned to see dark-skinned people arguing with airport officials. It seemed to be a pattern, and she wondered if these people were unused to traveling or if it was even their fault. Always the dark people, the ones who looked different. She smiled when they finally got to meet their families: shouting, hugging, kisses, and tears, all of it very loud!

She scanned the scene, her smile broadening when she saw them. They had even spelled her name right! Mr. Talbot was tall and good-looking, and she felt a twinge of unease when their eyes met and he gave her The Look. Just as quickly it disappeared, supplanted by the Appropriate Father Look she was accustomed to seeing in all but her most unguarded moments with men. She was getting used to the idea that men found her attractive and that The Look was normal, as long as it didn't become a stare or the man did more than look. Ms. Talbot was petite — shorter, even, than Millie — with a pretty face and twinkly, maternal eyes. Pretty in a striking sort of way, Justine was a gangly fifteen-year-old who had inherited her father's height. Her aquiline nose was her most arresting feature, more "French" even than Millie's, her long, slim arms extending from a sleeveless top. Something calming, down-to-earth about her smile, and it only seemed natural when she hugged Millie and called her "my French sister." Millie liked her immediately.

"Let's get a cart for those stylish bags of yours," Mr. Talbot said jauntily. "Our car isn't very far."

Justine shot her father an amused look. "Uh, Dad, suitcases have wheels now. What will they think of next? We can... like... roll them."

Mr. Talbot laughed. "My daughter, the future crime scene investigator."

Justine rolled her eyes. "Um, forensic scientist."

"What's the diff?"

"OK, here we go again. Crime scene investigation is field-based — as in at the... crime... scene. CSIs take photographs, put down evidence markers, sketch the crime scene, take notes, collect evidence — bagging the stuff that forensic scientists will be looking at — and interview victims and witnesses, while forensics is primarily lab-based. We make sense of the stuff the CSIs drag in from the field."

Mr. Talbot stifled a grin. "I see. Thank you for the edification, Justy.

"What is that supposed to mean?"

"Look it up, smarty-pants. Say, is anybody hungry?"

"I am," Millie said.

"Good," Ms. Talbot said. "We made reservations at an Italian restaurant. Have you ever had Italian food, Millie?"

"Mama makes spaghetti sometimes, and of course French bread is a lot like Italian bread, and the French and the Italians both love garlic."

Mr. Talbot couldn't help but marvel at Millie's accent, the way she pursed her lips as she shaped the words, as if kissing each one as she sent it on its way.

"I think you'll like it, then," Ms. Talbot said.

Millie couldn't remember a more satisfying meal. From the crusty bread dipped in salted olive oil to the Caesar salad, the lasagna, and the tiramisu with the little candle stuck in it — they pretended it was her birthday — everything was perfect. As they drove through the city at night, the strangeness of her new home dawned on her. Everything was so bright and quiet and neat. The city seemed much bigger at night, much bigger than it did from the plane.

"If you girls haven't made any plans for Saturday, I was thinking Forest Park," Mr. Talbot said.

"Where the St. Louis World's Fair was held!" Millie said.

"Yes!"

"Where they invented the ice cream cone... and the hot dog in 1904!" Millie said.

"Smart girl!"

"Not so smart. Madame Diaz told me that."

"C'mon, honey, give yourself some credit," Ms. Talbot said. "You were the top student in your class."

"OK, maybe I am kind of smart."

Everyone laughed.

As they drove, the yards got bigger, the trees got bigger, and the houses got bigger and farther apart.

"What part of the city is this?" Millie asked.

"Ladue," Mr. Talbot said.

"Ladue is very nice."

"We like to think so."

The car turned into a driveway that arced past a large, pillared house.

"Welcome home, Millie," Mr. Talbot said.

Millie had envisioned a room with twin beds or even bunk beds, shared with Justine. She was surprised to have her own room, with a queen-sized bed and attached bath. It was like staying at a hotel, with clean, white towels of various sizes (the letter "M" scripted on the corner of each one, no less!), a toothbrush wrapped in plastic, and a little bar of soap shaped like a seashell and smelling of lavender.

"This is the guest bedroom," Ms. Talbot said. "Grandma used to stay here."

"Where is she now?" Millie asked.

"She's getting up there, in her eighties. She fell and broke her hip — or her hip broke and she fell; we'll never know which. Anyway, she broke it pretty good.

A lot of pins holding it together, a lot of rehab ahead of her, and she's none too happy about it. Anyway, we're going to see her tomorrow when Dan gets off work."

That was it: 'Dan' Talbot!

"I'm afraid dinner tomorrow night will be pretty casual. Do you like pizza?"

"Yes."

"Good, we'll order you a pizza. There's some soda in the fridge."

"You will not be joining me?"

"No, honey. Sorry to leave you alone your second night here, but this is a family matter. Grandma hasn't been herself since this happened. She might not appreciate us bringing a stranger along. You'll meet her sometime, I promise."

"I understand."

"I'm glad. In the meantime, we have a great home theater system, lots of movies you can watch, including *The Horseman on the Roof,* a French movie Justy thought you might enjoy. Justy can show you how to use it. And don't forget Forest Park on Saturday! Usually, we do the museum in the morning, the zoo in the afternoon, and a baseball game in the evening if the Cards are in town — and they will be this Saturday. It should be a fun day."

"I will look forward to it."

"Oh, one more thing: Open your curtains in the morning if you want to see what Dan has been up to in the backyard and I've been up to in the garden. G'night, love."

"Goodnight, Ms. Talbot."

"Please, you're practically my daughter now. You can call me 'Sarah' or you can call me 'Mom.' Just don't call me Ms. Talbot: It makes me feel old."

"OK, Mom."

"Good girl! Better get some sleep now. First day of school tomorrow. G'night, love."

As she stood beneath the warm, pulsating jets of her personal shower, Millie reflected on the strangeness of travel, how small it made the world seem. In less than twenty-four hours, she had gone from the Brittany region of France to its capital city, itself another world, hopped on a plane crossing the Atlantic to New York, another world, then another plane to St. Louis and a nice American family, a yummy Italian meal, and a beautiful house with her own room, even her own bathroom. On the way, she had seen thousands of people from all over the world, people she would never see again. It was bizarre and exhausting, and even a little sad. All that travel, all those people, one world after another streaming past in an endless parade of life. The warmth of the water made her realize just how long her day had been, how tired she was. Yet another surprise when she saw a bathrobe with an "M" on the pocket hanging on the back of the bathroom door, a cushy-looking pair of slippers nearby. She put them on — everything was so soft — and opened her new toothbrush, brushing her teeth with toothpaste that had red and blue stripes in it.

In honor of France? I would not be surprised, she thought while reminding herself the American flag was also red, white, and blue.

The day's last surprise was a pair of flannel pajamas decorated with rosebuds lying on the bed.

This is how a princess must feel, she thought, smiling as she put them on.

Falling into a dead sleep with a smile on her face, even given the soft, strange bed she slept on.

***

Millie awoke the next morning to a tapping on her door.

"Sis? It's me, Justy," a voice said through the door.

Millie yawned, stretching deliciously. "Entre vous."

"What?"

"'Entre vous' is French for 'come in.' Your first lesson!"

"Merci," Justine said, laughing as she opened the door.

Smells of bacon and coffee wafting from the kitchen. The only things missing were biscuits, and she knew there was no time for that on a Friday.

"Mom told me to wake you up. We won't be leaving for a couple of hours, but she wanted to make sure you have time to get ready."

"OK. I will be ready soon."

Smiling faces as she looked around the breakfast table and realized she was really here, that it wasn't a dream.

Dan Talbot smiled as he looked up from his newspaper.

"How did you sleep, honey?"

"Very well, Mr. Talbot."

Talbot put down his paper in mock disgust. "OK, if you can call my wife 'Sarah' or even 'Mom,' you can certainly call me 'Dan' or 'Dad' or even 'Papa' if you like. I'm kind of funny about my age, too."

A shadow crept over her face at the word 'Papa.' Millie recovered and smiled.

"OK... Dad."

Talbot smiled back. "Much better. Most of the kids take the bus to school. Yours is number forty-seven. Justy will show you where to catch it after school. It's a very nice school, by the way. There's a soccer field — a 'football pitch,' I think you would call it (Millie nodded), tennis courts, and an indoor pool."

"And a library?"

"All St. Louis County public schools have libraries. Ladue has one of the best," Sarah said.

"It better be, seeing as how they keep raising our property taxes," Talbot said.

"C'mon, honey, don't start."

"Hey, I said it good-naturedly," he said, scanning the table for Justine's reaction.

Justine smiled and shook her head. Millie sensed a healthy bond between them, one that was gratifying to see after her experience with Papa. History, distant history. A different world, and nobody ever had to know about it.

"We'd better get going," Justine said to Millie. "Pen? Notebook?"

"Yes. Yes," Millie said.

Sarah held up a smartphone. "Do you have one of these?"

"No, Mom."

"Take this one. Do you know how to use it?"

"No, Mom."

"Justy can show you on the bus. A smartphone is a good thing to have, especially if we need to reach each other during the day. Especially since phone booths have nearly gone the way of the dodo bird."

"The dodo bird?"

Talbot smiled. "There used to be millions of them; now they're extinct. Look it up."

Millie smiled. "That is the same thing you said to Justy. Except you did not call me 'smarty-pants.'"

Talbot laughed. "Not yet. 'Look it up' is what I tell both of my daughters. Both of you are smart girls. Look things up and savor that… Moment of Discovery."

Justine rolled her eyes.

Talbot smiled and ruffled her hair just to annoy her.

"Gotta go, princess!"

Millie watched him go with a strange and deliberate clarity, as if trying to ingrain his image in her mind, if only to prove it was real. For a fleeting moment, Dan Talbot stood in the doorway, his tall silhouette framed by a rectangle of light, armed for the business wars with leather briefcase in hand. His shoes made a clicking sound as he headed down the walk, to the car parked at the apex of the curve — the top of The Arch.

Ditto Sarah Talbot, rinsing the breakfast dishes and loading them into the dishwasher, the sleeves of her pale blue shirt with dark blue pinstripes rolled up, her hair pulled back in a yellow scrunchie, and her back to the girls as they headed out the door.

"Be good, Mom," Justine said.

Sarah turned and wrinkled her nose in mock disdain.

"You know something? I'm tired of being good! It's not easy being a parent, you know. All this 'role model' stuff to live up to. Always the danger of your daughter putting you on such a high pedestal that you're afraid you're gonna fall off and hurt yourself."

Justine laughed. Millie smiled, the sarcasm eluding her.

"Such high expectations you have for your humble mother! If only I could be bad once in a while! Just to see if I can remember what it feels like! Tell you what, I'll be as good as you are. How about that?"

"How about, Mom, I think you're a hoot! See you later."

"OK, honey. Enjoy your first day."

"Not likely," Justine said. "The last time I checked, 'first days at school' and 'enjoyment' were polar opposites."

"Don't forget about Grandma."

"Ugh, don't remind me!"

"C'mon, honey. Grandma needs us."

"I know, I just feel like being… difficult, that's all."

"Then, tomorrow, Forest Park!"

"See you, Mom," Millie said.

"See you, honey."

***

The first day of school was as good as could have been expected, as good as the abrupt transition from balmy summer days that seemed to spill endlessly on like an extended canoe trip to swimming pools suddenly turning green, school buses appearing like yellow jackets through the trees, the first chill of fall in the air, clothes too scratchy and new to be cool, crisp textbooks stinking of printer's ink, and the familiar smell of pine disinfectant in bathrooms and locker rooms would allow.

Although some questioned the logic of starting school on a Friday only to shut everything down for the weekend and restart in earnest on Monday, there was no question about it in Justine's mind. Friday was a fluke, the swipe of disinfectant before the injection. Friday was the transition, easing the way for the grim reality to follow, buffered by that illusion of a mini-vacation, the weekend, squeezing two more days out of summer that could even be made to feel like three if you made Friday seem like the-weekend-come-early with dinner or a movie or a ballgame. Yes, starting school on Friday was a good idea, Justine decided, and it was all about psychology.

After school, Justine showed Millie where to catch the bus, but instead of getting on it with her, she got into her parents' gray Lexus that pulled up in front of the school. It being Cazh Friday, Dan and Sarah Talbot were able to get off early. Millie felt more of that strange and deliberate clarity as Justine Talbot turned and waved as she got into the car, looking very tall as the late afternoon sun formed a halo behind her. As she saw the impression of hands waving through the tinted glass, Millie feeling a sense of loss she couldn't explain as they pulled away with a smart tap of the horn.

***

The care center — politically correct-ese for "nursing home" — was a hectic place on Friday, everyone making plans for the weekend: in the families' case getting the chore of visiting their loved one out of the way so they could enjoy a guilt-free weekend; in the staffs' case getting through the paperwork that would only be worse if it waited until Monday.

Grandma did not like her new aide, and she felt the charge nurse was being dismissive whenever she complained about something, and there was always something to complain about. Plus, she was still having a lot of pain during physical therapy. Overall she wasn't progressing as quickly as she had hoped and, as a result, was feeling increasingly trapped and frustrated.

Her family was embroiled in an animated discussion about her care even as they were heading for dinner in the last of the evening traffic: "Do we need to find another place? Will Grandma be happy anywhere? Could we get her a personal nurse and an aide, at least part-time, so she could stay at home? Could we make some modifications to the house — like bathroom rails or a wheelchair ramp —

and take care of her ourselves? Then again, she would need an aide, if not a nurse, almost 24/7; I'm not strong enough to move her (Sarah talking), and we both have to work. This would be expensive, even for us. I'm not sure how much of it her insurance will cover," etc.

So comfortable were their seats, so smooth the ride, it was easy to imagine they were in their living room. It was dark out, and darkness was preferable to the late afternoon sunshine that could dazzle even the cleanest windshield, making it difficult to see the road. In the darkness, you could see the big, round taillights of the semi that suddenly stopped in front of you — that is, if your head wasn't turned as you were making a point to your wife in the passenger seat, your daughter's eyes on you as she hunched forward to join the conversation from the back seat.

Sarah Talbot uttered the only word that was spoken when she glanced over at the last second and screamed, "Dan!"

No squeal of good, new tires controlled by a computerized braking system, just the whoosh of airbags as the car met the rear end of the truck midway between its hood and rooftop.

Shearing off the airbags in one instant, the passengers' heads in the next as the car embedded itself beneath the truck with a metallic shriek that could have been death itself.

An hour later, Millie's smartphone rang, just as she was watching *The Horseman on the Roof* in French with English subtitles.

An hour later, a life that had seen an incredible change in the last forty-eight hours was about to change again.

Chapter VII

Maybe it was his business connections, his penchant for knowing things his competitors didn't and using them to full advantage. Maybe he had read the brief article accompanied by the striking picture in the paper and done some follow-up, but John Galvin found out. However he found out, helping Millicent "Millie" Fremont was all about PR, at least on the surface. Publicly it was a chance to come to the rescue of a promising young exchange student who would otherwise be sent home. Privately it was a chance to fill a void in his life that had long needed filling.

Her situation having suddenly become tenuous, it wasn't hard to facilitate. Millie was living in a detention center for troubled teens, there being no other place to put her. She was as miserable there as the staff was anxious to move her. Then along came John Galvin, an area businessman who had made a name for himself in a very short time. He was willing to give her a home, at least until Christmas break, long enough to see if it would work out. That would be the moment of truth because Galvin was in the process of buying the house on Lake Tanaka that would become his new residence, at once more pastoral and closer to his job as COO of Crystal Glass in Harper, twelve miles away. When he settled in St. Louis, he had made the seemingly curious decision of getting the house before the job — and the best fit was in Harper, an hour's drive to the southeast. Some people commuted all the way to Cape Girardeau, an hour or so beyond; by comparison, his commute was no big deal. The downside would be the need for Millie to adjust to a new home, though Galvin imagined rural Benson Junior High would be less of a challenge socially than upscale, suburban Ladue.

Their first meeting at the detention center was much like her first meeting with Dan Talbot: The Look quickly followed by The Shield of Fatherly Propriety, though she was well used to this by now. The two were even similar physically — tall and tan and lean — unlike her father, who was shorter and broader. Galvin had a sinewy quality about him, the animal litheness of a former athlete who still had his knees. Something about the way he moved, his healthy skin and easy smile, exuded confidence. It told her he was just as comfortable on a pair of water skis as he was behind a desk, which he was. There was no doubt in her mind he could have taken Dan Talbot apart — *if the truck had not beaten him to it*, her mind added the grim aside. At the same time, there was a sense of refinement about him. While looking as if they could crush anything, his large hands had buffed nails, neat half-moons rising from their cuticles. The blond hair of his youth had darkened to light brown, complementing the calm, penetrating gaze of green eyes that mesmerized women even as they intimidated men. The square watch he wore had a black face and a gold case and a lizard strap, costing as much as most cars, yet most of the time it lurked as a mere suggestion up his sleeve. John Galvin did not need to advertise. Millie was taken with him immediately, a first crush that surprised her after all she'd been through with men.

They had one more question at the detention center, one more question before they let him sign the papers and take Millie home. The question did not concern him because the only thing that could have derailed the process — the reason behind his divorce — had been silenced with enough money to ensure it remained silent. Since it was never a matter of public record, nobody would ever know, not even the snooping presstitutes who could have scuttled his career had they unearthed such information, especially in God-fearing Middle America.

"Mr. Galvin," the gray-haired social worker with the earnest expression said, "Millie is in this country on a one-year student visa. I understand you intend to move soon. What if her new school," she said, looking down at her notes, "Benson Junior High, doesn't have an exchange program?"

Taken off-guard by the question, Galvin compensated quickly with a winning smile. "Ms. Thomason, if it doesn't now, rest assured it will. It's a moot point, really, because Benson is a public school. As long as Millie speaks English — and I'll bet she speaks it better than most of the students there (at this Millie beamed) — they have to take her, don't they?"

Ms. Thomason smiled. "Yes, Mr. Galvin, I suppose they do." Then, to Millie, "Millie, are you ready to go home with Mr. Galvin?"

Millie's smile was that of a cat that always landed on its feet.

"I am ready."

***

Millie Fremont's association with John Galvin began with surprising ease, and therein lay the seeds of the problem. Things came too easily, too naturally between them, to the point Galvin ("Please call me John") was becoming ever less a father figure, ever more a friend. Part of the problem was his vitality. While he once confided to her his age (fifty), by comparison other fifty-year-olds were pale and paunchy and grumpy-looking, and when their faces were red — like Uncle Rene's — it was not from too much sun, but from too much alcohol. Their legs were strangers to sunlight, so white and smooth it seemed their pants had rubbed off all the hair. Meanwhile, John's legs were tan and hairy, his quads bulging over his knees, his calves cleaved into stalactites of muscle. John's legs looked as if he ran and biked and played tennis — because that is what he did — and he always invited her to join him. He bought Millie the best racket money could buy and a tennis dress made for a woman, a sleeveless number that flattered her budding figure. Occasionally she caught The Look as she flashed across the court on her slim, tan legs or lingered on the smooth hollow of her armpit as she lofted the ball to serve. Just as quickly The Look was gone, so quickly as to make her wonder if she was just imagining it. They didn't have to go far to play tennis because he had his own court, right next to a kidney-shaped swimming pool the occasional stray shot plunked into. She did not refuse the sexy little bikini he bought her, even though it elicited more of The Look whenever she wore it — or maybe even because of it. A foreigner as well as an adolescent, she was insecure about her appearance, especially since she wasn't as large-chested as some girls her age. The Look was no less than a balm for her insecurity. In time not only did Millie tolerate it, she welcomed it, enjoying the power she had over this handsome, powerful man. Because the context seemed different with John: more appraising than lewd; more appreciative than predatory. Other than the occasional, innocent hug — no back rubs, just a few platonic pats on the back — a fatherly kiss on the forehead, he never laid a hand on her. That was the important thing, and she loved him for this as much as anything.

Early on, it was apparent things were going well between them — well at school in spite of the social dysfunction that plagues all schools — and that she would, indeed, be accompanying him to Lake Tanaka during Christmas break. They had already been there a couple of times, the first time to close the deal. Convinced she was good luck, he took her out for dinner at Harper's only French restaurant to celebrate, and the second time when they determined who would have which room, where everything would go, and the kicker: what ideas she had for decorating. She was thrilled, never feeling more validated in her life.

On the first trip she noticed a subtlety she hadn't noticed before: with the real estate agent, he referred to her as his daughter while asking her to call him "Dad." She saw this as no more than an attempt at political correctness, defining their relationship for the outside world. Otherwise, it was always "Millie": "John" and "Millie" — as if they were peers, which they now saw themselves as despite a thirty-seven-year age difference. Galvin smiled a lot on that first trip as he looked to her for assent. Sometimes she noticed him gazing at her from across the room, a thoughtful look in his eyes. He certainly smiled more at the lake than he did at home, even more the second time. It was as if he could already hear the fire crackling in the hearth and the rain pattering on the roof, a cozy house and just the two of them, not father and daughter, but John and Millie. A smile as if he was thinking ahead, liking what he saw.

***

The one-hour commute gave him plenty of time to process his personal demons. The factors that had ruined things for him back East, forcing him to rebuild his life — very well, thank you — in the Midwest. He had violated a social more, acting on his feelings for a daughter who reminded him too much of her mother. His attraction to her clouded his judgment, gradually putting the feelings that surged through his loins in spite of the good sex life he enjoyed with his wife, above all else. The night it happened, the fateful night that forever changed his life, he had just made love to his wife (only once, though he was more than ready for a rematch. She said she was tired, and even their single union had "sympathy fuck" written all over it, and he would forever blame her for planting the seeds of what followed), she had just fallen asleep, and he was on his way to the bathroom. He had never met a woman who could equal his sexual appetite, the downside of his vitality. On a good night, usually on weekends when she was more rested, his wife came close, matching him for two and sometimes three rounds. But not that night. That night she was tired. That night he needed more, just to get to sleep, and an opportunity beckoned in the guise of a bedroom door that was slightly ajar.

He used the bathroom, and when he walked past his daughter's room, he was surprised to hear her say, "Daddy?"

It was all the excuse he needed, all he needed to justify his presence in forbidden territory at night and close the door behind him. Territory so forbidden it was like trespassing an inner sanctum while at the same time being wildly exciting. His heart beat madly. He knew he was coming dangerously close to The Line, the good judgment part of him battling the carpe diem part of him that was rapidly gaining the upper hand.

"What is it, love?" he asked, sitting on the bed. Looking for any excuse to be close.

"Daddy, I'm worried about tomorrow. I'm worried about starting a new school. Why can't I just go to public school with my friends? The kids I grew up with? The kids I'm used to?"

His eyes were adjusting to the light, the only illumination coming from the bar of light beneath the door of a bathroom that was always lit at night. Her face looked dreamily Impressionistic in the semidarkness, her dark hair spilling across the pillow. He touched her hair — it was very soft — and caressed the delicate ear lurking beneath it. They had always been close. His contact did not alarm her.

"Love, we've been over this before. First days are always the hardest at a new job as well as the ninth grade of a private school. Once you get through that first day, it's all downhill. This is a good school. You've been given an opportunity your friends don't have. Do well there and you're on your way to an Ivy League college."

"I'm still scared, Daddy. Kids do crazy things in school these days, especially to new kids who aren't members of The Club. Sometimes kids bring guns to school."

Galvin laughed softly. "Honey, kids bring guns to public schools. This is a private school, and a very good one. These kids come from good families."

"And they already know each other. They all went to elementary and junior high together. Ooooh, I wish I could stop thinking about it."

Galvin saw his opportunity. "And I wish I could make you stop thinking about it. Hold you in my arms and tell you everything will be OK and rock you to sleep, just like I used to do when you were a little girl."

"That would be nice, Daddy."

"Would you like me to?"

She laughed softly. "Yes."

He climbed into bed and slipped his arm under her neck as she lay on her side. Felt the smooth, warm litheness of her body in his arms. Put his nose into hair that reminded him of tropical flowers, launching his mental boat to faraway places — and tried to contain himself. He was losing the battle. Soon he was rock hard.

She noticed and laughed. "Ooooh, somebody is getting excited. Naughty, naughty!"

He laughed disarmingly, sensing an opportunity. "Do you ever feel like doing something naughty?"

"Only all the time."

"Do you ever hear your mother and me when we're…?"

"It's pretty hard not to."

"Does it sound like we're having a good time?"

She laughed softly. "Yes, I must say it does."

"I don't know how… experienced you are, but don't you ever get… curious? Wouldn't you like to have a good time, too?"

If it were light enough, he could have seen her blush. "Yes."

"Let's have a good time, love. Just you and me. As long as we're quiet, your mother never has to know."

Before she knew it, he was raising her nightie and caressing her bottom. Before she knew it, he was slipping off her panties. Before she knew it, he was lifting her leg and making contact.

"Daddy, you're serious!" she stage-whispered.

"Shhh! Of course I am, honey. Now just relax. Stop thinking about school for a while, OK?"

Before she could answer, he was nudging against her.

"Oh!" she said, her body tensing as he penetrated her.

"Sorry, honey, I didn't realize it was your first time."

She was tight: so tight! And dry: so dry!

Probably because she isn't ready. Probably because she never expected to be fucked by her own father, for chrissake! the thought intruded.

"Ahhhhh!" she cried when he moved inside her, the high-pitched scream of a little girl, making him grimace and clench his teeth.

Moments later, the door flew open and the light went on. His wife stood in the doorway, a wild-eyed Medusa with her mouth ajar.

"As of this moment, our marriage is over. You blew it, boy — and I do mean 'boy'; a man would never do this to a girl, much less his own daughter!" she cried, her voice rising to a shriek. "You've got a choice, mister: I can call the police right now, or you can call your lawyer first thing in the morning and see what kind of a divorce settlement he can draw up for your ex-wife and her fifteen-year-old daughter," she said, stressing the words 'ex' and 'fifteen.' "It had better be a goddamn good one, too, if you expect to walk away from this!"

While it was the only inappropriate contact he had ever had with his daughter, his wife had sensed it coming, saw how his eyes lingered on her maturing body, and it was a different animal than mere pride. She saw it and she waited, waited for a long fuse to make its way to a bomb, and when he finally acted on it, she realized with a hollow feeling in her gut that their marriage would be over. Their marriage would be over and, her anger mixed with sadness because she really did love him and didn't want to believe this could ever happen to a daughter she thought he loved as well, she would squeeze him for everything she could and take her daughter with her.

So marked the beginning of the end for him back East. The fact they looked good together and the Board knew her and there was marital discord (whatever the reason, it did not matter) was a serious problem for the image-conscious upper echelon of the corporate world. It translated into shaky, and shaky was bad for business. This alone was enough to shoot him down.

***

At fifty he saw the softness of men fifteen, twenty years his junior, confident he could mop up the floor with them. He refused to age gracefully, ever reminded of his time-defying youthfulness by the libido that raged within him. The high-priced "escorts" he met in Vegas, the sex tours he made to Bangkok and Pattaya, were poor substitutes for what he was looking for: sex — youthful, insatiable sex, with an intensity that equaled his own — how he wanted it when he wanted it. Sex on demand with a sensitive partner. A lustful, romantic lover he could control. Young and inexperienced, but passionate and eager to learn, grateful for whatever attentions he would bestow upon her. Ideally with some intelligence, the hint of an attitude that would make her more of a challenge. When he thought about these things, more and more Millie came to mind, and such thoughts became maddening to him. Here was a thirteen-year-old girl with the physical presence of a woman half a dozen years older. Someone he felt he could control. Someone he felt could please him. That was what made the temptation so strong, despite its risks. Young girls had no business being so attractive: the reason they called them "jail bait," he supposed. It was torture, and, as it had with his daughter, it was occupying more and more of his thoughts. Laying siege to his better judgment. Bringing the moth wings of his career, even his freedom, treacherously close to the flame once again.

It surprised him that he felt more embarrassed than guilty when his wife caught him in the act, his embarrassment morphing into anger when he lost his COO gig at MAGNUM, though the settlement was generous enough. Anger at being drummed out of Philly, where he was perceived as a leper in the rarefied air he once breathed and forced to rebuild his life in a rube city like St. Louis. But that was unfair. That was anger talking, as evidenced by the rashness of first impressions. St. Louis turned out to be a pleasant surprise with its reasonable cost of living and its general lack of pretense. There was a reason he came here, he felt with a growing certainty. He could make things work here.

He wanted it all. He was used to having it all, wasn't used to having his hand slapped when he reached into the cookie jar. He knew he could have it all, too, knew he could have anything he wanted if he only went about it the right way. Stealthily, deliberately, meticulously. Forgoing the forcefulness of personality one needed for success in the business world for the tact and sensitivity one needed for success in the personal world. Millie was a flower, more fragile and nuanced than he had realized. She had to be approached in stages before he could expect her to blossom into the woman he wanted her to be. But it would not be in Ladue, a place that was too proper, too quiet. A place with too many prying eyes, anything you did almost invariably frowned upon. No, it would not be Ladue, but it might be Lake Tanaka. As soon as he saw that big stone fireplace with the window curving around it, he thought it might. As soon as he sealed the deal on the house, he took anotherr step to ensure that it might, paying the neighbors on either side of him twice the value of their houses (he was prepared to go thrice) with immediate plans to demolish them. Freeing up plenty of space for him and his Millie!

The Christmas break came quickly. Millie had settled in at school, getting on as well academically as she did socially, at least with the boys, her association with the girls never graduating beyond the frosty stage. Older boys flocked to her, offering her rides home as they tried to impress her with their souped-up cars, ultimately needing to be chased off. At such times Galvin couldn't help but see himself as Humbert Humbert, enjoying the darkly funny innocence it lent to musings about Millie that were anything but innocent. It validated them, made them human, and therefore OK. Psychology — at least Western psychology — held that there was nothing abnormal about being attracted to children: so cuddly and cute, no different than being attracted to a puppy or kitten. It was only abnormal to act on this attraction, in the process violating one of the greatest taboos of Western society. Then again, it was only Western society, as child brides were common elsewhere. Ultimately, society, the highest court in the human realm, decided what was right and wrong. Then there was that part of him that questioned whether children, born of man though they were, could even be considered human. If they weren't, indeed, of God, their desecration a sacrilege. The thought troubled him, and he tried to push it away because deep down, conditioned as he was by a Western mindset, he knew his intentions for Millie were wrong, just as trying to consummate a physical union with his daughter was wrong. He admitted, if only to himself, that he had a problem, and the means he had for indulging it made it something to be wrestled with — but not too vigorously. Ultimately it wasn't the moral dilemma that concerned him so much as the embarrassment, the consequences, of getting caught. Millie Fremont was becoming an ever-greater fixture in his life. He wanted her to be happy; indeed, her happiness would make his complete. But first, he wanted her, all for himself.

Little did he realize that any happiness she might gain from such a union was a delusion on his part, that any such union was ultimately self-serving. If he had known the traumas she had been through, starting as early as age three, he would have better understood why. They would have told him that Millie had wounds to her psyche that were still healing and, if not stopping him outright, at least cause him to proceed with caution.

It began innocently enough, a dinner at a nice Italian restaurant on the last day of school before the break. On the surface, it was a father taking his daughter out for dinner, possibly for her birthday. Millie was radiant, looking like a young Audrey Hepburn, the candlelight that could have been a metaphor of her happiness bringing out the warm glow of her skin. He smiled at her, and she smiled back, and the stirring that was within him hung over him like a dark cloud that wouldn't pass. Afterward, he took her to a fancy ice cream place for dessert. There they shared a huge sundae, and she surprised him by ordering coffee: something very adult about that! At one point he took her hands in his, her fingers long and slim with a birdlike delicacy. He gazed into her eyes as he caressed the tender skin between her fingers. Making her hands feel as if they, too, were glowing. Making love to her in a socially acceptable way. Causing the pleasant tingle she felt between her legs to radiate through her entire being. That night before bed he kissed her: on the forehead and both cheeks while caressing her ears. More tingles, a warm, wonderful feeling opening up inside her. One she recognized as love. She went to bed with a huge smile on her face, never feeling more at home, more at peace. She had just had a great dinner with a kind, attractive man who was different than other men. A man who loved her for being who she was. A man she trusted. The following day they would move to their new house, the one she had helped decorate! Indeed, it felt as if they had already moved, the house in Ladue ghostlike in its vacancy. All they'd be bringing with them would be overnight bags containing a fresh change of clothing, their toilette kits, and some sheets and blankets and pillows. She drifted off into the deepest, most peaceful sleep of her life. Anyone who saw her head on the pillow could have easily mistaken her for God's prettiest angel.

All the while, Galvin lay in bed with his arms folded behind his head, his mind burning like the sign for an all-night diner.

My God, how tight she must be! He tried to stifle the thought.

His manhood was like a caged tiger thrashing against the bars, and it was all he could do not to scrap his game plan, barge into her room, and take her.

Chapter VIII

By the time Paul Mahr arrived at Lake Tanaka in FRM (Full Reporter Mode) — notepad open; pen ready; microrecorder in his shirt pocket; extra batteries in his pants pocket; camera with a lens like a toucan's beak dangling from his neck — there wasn't a hummingbird in sight. Although he'd been staying at a local motel and calling the Benson PD every hour, he knew better than to arrive until the "all clear" was given. Even the police and the paramedics wouldn't respond until then. Now that they had committed themselves to action, the so-called first responders — the neighbors would always be the first responders, except they weren't responding — were ubiquitous: nine pale blue tarps, the sunlight turning their peaks and valleys into the mountain range on a local beer can, were sprinkled around the lake, each of them separated from their environs by yellow crime scene tape. Sometimes the body had fallen on a graded surface, like Wanda Smith's at #258 North Lakeview Way, though the constant was the congealing pool of blood around it swarming with insects. The police were the advance force, the EMTs falling in behind, one of their vehicles sweeping either side of the lake, moving slowly with their lights off, in Cleanup Mode only, scoring brownie points with the county coroner for taking on the gig, as there was never any doubt the birds had done their work. While their vans were similar in size and appearance to mail trucks, the blue, asterisk-looking Star of Life was the antithesis of the abstract, vital-looking eagle, with the snake coiled around the rod of Asclepius, God of Medicine, somehow more sinister-looking than life-affirming. A paramedic would emerge from either side, wrapping a tarp that crinkled in the cool morning air around each body, securing both ends with a bungee cord, and loading it like cordwood into the back of the van. While there was no need to treat bodies with the same care as live patients, the scoop stretcher came in handy for gravel driveways that made wheeled stretchers a pain in the ass. Still in the early stages of rigor mortis, the bodies tended to sag when lifted, and here the scoop stretchers came in handy as well. In every instance, the neighbors stood watching, some with their hands over their mouths, their eyes wide with disbelief as they watched people they had known for years being bagged up and carted away like roadkill. Most of them kept a respectful distance, in death as in life trying not to get involved. Still, the police went through the motions of speaking with many of them, their responses universally unhelpful: a buzzing of wings deafening as a helicopter coming in for a landing, followed by screams. The EMTs met at the confluence of the North and South roads and left the lake together, a funeral procession of two, taking the bodies to the county morgue — gray and unmarked — behind Harper Memorial.

As you passed the entry gate, the Rod & Gun Club to your right, a steep grade led down to the lake, the road branching left and right into North and South Lakeview Way. If your brakes failed, you would run smack-dab into an expanse of grass that served as a park and separated the road from the lake. As you faced the lake, there was a small parking lot fringed by toilets and dumpsters, swing sets and a horseshoe pit off to the right, a slab of concrete big enough for a half-court game of basketball and a road for launching boats to the far right, with a small footbridge fording the creek that ran through it all. This grassy area was the lake's official meeting place, from fireworks on the Fourth to bonfires on Halloween. Today it was swarming with police and EMTs and their assorted vehicles. Some rain had fallen overnight, their tires carving deep ruts into the grass.

Mahr was in the middle of it all, bouncing like a pinball from uniform to uniform, gathering information. Getting the details any newspaperman needed for this sort of story: names; ages; addresses; next of kin; cause of death. While 'Death By Hummingbird' was the official cause, there were many variations. An older woman appeared to be killed by a single hummingbird, her neighbors claiming she had a heart attack. Others had been swarmed, with various parts of their bodies attacked, though always an area that was soft and vital: eyes, necks, veins, arteries, and, something new this year, genitals. An area rich with blood, especially in men where the veins ran along the surface like rivers on a relief map. Nearly every victim this year had been attacked in the genitals. Another pattern: In one case, an entire family was taken out as they set off in their boat, among them a three-year-old boy. Which told Mahr that familial association, not age, was what counted. Which brought him back to the first pattern he had noticed, the one that had caused him the greatest consternation, leading him to believe this was no freak occurrence of nature: Every person who was killed was a member of a family that had been present on the lake the night the Fremont girl disappeared. Mahr was standing there, looking dazed as he processed this bit of information, when a voice called out to him. Looking up from his notepad, he saw a familiar-looking face whose context escaped him.

Mahr smiled as an older man with the look of an aged cowboy, a hand he immediately recognized as prosthetic by the way the light glared off it, ambled up to him.

"I know I should know you, but...," Mahr began.

"Kevin Cousey," the man said, eliciting a look of wariness when he held out his artificial hand, probably because some of them could squeeze so hard, and Cousey looked like he could.

Overcoming his doubts, Mahr accepted his hand and received a normal handshake, albeit one that felt like squeezing a doll. His look told Cousey that he was still trying to place him.

"There was no reason to keep it," Cousey said with a grin, "the hand and the title of 'Doctor' when I... left my ENT practice twenty years ago."

"Of course!" Mahr said. "I did the story about your accident. I remember because it was one of the first pieces I did as a full-time reporter, also because it was so bizarre."

"Tell me about it," Cousey said.

"But I must admit I couldn't quite place you."

The truth of the matter was each of the twenty years Cousey had aged since then was like rolling a boulder uphill. Still, there was an undeniable sense of character about him, a sense not so much of being eroded by time as carved by it. The look of a man who had been through a war that hadn't beaten him.

"Well, I still recognize you, even without those Coke bottle lenses."

Mahr laughed. "Ah, the joys of laser surgery!"

"Would you recommend it? I've thought about getting it done."

"I would say if you can live with glasses — and I had reached the point that I couldn't; I was literally going blind, and my glasses felt like manhole covers on my nose — frankly, I wouldn't bother."

Cousey smiled. "Candid enough. Say, when you're done here, I wonder if you might care to join me for a beer. Save for the occasional medical article I publish, the occasional patient who comes to me on a casual basis, I'm no longer a practicing physician, per se. But I'm still a thinker and a researcher, with too much time for both. I might have something for you about our little bird problem."

Mahr smiled. "Our little bird problem… with little birds. Let me see now: leaving this hot field, talking to one fascinating person after another whom I can always call later, or having a cold one with you and technically still be working. OK, I accept."

"Good," Cousey said. "My ride is right over here. Doctors drive Beemers and their wives drive Range Rovers that never seem to get muddy on their way to the supermarket, but that was another life. Real guys drive old Chevy pickups."

***

Cousey's place was a postage stamp of perfection, a refuge from the fifties meticulously preserved. The house's three stories — actually two and a basement — were a gray wedge thrust from the hillside. A mammoth pair of black oaks bookended the deck that spanned the top floor while, midway between the yard and the lake, a life-sized statue of an angel spread its wings toward the water. Just uphill from the statue was the stump of a large tree, smooth and level enough to be used as a table, with one of those springy metal chairs from another era alongside and a well-worn path between it and the house. Forty yards into the lake was a swimming platform, the dam behind it. The stump, the statue, and the platform all lined up, and Mahr could see the appeal of sitting there with a cold one, watching bikini-clad cuties dive and sunbathe.

Cousey smiled as he followed Mahr's gaze. "The stump is my early morning base for coffee, my early evening base for beer. My job made me an early riser, you see, and in my retirement I've seen no need to deviate from it. I love the sight of morning mist rising from the lake when the first light of day hits it! Now the deck, the deck is for meals, the occasional midday beer when I'm entertaining, say, visiting dignitaries or just plain when I have more than one guest which, since my days at the hospital, isn't often. Paul, you're the first guest I've had in awhile."

"I'm honored."

"Ah, don't be! By the way, few people know this; probably not even newsworthy, but I have no less than three fridges: a little one upstairs for beer, a little one in the basement for beer, and a big one in the kitchen... for beer — and other things."

Mahr smiled. "Safe to say beer is a constant in your life."

"Ah, that anything should be so constant! Are you ready for one?"

"Certainly."

"Good, but just one for now. I want you sharp when I tell you what I'm about to tell you."

"Why me? Just curious."

"Because, save for that piece you did on charter schools a while back, I agree with most of your editorials, you're local, and if you've managed to stay local all these years, you're either in some kind of career rut or you actually give a damn about this area. Of course, you were also handy."

Mahr laughed. "I plead guilty... especially to that last! So, what's your issue with charter schools?"

Cousey laughed. "Some other time. I want you on my side for a while!"

Mahr followed Cousey into a house that was cave-like this time of day, paneled in knotty pine, with a massive stone fireplace in the lakeside wall. They thudded up the stairs, their footsteps cushioned by a maroon runner held in place by heavy brass strips. Upstairs the lake-facing wall was all windows, the sort of mini-fridge you'd see in a college dorm flanking a gunmetal gray table with a computer on top, pushed up to a window.

My God, what a perfect place to write! Mahr couldn't help but think.

Cousey opened the fridge, withdrew two long-necked microbrews, and handed one of them to Mahr. He pulled two frosted mugs from the fridge door, Mahr nodding in approval.

"There's an opener outside. I'm pretty Old School when it comes to beer. While I have been known to drink beer from a bottle with a twist-off cap, even a can if I'm in Redneck Mode or there's no other option — don't forget the cooler cup! I've always been of the opinion that good beer needs an opener — unless, of course, we're talking draft."

Cousey opened the door and they sat on a deck that alone was worth the price of admission with its perfect balance of shade and view. A nice breeze was coming off the lake, an unseasonable warmth creeping into the day.

Mahr withdrew his microrecorder. "I'm going to be lazy and just use this. I just want to have a beer and listen to you... if you don't mind."

"Not at all. Record away."

Mahr hit the button and placed the recorder on the small wooden table between them.

"I saw them come," Cousey said. "I always see them come because I'm already out there with my coffee, watching the mist coming off the lake. Brooding about things. I see them come, but of course I hear them first. It starts with a rustling the night before, in those trees behind the dam," he said, pointing, "but, judging by their numbers, probably extending far into the woods."

The beer felt good against the back of Mahr's throat. He could see drinking beer in a place like this being dangerously seductive.

"How many, would you say?"

"Hell, I don't know. Many thousands. Maybe a million. Some years there are more than others, but there are always a lot of them."

"And this year?"

"Hard to say. A little less than last year, I think. Last year they killed ten people, this year only nine, so maybe they figured they didn't need as many troops."

Mahr smiled but said nothing. "You speak as if they plan their attacks," he said finally.

Cousey looked him in the eye. "Of that I have no doubt."

Mahr's smile broadened. "OK, just to see if we're on the same page, why do you suppose they killed fewer people this year when their pattern has been to kill one more person every year?"

There was a sparkle in Cousey's eye. "You've done your homework, Paul. In most years there are lake residents or former lake residents — people who are either on vacation or who have moved — who come up dead on April 15th. Always killed by hummingbirds. I have no doubt this will end up being the case, and the birds will get their quota."

Warm glow of recognition as Mahr had a "Yes!" moment. Before him was no less than the ally he'd been looking for, a reputable sort who validated what to him had seemed crazy.

"You've done your homework, too. I'm impressed," Mahr said.

Cousey smiled. "I have the time, you see."

"Next question, one that strikes me as rather obvious: Why do you suppose the birds leave you alone?"

"Tell you what, Paul, there have been years when I've wished they hadn't, years I've wished they'd put this old sucker out of his misery. But, no, on April 15th, they don't come within ten feet of me. You'll notice I have two feeders, one at either end of the deck. Today they haven't been touched. They never feed on April 15th, which strikes me as odd given their numbers and the amount of energy they expend. It's almost as if April 15th is sacred, a day of fasting. Come tomorrow, those feeders will be drained in a hurry."

"So how do you explain it?"

"I can't prove it — not yet, anyway — but my gut tells me it has something to do with John Galvin and the little French girl who used to live with him before she disappeared, a year to the day before this all started."

"Millie Fremont."

"Yes, that was her name. Sweet kid. I used to run into them all the time in town. Beautiful little thing, the sort of girl a father has to keep a close watch on. Anyway, there was something going on in that house, and it wasn't good. Millie had bruises on her arms, sometimes even her face. Every time I saw her, she seemed more subdued, like she was afraid of him. As a doctor trained to be on the lookout for signs of abuse and a father who loves kids, I was determined to do something about it. Legally it got me nowhere. Galvin was smart enough, you see, to be pro-active. He always reported her injuries himself, and she never refuted whatever he told them. Mind you, and this is not for publication, doctors have been known to trade notes about their patients off the record, especially when a kid's welfare is involved and they don't feel like they're getting the full story. For example, once I was told she bruised her face on an overhanging branch when she was out riding bikes with friends. How unlikely is that, I ask you? If Millie had any friends, she certainly wasn't allowed to hang out with them, but she never said anything to the contrary. I suspected he used both positive and negative reinforcement: "I'll buy you a new dress" versus "I'll send you home on the next plane" to elicit her coop-eration. One way or another, he paid for her silence, just as I suspect he paid for the silence of his daughter and ex-wife."

At this, Mahr smiled. Another connection! "You suspect that as well?"

"Yes, I do. Maybe Millie was afraid of him. Maybe she was just confused, I don't know, but something wasn't right, and it stayed that way until the night she disappeared. Galvin being such a big shot has made it hard to get to the bottom of things.

"Then there's Galvin himself, an intimidating son of a bitch if I've ever seen one, and I'm no slouch. One time he ran me off the road in that big, black Hum-mer of his. That monster he calls a dog acts like it wants to tear me apart whenever I'm walking around the lake and Galvin is in his yard, gaping at me like Satan himself. Acting like he's enjoying every moment of my discomfort."

"Any other theories as to why the hummingbirds don't attack you?"

"Yes, and I'll tell you over another beer. You're getting this on tape, so no need to be sharp, eh?"

Mahr smiled. "Twist my arm."

Cousey reached over and touched him on the elbow. "Don't worry; we'll have some pizza to soak up the next one."

Mahr laughed. "You must think I have all day."

"C'mon, Paul, *The Harper Gazette* ain't exactly *London Times*. It's a biweekly, for chrissake. Tell me you're not killing yourself over this rag."

Mahr couldn't help but smile. "True enough."

"What I think is you may well be sitting on the biggest story this county has seen in a decade or more, one that promises to get even bigger by the time we figure it out. By the time we're finished here today, I think you'll agree your time has been well spent."

"Since you put it that way. Thanks, Doc," Mahr said as Cousey handed him a cold one.

"Besides, I can always use the company, and I have plenty of nice, cold brewskies to make sure I have it!"

The cassette ran out and Mahr dutifully flipped it over and hit the button. Frantically he patted down his pockets.

"Damn! I forgot to bring extra cassettes!" he said. "I guess I'm not used to interviewing someone who actually has something to say."

"You mean like those high school football coaches who spout such linguistic pearls as 'Our guys dug deep'? or 'Our guys left it all out on the field'? or 'Our guys gave it 110 percent?' As if they could give any less."

Mahr laughed. "It's like they have the same half-dozen phrases in their heads — I get this image of a few sheets tumbling around in one of those big laundromat clothes dryers — and they pick the one that best fits the discussion."

Cousey broke into a broad grin. "Another brilliant thought, fresh from the dryer! You can always interview me again. Honestly, Paul, I don't know how much of what I'm telling you is even newsworthy — at least in a provable, fact-based sense that won't, say, get your paper sued by someone with the financial means to take it for quite a ride through the legal system; word is Galvin is worth about fifty mil. My gut tells me we're talking about something that is beyond facts, beyond hard evidence. I know, kinda spooky."

Mahr smiled. "But you digress. Any other theories as to why they leave you alone, Doc?"

"Do you see that statue in my yard, the one with the eight-foot wingspan?"

"Gosh, I don't know how I could have missed it."

"Three guesses who it is."

"First, if I may, where did you get it?"

"There used to be a church in South St. Louis called St. Cecilia's. Fortunately, they took out all the good stuff before they tore it down. I bought the statue at what amounted to a church bazaar. Wait'll you see him close up. I stole that statue, but I still like to believe he protects me!"

"Aha! You just gave me a clue. The wings told me it was an angel, and angels protect people when they aren't kicking ass on God's behalf. Not being well-versed on the subject, I'm just gonna go for the obvious and say it's one of the three heavyweights of the angel — or should I say archangel? — world: Michael, Gabriel, or Raphael."

"As long as we're talking Roman Catholicism as opposed to Eastern Orthodoxy, which has thousands of them, yes! That would be Michael, God's Warrior Angel: protector of soldiers in battle, heaven's answer to Rambo, etc. I like to think Michael is protecting me, especially on a fateful night twenty years ago when I was ready to use the gun I'd bought for something other than target practice or home defense. When I saw Michael's wings illuminated by the setting sun and knew I still had some fight left in me."

"Let me guess: the night you blew your hand off."

"No, a year later, when my wife threw in the towel on our marriage and took the kids with her. I ended up sitting by that stump down there for the first time and drinking a good bottle of Scotch and watching the sun go down and the stars come out. The most memorable sunset of my life, let me tell you. Anyway, Mike and I have been bosom buddies ever since. The birds leave him alone, too; not a speck of bird shit on him. Not for publication, right?"

Mahr smiled. "Not for publication."

"Bring your beer. There's something I want to show you."

Cousey pulled a second chair up to the computer table and booted up the computer, navigating to the site he was looking for.

"As you know, I have lots of time to think. Why, I can run any crazy theory I want to, run it clear into the ground. Not surprisingly, my thoughts tend more toward hummingbirds than taxes come April 15th. Insurance payments and pensions and SSI are all pretty straightforward, and besides, that's what accountants are for. Before I show you what I'm about to show you, let me ask you: What time do the hummingbirds attack?"

"Based on eyewitness accounts, 7:00 AM or shortly thereafter."

"I checked my watch this morning, as I always do on April 15th. I've always believed in punctuality, so it's a good one. This morning the hummingbirds departed at the same time they always do — 7:15 AM sharp — from the same point they always depart from."

"The trees?"

"No. I'll tell you later if I don't forget."

"Rest assured, I'll remind you. The time thing alone is weird."

"Tell me about it. Anyway, the notion of Michael being a protector formed a segue in my mind — to patron saints and the various things they are said to protect. Ultimately, this train of thought chugged its way to the question: Is there a patron saint of hummingbirds? The answer is there isn't, but there are no less than four patron saints of birds, one of them being pretty obvious."

"St. Francis of Assisi."

"Yes! The patron saint of all animals, of nature itself. Trust me; the others are far more obscure. Unless you have as much time to burn on minutia as I do, you'll never guess them."

"OK, who are they?"

"St. Gall, not to be confused with St. Paul, is alleged to be the world's first bear tamer. He exorcised some blackbirds from the woman he was healing. Then there was St. Tryphon of Lampsacus, who began his life as a goose herder and a healer of animals. He exorcised a black dog from the emperor's wife, and prayed locusts away. The last of these saints is a woman. Before I introduce her, I have to ask: Do you believe in reincarnation?"

"Let's just say I've experienced dèjá vu too many times to dismiss it out of hand."

"Diplomatic answer, Paul," Cousey said with a smile.

With that, he opened the website, moved the cursor to one of the names listed there, and left-clicked his mouse.

"I'm not going to say anything. I'm just going to let you read it and see if you come to the same conclusion I have," he said, tilting the screen toward Mahr.

Mahr read the information, sometimes aloud. "St. Milburg: born in England to a king and a saint. Two of her sisters were saints. My goodness, it must have been in the genes! She became a nun, founded her own abbey. Hmm, she was considered a miracle worker, with a strange power over birds. One time she asked them to stop damaging crops — and they did! She died in the year… 715."

Mahr's mouth went slack. "715: a quarter after seven."

Cousey smiled. "Do you think?"

Mahr looked at him, dumbstruck.

"I thought you might see it that way. Anything is plausible if you believe in reincarnation," Cousey said.

Mahr snapped out of his daze. "Still, a couple of things don't add up: the name 'Milburg,' for one thing. While I suppose this could be shortened to 'Millie,' the girl's birth name was 'Millicent.'"

Cousey's smile remained. "I thought about that, too. I also considered the historical context. As we are well aware, the French have never been fond of the Germans, especially after they marched down the Champs-Elysees in the last world war. It strikes me as highly unlikely that a French family would christen their daughter with a Teutonic-sounding name like 'Milburg.'"

"Another problem: St. Milburg was English; Millie was French."

Cousey laughed. "Not a problem. If people can come back as rabbits and cockroaches, why not someone from another country?"

"I must say this is blowing my mind."

"You're not alone. Yet it may take a healthy suspension of disbelief to explain what is going on. All told, I figure some eight hundred lives depend on it."

"Eight hundred lives?"

"There were roughly eight hundred people — 792, to be exact — living in the lake's roughly two hundred households the night Millie Fremont disappeared."

"And at a rate of ten last year, eleven this year, twelve next year…"

"You do the math: It could go on for quite some time. Furthermore, if you were somehow able to communicate with her family in France, I'm sure you would find more evidence linking her to hummingbirds. It already exists here. One day a week I teach a biology class at the Benson Public Schools, circulating through each grade. One of the teachers had a gorgeous watercolor of a hummingbird on the wall behind his desk. I asked him who did it, already suspecting who."

"Millie Fremont," he said. "She lived and breathed them. One of her classmates told me she even had a hummingbird tattoo on her ankle, which I thought was rather strange for a twelve-year-old. Then again, kids are getting them at younger and younger ages."

"Help yourself to another beer and grab one for me, will you? I'm ordering a pizza. It's a long way to deliver, but I know the kid, and I tip well. 'If you're gonna spend so much money, why don't you just order two of them?' he asked me once. I love that kid; reminds me of my son." Cousey turned somber for a moment. "Any preference as to toppings?"

"None as long as my side includes anchovies."

"What, and deprive my side? Anchovies it is, and everything else except pineapple! I could never get into pineapple. Must be a California thing."

"Actually, it was invented in the other 'CA' — Canada. Probably a case of wishful thinking in the dead of winter. I like pineapple, but if there's enough other stuff, I can live without it," Mahr said.

"Let us repair to the deck, then, shall we? You're mine today, Mahr!"

"Fine with me, Doc. I was ready for a change of pace. You don't know the beating my eyes take staring into a computer screen all day."

"Oh yes, I do."

Mahr smiled. "No, my friend, I can assure you that you don't. Even if you spend all day, every day on the computer, you don't. Because you're only reading stuff, with a lake to rest your eyes on whenever you need to. I, on the other hand, am forced to scrutinize, to make sense of the tripe these illiterate bozos who call themselves 'reporters' churn out, lest their editor comes off looking like an ass. The buck stops with me, and sometimes I wish it didn't."

"Point well taken."

"Thank God the Gazette, as you've so kindly reminded me, is only a biweekly, or I'd be tied to my computer all the time. I don't know how those poor bastards at the dailies do it."

"Have a seat," Cousey said. "I'm not through blowing your mind yet."

Chapter IX

This time Cousey surprised the kid and ordered two large pizzas; they arrived just as they were finishing their third beers and getting a little punchy. Just as the lake was turning the fleeting fluorescent orange of pre-sunset. Cousey enjoyed the look on Mahr's face when he slipped the kid an extra twenty.

"I'd do anything for that young man, as long as it wasn't immoral or illegal," Cousey said. "Do you ever notice how life gives you Replacement People whenever you seem to need them?"

"Meaning what?"

"Meaning that kid is a replacement for my son who is alive and well — as far as I know. I never hear from him. He's a grown man now, with two kids, a great wife, and a job that keeps him on the road a lot. But I'm his father, goddamnit! One would think, in the course of his wanderings, the road might lead here once in a while! Hell, I'd even be willing to meet him in Chicago, if need be! I'm developing a theory: that he feels, on a purely subconscious level, the way I used to feel whenever I met someone with something wrong with him — that I'm a freak, and the thing that makes me a freak defines me to the point it's impossible to see anything else. A troubling reminder, perhaps, of my own mortality. Kind of like how you feel when you meet someone you know has had heart surgery: You can't see it, or maybe you can see part of it, but you know there's a surgical scar lurking somewhere beneath his shirt that looks like a kid's version of railroad tracks and, try as you might, you can't ignore it. Because the scar becomes him, just like for some people, my wife included, my missing hand becomes me. This probably sounds crazy, but it's the only explanation I have. I've always loved my son. We never fought. I was always good to him. But something must have happened, and it appears I'll never know what."

"Any other kids?"

"A daughter, also grown and with kids. I do get to see her, albeit at a time and place of her choosing: She's a busy mom, and I'm a retired old bum, so I have no problem with that. Sometimes it feels strange to see her, though. All grown up, in one restaurant after another."

"Probably because she seems out of context."

"Maybe so."

"Why doesn't she come down here? I should think it would be a great place for her kids to spend the weekend. I can't imagine a kid not wanting to come down here for a hayride and a bonfire."

"Frankly, I can't, either. She says there are too many memories here and, even though the vast majority of them are happy, the very fact they are history somehow makes them sad. I'm not sure I buy it, but that's what she says."

"You'd think she'd want to displace them with more happy memories."

"You would think. But she just gets miffed when I forget the way things are and invite her down. Anyway, pardon me for venting. My melancholy comes and goes, and I suppose it all starts with having too much time to think. Hey, I'll carry the pizzas if you'll grab that chair."

"And take it where?"

"To the only place to be on the lake at sunset, of course!"

***

Soon they were seated at the stump, St. Michael's wings transformed into a glowing medley of curves.

"Damn, but that tastes better than it should!" Cousey said, biting into his first piece. "Come to think of it, this is the first thing I've eaten all day. Just some coffee this morning."

"Do you think you'll contact the French girl's family?" Mahr asked. "Would you recommend I do?"

Cousey gave the matter several seconds' thought. "Honestly, I don't think it would help our investigation. I already know there was something special, maybe even miraculous, about the girl. Just for the sake of argument, let's say she is the reincarnation of St. Milburg, come back from the grave some fourteen hundred years later. Let's say something bad did happen to her — given there's been no sign of her for twelve years, I'd say that's likely — and the hummingbirds she loved are pissed about it, murderously pissed about it. Where does that leave us? We still don't know how to stop them. We still don't have any hard evidence on Galvin. It wouldn't affect the hic et nunc of the situation."

"Or the e pluribus unum, for that matter," Mahr said.

Cousey laughed. "Touché!"

The orange had risen from the water to the sky, where the clouds streamed past like tongues of flame. A small flotilla of ducks broke the calm of the water near the swimming platform. Mahr noted that Cousey's eye was repeatedly drawn there. Mahr looked beyond the platform to the trees, suddenly reminded of something.

"You never told me where the hummingbirds depart from."

"You're right. Must have been all this beer on an empty stomach. The birds congregate in the trees the night before, and there's nothing like the sound of them. Imagine a million pieces of chirping laundry flapping in the breeze: That's what it sounds like. By the time morning comes the trees are swaying — we're talking oaks with two-foot trunks — and it's not from the wind. Then, right at seven, as if on cue, God knows where it comes from or who their leader is, they rise en masse, changing color as they bob and twist and weave, filling the sky, only to come streaming back down to the swimming platform, as many of them as can fit. From where I'm sitting, it looks like they're balancing on Michael's wings. They crowd the platform, fighting and jostling for position as if it's a sacred place, some of them falling into the water only to scramble to regain their spot. All the while, the rest of them swirl around the platform like a psychedelic tornado that keeps changing colors as the light catches it, as far into the heavens as the eye can see. Hummingbirds can live as high as 17,000 feet: That would put them over three miles into the sky! A three-mile funnel cloud of hummingbirds over Lake Tanaka — imagine! This goes on for a good fifteen minutes. Picture the home team before The Big Game, crowding onto the team logo in the center of the field, jumping up and down, pounding each other's shoulder pads as they psyche themselves up: That's the vibe I get from these hummingbirds. Then, another signal, maybe from nature itself, and the birds rise from the platform, the tornado disperses, and the birds of hell are loosed all over the lake at seven-fifteen sharp. If there are boats on the water, they'll check them out first. It's only certain residents they target; they get them as soon as they go outside — and there's always a reason to go outside. Sometimes I think people forget, and on April 15th it costs them. Soon you hear the first screams: sometimes a few doors down, sometimes echoing across the lake. Amazing how sound carries on a lake! All the while, I'm thinking, 'Oh, shit! Here we go again!'"

Mahr listened, spellbound. "The obvious question, it seems to me," he said finally, "is why the swimming platform?"

Cousey beamed at him over his mug, the beer shimmering like topaz in liquid form.

"Just the question I've been asking myself. A while back I had a strange dream." Cousey looked around. "Is the recorder on?"

Mahr smiled. "You'll remember I ran out of tape — and the will to write this all down."

"Good! The dream was divided into three parts, one audio part sandwiched between two video parts. I know that sounds strange, but I'm a strange kinda guy. The first part featured the swimming platform, just floating there like there was something about it, but I didn't know what. The second part was the most telling, so telling that I wish I had video to go with it: a girl's voice, crying, sniffling, agitated, angry, saying she'd had enough. This was followed by the sounds of slapping and screaming, and a single, heavy thud. Then silence, soon followed by the sound of a man's voice: disbelieving; grief-stricken. The rest of the sounds were water-related: something being loaded into a boat; oars moving in the water; a loud splash followed by the sound of bubbles. Finally, the image that pulled it all together: the Archangel Michael wearing a scuba diving mask. Anyway, my dream, for what it's worth. What do you make of it?"

"I wouldn't have a clue. A woman I used to date took a course in dream interpretation."

"Why don't you ask her?"

"I'm afraid we're no longer on speaking terms."

"Paul Mahr: Heartbreaker!" Cousey said.

Mahr laughed. "That'll be the day! I can tell you this much, though: Dreams have been known to contain messages, albeit conveyed through an Alice in Wonderland-type filter. There is something about scuba diving and that swimming platform that bears looking into, I would say. Tell me, what kind of boat does Galvin have?"

"I understand he has a yacht on Chesapeake Bay. Word is it's a bit... much for the lake. A boat like that needs more than a fish tank to breathe in. All he keeps here is a rowboat, to stay in shape. Evidently, he was on a rowing team in college, and he's pretty vain about his physique. I see him going by once in awhile, making a complete circuit of the lake."

"What with all the coves and inlets, that must be five or six miles!" Mahr said.

"Galvin is a freak of nature, especially for a man of sixty-plus years. I wouldn't want to mess with him."

"If I were you, I'd start a scuba club," Mahr said, "an actual club as opposed to just poking around, which would only look suspicious. I start a scuba club, and the first thing I explore is the area under the swimming platform. I don't think you're going to be happy until you do."

"I tend to agree."

"Are you in good enough shape, though?"

"For deep-sea diving? Hell, no! To plunk myself into fifty feet of water, with plenty of people around to fish my sorry ass out if I get in trouble? Hell, yes!" Cousey said.

"I'd start one, then. I'd invite everyone to join, even outsiders, just to make it more unassuming. Can outsiders still use the lake?"

"Only if they're a guest of someone who lives here," Cousey said.

"Good, they can be your guest! Make it as big as you can and see who shows up, keeping an eye out for you-know-who. His reaction could be telling," Mahr said.

"Yes, in all the excitement I neglected to mention that Galvin was head of a Navy scuba diving team, for chrissake!" Then, withdrawing a piece of paper from his shirt pocket and handing it to Mahr, he said, "I might have some hard news for you after all."

Mahr smiled as he read the headline:

"First Meeting Planned for Lake Tanaka Scuba Club"

"You rascal!" Mahr said.

"I've already booked the Rod & Gun Club," Cousey said, smiling. "Only fifty bucks to use it during the week, half as much as Friday, Saturday, or Sunday. I figured I'd start small, shoot for a time when not much else is going on."

"Will you be electing officers?"

Cousey laughed. "Probably not the first night. Let us see if the patient has a pulse first."

Paul Mahr couldn't recall a productive day more pleasurably spent, ironically on a day marked by mayhem. Still, a somberness overtook him as the sky flamed through its nightly ritual — always more dramatic over water — and he thought about the nine family members missing from various lake households tonight, and would be missing from now on. He thought of the physical residue of the lives they'd left behind, tainted by the way they had died, but still usable, some of it boxed up to be hauled or stored away, most of it absorbed by family and friends — because a life wasn't a museum the contents of which you weren't supposed to touch.

What Cousey said made sense, albeit in a brutal sort of way. Nine lives that would become eleven lives, then twelve next year; all of them payment for a life he suspected had been snuffed out. A very special life. And it would go on like this until the debt had been paid with eight hundred lives, some of them children guilty by association only. The sins of the fathers were being visited upon the sons, and it was an inheritance that could not be disinherited. For eleven years this had gone on. For eleven years John Galvin had escaped judgment.

"Another question for you," Mahr said as the sun disappeared behind a hill forked with trees, the sky aching with color as if a fire were burning behind it. "Why do you suppose the hummingbirds haven't killed Galvin?"

The question shook Cousey from his private reverie. There was a meditative aspect to sunsets, a mood about them that encouraged reflection. Communing with nature as the sun was coming up or going down was as close to religion as he came these days, though the Creator of it all was never far from his thoughts.

"Good question, Paul, one that has often occurred to me. In fact, I have a few theories about it."

"The first of them being?"

"I'm dead wrong about him, and all that I'm doing is building castles in the sky. Maybe I am dead wrong, but my gut tells me otherwise."

"And the other theories?"

"That he's guilty as hell and they're saving the best for last, giving him time to think about it, the anticipation of an event often being worse than the event itself. Frankly, I like the notion of making Galvin think about it while people are dropping all around him, people who are only slightly less guilty than he is."

"How do you figure?"

"Edmund Burke said it best: 'The only thing necessary for the triumph of evil is for good men to stand by and do nothing.' Everyone on this lake damn well knew what was happening to that girl, and if we'd grown some collective balls and said 'Enough!' she'd still be alive today. She'd still be alive, the hummingbirds would be going merrily about their business, and the only thing we'd have to worry about on April 15th is the only thing you're supposed to worry about on April 15th: taxes."

"Any other theories?"

Cousey smiled. "Assuming Millie really was the reincarnation of St. Milburg, maybe she simply told the birds to leave him alone."

"Why would she do that?"

"I think you can answer that one, Paul. What happens to Millie Fremont if John Galvin is gone?"

"They send her to live with another family?"

"Maybe, but this was her second placement. In both cases, the people she was staying with died. My hunch is they would have sent her home, and I suspect returning to rural France would have been something of a letdown. Despite the abuse she endured, I think it is inaccurate to paint Millie purely as a victim. Every time I saw her, she was wearing a new designer something-or-other. Who knows, maybe he even promised to send her to a good college. In any event, Millie was getting something for her trouble, enough for her to tolerate the situation. She would have had reasons for wanting him alive."

"Yet now she's gone. It seems to me those reasons no longer apply."

"All I can think of is the birds are still honoring her request not to kill him," Cousey said.

"As they continue killing others."

"I know, that's the puzzler. Maybe it really is my second theory: that they're saving the best for last."

"Tell me, Doc, why do you stay here?"

"The lake is my home. I've been here for more than thirty years now, and I feel no desire to move. You've seen my house; could you leave this place, on this lake?"

"No, I don't suppose I could — as long as I had a job in the area."

"Funny, and I never noticed this before because I was never in the same place long enough, but the longer you live somewhere, the heavier, the more substantial everything seems. That metal table I work on upstairs couldn't weigh more than sixty pounds, but to me it weighs a ton. It's like it's been planted there; it belongs there, as much as those two big oaks at either end of my deck belong there. Finally, I've found a place where I feel settled, where I feel a sense of permanence, and there's something satisfying about that. The other part of it is the lake has unfinished business. As much as anyone, I'm a part of it. I want to see justice done. I want to see the spirit of Millie Fremont put to rest. A spirit that will not rest until it has vengeance, and we've seen what that vengeance is capable of. I have no doubt she's dead, but I want to know who did it, and I want to know where her body is.

Then I want to take up a collection and build a memorial for her and hang hummingbird feeders from it. But it wouldn't just be for her, it would be a reminder of what happens when you hunker down in your comfort zone, when you refuse to get involved in other people's lives even, when those lives are under siege. Millie would have liked that. The lake owes her at least that much."

Mahr sighed. "You know what I think?"

"What do you think, Paul?"

"I think you're a good man."

Cousey flashed him a sad smile. "Thank you for that, Paul. Just for the record, I think you are, too. Trouble is, it's a lonely world for good men."

***

Mahr got Cousey's announcement into the next issue, displaying it as prominently as advertising space allowed. The outpouring of interest was amazing to the point of being unexpected, amazing to the point the gathering was too big for the Rod & Gun Club and had to be moved to the field at the bottom of the hill. Cousey recruited some of the men to collect firewood, a bonfire breaking the evening chill while lending an earthy charm to the proceedings. Cousey stood on the edge of the basketball half-court, those in attendance sitting in the grass on their coats, trying to keep their butts dry as the bonfire warmed their backs. From time to time it popped loudly — most of the wood still being damp this time of year — and a couple of the men tended to it. John Galvin surprised everyone by showing up. It was the closest look many had ever gotten of him, as he was usually behind the tinted windows of his Hummer before disappearing into his house, his only other exposure being the boat trips he made around the lake thrice weekly. Here he was, front and center, looking strangely natural as fit men tend to as he sat on the grass with the others. Creating the illusion of average joe-ness.

Cousey was used to addressing medical conferences, doing so in a confident, resonant voice, but that was twenty years ago. Before him sat younger men with two hands, and there was something intimidating about their youth and their completeness, in spite of the fact he was in better shape than most of them. Galvin's presence was especially unnerving, staring brazenly up at him from the front row in a silent challenge no one else could see. The first thing Cousey did was deflect the attention from himself, buy the minute or two he needed to regain his composure.

"Please, let us observe a moment of silence for the nine people who were killed on the lake on April 15th."

He met Galvin's gaze, doing his best not to look accusatory. Galvin met him squarely and unflinchingly with the perfect poker face. The evening's first experiment had failed.

"Would anyone like to lead us in *The Pledge of Allegiance?*"

A good redneck ploy, a known crowd-pleaser, and a way to buy another minute. Once a grade school staple, nowadays it seemed strange to stand with your hand over your heart reciting *The Pledge.*

Once again Galvin surprised everyone by volunteering, springing to his feet with catlike ease.

"I pledge allegiance to the flag of the United States of America, and to the Republic for which it stands, one nation, under God, indivisible, with liberty and justice for all."

Cousey couldn't help but linger on the word "justice" as he watched Galvin in action. If it was strange to see him close up, it was even stranger to hear him speak: the booming, polished voice of the boardroom combined with the inflection of a jazz DJ rising above the others, leaving one with the unmistakable impression that Galvin liked to hear himself talk. Indeed, he recited *The Pledge* as if he were auditioning for a play. He was an instant hit, exchanging smiles with the others as he returned to his seat on the grass, Mr. Salt of the Earth.

Cousey sounded shaky by comparison, the broad smile on Galvin's face only feeding his discomfort. Then, as if he'd willed it into existence, something took hold and the Dr. Kevin Cousey of old asserted itself.

I have to face a hundred of you while Galvin has his back to you. Time to strut the old stuff! he thought.

He gained control of the meeting, soothing his vocal cords from time to time with the bottle of water slung on his hip.

"Gentlemen… and lady," he said, acknowledging the lone woman in attendance, "thank you for attending this, the first meeting of the Lake Tanaka Scuba Club. My name is Kevin Cousey, former head of ENT at Harper Memorial Hospital before I had… a little accident," he said, holding up his prosthetic hand. "But life goes on, and at least you don't have to call me 'Doctor' anymore. 'Kevin' will do quite nicely.

"I must say I'm pleasantly surprised by tonight's turnout. As you can see from our choice of venue, I wasn't ready for this many people. There's a clipboard going around for you to write your name, phone number, email, and mailing address. I'm not sure what I'll do with this wealth of information; it would just be nice to know who's here, as we may be electing officers next time. You'll recall the original notice said we'd be meeting at the Rod & Gun Club, just up the hill, but as you can see, it wasn't big enough to hold us. I'm glad you were able to find us. Still, seeing as how I paid fifty bucks to reserve the joint, that's where we'll be having our refreshments when the meeting proper is over; sorry, just coffee and cookies this time. While they certainly aren't mandatory, as the Scuba Club has no official dues in place yet — we need officers before we can decide things like that! You'll find a box on the refreshment table for donations: 'anything your heart moves you to give,' as they say in church, and it's fine if it doesn't move you to give anything.

"I don't have an agenda tonight; this meeting promises to be strictly informal. However, I would like to start by asking if anyone here has any scuba diving experience you'd be willing to share with the group. Don't feel bad if you don't have any. Other than falling out of a boat once, I don't, either."

General laughter from everyone but Galvin, whose stony glare never wavered. This would be the norm throughout the evening

"This was something I just got a wild hair to try, while I still can, kind of like the time I taught myself to ice skate. Bought myself a decent pair of hockey skates, padded my butt real good, put on a pair of gloves, and said, 'OK, I don't think I can hurt myself. Let's give her a go!'"

More laughter.

"All right now, please raise your hand if you have any scuba diving experience."

Of the 103 men and one woman present, about twenty hands went up. One of them belonged to John Galvin and another to the woman, who was built like a truck, her butch haircut a warning for men to stay away (not that many would have approached her), all decked out in a jeans outfit and cowboy boots. She was a guest, not a resident. The lake did not cater to her kind, once denying a lesbian couple what should have been a routine request to build a dock. They and the lake's only black resident didn't stay long.

Cousey motioned to the woman, whose gender was hard to determine in the semidarkness. "Ma'am, would you mind speaking first?"

Doris Kath spoke in a voice that was low, flat, and, to most of the men present, decidedly unfeminine. Like the owners of half of the hands that were raised, she worked as an underwater welder, repairing barges on the Mississippi. Most of the rest of them had dived while on vacation, one of them liked to poke around for valuable objects in shallow bodies of water, and a couple of them had dived in the military. Galvin spoke last.

No doubt for dramatic effect, Cousey's thoughts turned cynical as Galvin rose to speak.

"My name is John Galvin. I'm originally from the East, lived in St. Louis but got tired of the commute. I work at Crystal Glass in Harper, and moved to the lake about thirteen years ago."

'Work' at Crystal Glass? Cousey thought. *How unassuming! You're the fricking COO!*

A collective stirring of recognition when Galvin said, "thirteen years." As low-profile as he tried to be, Galvin's very presence at the lake was high-profile. Everyone knew the trouble with the hummingbirds began shortly after his arrival, vaguely sensing a connection between them. Tonight, though, Galvin's cordiality was winning some of them over.

"I needed a place to decompress from the corporate world, and Lake Tanaka has fit the bill nicely," he said, flashing his best salesman smile.

More surprises as, once again, Galvin went on the offensive.

"Some of you may still recall the sweet, young girl I moved here with: Millie Fremont, a thirteen-year-old exchange student from Nantes, France. She was originally staying with a family in Ladue who died most unfortunately in an auto accident on just her second day in-country. I found out about her situation while I was living there. Anyway, she came to live with me, and I loved her like my own daughter," Galvin said.

I'll bet you did, Cousey thought, unimpressed.

"Tragedy struck again when she disappeared, and I have grieved her loss ever since," Galvin said.

You slimy bastard! Cousey thought. *With the cheek to lay it on the table — though certainly not all of it. We're about to get to the "all of it" part!*

"Anyway, I've gone on quite a little tangent here. I'm supposed to be telling you about my scuba diving experience," Galvin said to scattered laughter.

"For ten years I was on a Navy scuba diving team, the last eight as its leader. Our training was similar to that of the SEALs and Delta Force, probably because we worked with them so often and needed to keep up with them — no mean feat, let me tell you. Our objective was primarily the sabotage of enemy targets, usually involving underwater demolition. Ships, bridges, pipelines, communication networks: that sort of thing. I can't tell you where because it might still be classified. Suffice it to say it was dangerous, demanding work, the sort of work that reminds you that you're a sailor fighting for your country. I won't say I loved every minute of it, but I loved most of it. Anyway, that's my story in a nutshell," he said to applause and even some whoops as he sat back down.

"There you have it. Some great diving experience here," Cousey said, once again trying to fend off his earlier feelings of intimidation. "Now, if I could just get one more show of hands before we adjourn for refreshments: How many of you own scuba diving equipment?"

This time only three hands went up: Doris Kath's, the treasure hunter's, and John Galvin's.

"Hmm, not many. OK, one last question that strikes me as especially important: Where can you get scuba diving equipment around here?"

Galvin rose to speak. "There are some good dive shops at the major lakes — Lake of the Ozarks; Bull Shoals; Table Rock — in the same vicinity and sometimes even in the same places that sell boats. It takes some digging, but you can find shops in St. Louis as well. Many of them will rent equipment, but of course you have to leave a deposit."

"Thank you," Cousey said. Then, to Kath, "Yes?"

"I got my equipment, the stuff I use for recreational diving, through my company at a nice discount. I could ask them if they'll sell to the public; I'm guessing they will. A buck's a buck, right?"

And a dyke's a dyke, at least one of them thought with a derisive smile.

"That sounds good. Now, if there are no further items, I want to close by saying our next meeting will be on the third Wednesday of the month. We'll keep them on Wednesdays as long as that works for everyone (general nodding of heads) at the Rod & Gun Club. We'll have to do it outside if this many of you keep showing up — and I certainly hope you do — but at least we'll have some extra chairs set up in the parking lot next time; I'll look into getting some. I just hope it doesn't rain; if it does, we'll all just have to squeeze inside for some quality Kumbaya Time."

General laughter from the group.

"Do we have a motion to adjourn? Good. Who will second that? Good, the meeting is adjourned. Thank you all for coming, and have a safe trip home — after you've enjoyed some refreshments up the hill, that is."

People were piling into their cars and Cousey was climbing into his pickup when the last person he wanted or even expected to see ambled up to him.

"Cousey, walk with me. There's something I want to talk to you about."

Ever the subtleties of loathing: "Cousey" instead of "Kevin" or even "Doc," a reminder of his past glory he never minded hearing. Talk "to" rather than "with" you; little things, but grating nonetheless, with it the prospect of climbing a hill he never climbed, the gentle ups and downs of the lake's three-mile loop well serving his need for physical exertion three times a week. The entrance road was much steeper, a quarter-mile grade that could wind anyone who wasn't in top shape.

There had no longer been any reason to climb it. The last time was over twenty years ago when he'd posted a notice on the community bulletin board after the family cat went missing. Now he was being forced to climb the hill again, and he saw it for what it was intended to be: a simple but brutal reminder of his physical limitations. Cousey felt trapped between knowing he couldn't refuse the challenge and knowing he couldn't let it defeat him. Anyone who could row a boat around the lake, anyone who looked as good as Galvin did at sixty-plus, could kick his ass on this hill, all the while doubling the effect with negative talk, enjoying the struggle that was playing out before him like a cat toying with a mouse. The thought of being toyed with, mentally or even physically, angered Cousey, and he steeled himself for the challenge. He would look the monster in the eye, even if he were sucking air as he did so.

"I'm sorry, this wasn't very considerate of me. Here I am, thinking everyone is an Olympic athlete when we could have just taken my car," Galvin said, all crocodile smiles as Cousey took his first deep breath.

This time it was Cousey's turn to surprise.

"You mean that big piece of shit you ran me off the road with?"

Galvin was a good four inches taller, and he kept his cool as he looked over at Cousey.

"That customized 220-thousand-dollar piece of shit I momentarily lost control of when I was answering my phone? Yep, that's the one," he said cheerfully.

"How inconvenient," Cousey said. "I suppose you also lose control of that monstrosity you call a 'dog' whenever I'm walking past."

Galvin's gaze was icy, his tone shifting abruptly as they mounted the hill.

"Dogs have a sense about people; not much I can do about that, either. So, what are you up to with this scuba club, Cousey?"

Feigning ignorance, Cousey tried to focus on the conversation.

"Oh, boredom, I suppose. The need for a hobby; I certainly have the time for one. And, I suppose, just plain curiosity. Do you ever find yourself looking at a body of water and wondering, 'What could be under all that?' I'm not just talking fish, The Lost Species that could be combing the depths like Nessie. I'm also not talking about the ocean; the ocean is too big to know what's on the bottom, and we already know there are lots of things on the bottom. I'm talking lakes: something more finite, more explorable. I'm talking about the things people dump into lakes, the things that fall out of boats. Maybe even the things people are trying to hide," he said with a sly glance at Galvin, who shot him a wary look.

Bingo! Cousey thought.

Galvin responded by increasing the pace, Cousey laboring to keep up.

Verbally Galvin recovered quickly. "Good luck finding anything at the bottom of this lake, let alone even being able to see down there. You might have checked with me before you launched this harebrained idea."

Cousey laughed. "As if we're on speaking terms."

Galvin pressed on. "The lake is polluted, silted up; more from runoff than anything, I suspect. Another fifty years and there will be nothing left. Believe me, I've had the tanks on. I've been down there."

"I'll bet you have," Cousey said, letting the uneasy silence that followed sink in. "Still, it's a starting point, a way to… get our feet wet, if you'll pardon the pun."

The cleverness of Cousey's banter contradicted the ordeal his body was enduring, an ordeal he tried to mask as best he could.

"I've had to pardon a lot of things about you, Cousey," Galvin said.

Cousey ignored him. "Anyway, it's always best to start in your own backyard."

Galvin glared at him. "As long as you don't shit in your own backyard."

"You should know about that."

"What are you implying?"

Cousey played dumb. Sort of. "Only that you're a… worldly guy with a broad knowledge of things."

"I'm afraid you're not making any sense," Galvin said, his eyes drilling holes.

Cousey had touched a nerve. They had almost reached the top, Cousey never more gratified than to see the windows of the Rod & Gun Club coming into view. He had fared better than he'd expected, suspecting anger and adrenalin — not to mention a strong desire not to be shown up — was part of it. Though Galvin was hardly winded by the time they reached the top, his triumph was hardly complete.

Cousey's mind was pumped full of oxygen. He smiled at the thought of planting one more seed of doubt.

"Another thing about diving here occurs to me. While you say visibility is a problem — and I have no reason to doubt your assessment — you can always feel your way around. The lake isn't that deep, and I've long been curious about the swimming platform. I have a good view of it from my house, and the hummingbirds seem to love it there. Anyway, I have a hankering to do some exploring, and that's the first place I intend to check out."

Galvin's smile turned icy. His eyes flashed warning.

Double bingo, you guilty bastard! Cousey thought.

"You may be aware that I watch the hummingbirds come in every April 15th, and I'll be damned if they don't swarm around that swimming platform like it's some kind of shrine; enough to make a fellow pretty darn curious, that's for sure. Anyway, I'm fixing to outfit myself with some scuba diving equipment real soon, do some poking around near my boat dock in the daytime, maybe wait until the next full moon to check out the swimming platform. Most of my friends still work, you see, and I'd be a fool to go out there alone. There's something... romantic about a moonlight dive, don't you think? If all I'm going to be able to do is feel around, it doesn't really matter if it's day or night, does it? A flashlight works better in the dark. Who knows, the moonbeams might even bring out a surprise or two."

Galvin's poker face was back, matched by his flat tone, though Cousey sensed the turbulence roiling just beneath the surface. Just as he sensed with a growing certainty that something was under the swimming platform.

"Suit yourself," Galvin said. "Just know that I think you're a fool for starting this club, wasting people's time."

"We'll see whose time is wasted, Galvin. We'll see who ends up the fool."

A little touch of defiance — just to piss him off! Cousey thought.

Galvin marched through the door of the Rod & Gun Club to score more points with the locals. Cousey leaned forward with his hands on his knees, sucking enough air to overcome his exertion before going in. Watching as Galvin worked the room like a boardroom veteran. What he didn't see was the look on Galvin's face on the drive home. Didn't see how utterly the smile had left a face that ached from smiling, the muscles involved in that undertaking being the least-developed in his body.

Chapter X

Her new life opened up before her with the bright green field at the foot of the hill, the gray-blue of the lake beyond. There were boats on the water, ducks paddling and quacking their way around them, with birds as large as Canada geese flapping everywhere. She smiled, mesmerized by the idyllic scene.

Already the change had begun. John Galvin's hand was on her left knee, caressing it gently, allowing it to linger there as a subtle symbol of entitlement. Given it might have been a portent of things past experience told her she should have been wary of, Millie Fremont was too happy to notice. At least at the time.

The house was a curious affair, and now that she lived here, she viewed it with greater scrutiny. It was as long and low as the house in Ladue. It was built into the hillside on the lake side of the road, a single-car garage the only structure that rose above a flat roof that was parallel to the driveway. Galvin pulled up to the closed door, big, new tires crunching to a stop on the driveway because the Hummer was too wide for the garage. The place was made of stone, the curved part of the roof facing the lake. As they left the Hummer with their bags — everything else was already here — Millie could see the large, curving window beneath it as they walked down the steps and around the front. Her first impression of the place was of permanence, solidity, an impression that was further reinforced now that their stuff was moved in.

Our stuff, she thought, never feeling more a part of something.

Galvin was exhausted, thoughts of Millie feeding his insomnia more than the logistics of the move. Familiar thoughts in which titillation vied with fear.

They were still full from brunch when Galvin said, "Love, let's rest awhile, and then I'll take you for a boat ride."

Millie beamed. "Sounds good to me."

And so they rested — or at least Millie did — drifting off to sleep thinking of the best places to set up hummingbird feeders. Galvin did not sleep, his eyes burning like embers under their closed lids. He rose to find the door to Millie's room ajar, seized by conflicting emotions when he looked in and saw her wispy body in repose on top of the covers, her angelic face on the pillow, her shoes tucked neatly beneath the bed. Feeling tormented as his demons waged war within him. It was driving him crazy, and it all boiled down to two choices, neither of which seemed viable: have her or send her away.

Take it slow, he told himself, remembering the lesson of his daughter. *Ease her into this or you'll freak her out.*

***

The late afternoon sun shimmered on the lake, tiny waves pulsing like the bulbs in an old marquee. Galvin rowed, Millie seated across from him in a tight pair of jeans, her legs parted slightly. The Look was there. Millie noticed it and shrugged it off, and he caught himself doing it and looked elsewhere, smiling his Benevolent Father Smile.

"John, you look tired," Millie said with the French accent that sounded so sensuous coming from a female, so wimpy coming from a male. "Did you sleep?"

"A lot on my mind, I suppose. Moves are always stressful, even when they go as smoothly as this one. So many details to consider."

"Well, we are finally here," she said. "Things will get better once we are settled in."

"Of that I have no doubt, my dear."

They rowed around the lake, the sun giving Millie a sleepy, dreamy look as it danced off her hair.

She pointed to a gray wooden platform about eight feet square floating on the water up ahead.

"Can we get a closer look at that?" she asked.

"Of course we can, love. The day is your oyster."

Millie looked at him inquisitively. "What does that mean?"

"It means my girl can do anything she wants to."

Galvin rowed close enough to reach a small bollard, holding the boat steady as Millie climbed the metal ladder that ran up the side and looped over the top. The platform was wet, her feet slipping on the planks. She stood there with her arms akimbo, smiling out at the lake. Today she felt as if it were her domain. As if to prove it, she held out her hand and a hummingbird with a shimmering red head alighted upon it.

Galvin was dumbfounded. "My dear, I have never seen a hummingbird do that!"

Millie smiled. "Oh, they do it all the time with me. Hummingbirds are like children: They can tell if you love them — and I love them so! This one reminds me of Pierre."

"Pierre?"

She pulled up her pant leg, the hummingbird still perched on her other hand, and showed Galvin her tattoo.

"This is Pierre; I knew him back in France."

Galvin was struck by the exquisite slimness of her ankle, the notion that a tattoo was a very adult thing. His heart pounded.

"Whenever you're ready, love," he said.

"Adieu, mon chère. Say hello to your family for me," she said to the bird, and it flew away.

They hadn't brought any food — the opportunity for intimacy it afforded notwithstanding, Galvin didn't feel like cooking — so he took her to a Mexican restaurant he had seen on the way in. Afterward, he stopped at the liquor store, bought a nice bottle of whiskey for himself and a small bottle of liqueur for Millie.

I can't wait any longer, he decided. *One way or another, there must be a resolution.*

"A little housewarming gift for you," he said, handing her the bottle with a flourish. "I feel like celebrating tonight."

"But, monsieur, it is alcohol. I am too young!"

Galvin smiled. "We make the rules. It will be our little secret. It is sweet, just like my Millie. I think you will like it."

When they returned to the house Galvin made a fire, and they sat together on the couch watching and listening to the growing conflagration. He poured himself a small glass of whiskey, half as much liqueur for Millie.

He raised his glass. "To our new house!"

"To our new house!"

She brought the glass to her lips and coughed.

"Sip it, my love; it isn't soda. Just sip it and watch the fire."

She sipped it, and as she did Galvin watched her closely. She was smiling more, her eyes getting more of a faraway look as she gazed into the dancing flames: so playful, so mysterious.

"This is nice!" she said, laughing.

Time for a test, Galvin thought.

He caressed her hair, her sensitive earlobe, slipping his hand down her neck.

Pleasant tingle between her legs.

"Mmm, that feels good," she said, closing her eyes like a contented cat.

"I want you to feel good, love," he said. "I want you to feel very, very good."

Galvin refreshed her glass, and she sipped her liqueur, her mind drifting ever farther away. Galvin watched her, smiling, caressing. Waiting for the right moment.

"I'll be right back, dear," he said when it arrived. "Don't let the fire go out, eh?"

She beamed at him. Her smile was too big, and he smiled when he saw it.

"Do not worry, I will not!" she said, laughing.

He returned to the couch, shielding a small dish of olive oil from her view.

"My dear, I would love to see Pierre again. Could you slip off your pants for an unobstructed view?"

Everything John Galvin said seemed like a good idea. "Sure!"

Off came the pants, Galvin doing a double-take at the sight of her slim, graceful legs in the firelight, their lines unbroken even by a tennis dress.

"Ah, there he is!" Galvin said, tracing the lines of the tattoo with apparent appreciation.

This was his opening, the touch lingering in a caress.

"My dear, do you ever get cramps in your legs?"

"Sometimes, when I run."

"Well, I used to get them bad, sometimes so bad the pain would keep me awake at night. My dad, bless his heart, would get up and massage my legs with rubbing alcohol," he said, massaging Millie's lower leg. "Doesn't that feel nice?"

She smiled contentedly, her face glowing in the firelight. "Yes, it does."

"It was the nicest thing my dad ever did for me," he said, his hand rising to her knee, the soft, smooth warmth of her inner thigh. "Funny, but we were never very close. Here, let me give you a little more," he said, reaching for the bottle with his other hand.

Watching her as she gazed into the fire. Watching until the smile stayed on her face and a blankness came over her eyes.

Time to up the ante, Galvin thought.

"Love, I forget, what is the name of the town you are from?"

Millie laughed. "I do not live in a town, silly! I live on... I live on a farm. There is no town."

"Sure there is. What is the name of that big town near your farm?"

"Oh, the big town! Nan... Nancy! Nantes! Nantes Nanny Nancy!" she said, laughing.

It was time to make his move.

"Love, can you do me a favor? I want to buy you some new panties, some nice silk ones. Can you give me this pair so I'll know your size? Here, I'll cover you with the blanket. That's it. Just slip them off. Good girl!"

His heart was pounding as he reached under the blanket that covered them both and resumed his caresses, working his way to the space between her legs. He was very gentle. She didn't seem to mind.

"Ooooh, that feels so nice," she said as if it were natural for him to be visiting her Special Place.

His hand went to the oil. Soon he was caressing her with it and she was moaning words of pleasure, some of them in French. This excited him all the more. He could feel her growing excitement. She felt like she was being tickled, in the nicest way possible, the feeling increasing in intensity until she felt she was going to explode. In her mind a beautiful bird was flying toward her, the sun shining on its golden wings. Soft and feathery, the tip of one of them touched her, and she was rocked by a sensation she had never felt before: a bright, hot flash of pleasure that surged through her entire being.

"Wow!" she said.

"Does my love enjoy the fireworks?"

Galvin smiled. He considered stopping there, calling the evening a success, but his member was pressing painfully against his shorts, begging for release. It would not be denied, not this far into the game. He reached under the blanket and unbuckled his pants, lifting his buttocks so he could lower both them and his shorts. His organ had sprung up like a jack-in-the-box when he lifted the blanket, and for a fleeting moment he feared what her reaction might be.

She smiled at the mini-soldier standing at attention in his shiny pink helmet. She did not fear it, so far away did it seem, so disconnected from the past — and this was John. It was like watching herself in a movie, not something that was happening to her right now.

Not something that could harm her.

"Love, come have a seat on my lap," he said gently. "There's something I want to tell you."

***

Afterward, he used her panties to dry her off. He picked up her things and escorted her to her room. She was still laughing as he helped her out of her shirt and into her nightie.

"Good night, love," he said, kissing her on the forehead. Quickly returning to Benevolent Father Mode as if nothing had happened.

"Good night, John."

"Breakfast out tomorrow. Sleep as late as you want."

Damn, I forgot to keep the panties! He thought. *Oh well, maybe less suspicious this way.*

He went away smiling at the singularity of what he had just experienced, with it the peculiar satisfaction of attaining a forbidden thing, though the fear of being found out remained. If anything, it was stronger. Because he was no longer thinking about it, he had done it. Done it again. Crossed the same line he had crossed before. A line that had caused his life to unravel, with (he tried not to think of it) a girl two years younger than his daughter had been. Learning nothing from the experience but a better way to go about it the next time.

What have I done? he thought as he repaired to the couch and refilled his glass, gazing into the glowing log canyons that remained of the fire, hissing and crackling as they pulsated with a hellish glimmer.

Sick bastard, he thought.

Then he smiled, smiled because he had consummated his marriage with his child bride (all the while admitting it wasn't entirely consensual and she didn't see herself this way). Smiled at his refusal to be cowed by society and its seemingly arbitrary rules. It all depended on where you lived, he merely having the misfortune of living in the wrong place. Smiled at his refusal to be denied anything he wanted, however impossible it seemed.

Carpe diem! he thought.

Ultimately, he smiled because he had gotten away with something he had long thought about doing, and the girl had actually enjoyed herself, and he would certainly do it again. He finished his whiskey — *half a bottle, goddamn; if I can't sleep tonight something is wrong with me* — drew the screen across the hearth, threw some warm water on his face, rinsed the whiskey taste from his mouth, and turned in for the best sleep he'd had in quite some time.

***

For Millie it was A Tale of Two Sleeps. For four hours she slept the sleep of the dead, dreaming vividly. She was on a merry-go-round, a warm tingle between her legs as she rode up and down, deliriously happy as color and motion spun all around her, intense flashes of warmth that began between her legs and went deep inside her as she grabbed for the brass ring. But the ride was becoming painful, and she looked down to see she was sitting astride the saddle horn, her blood running down the sides of the brightly colored horse…

The image jolted her awake to a pillow soaked with drool, a head howling with pain, and a bladder swelled with urine. It stung when she urinated, and she was surprised to see a slimy discharge. She threw back two pain pills with some water, but the pounding in her head continued, feeling as if a giant hand was squeezing her brain. She tried to get back to sleep, but the pain wasn't the only thing keeping her awake.

She remembered what had happened, with a clarity she didn't have at the time it did. Remembered everything, starting with the hand on her knee on the drive down. Grown men didn't put their hand on the knee of a thirteen-year-old girl. Grown men didn't even put their hand on the knee of a woman unless they were intimate and she was OK with it and it was done in private.

The Look he gave her in the boat. Men were always looking there when they weren't looking at breasts, always pretending they weren't. With a strange clarity, she realized John was no different in this regard.

Then the couch, the caressing that started with her hair and moved on to her neck and ear, John putting more alcohol in her glass as she gazed into the fire, knowing now that alcohol was the key. It felt good at the time, and it didn't stop, and there was no reason to make it stop because it felt so good, even if she didn't realize what was happening.

Then his hand on her leg, starting at her tattoo and going higher and higher, more liqueur in her glass — it was funny; ha! ha! — until her pants came off, then her panties. Now he was really touching her, and at first it tickled and then it felt good, so good that it didn't seem strange when she saw him (it was like watching a movie), and before she knew it, she was riding up and down on him like that horse in her dream, looking into the fire — how warm and pretty and seductive the flames were! — and feeling very, very good so good that it made her forget the other times. Until now.

Oh my God, it has happened again! she thought, and that it should happen with John Galvin — the man she had trusted; the man she had looked up to — shook her to the very core of her being. One by one, the pillars that held up her life were crumbling.

The illusion of wellbeing she had let herself believe, as if she were overdue for something good, starting with the caring, sensitive man who had come like a shining knight to her rescue — different from the rest of them — the serene castle by a magical lake with hummingbirds he had taken her to live in happily ever after, making her feel like a princess for the first time in her life, all came crashing down like the body of a rare and beautiful bird shot from the sky, the wreckage of an impossibly beautiful dream. She cried hot, bitter tears, turning her pillow into a sodden mess. She flipped it over and cried some more. She cried so hard she was afraid she would awaken John and he would come to her aid, and now she was afraid of what that aid might be. Still, she slept no more that night, only cried.

Determined to prove to herself that she wasn't imagining things, she looked over at her panties when it was light enough to see, lying on top of her neatly folded jeans. She held them to her nose and smelled a familiar smell. Her cousin, her father: It was the same smell. Her head reeled and her stomach heaved, and soon she was vomiting into them.

***

She returned to her bed and the old habit of hugging her knees as she stared off into space, suddenly feeling herself in limbo. There was no returning home to a mother, a life that held no future save to cook and keep house and bear children, all the while ready to satisfy the sexual needs of a husband with rough hands and limited understanding. The sort of life a woman had to endure until she reached the pot of gold that was said to be at the end of it. Sometimes she wondered if anything good could come of this life. *Suck it up*, she told herself. It was the same here, except she could see the rewards if she were willing to play along. Nice dinners; nice clothes; the possibility of going to college. Once she was out of college, once she had a job, she could finally tell him "No more!" with a slap in the face for emphasis. But that was nine years from now, maybe ten. A long time to play the game, to pretend life was good when all the while you were biding your time. Suffering in the interim.

I must try, she resigned herself to the thought, *to life as it is*, a life she was determined to get something out of after all that men had put her through. *I must try. Because there is nothing else.*

She managed a smile. *Hummingbirds. I still have my hummingbirds.*

A tap on the door gave her a start. It opened and Galvin's smiling face was reminiscent of a jack-o'-lantern as he thrust it into the room. A face that no longer seemed handsome.

"Good morning, princess. How did you sleep?"

She forced a smile. "OK, I guess."

"How's the head?"

"It hurts."

"Sorry about that, honey. Now we know why drinking is for adults only, though rest assured adults can overdo it as well. My head hurts a little, too. Get cleaned up and we'll go have breakfast. I'll give you a couple of my pain pills."

"OK."

A feeling of elation swept over Galvin as he closed the door. *She seems OK. Maybe she doesn't remember.*

At breakfast she found it difficult to maintain a facade of normalcy. She found herself hating the would-be kind, fatherly face that smiled across from her, for the first time seeing the evil behind it. She dreaded that smile, even as it was making plans for a day at the zoo. Dreaded the passage of time that would make the day dark and cold again, cold enough to light another fire in the hearth.

Cold enough to bring them together for another snuggle on the couch.

That night, after they did go to the zoo and eat out, bought some things for breakfast on the way home, he surprised her.

"Sorry, honey, no fire tonight. I'm really bushed. You can stay up if you want. I'm going to turn in early."

He took her by the arms, surprised to feel her body stiffen as he kissed her on the forehead. That night, as he was turning off the lights, lowering the thermostat, shutting the house down for the night, he heard a sound he never expected to hear, a subtle sound that spoke volumes: the click of the button on the doorknob to her room. It told him something wasn't right, that her calm sense of ease that day was no more than an act. If he had been more perceptive, he would have noticed the dried tears that streaked her face when he entered her room that morning; noticed she had moved her panties from the chair, with the added suspicion that she had inspected them; detected the faint smell of vomit. Locking her door conveyed the unmistakable message that she was onto him, and, at the very least, he'd better give it a rest. Wait until next weekend before approaching her again — and, despite this warning sign, he couldn't help but think of doing so. Better to give her time to heal, to get used to the idea of being what he expected her to be.

***

The week that followed was a much-needed respite, pushing the happenings of the previous weekend so far away as to almost make them seem an aberration. As she saw it, he had satisfied his curiosity; maybe they could move on now. Maybe their relationship could return to the way it was, she tried to sell herself, all the while realizing the impossibility.

Once your eyes are opened..., she thought.

On Thursday night of that week, she dreamed, and the dream was so vivid, so unlike any dream she'd ever had, it felt like there was something to it:

She dreamed of olden times when men and women wore heavy, shiny clothing that looked better than it smelled. Most of the time it was too chilly to bathe, easier just to mask body odor with another layer of powder and perfume. Her father was a king, wearing an English crown. Everyone spoke English, and it wasn't the soft, friendly American English that she had grown so accustomed to, but the clipped British English that sounded like someone announcing a public flogging.

Young men noticed her, and she gazed into a mirror with a beveled edge and saw why. Her parents scolded them away, and soon she realized they had other plans for her: the convent. There her unmet physical needs roiled within her, assuaged somewhat by the peace she felt among the sisters, by the way the gray light of dawn sifted through the chapel windows during lauds, bringing out bits of the woodwork that soothed her with its feeling of permanence. She came to see the convent, the spirituality behind it, as an anchor in her life. It and the birds she befriended gave her an ever-greater pleasure through the years. The power she felt within her grew on two fronts, leading her to found her own abbey and to control the birds she loved so. She thought, she prayed — and the birds… did things. She was sure of this (awestruck, in fact) when a lack of rain had all but ruined the crop, and the farmers, trying to protect what little they had left, asked her to intervene against the crows. She stood in a field, extending her arms like the most beautiful of scarecrows as her habit billowed in the breeze, visible to all among the broken sheaves of corn.

"Heavenly Father, You who minister to the crows as You minister to us all, feed them with Your manna so Your crops may feed our children. In Your mighty name, I pray, amen."

She smiled as she finished the shortest prayer she had ever prayed — and the crows departed as if blown by a great wind.

Her dream followed the nun's life to its end. Many mourned her when she died, the word "Saint" carved on her crypt.…

Millie awoke with a shudder and a sense of determination. It was Friday morning, and she was leery of the weekend that lay ahead. The dream made her feel special, that there was more to her than she was aware of. It wasn't the first time she had thought about nuns, certainly not the first time she had thought about birds, but it was the first time she had put the two of them together and linked them to herself. There was something to it, she just didn't know what. Yet. All she knew was she was tired of men. Men who had robbed her of her childhood, even her dignity as a human being. Men who didn't have the decency to wait until she was a woman. Having a period didn't make a girl a woman, it merely created that illusion in their minds. Whatever was in their minds, it needed to stop, and in John's case it needed to stop now.

***

John Galvin had other ideas, his money and his confidence and his physical power combining to make him an irresistible force, if only in his own mind. Unused to the word "no," he wasn't about to hear it from a thirteen-year-old girl. When plying her with alcohol no longer worked, he used force and harsh words — a squeeze of the arm; a slap in the face — with the threat of greater force and what had always been his trump card: the ability to send her home. One time she ran off into the woods, and when the men from the lake found her and brought her back, she dared not say why she had left. It didn't save her from the second-worst beating of her life, but it did save her from getting beaten to death. From then on, she accepted the many kindnesses he bestowed upon her — usually clothing, sometimes jewelry, once a nice watch — even though they were never enough to compensate for the pain, both mental and physical, of his repeated violations. He was taking less time with foreplay, more time with the act itself, an act that was becoming less an act of love (if it ever was) than an exercise in satisfying his physical needs, an exercise in control that, if his blinkered perception would ever allow him to see it, surely crossed the line into rape. At last he had someone he could manipulate for his own pleasure, the feelings of power he derived from it a heady intoxicant.

Millie had a trump card, too, one she dared not play. The red-headed hummingbird reminded her so much of Pierre that it might well have been Pierre, hummingbirds being known to live for a dozen years — she had known Pierre since she was three — and travel distances of four thousand miles, more than the width of the Atlantic between the U.S. and Europe. Another green-headed bird did, indeed, remind her of Jerome, and an all-brown bird looked and acted uncannily like Madeleine. She gazed at them, transfixed, as they visited the feeders. Her friends. Her protectors.

Could it be? she thought, admitting it was far-fetched but possible.

"Pierre" hovered in front of her face, the tiny jewels of his eyes meeting hers as he tilted his head the way Pierre used to, somehow understanding what she felt but didn't say, awaiting her instructions. Just like the original Pierre.

Millie frowned as she realized what he had in mind. "No, do not hurt him! Hurt him and my dream is over. I can endure. Some day I will be free."

And so the hummingbirds left John Galvin alone.

The only choice that remained to Millie was passive aggression. Even when it cost her a slap across the mouth, she cried out more often, more shrilly, in the hope someone would hear and facilitate the rescue she was unwilling to facilitate, even though it was one that would undoubtedly have consequences, his loss ultimately resulting in her own. Part of her doubted her ability to accomplish even that, and for this reason she was afraid of him. Afraid she could not get him into enough trouble to make it stick. Afraid his money, his power to manipulate others, would keep him out of trouble and maybe even get her killed, with him wriggling out of this as well. Yet she could not kill herself; something about the dream, about suspecting who she truly was, would not allow it. If a saint could suffer, then so could she.

Still, it occurred to her with a nagging frequency that someone should have heard her cries. Someone should have heard and come pounding on the door — at least that's how it was in the movies. But shortly after moving in, John had bought a massive Rottweiler he named Fritz, and it would have taken the most strong-willed of neighbors to deal with that hellhound at night.

Sound carried on the lake; she was surprised how well it carried. While John had razed the houses on either side of them — she suspected so he could do the things he was doing to her now — and the houses across the road were situated far up the hill to cheat a better view of the lake, the lots here were too expensive for any distance to be very great. She was sure people heard her screams, but the only one who had ever done anything was a "meddlesome old bastard" (as John called him) across the lake. Every time Dr. Cousey saw a new bruise on her, he reported it to the authorities. Every time John beat him to the punch, explaining away what had happened, and she knew better than to contradict him. It was common knowledge that John and Dr. Cousey didn't like each other. She noticed that John seemed to take great pleasure in Fritz's behavior whenever they were in the yard together and Dr. Cousey was coming by on one of his walks, the knuckles on the hand that held his hiking stick turning white as if he expected the gate to swing open and Fritz to come barreling out. Dr. Cousey, she realized, was a warning to others who would stick their nose into John's business.

Three months into what had become full-fledged weekends of torture, Millie's body finally blew the whistle.

"John, I am pregnant," she broke the news at breakfast one Friday.

She had known about it for a couple of days, an early pregnancy test confirming her suspicion. Nevertheless, she had deliberately waited until Friday to tell him, hoping it would put a damper on his weekend plans.

It was as if someone had hit Galvin across the face with a two-by-four. He stared across at her, open-mouthed. Finding himself in the unfamiliar position of not being in control. Trying to be civil. Trying not to freak her out as much as he was freaking out.

"How far along, love?" he asked in the vocal equivalent of a poker face.

"Probably not very far. I just missed my first period. I bought a pregnancy test and found out."

Her eyes were tearing up.

Then the stupid question. The ridiculous question.

"Are you sure I'm the father?"

Millie looked over at him, clearly hurt. "Do you think I would let other men do this to me? I am thirteen years old. You are the father, John."

Galvin sighed, shaking his head. "This is not good, love. Not good for you. Not good for me. Not good for the child."

Millie eyed him intently. "You seem surprised this happened. I am still a child, but I am a child who menstruates. Can someone who menstruates not get pregnant? You should have known this would happen."

"This will not do, love. People will talk."

Millie's eyes glittered through her tears. "Yes, John, people will talk. People will talk, and they will know what you have been doing to me."

For the first time, his eyes flashed warning. "That would be an embarrassment — for both of us."

"For both of us, yes, but especially for you."

"You are too young to raise a child. You should be thinking about school, the fine college I will send you to some day. I already have a child, a daughter, all grown up."

"A daughter you never see. A daughter you never even talk about. Maybe you did this to her, too."

"Shut up!" Galvin cried, backhanding her across the mouth.

Millie was in shock. "So, I am not the first! You are a monster!"

As if to disprove this, Galvin clenched his teeth but stayed his hand, his anger transforming his face into a wretched, twisted mask.

"Listen to me and listen well," he seethed. "Raising another child is not in my plans!"

"Then you should have taken precautions."

"I am taking precautions. You will have an abortion."

"No!" she said. "You have made the mistake, not the baby. You must take responsibility. Do you not love me, John? Is this not what a man wants when he goes into a girl? I will have this baby, and if she is too much for me to handle, I will put her up for adoption."

Galvin glared at her. "Did you just say 'no' to me?"

Her eyes flashed defiance. "Yes."

He slapped her across the face, splitting her lip.

She rolled her lip, tasting blood. Crying softly.

Galvin thrust his finger at her. "You will get an abortion; do you understand?"

Millie dried her eyes on her sleeve, once again daring to look him in the eye.

Her voice quivering, she gathered herself and said, "It is my body, my decision! Even if I were carrying the baby of Satan, I would not kill it!"

He rose so suddenly that he knocked over his chair, knocking Millie off hers and two of her teeth loose. Her mouth was bleeding in earnest as she lay on the kitchen floor, her body convulsing with sobs.

"We'll see about that," he said as he left the room.

That night there was another fight, one that everybody on the lake couldn't help but hear. Sounds of a man yelling, a girl screaming, and everyone knew who it was. Sounds of slapping, of things being knocked around. The only thing they didn't hear was the punch that ended it, though the "Oh my God!" that followed was clear enough. The whole lake heard it, but no one came to investigate. Fritz, the first hurdle in a parade of excuses, saw to that. One hand, and one hand only, reached for the phone — lonely; disgusted; impotent, but still trying — and called the police.

"Are they still arguing?" the officer asked.

"No, it's quiet now."

"Then it's probably over," the officer said. "No reason for us to come out."

"Not even to make an arrest?"

"Good night, Dr. Cousey."

Kevin Cousey's hand was shaking as he put the phone down. He took a deep breath and gathered himself, and picked it up again.

"Did you contact the Benson PD?" the deputy asked.

"I did, but they're kind of sketchy about jurisdiction when it comes to the lake, seeing as how it isn't within city limits. They refused to come out."

"Sir, we're having a pretty busy night. It might be a while before we can get someone out there."

Cousey sighed, sensing the runaround. "OK. Please call me when you do, whatever the time. Here's my number."

"Will do."

Dr. Kevin Cousey slept fitfully, anticipating the call that never came.

April 15th: the night Millicent "Millie" Fremont disappeared from the lake forever.

Chapter XI

Kevin Cousey looked at the calendar — the kind that showed moons: full, half, and new — and smiled. He had tipped his hand deliberately enough that it would be noticed and, he hoped, subtly enough that its deliberateness wouldn't be suspected. A week before the next full moon. The trap had been set, and now it was just a matter of waiting for the rat to take the bait. For the last twenty years he had struggled to find a purpose in a life that had gone horribly awry. Part of the rush he was feeling tonight as he sat on his deck, watching a moon the size of a nail clipping partially obscured by clouds, was the feeling his mission had finally arrived, in a way he never could have imagined. Part of the beauty of his plan was he didn't need scuba diving gear, just the ruse of a scuba diving club. It was very likely he would never buy any, never have to search for whatever was under the swimming platform — because Galvin would do it for him. When he brought up what Cousey suspected with a growing feeling he would, he would catch Galvin red-handed. His whole purpose for starting this club was about to be realized, and who gave a damn what happened to it afterward?

He would go on an all-night stakeout every night until the full moon. He hadn't pulled an all-nighter since his residency, and here he was forty years later planning a whole week of them. Of course, there were ways to cheat sleep, and unfortunately one of them wasn't coffee. Coffee left you more tired than before when its initial boost wore off; Lindberg had the good sense to forsake it on his transatlantic flight, opting instead for water and ham sandwiches. Candy bars were better or, his old standby on long car trips, chocolate-covered coffee beans — with the radio up and the windows down — popped one at a time whenever he felt himself nodding off. Small, frequent doses of energy were this doctor's orders for staying awake. Of course, there couldn't be a radio, though at least there was plenty of cool, oxygenated air to rejuvenate him. He also didn't need to get up for work in the morning, so he could rest up during the day.

A chill swept through him as he contemplated embarking on such a plan alone, wondering if he was up to it. He had two boats, and he debated on the speed of the pontoon boat versus the stealth of the rowboat. Finally, he decided on speed because Galvin could certainly outrow him, not to mention hear him coming a mile away with his military-trained ears. Better to let him do his thing then roar up and apprehend him.

Apprehend, he thought. *Listen to me, talking like a cop! But hey, somebody's gotta play cop around here!*

It occurred to Cousey that he needed to be in the boat, ready to go night after night, and that the pontoon boat scored another point for being more comfortable. He could sit on one of the padded benches on the far side, out of sight should Galvin shine a light his way, though he dared not lie down. More thoughts of Lindbergh, deliberately making his seat uncomfortable to help keep him awake. He would also need a good flashlight — his big camping light would fill the bill nicely — his smartphone to call the police, and a gun to hold Galvin until they arrived.

With the latter, there was a problem: Was he prepared to take a man's life? The answer was "no." The gun was a bluff; Galvin would see it, if not in his eyes then in the way the gun trembled in his hand. He might even have a gun himself and claim self-defense. The acrimony between them was well known, after all. Grudgingly, Cousey realized he couldn't do this alone. At the same time, he wondered who on the lake he could trust. While Galvin wasn't universally liked, he was universally respected or at least feared. Who knew who he had in his pocket?

Then he realized it didn't matter. That it would be dark and he didn't have to tell anyone who he was after, merely that he was trying to catch someone in the act of doing something and would pay him well for his help. Maybe some out-of-work young guy; he could make it worth his while. A young guy who was good with guns and up for an adventure. Certainly, the redneck spirit was alive and well here. Surely there was someone. The biggest challenge would be to keep him from blowing their cover. Because everyone knew how sound travels on a lake.

I have to move quickly on this, Cousey thought. *We're talking tomorrow night. God help me if it's tonight, the same night I tipped him off. Then I'm really screwed.*

***

Finding a partner wasn't as hard as he expected, just a matter of combing the lake for vehicles still parked in their driveways after 9:00 AM: time enough to give everyone except those who worked graveyard a chance to get to work. If there was a dog, make sure it was behind a fence, then knock on the doors of houses with a pickup out front.

Please, no more Fritzes, he thought.

By the time he had knocked on his fifth door, he knew he had found his man. A large, young guy answered the door, looking as if he had just woken up. He had a beer gut and a red face, and he was wearing a black concert T-shirt.

"What can I do for you?"

"Good morning. I'm Kevin Cousey and I live on the lake. I used to be a doctor before a firecracker blew my hand off," he said, holding up the fake one.

"Yeah, I heard about that. Sorry."

"One of those things. Anyway, sorry to bother you, but would you happen to know anyone who's good with a gun and can stay awake all night? Someone who wouldn't mind earning a few extra bucks?"

"How few?"

"Two hundred a night, paid in cash, with a five-hundred-dollar bonus."

"A bonus for what?"

"Catching the guy I'm looking for. You see, I'm conducting a stakeout here on the lake, and I can't do it alone. I don't intend to kill anyone, but I do need someone who knows how to use a gun to hold the guy until the police arrive. Do you know anyone who might be interested?"

The man smiled, his teeth advertising chewing tobacco. "I'm your man, Doc. I never killed nobody, but I sure as hell can hit a target. Practice down in the woods durn near every week."

"Good. What's your name?"

"Calvin Maxwell, but my friends call me Buddy."

"Can I call you Buddy?"

"Sorry, you gotta be my friend. Can't we just keep it… professional?"

Cousey's mouth fell open.

Maxwell laughed. "I'm just shittin' you, Doc. Of course you can call me Buddy."

Cousey smiled. "Can you start tonight?"

"For two hundred dollars I sure as hell can."

"Good, here's my address. Be at my house by 10:00 PM; the guy I'm after would be a fool to show up any earlier than that."

"Anybody I know?"

"Possibly, but I'd really be surprised if he were a friend of yours. I'd like to keep his identity secret for now."

"OK."

"I'll pay you a hundred when we start, a hundred when we finish, and that bonus if we catch him."

"Sounds good."

"Buddy, one more thing: please, not a word of this to anyone, not even your wife."

"Shee-it, I ain't got no wife."

"A keeper like you? Get outta here!"

Maxwell cut loose with a belly laugh.

"See you at ten," Cousey said.

***

Calvin "Buddy" Maxwell arrived at 9:46 looking like he meant business in the same black T-shirt and a pair of Desert Storm cammies, the AK-47 the most serious part of his look.

"Is that what I think it is?" Cousey asked.

"If you're thinking 'Kalash,' it is."

"Shit! Are those things even legal?"

Maxwell grinned. "Hell if I know. Probably not if'n it's fully automatic like this puppy. I ain't too worried about it. All I know is the dude I bought it from at an Army/Navy surplus shop in St. Louis told me they're normally expensive as hell — like around then thou — and seemed in a big hurry to get rid of it. Long story short, he made me an offer I couldn't refuse, and told me to forget where I got it. You wouldn't believe some of the shit they got on this-here lake. One guy's got a frickin' machine gun straight outta Vietnam: It takes two guys to move, with these long belts of shells you feed into the sucker that look like little missiles. Not with the intent to kill no one, mind you, just to defend hisself the day The Man tries to take our guns away. I say let him try! What are you packin'?"

"Just a .38."

"Can I see it?"

Cousey handed it to him and Maxwell spun the cylinder like a seasoned gun handler and slapped it back into place.

"Nice piece! Looks brand-new."

"It isn't, but it's never been used."

"Why not?"

"Long story, better saved for another time. Anyway, it's basically a prop. That's why I need someone who knows guns."

"I'm your man," Maxwell said.

"A couple more things before we head for the boat: That's where we're going to wait him out, ready to turn on the engine and go out there if we need to. No talking and no coffee."

"Shit, I brought me a Thermos fulla jake."

"Trust me, candy works better. I'm bringing along some chocolate-covered coffee beans. The 'no talking' part is obvious."

"You're the boss."

"No, Buddy, from this moment on, we're a team — but I'm dead serious about this. Here's your first Benjamin."

"Thanks, Doc. Money always perks me up."

***

It was harder than they thought, staying awake without the natural inclination to talk that would have made passing the time so much easier. Popping the occasional chocolate-covered coffee bean — "Damn, these are good!" Maxwell said before Cousey shushed him — as they busied themselves scanning the sky, trying to remember any constellations other than the Big Dipper and any planets other than Venus and any stars other than the North Star they could see in the intermittent cloud breaks, all the while attuned to the sound they expected to hear: of oars dipped into water. A subtle sound, to be sure, as Cousey was certain Galvin would be drawing upon his naval training. Native American hunter/warriors showed it was possible to move almost soundlessly on water, and the best he could hope for was carelessness born of overconfidence on Galvin's part.

I'm sure he thinks we're all rubes; let him keep thinking that, he thought.

A little moonlight fell on the water, and it was exhausting to focus on what little it revealed. Tonight's was primarily an exercise in hearing, made more difficult by the lulling effect of night birds, the call of a whippoorwill deep in the woods, and spring peepers. They listened intently, and it was a taxing exercise. Perhaps due to the frequent checking of their watches, time crept by. Finally, the first rays of morning, the fog that accompanied them giving the lake a primordial look. Early Friday morning and utterly quiet.

Cousey finally broke the silence. "OK, I'm calling it. Here's your other hundred."

Maxwell took the money, stretching his big arms with a mighty yawn.

"Good enough. Same time tonight, Doc?"

"Same time, but don't hold your breath about catching him tonight. People like to party on Friday nights."

"Tell me about it," Maxwell said.

"Anyway, not a great time to be secretive."

"Unless you look at the flipside, Doc. The lake is gonna be one noisy place tonight, and noise is a good distraction. Plus, half the people on this lake are gonna be outta their frickin' gourds. When they pass out it'll be like wakin' the dead.

Friday night might be a better time than you think. I'd sure as hell be thinkin' about doin' somethin' sneaky tonight."

Cousey smiled at Maxwell's simple logic. "Good point. See you at ten."

***

Friday night held other advantages and disadvantages, one advantage being there was so much commotion on the lake they could actually talk for the first couple of hours. One disadvantage was it made it harder to hear such subtleties — as oars in the water, the splash of something entering the water, or the thump of something being tossed into a boat. Several boats were out tonight, each of them captained by a shouting drunk with a crew of rowdies. Yet there was also more light tonight: from a moon that was getting ever closer to full; from the beams of light that occasionally swept across the lake. One bunch even went skinny dipping, dismayed by how cold the water was.

"Commotion or no, he won't come out while other boats are out," Maxwell said.

"Buddy, you're even smarter than you look," Cousey said.

Maxwell chuckled. "I sure as hell hope so."

By midnight there were no more boats, though parties all around the lake were still going strong. Bright glare at the far end; apparently someone had lit a bonfire.

"Now's when we need to be quiet," Cousey said.

Two nights of surveillance were beginning to weigh on them. Like driving in a blizzard, it took utter concentration, leaving the fatigue of adrenalin burnout in its wake. Finally, at 3:00 AM, when all was nearly quiet, when the fire at the far end of the lake was out, when Cousey's eyes were closing and his head was nodding, Maxwell clapped him on the shoulder.

"Shhh!" he whispered. "Listen."

They both heard it, the sound of oars dipped into water. One didn't so much hear the oars as the droplets that came off them when they were lifted from the water. At some point there had to be a space, a space in which the oars were lifted from the water and the boat was propelled forward. They were fully awake now as they heard signs of activity on the swimming platform. Maxwell lurched forward, ready to spring into action, but Cousey put his arm out.

"No!" he whispered. "Wait for him to finish whatever he's doing and pull away."

They waited with pounding hearts, listening as a rope was tied to the platform, a splash as something large went overboard, followed by the sound of bubbles. Then silence.

"He's underwater, bringing something up," Cousey whispered.

For several long minutes they waited. Deep beneath the platform a bar of light undulated in the murk. Suddenly there was a splash and a rush of bubbles, the loudest sounds in the whole sequence. Cousey expected to hear a thump — as of something thrown into the boat — before physics reminded him that even someone as strong as Galvin would have trouble hoisting something as heavy as a body, possibly weighted, into a boat while treading water. Instead, there was the sound of rope thwacking against wood, something being tied, followed by the rope-like sound of something being loosened. Once again they heard the sound of oars in the water, fading into the darkness as the boat pulled away.

"When?" Maxwell asked.

"Let's give him a minute."

They gave him a minute.

"Now!" Cousey stage-whispered.

He turned the key, and the boat roared to life. Pontoon boats weren't fast, but they could still outrun a rowboat. Cousey drove while Maxwell shone the light, his weapon at the ready, and soon the rowboat was in view.

"Hands up, Galvin!" Cousey said to the broad-shouldered man rowing the boat.

Instead of acknowledging them, the man draped his torso over the far side, his right arm moving, and straightened up. Only then did John Galvin turn and face them with a derisive smile, knowing damn well he was dealing with amateurs. Raising his hands like a mobster in a James Cagney movie as a pontoon boat that looked every bit as threatening as a parade float drew near.

Cousey withdrew his smartphone and began snapping photos.

"What's the charge, officers? Is there some law I'm not aware of against being on the lake at night?"

"Hand me the light," Cousey said, shining it inside Galvin's boat to find an oxygen tank, flippers, a mask, a flashlight, a coil of rope, a pair of pliers, and a knife, all of which he photographed.

He handed the light back to Maxwell and circled the boat, a pair of ropes dangling from the other side.

"Shine the light on those ropes," Cousey said to Maxwell.

Maxwell did and Cousey examined them: Their ends were flared.

"These ropes have been cut," Cousey said, taking another picture. "Looks like our friend has jettisoned his cargo. Mark this spot as well as you can."

"I'll never be your friend," Galvin said.

"And I'll cry myself to sleep thinking about it," Cousey said.

Galvin was no longer smiling. He lowered his arms, realizing they had nothing on him.

"I repeat: Officers, what is the charge? You, fat boy, lower that goddamn pea shooter before I shove it up your ass!"

Look of recognition as Maxwell lowered his weapon and flashed a bewildered glance at Cousey.

"John fuckin' Galvin? Are you kiddin' me? What the fuck is goin' on here, Doc?"

"I'll tell you later," Cousey said.

"'John fuckin' Galvin' is right. I'll tell you what the fuck is going on here: You just threatened an unarmed man who was minding his own business with an AK-47, which was illegal in this country last time I checked. Good night, gentlemen. Get whatever sleep you can because you'll be hearing from the police and my lawyer, in that order, very soon."

And with that, he rowed away.

Ten minutes later Cousey was pulling into his dock.

Maxwell was hot. "OK, Doc, would you mind tellin' me what the fuck is goin' on?"

"Do you remember the French girl who disappeared on the lake?"

"I heard somethin' about her."

"I have reason to believe John Galvin killed her and hid her body under the swimming platform. I baited him, and tonight he went back for it. I suspect that was what he was cutting loose. That was why I asked you to mark the spot. Because I'm going to call the police and have them dredge the lake."

"But ain't a body supposed to float?"

"Not if it's weighted down. It was too heavy for him to get into the boat. That's why he tied it to the side."

"How much you gonna pay me tonight?"

"Another hundred. Plus your five-hundred-dollar bonus."

"Thanks, man, but we didn't get him."

"Yes, we did. He just doesn't know it yet."

Maxwell returned to his house across the lake. An hour later, just as he was getting to sleep, the Benson police pounded on his door, confiscated his AK-47, and hauled him off to jail. He had one phone call, and the only person he could think of, the only person who might be up at this hour, was Cousey.

There were a couple of police officers in his living room when Cousey took the call. He had made coffee, and they were asking him questions.

"Excuse me, officers, but I need to take this: Buddy Maxwell's one call." Then, to Maxwell, "Buddy, I'm sorry about this, I really am. Really? Sounds like they're more pissed about the weapon. When is your hearing? Shit, a weekend in jail! I should have figured. Look, just hang tight and I'll bail you out Monday. You don't strike me as a hardened criminal, so you should make bail. I'll get you the hell out of there, I promise. This is my fault, but trust me, something good will come of it. Damn right I'll reimburse you for your weapon. OK, you take care now. Again, I'm really sorry."

He turned back to the officers. "Sorry, but that was kind of important. I got this young guy in trouble, and I feel bad about it."

Even though they were young, they knew about Doc Cousey, and most of those who knew him respected him. He was a local as opposed to a yokel, with a rep for caring about people. The last thing they wanted to do was run him in. Locking up a good old dude like this was bad karma. Still, there were questions that had to be asked. Galvin had lunch with their chief on a regular basis, after all, and they suspected there was more to it than a mutual craving for café-style food. Cousey answered their questions, was as cooperative as he could be at 4:00 AM, and they seemed satisfied.

It was time to ask a question of his own.

"Officers, I was actually planning to call your department first thing in the morning. I can pretty much remember where Galvin dumped the body. I was wondering if you could arrange for someone to dredge the lake."

The fat officer shook his head. "Sorry, Doc, it ain't gonna fly. The lake is private property and, what with all these budget cuts and it technically bein' out of our jurisdiction, we'd need a much stronger case to justify comin' out here. You're doin' a whole lotta theorizin' and, while it sounds good, from a legal stand-point it's all hearsay."

"Would I have better luck with the county?"

"I doubt it. Those guys are even busier'n us."

Cousey gazed at him sadly. "Then he gets away, and the hummingbirds keep killing more people every year. There's a link between the girl and the humming-birds: I'm not sure what it is, but I know there is, and some day I'll prove it. She meant something to them, and they're none too happy about what John Galvin did to her."

The tall, skinny officer laughed. "I've heard that one before. Old Lady Baxter thinks there's sin with a capital "S" on this lake, keeps spoutin' it to the point folks think she's gone bats. C'mon, Doc, you don't really believe that BS, do you?"

"Officer, until someone gives me a better answer, yes, I do."

The fat officer said, "Sorry, Doc, but I'm afraid we can't help you. It would have to go through the chief, and you know how that'll end up. This ain't common knowledge — please, keep it under your hat — but Galvin just donated $100,000 to the police retirement fund, even asked them to keep it outta the papers, real modest about it. John Galvin walks on water as far as the chief is concerned. So, hey, anything you're plannin' will have to be on your own dime. Please, keep it legal, though. We might not be able to keep from arrestin' you next time, OK?"

The officer smiled. Cousey's own smile tight-lipped as he shook their hands and showed them out. It was 5:00 AM, and he was a walking zombie. Those sleepless nights of his residency were the little gift that kept on giving, one he couldn't escape even in retirement. For the next three hours he fell into a bludgeoned sort of unconsciousness, feeling strangely refreshed when he awoke — because an idea had come to him. He got the roster from the scuba club meeting, ran his finger down the list, and found the number he was looking for.

Chapter XII

"Ms. Kath? Good morning; this is Kevin Cousey. We met a few days ago at the scuba club meeting. Sorry to bother you at home, especially at this hour. You were already up? Good! I'm an early riser myself. Hey, I remember hearing you say you're an underwater welder. Question: You said you have your own scuba diving gear, but do you have dredging equipment? Nighttime illumination? The reason I'm asking is I'd like to hire you to retrieve something from the lake, today if possible. I'll pay you well. No, nothing that big, more in the one-hundred-to-two-hundred-pound range: non-toxic; non-metal. You don't have dredging equipment, but you know where you can get some? Yeah, Belleville does kind of chew up your morning; rest assured I'll pay you for your trouble. How about this afternoon? Say… one o'clock? Good! That should still give us some daylight to work with but, just in case, you do have illumination? Good! Don't worry, I'll pay you double for any work we do after dark. Yeah, I'm afraid this is time-sensitive; it's important we find this… item — pardon me for being so mysterious — before anyone else does. Well, good. I, for one, am glad you postponed your trip. OK, sounds good. Please, call me Kevin. OK, Doris, I will. I'll meet you at the gate at one o'clock. Thanks!"

***

Doris Kath defined the term "brick shithouse," looking even more formidable in the daytime. There was no give in the arms that filled the sleeves of her jean jacket like water surging through a fire hose. She looked every bit of 250 pounds, and it would have been unwise for any man short of a wrestler to antagonize her. She had liked Kevin Cousey immediately; in his eyes she didn't see the judgment she had seen in so many others. The charming little grin that played on her mouth seemed incongruous with the rest of her when Cousey drove up the hill to meet her, all the while the glint in her eye said, "Let's get rolling!" Soon she was driving a massive DRW that could have been the symbol of female empowerment hitched to the flatboat she towed through the gate.

Cousey eyed the boat doubtfully. "That's all you need?"

"As long as we ain't talkin' no rusty ol' Edsels, that and a little luck. Dredgin' is like fishin' except you can't make the fish come to you. That's why it pays to know where you're lookin', at least the general area. It's tedious, time-consumin' work. You can be out there for hours, or you can snag somethin' right away. How deep are we talkin'?"

"About fifty feet, I'd say."

"No problem. I brought enough line to go down two hundred."

He led her to the boat launch and parked his truck. "If you would be so kind, take me to my boat and I'll join you. I'll show you the area we'll be dredging along the way."

***

John Galvin had his binocs out, intently watching the proceedings from his deck. Cousey's truck was parked at the foot of the hill, and he suspected that was him venturing out in a strange boat, one that was traversing the area they were in last night. Sure enough, the boat made an arc around the spot before proceeding on to Cousey's dock. It returned to the spot, and he realized it was the Diver Dyke from the meeting, followed by Cousey in his pontoon boat. With disbelief, Galvin realized what was up.

Cousey's sheer doggedness was daunting. Most men would have backed off when deputies paid them a visit at 4:00 AM and hauled their partner away, but not Kevin Cousey. He was right back at it--an old guy who sure as hell wasn't getting much sleep these days — beating him to the draw. Galvin was tired. As much as he needed to retrieve his cargo and be done with this, he needed sleep, needed time to think through his next move. So did Cousey. Except he had already made his.

For the first time since it happened, a chill swept through him. Even now, he thought about running, which he could still do in an orderly way. No arrest warrants had been issued. He could call his office, tell the secretary he was taking a leave of absence, give Ted his blessing to run things in the meantime. He had groomed Ted well, was confident the ship would not founder in his absence. Part of successful leadership was knowing how to surround yourself with the right people, like chess pieces protecting the king. That way, you could carve out some time for yourself whenever the situation demanded.

Funny how I still care about such things. Corporate pride, I suppose. Probably one of the reasons I'm a multimillionaire, he thought.

He could pack two big suitcases with tropical clothes, his camera, his laptop, and an overnight bag, and be in that great little place in the Bahamas by day's end. He could extend his leave of absence for one month, then two, until eventually they'd get used to the idea he wasn't coming back, and Ted would take over, the luckiest break in his life tumbling into his lap. They could always work out the severance package later, Galvin mindful of the fact a big company in Harper wasn't the same as a big company in Philly, adjusting his expectations accordingly. Not that he needed the money.

Running was an option he retained as a last resort, if only because it wasn't in his nature to run. To be driven out as he was back East, with no other choice, regrettably, yes. To run, voluntarily and outright sans legitimate pursuit, hell no. He would allow them the head start they had earned, and if they didn't find what they were looking for today, he would be out there tonight with the dredging equipment he was about to arrange for, and he would keep at it until he found it. Just as running from things was not in his nature, neither was running around half-cocked. He would wait them out, and if they found anything he would be on the phone with Dave, assessing the legal options that were among the many he had. Including a call to the chief, and maybe another generous donation to the retirement fund would make the evidence... disappear. Unless they took it directly to the county; it all depended on who showed up. Complications, always complications, but it was no big deal. Who cared about a French exchange student who had been gone for as many years as she lived?

Beautiful as she was, the sex wasn't even that good, he thought, in the next breath admitting, *as if sex with a thirteen-year-old girl is supposed to be good. Let's get real, John.*

Certainly she wasn't worth all this nonsense, nonsense he was about to put behind him. He smiled in spite of himself, a gambler who knew he couldn't lose.

***

Cousey watched Kath at work, surprised at how primitive the process was. Over and over, she threw a three-pronged object called a "drag" over the side, combed the bottom with it, and hoisted it into the boat whenever she snagged something. More often than not it was kelp or an abandoned car tire. These she handed over to Cousey. When he had a full load he ferried it to the shore, where it accumulated into a considerable pile; indeed, the operation took on the secondary purpose of clearing the lake of debris. Kath was tireless, her expression flat and grim as she bent to her task. She had already had a good lunch, allowing herself only an hourly water break. Her boat was like the hub of a giant clock as she launched her over-sized fishhook from each hour of its face. Only when she finished each circuit did she move her boat, and only then as much as one clock-width. In this way, she saturated a particular area before moving on in an ever-broadening circle. Cousey was convinced she would eventually find Galvin's cargo — but not while it was still daylight.

The sun was plummeting fast.

Galvin saw it and smiled.

Kath saw it and bore down.

Despite her best efforts to outpace nature, the sun went down in a celestial blaze of glory. Galvin smiled and put his binocs away, letting out his breath for the first time all day. The dredging equipment had arrived, and his thoughts turned to dinner — a nice, grilled steak, a salad, and a big old spud, all washed down by a bottle of Norton, a local red he had acquired a taste for, and dredging the lake afterward. He smiled because he remembered exactly where the body was; he, too, had marked the spot, and not only was Kath not there, she was moving farther away from it.

He lit a candle inside a webbed holder and ate on the deck, watching as the lights came on like the jewels in a necklace around the lake. He loved it here and did not want to leave. He certainly did not want to be forced to leave.

A flash of light over his shoulder told him a boat had changed direction. Her boat, working on in the encroaching darkness. His brow furrowed as he pictured Cousey telling her she was going the wrong way.

In reality, Cousey was telling her, "I'll order some pizza. What toppings do you like?"

In Doris Kath was a determination to proceed, no matter what. She was getting caught up in this, as stubborn as a fungal infection. Her instincts about what she was searching for, combined with her will to overcome the male world, to make it pay for her stepfather raping her at age fifteen and ostracizing her for the choices she had made because of it, both played into it. Good thing he was dead because it saved her the hassle of ending his miserable life. In a matter of hours Doris Kath cared as much about the search as Kevin Cousey, in spite of not knowing what she was looking for. Sensing that whatever it was, it was important enough to make her work into the night on her day off.

Galvin's uneasiness returned as he picked up the binoculars he hadn't thought he'd be needing any more that evening. Waiting for them to give up for the day. What they were doing was pure drudgery, she filling his boat with trash, he hauling it away, the pile of debris at the far end of the lake growing into a small mountain. But they worked on: tireless; driven. Then, just after 11:00 PM, an hour before they decided to call it quits for the day, she gave out a shout, one he could hear all the way from his deck. He shuddered as he realized she had found something too big to be pulled out by hand.

"I'm going down for a look," she said, donning her gear, underwater flashlight in hand.

That was when Cousey told her.

"Look for a body bag, probably weighted."

She disappeared beneath the surface. Cousey could see her torch wavering far below. She came up in a roiling of bubbles.

There was a triumphant smile on her face when she lifted her mask. "Bingo!"

It was too heavy to haul up by hand, so she went back down to attach the cable for the drag well. She came back up and shed her gear, set up what resembled a mini-oil derrick on the far side of the boat to compensate for the weight of an object that would cause it to list, and with a clicking of metal teeth winched it up and over the side. The rubber bag was slimy with algae, the zipper that ran along its length rusted shut. Thinking "tampering with evidence" — *I don't want to give this bastard any breathing room* — Cousey resisted the urge to cut it open.

Who to call? he thought. The Benson PD had hardly distinguished itself of late, Cousey harboring a growing suspicion Galvin had them in his pocket. The county sheriff's department was at least an unknown, Sheriff Tate coming off as no-nonsense and thoroughly unimaginative, a redneck's redneck if ever there was one.

He got out his smartphone and called the latter.

"This is Kevin Cousey. We just pulled what I suspect is a body from Lake Tanaka."

Then he called a few friends on the lake, told them to spread the word and meet him at the boat launch. No longer trustful of law enforcement, Cousey was taking no chances when it came to witnesses. As he hung up, he noticed a growing murmur emanating from the trees behind the dam. A sound he was well familiar with, even if its context puzzled him.

The hummingbirds were assembling... and it was neither morning nor April 15th.

***

A pair of deputies had already arrived, an EMT van right behind them by the time Kath and Cousey pulled up to the boat launch. The deputies insisted on carrying what appeared to be a body bag off the boat, intent on removing it from the lake without opening it. Cousey smiled to see the crowd that had gathered. Some of them were Saturday night revelers, and John Galvin was among them, watching from the rear.

"Hey!" Cousey said to the deputies, "that's my property until you can prove otherwise. You have my permission to open the bag, but only if you do it here. Then, if we determine that it is, indeed, a body, we've got a potential murder on our hands, and I can't legally stop you from taking it away."

The doc knew his stuff, and the deputies knew it. Neither would the citizenry, drunk as many of them were and further sensitized to their rights, allow the bag to be removed without their inspection.

Grumbling, the deputies relented. They tried the rusty zipper, managing only to break off the puller. The only alternative was a knife, and they pulled the zipper taut to separate the bag from its contents before cutting into it. The unmistakable reek of organic decomposition emerged, but all they could see was gravel. Donning rubber gloves, they removed it by the handful and piled it outside the bag, and left it there, focused on whatever else might be inside. Cousey's eyes searched the crowd and met Galvin's.

I've got you now, you bastard! his unsaid message went.

Enough gravel had now been removed from the bag to reveal a skeleton small enough to be a child's.

"Folks, I give you the remains of Millie Fremont!" Cousey said to the group.

"Please, Doc, we won't know that for sure until we check the dental records," the deputy in charge said.

Cousey persisted. "If it looks like a duck…," he said, looking triumphantly over at Galvin, who turned away.

The deputies had what they needed, and Cousey had what he needed: a body and witnesses to the fact it had been pulled from the lake. God only knew how far Galvin had his hooks into local law enforcement, but this evidence wouldn't be disappearing without a major scandal.

"Doc, can we agree this is our property now?" the deputy in charge asked. Technically he didn't have to, but the size and temperament of the crowd made it a wise gesture.

"Yes, Deputy, be my guest," Cousey said.

The deputy in charge addressed the crowd. "Folks, this is officially a homicide investigation. We need to take the remains to the county morgue."

Because Cousey had complied, the others did as well. The only things that didn't comply were the hummingbirds. If it were daylight, people would have seen the tornado that had formed over the swimming platform, extending three miles into the sky. They would have seen it and been horrified. But it was dark out, clouds blocking the stars, a moon that was just past full. Instead, they heard them, whirring and buzzing and chirping. A dark sky that had cloaked their movements was teeming with life. The hummingbirds came streaming down onto the two EMTs who carried the body bag to their van. Opening the veins on the backs of their hands, driving their beaks under their fingernails. Doing anything short of killing them to liberate the bag, ultimately causing them to drop it and run for cover inside the van, where some of them proceeded to hammer the windows in a hailstorm of blows. The others stood watching, mesmerized, and the birds left them alone, focusing on the bag. They swarmed it, and although the bag had been relieved of much of its gravel, it still weighed a hundred pounds. Cousey watched in disbelief as hundreds of tiny birds lifted the bag with their beaks, and claws, straining their hearts, their wings, to carry it away. They were both determined and multitudinous, falling away dead only to be replaced by others. Their progress was one of attrition as they lofted the bag, Cousey looking on in dismay as it disappeared across the lake and was swallowed up by the night.

"Well, I'll be damned!" one of the deputies said.

Cousey glanced over at Galvin, who met his gaze.

No corpus, no crime! Better luck next time, bub! his eyes seemed to say.

Galvin went home and slept the satisfying, bone-weary sleep of dead kings.

Cousey paid Doris Kath for her trouble, thanked her for going above and beyond. Then he went home and cried like he hadn't since his family left him.

***

Galvin awoke the next morning feeling reborn in spite of the unusual sight that greeted him on the lake. At first, he thought the water was littered with autumn leaves before remembering the year was well into spring. He walked down the hill for a closer look, Fritz wagging a tongue the size of a slice of ham as he tagged along. Many of the "leaves" had washed ashore, and he was taken aback when he saw they were hummingbirds. Thousands of hummingbirds that had died in the course of evacuating Millie Fremont's body — and, most ironically, freeing him from all responsibility. He would take whatever breaks he could get, smiling at how it had all panned out.

We make our own breaks, he decided, ever the captain of his own ship.

It was over, ending in the most unlikely of ways, but it was over. A moment of decision as he gazed at a lake strewn with birds, enjoying breakfast on the patio: a three-egg, bacon, tomato, pepper jack, and avocado omelet accompanied by four planks of sourdough toast swimming with butter, fresh-squeezed OJ, and plenty of fresh-ground coffee. Much as he had tried to push it away over the years, Millie Fremont's memory came rushing back with the discovery of her body. Her spirit inhabited this place — even the hummingbirds felt it — and somberly he realized it would always be this way.

The spirit of the murdered will not rest until the murder has been avenged, he thought.

But it was an accident, his mind countered, ever with the need to rationalize.

The type of accident that happens when a big, strong man loses his temper and punches a thirteen-year-old girl, he amended the thought.

The birds had seen him. Maybe, possessing their queen, they would forgive him and move on. Maybe they, too, felt closure, inasmuch as anything of nature could embrace a human concept, but this was a chance he was unwilling to take. Not that he was running; he wasn't running but leaving by choice. Millie was part of this house, part of this lake, a significant part of his reason for being here, and she was long gone except for that part of her he had no use for: her spirit. Save for putting him closer to a job he had never needed save to sharpen his professional teeth on, it dawned on him there was no longer any reason to stay.

His thoughts returned to the Bahamas. Suddenly it felt like the right thing to do, albeit with circumstances that were now more appealing. Because he was choosing it voluntarily. No longer running but embarking on a new life. He would leave this place, but not yet. Spring was a nice time of year in Missouri, and even the muggy summers had their perks if you lived on a lake. Maybe a pontoon boat; they were cheap enough. Getting a pontoon boat would be a way of telling the locals none of this had fazed him, that he felt comfortable here, and that he wasn't going anywhere. At least not yet. Not until he was good and ready.

I'll finish my spring here, have my summer. Then, come Labor Day, I'll put the house on the market and wait until I get my price, even if there's a nip in the air by the time I sell it. All the while I can groom Ted to take over the company, give them a heads-up that I'm leaving, and start negotiating my severance package. Then, and only then, when my ducks — not hummingbirds! — are in a row, I'll blow this joint. My way. When I decide.

The notion of a controlled exit pleased him. It was a microcosm of John Galvin himself: calm, deliberate, calculating… and ultimately in control.

***

Kevin Cousey awoke from a bruised sleep, beaten into eleven hours of unconsciousness his body was determined to have, finally overruling a troubled mind that had given in to defeat. Or so it seemed. Despite the initial shock that greeted him upon awakening, that told him what had happened last night was, indeed, real, he, too, awoke feeling refreshed. Even as he drank the day's first coffee, he was coming to grips with losing The Big One, ready to see if anything existed beyond Plans "A" or "B."

The day blazed and he waded into it, bringing a pancake breakfast and a pot of coffee and his metal cowboy mug to the deck. A brisk breeze ruffled the surface of a lake that appeared to be scattered with leaves, though, remembering last night, he soon realized what it was. Bolstered by sleep and the sobering effects of coffee, he assessed what had happened, trying to reassure himself that something good had come of what seemed a day of futility, and damned if he wasn't able to come up with a few things:

First, the look on John Galvin's face when they opened the bag and revealed its contents.

Second, as evidenced by the thousands of tiny bodies floating in the water, hummingbirds were small creatures with limited strength regardless of their numbers. It was hard for them to carry heavy things. Very possibly they didn't get far. Very possibly Millie Fremont's remains were somewhere in the woods. He would explore those woods with Buddy, whom he suspected knew them well.

Third was the gravel, and this put a smile on his face because it was something he could address immediately.

And you'd better, bucko, before someone beats you to it! he thought.

Not that such a thing was likely. The last thing Galvin would be doing this morning was return to the scene of the crime. Besides, it would only be natural for him to feel complacent, the most damning piece of evidence having disappeared. The missing skeleton put him far ahead in the race, and if you were far ahead there was no need to worry about whoever was behind you.

God only knew how it would end, but the beginnings of closure were in sight. He sensed it, smiling when he felt a faith that had long been dormant kicking in.

He finished his coffee, brought his dishes back to the house — no pressing reason to wash them now — and went to his carport. There he got a couple of potato sacks and a shovel, threw them into the back of his pickup — no namby-pamby bed liner to worry about cracking; the nephew of the guy who brought you the slipcover (someone from the city, no doubt) must have invented the damn thing — and headed for the boat launch.

Maybe, just maybe, he thought as he drove.

Five minutes later he was pulling up to several small mounds of gravel the deputies had removed from the bag, about a hundred pounds' worth from the look of it. Galvin struck him as a careful man: cool, methodical, meticulous. But even cool guys weren't cool all the time, couldn't be a hundred percent objective when they had just killed someone, especially if they weren't professional killers and there were feelings involved. Killing tended to upset people, and people who were upset made mistakes. They left evidence behind, and in these days of forensics it didn't take much. While Cousey didn't kid himself about knowing what to do with any DNA-containing samples he might find, the possibility of finding something in the gravel that might be useful as evidence burned in his thoughts. Alas, these thoughts were tempered by the notion the gravel had been removed from the top of the bag, evidence as small as he was looking for tending to sift to the bottom.

But the bag had been turned, shifted, rolled. There existed the possibility he might find something.

The gravel stank nearly as much as the body, and he resolved not to handle it until he got home and put on some rubber gloves. He shoveled half of it into one bag, half of it into the other, and loaded them into the truck. He got all but the smallest fragments; he was sure of it. Then a thought struck him as he was pulling away.

If something can settle in the bag, something can settle on the ground while I'm shoveling gravel.

He went back to the boat launch and knelt down, running his hands through the grass in spite of the residue, looking for anything that didn't belong. His heart pounded when he saw a round object coated with dirt or decomposition.

A ring! he thought, only to flip it over and see it was a bottle cap.

The occasional cigarette butt teased him, a blackened penny. He found himself wishing for the obvious, the impossible: a hummingbird pendant on a chain so thin it could have been overlooked; a hummingbird pierced earring, its French wire gleaming in the sun like the question mark that precedes the answer that solves the case; unmistakable tie-ins to a murder.

A thought occurred to him as he set his mind to the unfamiliar task of thinking like a criminal: *When you kill someone, assuming you are still somewhat rational, the first thing you do is remove all forms of ID from the victim's body, starting with a purse or wallet, a cell phone, and ending with valuables or something personal, like a monogrammed hankie. That seems pretty obvious. But when you kill someone, do you undress her, especially if she is a child and you're already self-conscious? No, you leave her clothes on because you already feel guilty.*

Cousey searched for clothing-related items. Still nothing. He combed the ground thoroughly, painstakingly. There was nothing there.

Still the bags to go through, he thought, squatting beside the lake to wash the stink off his hands before committing them to his steering wheel.

He brought the bags to his carport, pulled a wheelbarrow up to his workbench, moved various tools and a couple of projects he was working on out of the way, dumped the contents of the first bag onto the bench using a trowel to spread its contents to a uniform depth, donned some rubber gloves, and methodically sifted through it, creating a growing pile of gravel in the wheelbarrow. Nothing by the time he had gone through it.

Shit! Still the other bag, he thought.

He wasn't hungry; the pancakes were staying with him, as pancakes tended to. He dumped the second bag onto the workbench and, as he was spreading out its contents, he saw something: an ivory-colored button with a small shred of fabric — wool? — clinging to it. He smiled as he saw the word "CAISSON," a brand he wasn't familiar with, curving around the button.

The discovery caused him to slow his pace. Because he knew a button, even a button with a French-sounding name, wasn't enough. It would take too much to fortify such evidence, like a hi-def picture of her wearing the sweater, sharp enough to see the writing on the buttons, which was ludicrous. He needed more, and he damn well knew it.

The wheelbarrow was getting full, the workbench almost bare when he saw an object he nearly mistook for a piece of gravel, except it was smoother, shinier. He smiled as he picked it up: a tooth! A front tooth!

Finally, something conclusive! he thought. *Something to put this bastard away forever!*

Already his mind was racing ahead. Monday promised to be a busy day. First, he would spring Buddy. Second, with Buddy as his witness, he would deliver the tooth to the forensic lab that adjoined the morgue, determined to think county instead of local. Third, if Buddy was game — with lunch to elicit his cooperation, beer to reward it — he would comb the woods for Millie Fremont's remains.

If she's still in the area, it shouldn't be hard, he thought. *Just follow the trail of dead hummingbirds.*

Chapter XIII

Monday, after a fast-food lunch of Buddy's choice, Kevin Cousey and Buddy Maxwell were walking along the top of the dam to the woods. Maxwell was an experienced hunter, well able to follow a trail of hummingbirds. Cousey winced when he stepped on the occasional hummingbird body: like stepping on a marshmallow with spaghetti noodle bones. More often, their feet plunged into mud, forcing them to the edges of a trail still wet from the spring thaw. The leaves shimmered with movement, sunlight dappling the forest floor. Winter was gone, but its presence lingered, snow-become-meltwater forming puddles that smelled like an amalgam of caves and peat moss and the rawness of new growth on the trail.

After its smell, the forest was all about sounds. The birds were a constant, and there were all kinds of them, making up for the lost time of a winter that had persisted almost until May with a jubilant riot of socializing. Their cries were joined by the distant yapping of dogs, the occasional truck rumbling past on a distant highway, a lonely jet scratching against the sky. The wind generated its own array of sounds, its pitch and nature changing depending on what it was passing through. It whispered through the pines like Indian breath. It turned the oak leaves into fibrous rattles that would morph into scratchy husks as the year drew to a close. It whistled and hissed through the clear-cuts that were sprinkled lesion-like through the forest.

As they walked, Cousey became aware of a sound that put him on his guard, the sound of a great conflagration, and from a distance it sounded like a cacophony of buzzing insects. As they neared it, the buzzing was interspersed with clicking, thumping, and chirping. The forest canopy had obscured the sky for most of this walk, and as they entered a clear-cut, it opened up at last, teeming with hummingbirds.

Maxwell's first instinct was to run. Cousey grabbed him.

"Every year, I watch the hummingbirds come in. Every year they leave me alone. Since you're with me, you're probably safe. You're also fairly new to the lake; that seems to make a difference. Just don't touch anything. I'm not even going to chance that."

"What's my bein' new to the lake got to do with anything?"

"I'll tell you on the way back," Cousey said. "Right now we need to concentrate."

The forest on the far side of the clear-cut was dark and murky, their eyes adjusting to the light as they passed through it. Then, as they were crunching along, they saw it: swirling with hummingbirds, a bier upon which they suspected lay the earthly remains of Millie Fremont. Elevated on a waist-high ahu that made Cousey shudder as to the energy it took to move stones that must have weighed ten pounds, the skeleton lay in an oblong wreath of twigs, edged in moss wherever it contacted the bones. The ground was carpeted with hummingbird bodies in a grim testament to the labor of love it had been to bring her here. There was a commotion high above, and they looked up to see a giant nest in the crown of the largest tree, shimmering in the light that filtered through it.

Millie's final resting place, Cousey couldn't help but think.

The body bag lay behind a tree, and as he reached to have a look inside, he was immediately converged upon by hummingbirds. They did not attack, but he had the distinct impression they would have had he proceeded.

"It's OK, babes," he said, backing away.

Moving to the bier where Maxwell stood, gawking in disbelief.

"Buddy, a word to the wise: Don't touch anything."

What he saw brought a smile to Cousey's face: The skull was missing its two upper front teeth. He withdrew his smartphone and leaned in, more hummingbirds pressing around him the closer he got. The air was charged, their wings roaring. Needing his flash for these dark woods, he chanced a picture of the skull, hoping it wouldn't upset them. The hummingbirds wavered like a disruption in a colored stream of air, some of them inches from his eyes, but they did not attack, evidently satisfied he wasn't a threat. He snapped a few more pictures, then stood back and snapped one of the bier, the body bag, the nest they were assembling high up in the canopy of the tree.

"Let's get out of here," he said to Maxwell. "I think I have what I need."

***

Earlier, they had delivered the button and the tooth to the forensic lab, glad to have the evidence beyond local jurisdiction. Now he went home and burned the photos onto a disc, making a copy for himself, and delivered it to the same authorities, cautioning the man in charge not to let anyone from the sheriff's department investigate the site without calling him first.

"Do that, and someone may get killed. I'm sure you heard about how the hummingbirds wrested the evidence away from the EMTs. I'm normally on friendly terms with them, but even I was uneasy in those woods. It's become a shrine, I'm afraid. Have them call me when they're coming out, and I'll be happy to join them. I wouldn't send any more than a couple of men. While they should definitely bring a camera, they must not remove any physical evidence."

The man smiled. "OK, Doc, thanks for the warning. I think we can live with that."

Cousey had his doubts, well versed as he was in man's tendency to meddle. Still, with the tooth and now the photos, he felt he already had enough to bust Galvin.

Someone else evidently agreed.

Miffed that Cousey had bypassed the Benson PD, with it the clear implication he didn't trust them, Chief Larry MacEnerny made a phone call — from a roadside phone booth that made it harder to trace.

"John, this is Larry. We've got us a problem. You've got a problem because Cousey found evidence linking you to the Fremont girl, namely a tooth he found in the gravel from the body bag that matches her dental records. He also located and photographed her skeleton; it was missing a couple of teeth, and one of them corresponds to the tooth he found."

Internally Galvin was beside himself. *Goddamn those boneheaded deputies! Goddamn them for not keeping the gravel as evidence, as any department with any fricking brains would have!*

Externally he maintained his poker-faced facade. "Larry, what do you suggest?" he asked blandly.

MacEnerny sighed audibly. "John, you need to get out of Dodge ASAP — because here's where my problem comes in: County is telling me I need to send a couple of officers to your house first thing tomorrow morning and bring you in. Normally they'd be sending their own, but there's a deputy training exercise in Jeff City tomorrow, and they can't spare the manpower. I don't send my officers and my ass is in the grinder — in an election year, no less. I don't have a choice, pardner."

"So you're giving me a heads-up."

"Absolutely, as your friend. Don't worry, I'm not obliged to block your avenues of egress until 6:00 AM tomorrow. John, I know what a shocker this must be, but it's the best I can do under the circumstances. Get the hell outta here, and invite me for some pina coladas on that island hideaway of yours some day."

As if that is ever going to happen, Galvin thought.

Shock and anger and gratitude all roiled within Galvin, like emotions playing tag. Gratitude finally won out as the reality of what he was up against dawned on him.

"You've got it, Larry. I'll email your private mailbox when I get settled. In the meantime, thanks for the heads-up. Guilty or no, I don't relish the thought of being made a public spectacle of."

"John, I must admit I could never picture you in handcuffs. A Rolex watch, maybe, but never handcuffs."

Galvin forced a chuckle. "Thanks, buddy. Hey, do me a favor and take care of Fritz. I don't know what kind of police dog he'd make, but he's one hell of a watchdog."

"You got it, John."

"Another thing," Galvin said. "I'll leave my Hummer in long-term parking at the airport. There's a magnetic key holder under the rear bumper. I'll put my ignition key in it and my house key and the parking receipt under the driver-side floor mat. The title is in the glove box. I don't know what you'll want to do with it, but I've signed it over to you and it's all yours. Call it a little going-away present."

"Thanks, pardner."

"Thanks again for the heads-up, Larry. See you on the island."

And with that, John Galvin cut his last connection with Benson, Missouri.

"Fuck!" he said when the call was over.

Goddamn that Cousey! I ought to put a bullet in the son of a bitch on my way out! he thought.

It wasn't so much about being caught as being in a situation that was beyond his control. The methodical nature of his plans had suddenly been supplanted by the necessity of flight, one that hinged on the kindness of a friend at the risk of his job. He would lose money on the house, no doubt. He would lose more money hoteling it in the Bahamas until he got settled. It was all so rushed, and rush inevitably entailed waste. But the alternative was prison, he reminded himself, where they were none too charitable when it came to child predators.

He winced at the notion of John Galvin, Child Predator.

Still, part of him was secretly pleased he had the presence of mind to tend to a couple of details — the dog and the vehicle — which a lesser man would have overlooked. It was all about being in control, and control, he realized, was a double-edged sword.

No, there was nothing to do now but cut his losses and run, seize whatever chance of freedom he had, and there were certainly far worse places to be free than the Bahamas. He smiled at the thought of an island beauty with dark hair and eyes, dancing with sinuous, golden limbs in the light of Tiki torches on a beach framed by palms. The younger, the better.

I can write a book, How to Tackle the Corporate World, *and it would sell,* he thought, though filling two large suitcases was what dominated his thoughts at present

I can always buy more stuff when I get there, he thought.

Freezing his accounts would not be an issue, as he'd long been putting his money in offshore bank accounts.

The process of leaving was underway, Galvin flipping on the stereo to make his last moments in a house that suddenly seemed occupied by a single, huge ghost more pleasant. The music became his world, blotting out the outside world as surely as the Hummer's tinted windows — until he chose to see it. Isolation with the option of company was a way of life he preferred, a right he had cultivated to separate himself from the vexing presence of lesser men. This evening it only served to separate him from the growing ruckus outside, one that began soon after he turned on the stereo. It began as a rustling in the trees beyond the dam, wheeled around the swimming platform, and waited. Waited for the agitated barking that signified an invasion of territory, the squeak of a storm door opening, and the thump of a front door closing.

***

His bags were packed, the TSA locks in place, their contents as meticulously folded and organized as only an ex-sailor with a touch of OCD could fold and organize them. He turned off the lights as if painting his way out of the house he'd had such high hopes for — until those hopes were dashed by one Millie Fremont. Yet why should he be surprised to be undermined by his less than honorable intentions toward a thirteen-year-old girl? Just before he turned off the nice stereo he hated to leave behind. *A housewarming present for Larry,* he assuaged himself with the thought. The last light in the living room. He gazed longingly at the fireplace with the big, curved window behind it, scene of so many good times with Millie. At least for him. A feeling of somberness was creeping into him, and he fought the tear that insinuated its presence in his eye.

Millie, I am so sorry it ended this way. Why did you have to fight me? Why couldn't we just go on living happily together here, away from a society that doesn't realize true

love cannot be caged, true love has no boundaries? Why couldn't you grow into the lover I always dreamed of? Why did you have to ruin everything? Why did you have to put me, the man who was so good to you, in such a desperate position? Why did you turn out to be such an ungrateful little bitch?

Leave it to John Galvin to allow regret to morph into self-righteous anger.

No sooner had he turned off the stereo than he heard the low, warning growl that told him something was amiss in Fritz's world.

Accompanied by a strange buzzing sound.

While never intended to be, Fritz became the target when he got between them and John Galvin when he thumped open the storm door carrying his bags — and came face to face with vengeance. With the selflessness of a Secret Service agent, Fritz put himself between his master and the hummingbirds, three of them immediately going to work on him. One bird poked him on either flank while two others flanked his head. When he spun to address the attacker, one of them plunged its beak into his right eye. When he spun the other way, the other bird took out his left eye, reducing the dog to a howling, pathetic mess.

Galvin threw down his bags and tried to reenter the house, his hand taking a ferocious pecking as he fumbled with the lock, his size preventing the storm door from closing as he found himself wedged between the two doors. Finally, the front door opened and Galvin tumbled inside, a couple hundred hummingbirds streaming in behind him before he could get up and close it. Unnerved by Fritz's yelping, he opened the curtains to see the dog spinning in circles. At least they were leaving him alone now.

His hand reached for the light switch, horror rippling through him when he saw what he was up against. They converged on him, and he shuddered when he saw in their fierce, dark eyes an amped-up version of Millie's eyes in their last fateful meeting. Briefly, he debated on whether to turn on the light, deciding his only chance was to be able to see his attackers. At the cost of them opening a vein on the back of his hand, he found his shades: the wraparound kind, well-made, with shock-resistant lenses.

You're not getting my eyes, you sons of bitches! he thought, regaining control.

Searching for a suitable weapon.

A fireplace shovel: that'll work, he thought.

Ping! Ping! He made contact with one tiny body after another. Indeed, there were so many of them it was hard to miss them.

Birdie baseball, anyone? he thought with a wicked smile, embracing the challenge as he had all others.

But every swing came at a price. Even as he dispatched birds, others targeted the veins in his arms that rose like clinging vines from his exertions. Soon he was leaking from half a dozen places, the flow increasing as the battle raged on. Most maddeningly, they were going after his genitals, a dozen at a time, pecking through his smooth, silk pants.

"Ugh!" he cried as a beak found a testicle, staining his groin red.

Ping! Ping! He was making progress, but so were they in what had become a war of attrition.

"Nyah!" he cried as a hummingbird drove its beak into an ear canal and drew blood.

Even as he cried out, another bird flew kamikaze-style into his mouth, lodging itself in his throat. He stumbled to the kitchen, leaned over the back of a chair, and ejected the intruder Heimlich style. Even as he was doing this, another bird opened up a vein on the back of his other hand.

Briefly, he scanned the room, figuring he was halfway there.

Gotta keep on the offensive! he thought.

The flipside of their diminishing numbers was the fact it was making them harder to hit, prolonging a battle that had become time-sensitive, a hockey game as opposed to a baseball game. The longer the battle went on, the more blood he lost, and there were no time-outs to staunch the flow. Badly outnumbered by a smaller, more mobile foe, he couldn't protect all of himself all of the time. He couldn't keep fighting with one hand moving between his neck and groin, trying to protect the two blood-rich areas the hummingbirds were focusing on, redoubling their efforts whenever Galvin dispatched them. This, all parties seemed to realize, was how it would end, one way or the other. A beak punctured his carotid artery and was promptly crushed, only to be replaced by another that laid it open. Galvin's world spun as the blood spurted out of him in earnest. The single living room light filled his perception with otherworldly brilliance... not of a heavenly deliverance but of the flaming lake filled with distant cries that awaited him. The pecking continued, ever farther away in his waning consciousness. He did not hear or even feel his body as it crashed to the floor like a tree coming down. Soon he was lying in a pool of blood with his shades still on, the world's coolest dead guy.

***

After first putting Fritz out of his misery ("Sorry, folks, but we need to put this animal down; please don't look if you're squeamish"), the arriving officers were taken aback by the sight that awaited them inside: Galvin's body crosshatched with red, his pants soaked with blood. It was strange to see him humbled so, like the statue of a dictator toppled in a revolution.

Upon closer inspection, it was hard to determine the presence of male genitalia in the bloody maw between his legs. It was as if someone had exploded a grenade there.

As with everything they undertook, the hummingbirds had played their collective hand to the last reserves of their energy. Not one bird that had entered the house remained alive.

"Looks like our man was fixin' to go on a little trip," one officer said.

"Looks like the birds canceled his flight," the other one said.

***

Kevin Cousey found himself torn between the horror of anyone dying in such a way and the satisfaction of someone finally getting his just desserts. The satisfaction of the lake community, in general, was more unqualified, the scourge of their collective guilt removed, with it the curse Galvin had put on the lake — or so they thought. Tempered though it was, Cousey's satisfaction was limited to the removal of a single, egregious party... but it was only one. Some 792 people were living on the lake at the time of Millie Fremont's death. Of these, only sixty-six had been killed by hummingbirds, another twenty or so dying of natural causes. That left over seven hundred people still to be reckoned with. Cousey remained unconvinced that the hummingbirds' yearly ritual wouldn't continue.

Most of the time the thought of it didn't bother him. As far as he was concerned, anyone who turned a blind eye to pedophilia wasn't fit to live. He could think of few character flaws as glaring. What did bother him, though, were the innocents, children too young to know what was going on at the time. The two families that had perished in the double boat attack showed him there was something cold and indiscriminate about their attackers, as cold and indiscriminate as nature itself. While he had earned their respect, there was an agitation about them, held in check by a single thread. There was no doubt in his mind they would have attacked him had he touched Millie's remains, an act they no doubt would have perceived as a sacrilege to her shrine: He had no doubt that was what they were building in the crown of that tree deep in the woods, and God help anyone who defiled it. He hoped they would finish soon, move what was left of her body to its treetop nest before some fool hunter or motocross rider happened upon her bier and paid the price for his indiscretion.

It was with some ambivalence that Cousey sat by his stump, sipping good whiskey and plenty of it as he watched the sun set over the lake. This evening the sky was a flaming riot of color, looking vengeful in its holiness. This evening the sky was nature telling mankind, "Fuck with me at your peril!"

A certain measure of satisfaction, but hardly relief — because instinctively Cousey knew the debt had yet to be paid in full. First, though, there was a decision to be made, albeit a comparatively mundane one: The scuba club's next meeting was fast approaching. Should it be the last one?

***

"Lady," he said before an amphitheater of chairs in the gravel parking lot of the Rod & Gun Club, nodding to a smiling Doris Kath, "and gentlemen," he said, nodding to the fifty men who had assembled, "I have a confession to make: I began this group as a ploy to draw out John Galvin, whose exploits many of us are well familiar with. I suspected Millie Fremont's body was buried under the swimming platform here at the lake. The ploy worked. I was right."

Kath rose to her feet. "Dr. Cousey hired me to dredge the lake. I was proud to help him catch the son of a bitch."

Buddy Maxwell stood up. "So am I. I was with the doc the night we busted Galvin, the night he done cut the body loose and dropped it back into the lake."

Cousey smiled. "Thank you, Doris and Buddy, for coming forward. I intended to acknowledge both of you publicly for your invaluable assistance, but was concerned I might embarrass you. You've resolved the issue for me. Now, another confession: Since it was never my intention to actively partake in scuba diving, merely to catch Galvin, I have yet to invest in any gear."

A smattering of grumbling from the crowd.

"Hmm… from the sound of it, some of you have made that commitment. Please, let us have a show of hands for anyone who has purchased scuba diving equipment since our last meeting."

He scanned the crowd, moving his mouth as he counted. "OK, I'm counting eight, and that's in addition to those of you who already have equipment. I think you've already answered my next question: My original intention for starting this group notwithstanding, should it continue? I can assure you, now and with all sincerity, that this baby will not die because of its father's negligence. I, as the group's first and somewhat chastened president, will commit to buying some gear and learning how to use it if we decide to continue."

Several cheered. Cousey smiled and bowed.

"I'll take that as a 'yes.' While I am told the lake isn't a good place for scuba diving, it is nonetheless a good project, as evidenced by the amount of junk Doris retrieved from the lake while dredging for Millie's body. I can see the group continuing with this most useful function. I suspect I could finagle a budget from the Board for this purpose. Perhaps divert some of the lake's road maintenance monies, seeing as how we had a light winter snow-wise. I'll let you know how it went at our next meeting. When we run out of options here or just get tired of picking up trash, I'm sure there are other waterways in the area to explore and clean up. Why, this could become Operation Cleanstream — the country's largest annual river cleanup, of the Meramec River — all year 'round. In the meantime, assuming those of you who have come this evening intend to be regulars, I would like to take this opportunity to elect officers… for vice-president (to assist me and in case I am indisposed), treasurer (to collect dues and open a bank account in the club's name), and secretary: to record the minutes and keep track of attendance. These positions would all be for a year, including mine as president. Which leads me to my final question before we vote for our officers: What would be a reasonable amount for our annual dues?"

"Fifty bucks," someone said.

"Make it a hundred," someone else said.

"No, fifty is better. A hundred bucks is even more than Lions Club, and I'm already paying dues to two other clubs," still someone else said.

"How many people like fifty bucks?" Cousey asked. "Let's have a show of hands. OK, it looks like a majority. Fifty bucks it is. You can pay it next time when our first treasurer has been installed."

"What will the dues be used for?" someone asked.

Cousey smiled. "Good question. I must admit it's something I haven't given much thought, probably because I wasn't even sure the group would continue. I guess it just strikes me as natural that a group should collect dues. Let me ask you: What do you think we should use the dues for?"

"Guest speakers," someone said.

"Parties and refreshments," someone else said.

"Entrance fees to other diving places," still someone else said.

Cousey smiled. "Good suggestions, one and all. Mind you, we won't be spending them on anything without a majority vote. As other suggestions arise, rest assured we'll vote on them."

"Fair enough," the guy who asked about dues said.

"Keep in mind we're already taking donations for refreshments," Cousey said. "Maybe we could do a potluck next time. How many of you want to have a potluck dinner next time? Most of you? Good, let's do one. I see no problem with bringing beer and wine; the Rod & Gun Club certainly does. Now, if there are no more issues, would anyone like to nominate our first vice-president?"

***

Cousey's fears about the lake were shared by a party whose philosophies, it could safely be said, were well removed from his on the ideological spectrum.

"The lake is a den of sin," Thelma Baxter told anyone who would listen, all the better if it were a captive audience.

Usually, this meant the members of Women Aflame, a group comprised of the spouses of church elders who met monthly for tea and spiritual support. Being the pastor's wife made Baxter the group's permanent head, its members her favorite kind of audience: one that was forced to listen, dared not shake its head at anything she said.

"Mark my words: John Galvin was just the tip of the iceberg. He was the devil, but the devil never works alone. He isn't powerful enough to vie with The Almighty by himself, you see. He needs help, and there's plenty of it on the lake."

One of the members put down her cup. "What do you suggest, Sister Thelma?"

"I'm glad you asked, Sister Jane. Eustace and I were thinkin' the other night, and do you know what he said? He said, 'I think it's high time we brought some Old Time Religion to Lake Tanaka. I envision an all-night tent revival, right on the lake. We'll start at midnight — when April 14th becomes April 15th — and we'll stand and we'll join hands. We'll pray and we'll sing and we'll speak in tongues... whatever The Spirit moves us to do. We'll see in the new day. We'll pray until seven o'clock when the birds are comin' in, and then we'll pray some more. We'll pray until those birds are fillin' the sky, and we'll sing and we'll pray and we'll speak in tongues until we drive every last one of 'em away by the power of almighty God!'"

"Amen!" somebody said.

"Praise Jesus!" somebody else said.

The women's enthusiasm seemed earnest enough. A few of them were saying "Amen!" and "Praise Jesus!" even while Baxter was talking, turning her words into the impromptu sermon it was meant to be.

Too bad women can't be pastors, Thelma thought.

She surveyed the smiling faces all around her, pleased at the validation she saw in them.

"It sounds like a 'go,' then. All we need is permission from the lake. A couple of our parishioners are on their Board. I don't think it'll be a problem."

"Will we take up a collection, Sister Thelma?" a member asked.

"Of course we will, Sister Alice. Why, we're performin' an invaluable service: doin' the Lord's work in a den of iniquity, a cesspool of sin."

Chapter XIV

John Galvin's death was the talk of Benson, making him even bigger in death than he was in life. The mystery surrounding him only deepened when his death wishes became known: cremation rather than burial, his ashes to be spread over a certain address in the Philly suburb of Ardmore, where he once lived. Some suspected it was to make his ex-wife sneeze, even though she was now living with their daughter on the Oregon Coast. No memorial service, with flower money donated instead to Galvin's pet cause: the Benson PD Retirement Fund. Like a suicide without a note, it all created a sense of unfinished business in the minds of the locals.

Country folk tended toward concreteness when it came to death — like the need to see the dead person in his coffin, even if he looked like a mannequin. They needed the ceremony, a eulogy, even if it was all fluffed up with pretense, black clothing and a caravan of vehicles with their lights on, police stopping traffic to let it pass if the person were important enough — as John Galvin surely would have been. If the day was cold or rainy, so much the better. As long as there was a rectangular hole in the ground with dirt piled around it, a couple of scruffy-looking guys leaning on their shovels, waiting for the ceremony to end so they could do their work and compare this funeral to the last one over a beer or three. A tombstone with flowers, both fake and real, banked up against it: a physical reference point for communing with the dead. Country folk needed closure, and John Galvin's death denied them that.

There was no closure, not with Galvin's death or Millie Fremont's death, and people were beginning to wonder if there ever would be. Too many deaths had passed between hers and his, with plenty of sendoffs in between. Lake residents were getting a clearer, ever more dreadful sense of what it was all about, with it an increased suspicion of the role they played. As long as guilt managed to claw its way through the calm facade of rationalization, there would be no closure. Perhaps most troubling of all, the hummingbirds had not waited until April 15th. Word was they were congregating down in the woods near the lake. While before their attacks could be anticipated, with a full year of calm between them, the tentative order that had been erected in the minds of lake residents was shredding. A feeling of closure about Galvin's death remained elusive, an undercurrent of anxiety humming just beneath the surface. A sense of anticipation for the sleeper to awaken and this nightmare to end — if it ever would.

While far different than Kevin Cousey's, Larry MacEnerny, too, had mixed feelings about Galvin's death. On the one hand, he had to admit the passing of a creep, one whose guilt he never doubted, while on the other, he had to acknowledge the benefits of their association, benefits he was reaping even now.

"He wanted us to have it," he said of Galvin's black Hummer, a vehicle MacEnerny offered for departmental use during the day but drove home every night, further separating himself from and justifying its "official" use by adding a two-way radio and an onboard computer.

There was no one to will Galvin's house to, his daughter and ex-wife already well provided for and uninterested in living in the place of his disrepute or even vying for his property, so the Benson PD assumed its upkeep and property taxes — presenting it as a civic gesture, no less, and MacEnerny moved in. He justified his presence with a stronger commitment to the lake on behalf of the police (if only symbolically, as it was beyond the city limits and officially in the county's jurisdiction), including the departmental barbecues he hosted every month and the occasional retreat. He even offered it as a crash pad to those who over-imbibed at the monthly meetings of the Benson PD Retirement Fund at the Rod & Gun Club. Alas, there was no chance of getting a yacht that would have been too much for the lake, anyway, or a piece of an estate valued at fifty-five million dollars, from which Galvin's daughter and ex-wife continued to receive a monthly stipend.

MacEnerny's days at the house were pleasant enough, especially weekends when he made the rounds in his boat like a king surveying his kingdom. He was a major celebrity here, managing with the PR of someone accustomed to running for office to eclipse the unassuming Kevin Cousey as The Man Who Busted John Galvin. No one seemed to remember their many lunches together, the large sums of money Galvin had donated to the retirement fund. No one seemed to notice the fact he was living in The Bad Guy's house and driving The Bad Guy's vehicle. If Fritz were still alive, he would even be taking care of The Bad Guy's dog. To the victor went the spoils, and most on the lake bought into the notion they rightfully belonged to MacEnerny.

There were, in fact, only four people who didn't: Kevin Cousey, Paul Mahr, Buddy Maxwell (both of whom Cousey kept in touch with), and MacEnerny himself. Even as he returned home at the end of the day for his ritual beers on the deck, MacEnerny could feel a pall settling over the sunlight of early evening, undiminished by more alcohol and the invigorating smells of the hearty, simple things he liked to grill. Every day was a cookout, a celebration, though more and more it felt like a marketing ploy that was getting ever harder to sell.

Everywhere he looked, he saw Millie Fremont: looking girlishly slender in a bikini made for an adult as she dived from the swimming platform; screaming like the girl she was on a pair of water skis, water pluming from her heels like the wings of Mercury; gazing at him through the intent brown eyes of the hummingbirds that frequented the feeder on his porch. Everyone at the lake fed them now — as a peace offering? A bribe? And although he couldn't care less about the little suckers, the feeder was his concession to conformity. Feeding the hummingbirds had become a superstition, no less than animism in a Western context.

What with his proximity to the place where she had lived and died, Millie Fremont was rooted in his consciousness, a soundtrack played on an endless loop. Lessened by the distraction of work blunted by beer, but returning to full strength when the beer had worn off and he was alone with his thoughts, free to soar in the night's yawning chasm. Seemingly averse to being pushed away entirely.

He was not sleeping well, did not look well, and did not feel well. He was drinking too much. He was eating too much greasy barbecued food. And he was haunted by the spirit of Millie Fremont that continued to inhabit his house.

He was circling the swimming platform on a fine Saturday morning, having once again compensated for a poor night's sleep with a nice breakfast and lots of coffee, when a hummingbird suddenly darted before his eyes, hovering there. In it, he saw Millie's face, not in life but in death, a leering skull with two front teeth missing; he had seen the pictures. Its tongue flicked out, and to him it was a snake, its fangs headed for his eyes. He felt a crushing pain in his chest, a bolt of lightning surge down his left arm. He lurched forward, inadvertently turning the wheel and sending the boat crashing into the swimming platform.

One of the two boats in the vicinity responded, a burly man tying up to his and engaging in a dubious exercise called CPR.

While the hummingbirds weren't blamed for this death, there was a collective sense as to what had happened. Something about bad karma. Galvin's (and now MacEnerny's) house was put up for sale, but no one would buy the nicest house on the lake.

***

It is time, Kevin Cousey thought, *time to use whatever influence I might have.*

He invited Paul Mahr and Buddy Maxwell over for breakfast, filled their bellies with food and their minds with his intentions, and they were OK with it. Anything seemed worth a try. After breakfast and led by Maxwell, they headed into the woods.

Cousey's mouth hung open when they arrived at Millie Fremont's shrine. The bier was gone, every sign of it, including all the rocks. Every sign of it but the bodies of hummingbirds decomposing on the forest floor. The body bag was gone. The nest hovered high in the tree like an alien spacecraft, filling half the crown. Were it not built built at the junction of the tree's two sturdiest branches, its stability would have been a matter of concern for Cousey. So many tiny, crumpled bodies littered the base of the tree as to make it appear like the canopy in negative. He had a strange urge to see what was up there, to pay homage at the shrine. Even though it wasn't safe to do so, it saddened him to think he would never see it, that it would take someone with a tree topper's strength and agility to make such a climb.

Let it live in your imagination, Cousey resigned himself to the thought, imagining a grandiose version of what he'd seen in the bier.

All around them the hummingbirds, diving and whirring and chirping, concentrated in the treetops as if guarding the shrine. Unconcerned by the presence of the three men gazing up at them from far below.

"Gentlemen, now is as good a time as any," Cousey said. "Don't let the statue in my backyard fool you. Though I like to think I'm a spiritual kind of guy, I'm hardly the praying kind. Believe me, this is destined to be more of a plea than a prayer. If you feel like chiming in, please do, even if it is a prayer. I have nothing against prayers, even if I don't pray them myself.

"Millie Fremont," he began, lifting his face to the nest, "I appeal to your spirit, to whatever aura remains of you here, to exert whatever influence you might have on these birds. Some say you are the reincarnation of St. Milburg, and I have no cause to doubt this. You were a special girl and, had you been given the opportunity, I have no doubt you would have blossomed into a very special woman. Know that in my way I loved you, and I grieve your loss. I did what I thought I could at the time to stop what was happening, but, in hindsight, I wish I had done more.

"I am human, just as you were human, and all humans make mistakes. I am sure there are few on the lake who do not feel your death, people who, like me, regret the events leading up to it and wish they had done more. Unfortunately, the birds I believe you control, even more powerfully in death than you did in life, have killed many people, Millie, including the perpetrator of these horrible crimes against you... crimes made more horrible by their being played out over a period of months for all to see or, more appropriately, to pretend not to see. And hear. Fear kept us away, Millie. Fear of Galvin and his physical presence. Fear of enough money to hire predatory lawyers and keep them busy for a long time bleeding people out. Fear of a big, black dog that seemed ready to tear someone's leg off. Doing the right thing is never easy, as our collective lack of involvement shows, but we were wrong, horribly wrong not to do more. Still, does our punishment fit the crime? Gradual but inevitable death, year after year until everyone who lived on the lake during your time is dead? That's nearly eight hundred people, Millie! Eight hundred lives in exchange for one, and your birds have already taken sixty-six of them.

"Children are dying. Last year the birds killed several of them, and that is why I am imploring you to stop them. I know you can stop them, Millie. I also know you were grievously injured, not just by Galvin but I suspect by others who saw your beauty as a target. It seems people are intent on destroying the beautiful things of this world. You were a flower of rare beauty, handled so often and so roughly that it withered and died. Please, Millie, forgive our foolishness. Put an end to your vengeance, if only for the sake of children whose only crime was to have parents who knew what was happening and did nothing to stop it."

Cousey lowered his head, wincing at the crick in his neck, and looked at the others.

"Anyone else?"

Maxwell returned his look, raising his eyebrows. "I'll give 'er a go. I sure as hell ain't gonna sound as good as you, but I reckon I oughta say somethin'. It ain't gonna be very nice, though.

"See here, Millie, it's like this," he said, gazing up at the tree. "You done killed sixty-six people so far. Sixty-six deaths versus one. I'm sorry, Millie, but that kinda math don't add up, especially when some of them deaths we're talkin' about is kids. Now I ain't got no kids, but I'd be none too happy if I did and your birds killed 'em. They ain't done nothin' wrong. In fact, I'd be so goddamn mad I'd come out here with a can o' gasoline and burn down this fuckin' tree. I don't care if your 'shrine' is in it, and your birds could peck the holy fuck outta me and I wouldn't give a shit. Because if they killed my kids, wouldn't nothin' matter to me no more. I don't go into their nests. I don't crush their tiny li'l eggs. Please... I ain't demandin', just askin'... please make 'em stop killin' people, especially kids. They done killed five dozen people already. Please, we're sorry; at least some of us are. Now tell 'em to leave the rest of us the hell alone."

Maxwell glanced over at Cousey, who nodded his approval and turned to Mahr.

"Anything to say, Paul?"

"Just this," Mahr said. "Millie, if you are truly the reincarnation of a saint, please act like one and rise above your martyrdom. Tell your birds to have mercy, even as Jesus forgave the idiots who were pounding nails into Him. You can do it, Millie. Call them off. We all grieve what has happened to you. If I'd been living on the lake at the time, what with Doc here and my media connections — writers are never good people to screw around with — together we might have been able

The Death Tax   187

to stop this. We didn't, though, and now we have to live with it. It's a tragedy every adult who lived on this lake at the time must live with. Mind you, it is far more difficult to live with something than to be put to death for it. I say make the bastards live with it, Millie. Haunt them. Punish them with your memory. Remind them of the weakness they'll have to answer for on Judgment Day. Believe me, that will be punishment enough, more than man or even your hummingbirds can ever mete out."

Mahr looked over at Cousey.

"Good enough," Cousey said.

They crunched away, their mood lightening as they left the dim woods and entered a clearing.

"Last one for beers is a rotten egg!" Cousey said, further lightening the mood when he pretended to run like an old man, his arms moving faster than his legs.

***

If anxiety were a mountain, the rest of the year would have been its downward slope as spring went peacefully about its business, giving way to the sunscreen and sunbaked asphalt smells of summer, passing into a fall of swimming pools suddenly turned greened and school buses patrolling the roads like child-eating sharks, with it an edge to the air. Then winter and its deceptive blanket of white: soft and snug when viewed from inside; stinging and slippery when you were forced to venture out into it. With it the new year and the gradual climb up Mt. Anxiety, April 15th a red flag fluttering at the summit, this time with the added wrinkle of a religious intervention.

No one was more anxious than Kevin Cousey, not that he had any more to lose than a few more acquaintances: faces fleetingly seen and waved to along the road or in the boats that passed; people he'd talked baseball and politics with at various lake events, not to be seen again until the next one rolled around. Rather, he was anxious to see if their intervention had worked. As April 15th approached, he found himself as revved up as a kid at Christmas.

During the hiatus the rest of the year had become, a couple of curious things had happened at the lake:

Sheriff Randall Eugene Tate did, indeed, call and inquire as to when it might be convenient for Cousey to accompany him and two of his deputies to Millie Fremont's burial site, even though Cousey told him her bier was gone. One of the deputies arrived with a camera, the other eliciting a frown and a warning from Cousey when he brought along rubber gloves and evidence bags.

"Just take us to the spot, sir," the deputy said with maddening officiousness.

Cousey sighed and shook his head, Maxwell leading the way. They took the only photographs they could, of the place where the bier had been, of the nest high up in the tree, marveling at how large it was. Although they were big, strong country boys, neither of the deputies wanted to scuff his boots or snag his double knits climbing the tree. Cousey smiled, and the sheriff threw back his head and laughed when a deputy put on a pair of rubber gloves and got a good peck on the hand when he tried to bag a decomposed hummingbird.

"Son of a bitch!" the deputy said, shaking his hand.

"Not a good idea, Deputy… as I tried to tell you. Trust me, it'll only get worse if you continue," Cousey said.

The deputy responded with a dirty look.

"Damned if I've ever seen anything like it. Alan, it might be a good time to give 'er up," said a sheriff who brought to mind a gnarly old oak, a man who had seen his share of hard knocks growing up near Kennett, where Missouri ground its boot heel into Arkansas.

Could Galvin ever have had this man in his pocket? Cousey couldn't help but wonder. *East versus South. Privilege versus hardscrabble. Somehow I doubt it.*

The other curious thing was that John Galvin's house found a buyer, though, really, it shouldn't have been such a surprise. It was, after all, a very nice house, with ample shade and a commanding view of the lake. But, with no offers and no owner to insist on its upkeep, its price continued to plummet until it sold for less than its previous owner had paid many years ago. Until a person with a normal income could afford it.

Funny to think people still believe in haunted houses, Cousey thought.

The "person" who bought the house was Doris Kath, the lake, quite simply, having come to accept her. Through the scuba club meetings. Through her diligent cleanup efforts almost every Saturday, more than anyone but Cousey, who never failed to join her, seeing it as a perfect excuse to try out his new scuba diving gear. For being the one to find Millie Fremont's body and unraveling the mystery of her death.

Unlike the lesbian couple who used to live there, flaunting their sexuality with the sort of "Fuck you!" brassiness that worked better in the city, Kath was sensitive to her surroundings, knowing full well that being "accepted" was different than being "embraced." She lived alone, entertaining her partner, a wisp of a woman named Sheila Norwood— of such exquisite feminine beauty as to make men sigh and exclaim "What a waste!"— on weekends, with no public displays of affection. Knowing they were under a microscope, they acted accordingly. In this way, Kath became a highly tolerated, marginally respected member of the lake community, one who slept peacefully in a house that was said to be haunted. Sincerely enjoying their company, not to mention Sheila's recipes, she being a would-be gourmet cook — Cousey further validated Kath by trading invites with the couple. Maxwell even got on well with them, finding in the macho Kath an unlikely soul mate. He took them hiking and shooting, and once Kath joined him on a deer hunting trip. She won his respect by trashing him in horseshoes and even beating him in arm wrestling.

"Damn!" he told her. "Nobody beats me in arm rasslin'! Remind me to never get you mad!"

Kath flashed him her best Cheshire Cat smile. "You can rest assured I will."

All in all, Cousey was pleased with the strides the lake had made over the past year. Maybe it was enough. Maybe the Hummingbird Goddess would smile down on them at last.

***

The first signs of activity appeared on April 8th with the arrival of a monster tent on a flatbed truck. A blue school bus followed close behind, filled not with the faithful, but the manual: scruffy, petty criminal-looking types, probably hired from a local carnival, to set up the tent. Considering the tent was large enough to accommodate five hundred people, their ability to erect it sans the use of heavy equipment was remarkable. Cousey watched them, fascinated. The biggest challenge was assembling and raising the two central towers, which they undertook by using a massive rope as a pulley. Around these the tent was spread out, garish red and yellow panels that clashed with the grass, the sky, everything, finally lifted into place by the two huge rings that circled each tower. More partitions were fastened around the tent to enclose it, and the whole thing was tied down with an army of stakes. The final product looked so surreal in the field at the bottom of the hill that Paul Mahr came down for a photo op. He came down a day before The Event as well, as Cousey's guest, intending to cover it from start to finish as a human-interest story while assigning staff reporter Tom Patterson to cover it as a straight news story. Mahr saw The Event for what it was: the year's biggest, with the added dynamic of Galvin's death an unknown as to how it would all play out.

Mahr was skeptical of such gatherings ever since the first one he attended at age twelve. Something about their frequent requests for money, collected unabashedly in big plastic buckets. They always came out after a healing; always of someone he had never seen before, usually suffering from a malady like lameness — for dramatic effect, he figured — only to receive a miraculous cure and disappear soon afterward.

"Come up and receive your miracle!" the preacher would say in a ritual that saw a metamorphosis from that fearful initial rising from a wheelchair, to a tentative hobbling, to a "Praise Jesus!" victory dance up and down the aisle. All of which left a strong impression on a twelve-year-old — until he saw one of the "healed" sharing a grin and a cigarette with the preacher behind the tent while the buckets made their rounds. The trick to attending such events, he soon learned, was to give little and often. Ten dollars, tops, divided into ones. Yet even if most of the faithful adhered to this strategy, as he suspected most of them did, there was still a killing to be made.

Cousey sat with Mahr by the stump, watching as the light changed in color and intensity on the brow of Michael's wings. The statue imparted a sense of presence on the small yard, along with it its owner. Flawed though he was, Cousey was the closest Lake Tanaka came to a guardian angel. Maybe it was his rubber hand, but people who didn't know him tended to underestimate him. As with Columbo, they did so at their peril, as even a formidable adversary like John Galvin had found out. The respect for him at the lake was almost universal, even among those who couldn't get past his doctor's credentials and initially wrote him off as a snob, a dynamic of social distancing he'd always tried to downplay. Mahr beheld the man who had become a close friend with a seeming incongruity of both admiration and sadness, musing on what might have been had fate not intervened.

Cousey reached into an ice-filled cooler, a dozen beers lining the bottom like cylinders in an Arctic engine: cans, but at least it was a good import. None of those *Look at Me, I'm a Beer Connoisseur!* frosted mugs today, just the cooler cups favored by real men. Crush the empty and toss 'er on the ground, slide in a new one and you're back in business, redneck style. Better bring the kind with a string for float trips, though.

Sometimes it's fun to adopt the local mindset, Cousey thought with a whimsical smile. *All we need now is a good dogfight.*

Mostly good people lived on this lake, after all. A little narrow, a little thick, a lot CYA, but good people overall, probably no different than most. People who would all but ignore you — until your house burned down. Then they'd come out of the woodwork with a degree of kindness you never would have thought possible, then feel compelled to tell everyone about it afterward. The *Bible* said it best: "They have their reward." Self-serving, to be sure, but hardly evil.

Yet there was a crisis on this lake they had ignored, all of them. Maybe not entirely, sharing their burden with "Did you notice?" tales of suspected abuse, followed up by nothing, but at least getting them out in the open so someone could do something about it, the very process of venting them easing their guilt. Praying to their God to deliver this girl while doing nothing to help Him. Never realizing that perhaps God had put them, as stewards of His Creation, there to intervene.

No, Cousey thought, *these people aren't bad, just weak.*

"A beer for your thoughts," he said, touching cooler cups with Mahr.

Mahr eyed him grimly, two weaving lines of Canada geese undulating brown and white as they honked their way across the sky just over his shoulder.

"Doc, shoot me for being cynical, but I think we're looking at more of the same come April 15th. I say this because I'm looking at it from the viewpoint of

Millie and the hummingbirds. I mean, you've tried to stop this, tried to get to the bottom of this. You've been doing this throughout, and God bless you for it, Doc."

Cousey smiled and raised his beer.

"Then we have our buddy, Maxwell — or is that Buddy Maxwell?" Mahr said with a smile. "We have Doris Kath."

"Don't forget yourself," Cousey said. "You've always taken an interest, done what you can to publicize the situation."

"I've played a minor role, let's face it, Doc. I'm only peripheral to what's happening here, more observer than participant. I don't live here now, and I didn't live here when it happened — so, the way I think Millie and the hummingbirds see things, I don't count. OK, for the sake of argument, let's say I do. Doris didn't live here, either, but let's say she counts as well. OK, let's be real generous and say half a dozen people count. We'll include the Baxters, even if I question their motives. That's only six people, six out of eight hundred who've shown they give a damn about what's happening here. If I'm the spirit of Millie Fremont, whom we believe controls these hummingbirds, I don't see any great outpouring of remorse here, certainly not enough to change my mind. With most people it's business as usual, with the cheek to think they can atone for their sins by allowing outsiders to come in, throwing some money at them, and thinking they can pray their troubles away — all of which strikes me as a bunch of sanctimonious bullshit. Even from here that tent looks like a big ol' target."

Cousey was impressed. "Paul, I'd say that was two beers' worth. Perhaps I've been naïve about my own impact. You know, playing amateur sleuth and letting it go to my head when we finally busted that lowlife. I never liked his dog, either; no great loss to the animal world when they put that monster down. Playing amateur sleuth while deluding myself into thinking a statue of an angel superhero could somehow impart its powers to me by osmosis, give some spiritual 'oomph' to my non-prayers. Listening to you, I realize how full of shit I've been."

"Come on, Doc, cut yourself some slack."

"But it's true."

"No, it could be true. We won't know for sure until April 15th."

"Fair enough, though I nonetheless subscribe to the belief I've succumbed to selfish thinking."

"You, selfish? How do you figure?"

"Seated before you, Paul, big as life and shrunken as defeat, is all that remains of a promising young doctor who went from a foothold near the summit of the medical world to a self-pitying freak on the verge of suicide. Someone who, ever since the accident, has desperately tried to salvage a feeling of self-worth, a sense of purpose from whatever remains of his pitiful life. I've been kidding myself with the notion that I've found it. To my knowledge, I was the only one who reported Galvin's abuse, the only one who called the police the night Millie disappeared, paying the price for my boldness with the strangely satisfying pain of martyrdom. Being clever enough — or so I thought — to have Galvin lead me to the body only to ditch the evidence. Then, with Doris's help, finding the body only to have the birds carry it away. Again through my own wiles, sifting through the gravel the deputies had left behind to find the evidence that busted Galvin. Lord, how mightily I've tried to make myself important! Lord, how I've needed to! These days my insecurity has bubbled to the surface… to the point I badly need to feel I still have some value, badly need a victory after all these wasted years. I desperately need to be the hero that comes to the lak"s rescue and saves the day. Not a big legacy, certainly not the one that could have been had my life proceeded as it should have, but a legacy nonetheless. Alas, you can see how this mindset has skewed my thinking."

"Sorry, Doc. The last thing I want to do is shoot holes in your accomplishments."

"Don't be sorry. The truth is bitter, but it's still the truth, and there's a cold beauty to the way it goes down. I'd sooner embrace a bitter truth than blind myself with a lie. Really, you've done me a service."

"I'm not sure how true that is," Mahr said, "but thank you for saying so. One thing you said bothers me, though."

"What might that be?"

"You talked about how your life should have proceeded. Who are you to say how your life should have proceeded? Are you God, or at least presuming to second-guess Him?"

Cousey smiled, gazing down at the beer through the hole in his can. Something satisfying about the give of foam rubber, the sloshing of the liquid inside an earthly counterpoint to a sky streaming with purple clouds.

"The beer seems to be having the opposite effect on us, turning you into an oracle and me even foggier than usual. Where do we stand on the beer count, by the way?"

Mahr lifted the lid. "Four."

"Hmm, not enough for pizza. But never fear, there's real beer in the house, the kind you need an opener for. Again you're right on target, Paul. God only knows how my life was meant to be. The trick, I suppose, is to make something good of it, no matter what. To realize my purpose here, whatever that might be."

Mahr nodded. "Life is a broken play. I tell myself that at this point in my career I should be working for one of the big Chicago dailies. Something keeps me here, though. Some day I suspect I'll do something — I have no idea what it will be — that makes it clear why I've stayed. In the meantime, I feel like I'm where I need to be. And deep down, I think you feel that way, too."

"I do," Cousey said. "Even with a fake hand and the faintest glimmerings of the family and career I once had, there's no place I'd rather be. I care about this place. I want to do whatever I can to protect it. And yeah, if I could somehow manage to feel good about myself again somewhere along the line, that would be nice."

"Everyone needs to feel important," Mahr said.

The sun had dipped beneath the hills, the curve of Michael's wings edged in faintest pink, forming the bottom of a Baroque picture frame for the swimming platform, the lake around it, the dam with a figure no larger than that of a boy fishing from it, and the trees behind it. Various mementos of MacEnerny's passing — from pictures to mini-Teddy bears to plastic flowers — were visible in the twilight on a platform still splintered from his crash. With spring still in its rawness, there was no urgency to make repairs. Cousey gazed at the platform, the boy on the dam beyond it, a shudder passing through him as he contemplated the kids who might not be swimming or fishing there this summer.

Chapter XV

April 14th saw the lake at its cheesy worst, a carnival atmosphere radiating from the hub that was the red-and-yellow-striped tent. A Special Use permit allowed the Baxters to keep the gate's entry arm up today, waiving the usual requirement to be a guest of someone at the lake and, as a result, all manner of people streamed in. Everyone who wasn't out trying to make a buck was out gawking at the spectacle sprawling out on the field before them. Most saw it as a welcome distraction, a symbol of proactivity displacing the siege mentality of previous years. Others, Kevin Cousey among them, saw it as an exercise in decadence, a big sign to the hummingbirds that said, "Kick me!" The Rod & Gun Club had reclaimed their building, cooking up barbecued chicken and burgers and brats on a phalanx of barrel grills while people helped themselves to cold drinks and all the trimmings inside. The day was unseasonably warm, many availing themselves of the tables under the awning.

"No Parking" signs sprouted like dandelions in the field at the foot of the hill, the tent taking up a good chunk of the space and the booths most of the rest, anyway. The adjoining lot was prime real estate, with space for only twenty cars. "No Parking" signs lined the narrow roads that nearly circumnavigated the lake, necessitating the parking of cars in the yards and driveways of residents, an opportunity they were quick to seize upon. Thirty dollars was the asking price for a spot close to the venue, people grumbling but acquiescing to rates comparable to sporting events in the city. Ten dollars was the lowest price, for a spot a mile away.

A variety of carnival games had been set up, the same scruffy-looking bunch that had set up the tent manning them with the bored, weary, hungover look that was universal among carnies. There was a dunking booth and rides for the kiddies, a clown making balloon animals, and food stands selling funnel cakes and sno-cones and cotton candy. The next largest thing after the tent was an inflated kiddie slide three stories high.

Far more came than expected, a few thousand from the look of it, and it was apparent that many of them intended to make a day of it and stay for the revival. As daylight waned, the pale burnt sienna that remained of the sunset giving way to the blare of floodlights, Pastor Eustace Baxter decided to remove the sides of the tent, thereby increasing his audience and ultimately the reach of his buckets. The downside was the chill breeze that blew off the lake, a veritable wind tunnel that started beyond the dam and skimmed across the water, the tent in its path as it continued on up the hill.

Yes, the pastor thought, *this could be a good night, in more ways than one!*

Utter chaos on the lake roads as the day-trippers who were departing converged with the all-nighters who were coming in. The Benson PD had all it could do to keep things moving in a place its officers had never directed traffic before. By midnight they were gone — save for the few who were members of the church or harbored a morbid curiosity about what would transpire — most of those who were coming or going where they wanted to be. Soon every seat was taken and the tent was ringed with onlookers, leaning against poles or sitting in the camp chairs some of them had thought to bring. Some of them threw blankets on the dampening grass.

Promptly at midnight, the proceedings began with a hymn, followed by another hymn and then three more hymns. Each of them delivered as people stood and swayed and clapped. Each of them at least five minutes long and consisting of roughly seven words repeated roughly eleven times, a video screen above the stage reminding the faithful what they were. The inclusion of a stage made this a far cry from the early days of tent revivals. Wearing a clip-on mike, Pastor Eustace Baxter orchestrated the proceedings from behind a Plexiglas dais flanked by twin eruptions of flowers in the center, three tiers of risers behind him. He frequently ventured from his "base" to encourage participation as well as to "connect" with the faithful. Seven seated church elders formed a row to his right, his wife Thelma nearest him, beaming at her husband with her head tilted and her gloved hands folded in her lap. The pastor's sound/video man sat behind a mixing console to his far right, Up With People's answer to Led Zeppelin grouped around a drum kit with a glitter finish and a Plexiglas shield in front of it to his far left. A batten, sprouting multicolored lights and massive enough to build a bridge with, spanned the stage, echoed by a procession of footlights. Not just a service, Pastor Eustace wasn't ashamed to admit, but a Broadway production. It needed to be to keep folks with an attention span compromised by video games entertained. Even as the last of the hymns was finishing, it being hard to tell if the assembled were aglow with perspiration or The Spirit, the buckets came out like the privilege of sitting down.

Long-winded though he was, there was no way Pastor Eustace could hold up for eight straight hours. The trick was to mix things up, come at them in bursts, using the hymns to reinforce the sermon and the sermon to reinforce the hymns and everything to reinforce the "gift offering," whatever was in people's hearts, as long as it was something and kept coming, in what amounted to an endless cycle. In this way, the rut that would ensue by doing anything for more than fifteen minutes would be avoided, and what amounted to a fundraising marathon would be a runaway train. Pastor Eustace was realist enough to realize he couldn't "save" anyone; that was God's work, and the best he could do was create an atmosphere where the two parties could come together. In addition to raising money for the church and save for the occasional "miracle," the primary purpose of these services was social. Expect anything more and you were bound to be disappointed. Ultimately, everyone was on his own when it came to God.

The time for Sermon Burst Number One had arrived.

"Friends, welcome to the first-ever Lake Tanaka Tent Revival. Let's have a 'Praise Jesus!' for that, shall we?"

A cheer from the crowd.

"Praise Jesus!" the pastor roared.

"Praise Jesus!" the crowd responded.

Two more "Praise Jesus-es!" for each, two more than necessary. It was all about repetition. In addition to having a lulling effect, repetition killed time, just as hymns that repeated the same seven words eleven times — their lack of a chorus making them further repetitious and, as a result, lulling — killed time.

"Friends, this is a joyous occasion! How could worshipping our Creator not be joyous?" Pastor Eustace cried, prompting a response that was programmed to come.

The crowd cheered, some of them moved to tears, "Amen!"

It was always a rush, a power trip that massaged the pastor's spine like a pair of divine hands. And, as it always did, the music had primed the spiritual pump.

"Friends, this is a joyous occasion, but it is also a somber occasion, one I would like to call an Occasion of Faith. As most of you are well aware, Satan has stretched out his black hand over this lake. Every year at this time he looses his minions over it in the form of hummingbirds, killin' innocent folks."

At the last minute, Cousey had decided to come, his frequent head shakings less visible on the periphery.

"All told, some sixty-five souls have been lost here thanks to these hellish vermin (although the number was in fact sixty-six, he refused to acknowledge John Galvin had a soul). Some say the devil's thirst for blood won't be quenched until every last soul who was livin' here at the time of Millie Fremont's death has been exterminated. This is wrong, friends. Wrong! These folks have the same right to their lives as any God-fearin' folk! The man who abused this dear little girl is gone, no doubt doin' the breaststroke in the Lake of Fire even as we speak! Join with me now, friends. Join with me in prayin' this curse off Lake Tanaka. Returnin' these hummingbirds to the cute little creatures God intended them to be. Do I have an 'amen!' on that?"

"Amen!" a few people said.

Pastor Eustace tapped his microphone and looked over at the sound man.

"Is this thing on? Do I have an 'amen!' on that?" he cried.

"Amen!" the crowd roared.

"Are you sure God can hear you?" the pastor cried.

"Amen!" the crowd thundered.

And so the revival began in earnest, Pastor Eustace with practiced skill interweaving snippets of sermon with hymns, fragments of video with Christian rock. At 2:00 AM, a black choir "from our 'sister church' in Ferguson" composed almost exclusively of big women and skinny men, filed down a side aisle in a peacock shimmering of robes and mounted the risers at the back of the stage. They sang for a rousing half-hour and were well received as the service took on a gospel flavor. Never one to miss an opportunity, Pastor Eustace sent out the buckets during the last hymn, implying that this collection was for the choir. In reality, all they would get was handshakes and broad smiles and photo ops, coffee and donuts, and some gas money for the bus ride home.

Cousey was ready, a wad of twenty crisp ones in his shirt pocket. He yawned when the choir's last hymn was over, popping the first of many chocolate-covered coffee beans.

Soon the reverend was back at it. "You have the power, friends. The power to say, 'Get behind me, Satan!' and drive this evil away! Just last year, we lost most of the Armbruster family — in the midst of a swimmin' party, no less. Innocent kids, just havin' fun. The Armbrusters were members of our church family, and little Jenny was always a favorite of mine. She was ten, but you'd swear she was twenty the way she looked at you through those little pink glasses; like a pretty little owl, she looked. But Satan didn't pay her any mind, no sir. He snuffed out this innocent kid along with the rest — and these are the kind of lives we're fightin' for, my brothers and sisters in Christ! Can I hear an 'amen!' on that?"

"Amen!" several people cried.

"God's a little hard of hearin', friends, at least that's how He lets on sometimes. How about an 'amen!' loud enough for God to hear all the way up in heaven?" he cried.

"Amen!" the crowd roared.

"Friends, believe it or not, but it's already 4:00 AM. We're past the halfway point, figurin' we'd pray 'til eight o'clock if we need to. Now many — quite charitably, I'm sure — consider me a rather… long-winded fellow (general laughter), but even I can't yammer all night long without some refreshment. Please, let us break for thirty minutes and replenish ourselves with some coffee and donuts. When you hear *"When the Saints Go Marching In,"* that'll be the signal we're startin' up again and to come on back. Please note the collection buckets on the refreshment tables. Donations are always welcome…"

"Whatever your heart moves you to give," Cousey mouthed his next words before they came out, finishing the expression that symbolized fundamentalist giving.

Pastor Eustace mopped his brow and hopped with unusual spryness for a man his age off the stage, working his way to tables piled high with donuts while coffee urns stood watch like gleaming sentinels, flanked by stacks of paper plates and napkins, boxes of plastic spoons, and veritable silos of creamer and sugar.

Cousey peeled off a bill and helped himself to some coffee and a donut, hoping to see a familiar face in the crowd. He saw Doris Kath solo, a wise move, and spoke with her briefly. But not about Sheila. Occasionally a scuba club member came up and said, "Hi." He was looking for Paul Mahr, his eye gravitating to the middle of the action, where he expected to see him interviewing someone. Sure enough, there he was with Pastor Eustace. Cousey drew near enough to eavesdrop, Mahr holding a microrecorder under the pastor's wagging chin.

"Pastor, has anything like this has ever been tried before?" Mahr was asking. "I always thought prayer meetings were for... non-specific purposes."

Baxter was leery. "Au contraire, my friend. Prayer meetins have a very specific purpose, and that is to communicate with The Almighty."

"Perhaps I should have phrased it better. What I meant to say is the timing of this meeting coincides with the yearly arrival of the hummingbirds at Lake Tanaka."

Baxter remained prickly. "I'd say the yearly 'attack' is more like it, wouldn't you? And yes, in that regard this meetin' does serve the additional purpose of so-licitin' God's intervention to ward off the evil that has afflicted this lake community. Mind you, the lake's Board of Directors invited us to come on behalf of the folks who are sick to death of bein' victimized by these birds year after year. So, yes, we are definitely performin' a community service here, in addition to a normal prayer meetin'. Now, if you'll excuse me, I need to fetch my wife some coffee," he said, ending the interview with the fake graciousness of a politician's smile.

The shaking of Paul Mahr's head was barely perceptible. Cousey saw it and smiled. Sensing he was under scrutiny, Mahr turned and met his gaze.

"Tough interview?"

"I've had tougher. At least the pastor was interesting."

"As opposed to... say... a football coach on autopilot, the laundry spinning around in his head?"

Mahr laughed. "You know it! Sometimes you have to piss them off with a smart-alecky question just to stay awake."

Cousey grinned and handed Mahr a dollar bill. "Get yourself some coffee and a donut and join me outside. There's something I want to run by you."

Soon they were standing by the water under a moon that shone like a light through heavy gray paper.

"Simple question," Cousey said. "How do you think this is going to end up?"

"Simple answer," Mahr said. "I don't think anything has changed. I think the birds are going to take one look at this little shindig and tee off. I'm seriously thinking about getting out of here before seven, yet I'm torn."

"By what, pray tell?"

"By that damn, irrepressible reporter side of me, of course. Provided I survive to tell the tale, I'd sure like to see what happens."

"Honestly, Paul, I don't think you'll score any quality interviews while people are... say... running for their lives. Every year I watch them from my backyard, and every year they leave me alone. How about we leave for my place at six-thirty, grab some coffee, and watch things unfold — unravel? — from there. I've got some binocs; you can see the tent from the end of my dock. Trust me, it's as close as you want to get"

"OK, my turn to ask you a question," Mahr said.

Cousey smiled, noting the microrecorder. "Off the record?"

"Don't worry, it's not on."

"Shoot," Cousey said.

"Where is your faith in the power of prayer?"

Cousey laughed. "Because there has never been an admission of guilt. No resident living on the lake at the time of Millie's death has ever made a public apology.

I agree with the pastor; there's evil here, but we can't hang it on Satan like we do everything else. Not this time."

"I agree. To quote Pogo, 'We have met the enemy, and he is us.'"

"As for the Power of Prayer, let's just say I'm cynical, especially in such a contrived setting. Somewhere in the *Bible* — I think it is James — it says something to the effect of, 'If you want to pray to God, do it behind closed doors. Don't advertise your piety.' Somehow I don't think a public outpouring of prayer will cause a million hummingbirds to tumble from the sky like shot clay pigeons. I tend to think miracles happen behind the scenes."

"I couldn't have said it any better," Mahr said. "Say, isn't that the opening strains of *"When the Saints Go Marching In"* I hear?"

***

There were two highlights in the second half of the service: At five-thirty, the power went out for precisely twenty-two minutes. Pastor Eustace passed the time cleverly enough, leading the congregation in a medley of light-themed hymns — from *"A Light from Heaven Shone Around"* to *"Oh Heavenly Word, Eternal Light,"* after which, in celebration of his soundman getting the power back on, the ubiquitous buckets made their rounds.

Leave it to Baxter to turn an inconvenience into an opportunity, Cousey thought with grudging admiration.

The other highlight was the overlarge woman who succumbed to heat exhaustion. While the night had turned chilly, the action inside the tent was heating up. Too much activity combined with fatigue and dehydration to do her in. Although no one realized it at the time, her demise was a blessing in disguise when a resident who'd been on the lake at the time of Millie Fremont's death was whisked away by the EMTs.

Cousey and Mahr had agreed to meet at the tent pole directly opposite Baxter. Mahr dropped three dollars into the kitty and helped himself to half a dozen glazed donuts wrapped in the church planting mission flyers they'd been handing out, the only things they had to wrap them in, and found Cousey, more leaning than standing against the pole. The sun was a stark yellow disc in a cloudless red sky as they slogged across the wet grass to Mahr's car. He had arrived early, using his press credential to park in the lot for free. Meanwhile, Cousey lived less than a mile away and had walked down.

Cousey shuddered at the old superstition: red sky at morning...

They climbed into Mahr's car. "I wouldn't want to have to scrub all the shit off this thing if you left it here," Cousey said, and twenty minutes later they were sitting in lawn chairs by the stump, eating donuts with a cowboy-sized metal pot of coffee and some milk and sugar between them a real cowpuncher would have curled his lip at. The din of the revival echoed across the lake — they were singing again — and they were glad to be far away.

"Donut for your thoughts," Cousey said.

"People tend to stay inside on April 15th," Mahr said. "A tentful of people, open on the sides, is like waving a red flag. If I'm the hummingbirds, I take it as a provocation. I don't think they'll have any trouble reaching their quota today."

Cousey laughed. "More like a cherry cheese Danish's worth, I reckon," he said, cowboy style.

Mahr joined him. It felt good to laugh, even if it was gallows humor. Anything to cut the tension that grew with the rustling in the trees behind the dam.

"Oh my God, is that what I think it is?" Mahr asked.

"Yep," Cousey said. "It starts the night before, and it's actually kind of soothing, though not so much the next morning."

"This is the first time I've heard it."

"They're assembling," Cousey said. "Thousands of them. Maybe a million. Maybe more. Come seven o'clock — four minutes from now by my watch — they'll congregate on the swimming platform. You watch. It's quite a spectacle."

Four minutes later, there was a great flurry of birds spilling over the trees like waves over a breakwater, jostling for position on the platform while the rest of them wheeled around it in a shimmering whirlpool of red and blue and green depending on how the light caught it, thrusting ever higher into the sky.

"That's where you found her body, wasn't it?" Mahr said.

"Yep."

"Heaven help us. They've turned it into a shrine."

"One of them, at least," Cousey said, "The one down in the woods is their Mecca."

"Ho-ly shit! Look at them all! I can't believe what I'm seeing!" Mahr said.

"There they go: seven-fifteen; right on time!" Cousey said, glancing at his watch. "God help those people. He's the only one who can help them now."

As if on cue, the birds on the platform rose to meet the birds in the air. Interspersed with chirping, the collective beat of their wings was deafening as they surged as one toward the far end of the lake, not sub-dividing as they had in previous years, just as "Morning Has Broken" was drifting across the water. Somehow it was strange to hear anyone but Cat Stevens singing it.

The irony of the lyrics wasn't lost on Cousey. "'Blackbird has spoken, like the first bird,'" he sang along.

***

There was one thing that didn't happen and one thing that did, both of them thoroughly un-Hollywood, as the birds bore down on the tent:

They did not tumble from the sky, stopped dead in their tracks by the Power of Prayer, grateful faces gazing heavenward to the soundtrack of *Ben-Hur*.

They robbed the scene of what should have been its "dramatic buildup," a myriad of little beaks breaking the surface like shark fins on water by not expending needless energy pecking their way through a heavy, rubberized tent.

Because even though it often manages to be dramatic, ultimately, nature is all about efficiency. That the sun should also be beautiful as it rises is merely a by-product of its primary purpose to warm the earth and facilitate photosynthesis, a subjective event appreciated by man alone.

What did happen was a greater sense of urgency as the birds approached the tent, a growing frenzy as they beheld what resembled a sunburst clown face as seen from above, the two rings with the support poles passing through them an idiotic pair of eyes, mocking them even as their queen lay dead, her murder unatoned for. It was as if someone had broken a window of cosmic proportions, shards of glass raining down upon the faithful. They streamed through every opening — through the "eyes" and from all sides — like hell in all its fury falling to earth in a world inverted by evil.

True to form and, at least initially, oblivious to the danger, Pastor Eustace seized the moment for dramatic effect.

"Friends, the evil is upon us!" he cried. "Quick, join hands and pray! Pray like you've never prayed before!"

With that, he turned off his mike and his attention to self-preservation.

The birds whirled and rose and swooped like a vast and feathery knot tying and untying itself. Rising and swooping with a thunderous roar as they poured into the tent en masse. Though some claimed it might have been the lighting or the "red eye" effect of photography, many of those who survived would note the blood-red look in the birds' eyes, glowing as if lit from within by an unholy fire; portals to the devil's cauldron. The shrieks of women, the shouts of men could be heard above the din as the birds pecked and pecked and pecked — at the soft, exposed necks and the veined hands that rose to protect them; the pale, bare legs with their tributaries of blue veins; the three inches of potbelly that hung over their belts like too much soft-serve spilling over the lip of a cone. Pecking and drawing blood. Pecking their way toward The Guilty Ones, blazing a trail through anyone who got in their way.

Their targets must be removed, Pastor Eustace realized.

Many were incredulous when he turned on his microphone, shielded his face with his forearm, and said, "Friends, by the power of Almighty God, I implore those of you who are residents of the lake to leave this tent immediately! Leave this tent now — before they kill us all!"

More incredibly, most of them obeyed, and a chaotic exodus ensued, chairs falling like dominoes as the faithful disembarked a sinking ship for a roiling ocean. Leaving no doubt as to their guilt. With a level of patience that was peculiar to predators, the birds waited until a sufficient number of them had spilled out onto the grass. Giving themselves room to operate.

The first of the dozen to fall this morning was a woman, a bird burying its beak into her jugular, all the way to its head, severing it. Sparing its mates another kill when she fell and drove her elbow into the neck of the three-year-old daughter whose hand she held.

Kill Number Three was a young guy swatting at the birds with his *Bible*. Grunting with satisfaction when The Word of God made contact with their little birdie bodies. But negative attention begat negative attention, and soon he was a living pin cushion, the birds pecking everything from his eyes to the veins in the back of his hands, his testicles to the arteries in his neck. Soon his blood was watering the grass like one of those ring-type sprinklers on an old lady's lawn. His *Bible* had fallen to the grass, its blood-soaked pages open to verses that included Genesis 1:28: "And God blessed them, and God said unto them, Be fruitful, and multiply, and replenish the earth, and subdue it: and have dominion over the fish of the sea, and over the fowl of the air, and over every living thing that moveth upon the earth."

Kill Number Four had flattened one of the folding chairs into a makeshift club, though he had neither the stamina to keep swinging it nor a shirt capable of containing his belly. Even as his chest was tightening up, half a dozen birds drove their beaks into his exposed navel even as their claws ripped open the fissure they had created. The official cause of death was a tossup between disembowelment and cardiac arrest.

Kill Number Five was merely trying to escape on sixty-something legs unused to running, especially in high heels on wet grass. No sooner did she slip and fall than three birds converged on her, two of them driving their beaks into the soft hollows behind her knees while the third one drove its beak into her left temple.

Kills Number Six and Seven were a young couple who didn't know when to unhitch. He might have even escaped — they had arrived late, and, not thinking it would matter at that hour, he had parked along the road near the tent — had she not stumbled a couple of times. Ten feet from a car with its doors unlocked, a hundred birds rose up before them like a shimmering red tsunami, surging into their esophagi and tracheas when they opened their mouths to scream. Tiny puffs of feather emerging with the little whistling sounds of their last breaths.

Kill Number Eight was packing heat, though why anyone would bring a handgun to a tent revival and what he planned to do with it now was anybody's guess. Half a dozen loud reports succeeded only in momentarily scaring the birds, winging a couple of them, and ultimately stoking their ire. By the time he was empty, they had regrouped, and the smile he died with was echoed by the "smile" of his ripped-open throat.

Kill Number Nine was a woman who turtled with her head between her knees and her jacket pulled over her head, determined to weather the attack with her secret weapon: prayer. Forgetting that prayers — including the many that Millie Fremont had made in the months before her death — tended to go unheard on this lake. Still, her prayers were able to transport her to another place, the sensation of tiny stab wounds all over her body morphing into thoughts of her Lord's final suffering, from the bite of His flagellation to the sting of the crown of thorns, the barb of pain when they thrust the lance into His side to the bright flashes of agony when they drove the spikes into His hands and feet. Look of peace on her face when she finally bled out, much like the faces of the martyred saints she had seen in religious art. She would be the only one who died in peace that day.

Kill Number Ten was the smartest sixth-grader at Benson Elementary, though not smart enough to stay home or follow his parents' instructions to accompany them out of the tent. Instead, he ventured deeper inside, all the way to the drum kit on the right side of the stage. He unscrewed the largest cymbal. Then, taking a visual measure of the bass drum, he withdrew his pocket knife, cut off the rear skin, and crawled inside, the cymbal forming a door behind him. It was a good fit: hardly any room for a hummingbird to peep its head through. However, the problem was the other side of the drum when one of the birds noted a shadow moving inside. Soon the boy was wincing at a multitude of pecks against his back as the birds breached the drumhead and widened the opening. Realizing he was a goner if he stayed put, he burst from his hiding place and ran, a would-be Captain America with a cymbal for a shield. One that prevented him from seeing the cord he stumbled over, ultimately decapitating him.

The last two kills were both the lake's longest remaining residents and John Galvin's next-door neighbors, a couple who were universally liked because they were friendly and minded their own business. Minded their own business when that black guy and that lesbian couple were drummed out of their homes for no other reason than being who they were. Minded their own business when they were the only ones who ever saw Galvin hit the French girl — calling her "Millie" made things too personal — with it a nagging compulsion to do something about it, a slap across the mouth followed by a stern-looking pointing gesture as they were pulling out of a parking lot.

"Oh my! Did you see what I just saw?" the wife asked.

"Yes, I did," the husband replied, and that was as far as it got.

That was as far as it ever got, including that fateful night of April 15th, when they were as close to what went down as anyone.

They died as they had lived, the voice boxes pecked out of their throats.

By the time it was over, bright arterial blood had splashed the grass in the harsh morning sunshine, had puddled in the murky light of the interior like a bad oil change. Trickled down the side of the stage, where a dismembered head teetered on the edge. Depending on how one saw them, these were either the martyrs who gave their lives for the lake that day or the guilty whose time had come, in either case buying the more fortunate among them another year.

As if on cue, the birds rose as one and spilled across the heavens — a teeming, dazzling curtain of light and color and sound and movement that was the daytime's answer to the nighttime's aurora borealis — over the dam and the trees beyond, leaving in their wake the sounds of bewilderment and suffering that were peculiar to the human condition.

Cousey and Mahr watched them depart with their mouths ajar. Mahr had never seen anything like it and, even though Cousey had, the spectacle that unfolded against the broad canvas of the sky never failed to leave him awestruck.

Cousey finally broke the spell. "Safe to say it's over, at least for another year. I'll call the EMTs while you go down there and get your story."

Chapter XVI

In all his years of reporting, Paul Mahr had never reached a crime scene, let alone a murder scene, before the police. Something unnerving about arriving where something has just happened, like a car crash with the dust of impact still rolling off it.

Safe to say, the prayer meeting was a wash. *All it did was make it easier for the birds to reach their quota*, he thought, doubting the need for any "homing pigeons" this year.

It was easy to tell the living — the ones who were still sitting up and groaning and being tended to — from the dead: the eleven bodies lying in various stages of defilement on grass "rugs" tacky with their blood.

There should be twelve, he thought, counting them, before grimacing at the discovery of a boy's body separated from its head in the eerie depths of the tent.

A mass evacuation was underway, even though many of the faithful who weren't injured or tending to the injured had remained, drinking coffee and eating donuts and trying to process what had happened as the first sirens could be heard in the distance. Mahr knew his window of opportunity was about to close, using his time to take as many photos as possible. Unlike interviews, which could always wait for later and were sometimes even improved by the wait, photo ops were invariably a fleeting thing. Something objectifying about a camera. Much like TV, it created the illusion of distance between the viewer and his subject. He supposed this was how documentarians were able to shoot starving people in Third World countries. A camera turned whatever you were shooting into something as objective as a movie or TV show.

Decency prevented him from taking pictures of Eustace and Thelma Baxter. Most seasoned paparazzi wouldn't have hesitated to capture someone at his most vulnerable, though Mahr had never subscribed to a philosophy he likened to killer instinct, devoid of empathy. He could never eliminate the barrier between himself and his subject entirely; one of the "character flaws" he suspected kept him from The Big Time.

Shoot me, I still have a conscience! he thought, unrepentant.

The pastor and his wife were huddled together in a pair of folding chairs. The pastor's suit was sliced to shreds, the damage continuing on to his hands, a badly pecked ear crusting over with blood. His wife sobbed quietly as her husband held a bloody square of handkerchief to her eye. Seeing Mahr approach with his camera, Pastor Eustace held up his free hand as if to fend him off.

Mahr raised his hands and smiled disarmingly. "Never without your permission, Pastor, and I'm not about to ask you for it in this context."

Pastor Eustace smiled gratefully.

"Can I offer you a fresh hankie?"

"Yes, I think we need one. Thank you, Paul."

Pastor Eustace took the handkerchief, Mahr impressed that he had the sense to put it on top of the old one.

"Your editorials have always been a bit… liberal for my tastes, especially that one about charter schools," Pastor Eustace said, forcing a smile. "I may doubt your judgment, but never your morals."

Mahr smiled back. *What was it about charter schools that stuck in people's craws?* he thought, mystified.

"I'll take that as a compliment, Pastor. Can I get you folks some coffee?"

"Yes, Paul, that would be nice."

"How do you take it?"

"Black for me, milk and sugar for her, if you wouldn't mind."

"Of course not." Then, to his wife, "Ms. Baxter, are you OK?"

The pastor answered for her. "By God's grace, she will be."

Just as Mahr was coming back with the coffee and a couple of donuts — there were plenty of them left — the police arrived with an entourage of EMTs. One officer with a "Get the hell outta here!" look on his face unspooled a thick roll of the telltale yellow tape that transformed any scene into a Crime Scene, while another, with an unusual degree of tact for law enforcement, it seemed to Mahr, escorted people from the area.

Could these guys be taking notes from the Brits? the thought occurred to him.

Watching them in action, Mahr couldn't help but muse on the mercurial relationship the Benson PD had with a lake that alternately disappeared and reappeared on its jurisdictional radar depending on whatever suited it at the time: usually sexy, high-profile boating and shooting accidents as opposed to the more mundane domestic disturbances that always had an element of danger about them. While the sheriff's department would eventually make an appearance today, last night's gig directing traffic had paved the way for the PD's continued involvement this morning. Although as a member of the press, with more right to be here than the average citizen and well used to dealing with cops, Mahr realized the journalistic potential here had run its course.

***

Considering neither of them had died in the attack and the tent and its contents had suffered minimal damage, no one suffered more than Pastor Eustace Baxter and his wife, Thelma. Fancying himself a healer, a divine messenger of the first order, the pastor was smitten with doubt about himself and even God.

A curious thing happened at his church: An unprecedented level of gift-giving — he refused to call it a "take" — at the revival was followed by a spike in church membership, to the point a shocked Eustace Baxter contemplated building a larger church. Ultimately, it was a passing fad, a collective desire, he decided in a rare moment of candor, to "see the freak behind the freak show." Soon church membership had fallen to half of what it had been before the revival.

If he needed further proof of his failure, he needed to look no farther than his wife. Thelma lost her left eye, the pink, silken eye patch she wore giving her the look of a pirate dandy. The glass eye she ended up getting didn't quite jive with her good eye. It was somewhat askew, giving her the appearance of a brain-damaged person peering out at the world, made all the more unsettling by it being hard to tell who she was looking at. She was far quieter these days, an unexpected blessing for those accustomed to her former self. She declined to join her husband in

God's New Calling, a church planting mission in East Africa from which he was destined never to return. The last time they would ever see each other she asked him the question that would sting him like a spiritual barb on the plane:

"My dear, could it be the God you serve isn't the same God that created those birds?"

***

At the lake there was April 15th, and there was every other day, its residents making such deliberate attempts at normalcy as to make it seem manic at times. Taking a page from Psych 101, the Board hosted a free barbecue for lake residents on the same grounds as the revival the following weekend, desperately trying to supplant a bad memory with a good one even as the last traces of the dead were brushed and hosed from the grass. The death toll was seventy-eight now, rising as some had expected, and it was all people could do to put it out of their minds as they drank too much beer and ate too many hot dogs and laughed too hard and too often, because life was neither that goddamned funny nor that goddamned good.

Kevin Cousey attended the gathering, just as he made a point of attending all lake gatherings. Immediately he noticed the difference in the way people were looking at him — with a mixture of respect: "This is the guy who stood up for Millie and finally busted ol' Galvin," and expectation: "What the hell's he gonna do now?" All of it unsaid, though he sensed it just the same.

The lake was in dire need of a distraction, the scuba club fitting the bill nicely. Cousey embraced it wholeheartedly—to the tune of lake cleanups every Saturday, starting at 8:00 AM and going until dark—the one day of the week he couldn't enjoy his sunset beers, though it did make the rest of them more satisfying, and was surprised when others embraced it as well. Doris Kath's participation was invaluable. She almost never missed a cleanup, and nobody ever outworked her. Just as importantly, she was able to access heavy-duty dredging equipment in addition to the three-pronged drag she'd always used. Used by the lake's largest boats, this equipment was able to remove objects no one suspected were down there, never would have considered removing even if they had been aware, from the badly rusted Edsel that was, indeed, languishing in its depths, to half a dozen small boats.

Out of sight, out of mind appeared to be the modus operandi for disposal here. In addition, they pulled out a dozen fifty-gallon drums, about to rust through and found to contain toxic chemicals. While one would have thought much of the fish habitat would be destroyed in the process, fishermen were pleased to report fishing on the lake had actually improved. Kath became the group's second president, Cousey shifting to secretary in a move better suited to his modesty. So pleased was the Board, so eager was it to erase the debacle of the tent revival, it hosted a Thank You dinner for the scuba club at the Rod & Gun Club, with a five-course gourmet meal and an assortment of wines catered by the French restaurant in Harper. Cousey used the opportunity to propose that the lake dedicate a statue to Millie Fremont, an idea that drew a lukewarm response. It seemed no one else was of a mind to honor someone considered indirectly responsible for the deaths of seventy-eight people. Part of him saw the statue as an appeasement, all the while realizing it would do nothing to assuage the lake's communal guilt.

The year's Big Story, though relating to the lake, occurred elsewhere with the departure of Paul Mahr from the Gazette after twenty years as a full-time writer/editor and several years as a stringer. As much as anyone's job had ever been, the Gazette had been his life. No employee in its history had ever been more closely associated with the paper. Like his biting "no quarter asked/no quarter given" editorials or not, people were shocked by his "departure": the vague, PC term for the sacking of a popular employee.

Its connection with the lake was, in fact, two-pronged: the graphic photos he took of the post-revival carnage and the interview he conducted with a certain lake resident. It was enough to get a South County-based contingent of higher-ups — known in the newsroom as The Group — screaming down to Harper in a white stretch limo. The Group managed half a dozen biweeklies in the St. Louis metro area, white bread its baking preference. Mahr had been pushing the envelope, just to keep himself interested, he would have been the first to admit that for quite some time and, as far as publisher Charles Hastings, a man in his sixties who was an uncanny mix of Professor Kingsfield and the original Perry White, was concerned, he had finally crossed the line. Accompanying him was a dour, smartly-dressed woman with "Personnel" written all over her and an imposing, fortyish black man whose demeanor screamed "High-Priced Attorney!" Mahr smiled inwardly at the corporate artillery assembled against him. Having already been apprised via the grapevine that he was out and Tom Patterson, a solid if unimaginative newsman, was in, he felt anything but contrite. He had worked for these sons of bitches too long and too hard, years before they took over the Gazette and he'd been part of the deal as its ready-made editor: a one-time convenience that had morphed into a full-time liability.

How times have changed, he thought. *I've nearly gone blind for you sons of bitches.*

"Mr. Mahr," Hastings began, the very mention of his name sounding like an accusation. "If you would indulge me, what is a newspaper's primary purpose for existing?"

Mahr was in no mood for games. "Mr. Hastings, if you need to ask me that, maybe I should be the one running the show."

Hastings' face reddened. "I will not tolerate your impertinence, sir!"

"You won't have to, sir, if you refrain from asking questions that insult my intelligence. Very well, I will endeavor to humor you. The answer you want to hear is 'to sell advertising.' While I've always accepted advertising as a necessary evil that pays the bills, I would suggest a newspaper's primary purpose for existing is to serve its community by reporting things that are important to its readership."

"Just the sort of answer I would expect from you," Hastings said.

"Then why waste your time and mine by asking the question, sir?"

"Do you find these proceedings a waste of time, Mr. Mahr?"

"Yes, Mr. Hastings, frankly, I do. Because you and I both know why you are here and where this is heading. How about we cut to the chase, you give me my severance check, and we call it a day?"

Hastings smiled. "So you think that's what I'm here for?"

"Sir, seeing as how you're accompanied by a couple of 'suits' and haven't seen fit to visit our offices since you acquired us, I have no reason to think otherwise."

"Well, think again, because I'm here to offer you a new assignment."

"I'm listening."

Mahr riffled through the possibilities, the only assignment that would have appealed to him being an unlikely one — no less than a promotion — given the circumstances: editor of The County Journal, a paper with five times the circulation of the Gazette.

"It will be based in Melville," Hastings said. "We're planning to launch a consumer-based publication, something along the lines of The Tri-County Shopper."

"Sir, the Shopper is little more than a coupon book," Mahr said.

"That's not entirely true. The Shopper contains recipes and a column called 'Healthy Foods,' as our paper similarly will."

Mahr snorted with disbelief. "No doubt augmented by editorial cartoons featuring lean ground chuck flirting with ripe tomatoes. Sir, you've got to be kidding!"

"No, Mr. Mahr, I'm not."

"Then I'm not kidding when I say I'll take my severance check. This is a farce, and both of us know it!"

"As you wish. Janet?" he said, reaching for the envelope.

"No, sir, not as I wish!" Mahr said. "This paper has been my life, ever since high school. Something big is dying here."

"Not so much dying as being killed, I'm afraid — by your own hand," Hastings said.

Mentally counting to three, Mahr willed himself to remain calm.

"Sir, if you would indulge me kindly, tell me how I killed it."

"OK, Mr. Mahr. How does a graphic front-page photo grab you? An interview with a kook?"

Mahr shook his head. "The 'graphic' photo you reference of two people in the foreground, gazing at the body, is of a blurry figure lying in the grass."

"A blurry figure with blood on it."

"Sir, the photo I chose was the least graphic of all the ones I took that day while still conveying what happened."

"Couldn't you have gotten a more suitable photo from Mr. Patterson?"

"Halfway through the event, Tom felt he had his story; I told him he could go home. The birds were the real story. I merely captured a hint of what they did."

"And the interview?"

"Dr. Kevin Cousey is a retired ENT man from Harper Memorial Hospital, once highly respected in his field."

"Retired?"

"Forced into retirement when someone threw an M-80 through his car window and he lost his hand trying to throw it out."

"I'm sorry to hear that."

"In addition to finding Millie Fremont's body, Dr. Cousey has done extensive research on the possible causes of this phenomenon with the hummingbirds."

"And these causes are… paranormal?" Hastings asked a question that served as a trap.

Tired of the bullshit, Mahr waded in. "Yes, when hummingbirds kill one more person than they did the year before, in the same place and on the same date, and they've been doing it every year for a dozen years, I think it is safe to say there is a paranormal aspect to the event."

Hastings smiled in triumph, Mahr having made his point for him. "Since when is a newspaper a purveyor of paranormal news?"

Mahr would have the last laugh — not that he was laughing — as he leaned in and looked Hastings dead in the eye.

"When this paranormal phenomenon has killed seventy-eight of its readers, that's when."

Hastings emitted an exasperated sigh. The look he gave his two colleagues told them their business was finished here.

"Mr. Mahr, I'm afraid we've reached an impasse. I wish to take this opportunity to thank you for your many years of service to this paper. I can only hope you find another position that better suits your temperament."

"Mr. Hastings, we were at an impasse the moment you came through the door."

Mahr took the check and walked away in disgust.

He was so upset, so embarrassed to be thrust into a ritual understood by anyone who ever worked in an office — the dismissed employee gathering his things

— that he didn't open the check until later. When he did, he was pleasantly surprised to see a bank check for two full years' pay tucked inside a gold-scripted "Thank You" card with nothing written on it. A tear ran down his face as he considered both the amount of the check and what twenty-plus years of his life added up to. He could also file for unemployment, but he wasn't willing to endure that indignity just yet.

Give yourself a month to find something, he thought. *Not because you need anything right away, but because you need to keep busy.*

Two weeks later, he was working at the last place he ever expected to be working, enjoying the novelty of immersing himself in a foreign world of colors and shapes and smells.

***

Although Mahr had told him about it and it shouldn't have come as a surprise, Cousey couldn't get over the sight of Mahr in a green apron in the produce department of Harper's largest market.

"Hard to get used to wearing an apron instead of a camera, I'll bet," Cousey said. "So, are you the manager yet?"

"Nope, just the assistant. Don Schuster, that bald guy over by the tomatoes: He's the manager."

"Say, aren't those Romas?"

"Yes, they are."

"Man, you're a natural. I can already see it! Does it ever occur to you that you might have missed your calling, that maybe newspaper work was, I don't know, just a detour on the road to fruit and vegetable greatness?"

Mahr laughed, hard enough to get the manager's attention.

"Anyway, you've gotta work your way up to manager, here like anywhere else."

"Don still looks pretty... with it. It looks like that might be a while. Is that your intention — to wait him out?"

"I've had a couple of newspaper offers, but they're both out-of-state. My intention is to hang around here long enough to see how things play out at the lake."

"Really? Is it that big a deal for you?"

"Big enough to lose my job over."

"I'm sorry about that, Paul. I feel like I was the one who got you into this. I feel like this is my fault."

"Please, Doc, don't even start. This is my community; I care about what happens here, too. Truth be known, I've been treading water for quite some time. I was in a rut, but it was a comfortable rut, the evil that I knew; too comfortable to make me realize I needed to get myself out of it. They made that decision for me, that's all. While it's a little humiliating how they went about it, seeing as how I worked for them for twenty years, maybe it'll end up being a good thing, the kick in the pants I needed to move on."

"A good way to look at it, Paul; I can certainly relate to your humiliation after how I was treated at the hospital, and I admire your attitude. Hey, tapping into your new area of expertise, do you know anything about avocados? I was going to make some guacamole tonight. Doris and Sheila are coming over for a Mexican potluck dinner; you always have a standing invitation to join us, by the way. Sheila's got a knack for Mexican food, and I make a mean pitcher of margaritas if I say so myself: The trick is to use Triple Sec, fresh lime juice as opposed to pasteurized lime juice in a little plastic bottle, ice cubes instead of slush, and no salt. Whoever thought to salt the rim of a margarita glass deserves to be flogged. The salt just accumulates in the bottom of the glass and spoils the last few mouthfuls."

Mahr smiled. "My thoughts exactly. It's always an education with you, Doc. Thanks, but I'll have to take a raincheck this time. I have a date, you see."

"Oh?"

"Have you seen that little cutie who works in the deli?"

"The little cutie who caught my eye as I was coming in? You're kidding! She's a dish... but you must have twenty years on her!"

"Hey, it doesn't bother me if it doesn't bother her. A lot of younger women are into father figures, you know."

"Tell me about it," Cousey said. "I have to beat them off with a stick."

"Seriously, there are some silver linings to this job. Like regular hours, less stress, and fruits and vegetables being a hell of a lot easier on the eyes than trying to make sense of bad writing on a computer monitor all day. And now her."

"As long as things go well between you, that is," Cousey said. "If it doesn't, you have to face that little sweetie pie every day. You know what they say about shitting in your own backyard."

"True enough, but at least you can't smell it on the other side of the store. I can avoid her if I must. Now about those avocados?"

"Right. I never seem to be able to pick a good one. It's either so hard you can't eat it for a week or so bruised that half of it is ready for the trash. Any trick to picking a good one?"

Mahr grinned at him. "Yes, it's one of the first things Don taught me. I know it seems counterintuitive, but if you want one you can eat tonight, pick one a little harder than what you would normally consider ripe, because anything that feels ripe has already been picked over — squeezed; bruised — several times. Also, see if that little bud at the end will push in; push in as opposed to cave in. Pick one that is slightly hard, one that gives a little at the end, and I can almost guarantee you the skin will peel away like a beautiful woman slipping out of her negligee."

Cousey laughed. "Ooooh, I like the sound of that! You have a way with words, Mr. Mahr. You should have been a writer... or at least an editor."

"I'll take that under advisement," Mahr said. "Now, if you'll excuse me, Don has been flashing me 'When Are You Getting Back To Work?' glances for a couple of minutes now. I ask you: Does his head not look like a tomato? And I have some freshly dyed navel oranges that are dry and in need of stacking like cannonballs."

"You're kidding me."

"About the dyeing or the stacking?"

"The dyeing, of course."

"No, I'm not. America is probably the only country where you'll ever see bright orange oranges. In other countries they're usually green."

"And you thought I was an education. Pardon me while I go squeeze the Charmin," Cousey said.

Chapter XVII

For the rest of the year the days at the lake passed peacefully enough, even during its Next Big Sociological Experiment: the addition of another lesbian couple when Doris Kath did what she'd always intended — have Sheila Norwood move in with her. She couldn't have orchestrated it more perfectly, waiting until she had established herself as a solid citizen before pushing the envelope. She even ran it by Cousey beforehand, he informing her of the reception the lake's previous minority residents had received. Sharing his theories as to why it had happened and how it might be avoided in the future. Strangely, the lake was so taken by Sheila's beauty and social graces, so impressed that Kath could land such a woman, that the discreet addition of Sheila to Kath's household only enhanced her status on the lake. As a couple they were outgoing without being overbearing, ever putting themselves in the middle of things as if it were only natural to do so while keeping their sexuality behind closed doors — where the consensus here was that even heterosexuality should be. Having no houses on either side of them was, of course, a boon to their privacy.

After April 15th, the rest of the year felt like a great moving away from the anxiety that had built up and finally peaked, another series of burials its denouement. Yet when the new year rolled around, its arrival made more ominous by the dead, gray cold of winter, Cousey could sense a gradual ratcheting up of tension as the months peeled away and April 15th loomed like a black square on the calendar, with it a seeming acceleration of time. The first three-and-a-half months of the new year always bore down on the lake so fast, and this year a feeling of anxiety had overtaken even him. Especially him, given the bittersweet nature of getting The Bad Guy while failing to solve The Larger Problem, all the while being expected to have The Answer. All too soon it was April again. The Answer, if, indeed, there was to be one, came to him in his dreams, but like everything in dreams, it seemed strange, so troubling as to make him wonder if it were, indeed, The Answer. Still, these dreams were variations on a theme so constant as to make him believe there was something to them. Then, on the night of April 13th, he dreamed again:

Almost invariably he was seated in one of the two chairs flanking the stump — the second one a constant with Mahr's frequent visits — beer in hand as he watched the sunset. Millie Fremont was on the grass at Michael's feet, reminiscent of the girl in Wyeth's *Christina's World*. Like its polio-stricken subject, there was a sadness about Millie as she sat on the grass. Her arms were bruised, her face swollen and purple around her left eye, her two front teeth moving as she talked. There was a sadness about her — until he looked into her eyes. They were dark balls of fire, with a deadness and ferocity not of the human world. In them, he saw the pent-up rage of the hummingbirds, released in torturous increments, a slow progression of death that hung over the lake and, come April 15th of every year, collected its grim tax. She gazed up at him from the statue's feet, the sight of her chilling the blood in his veins.

He fought back his fears and addressed her. "Millie, come sit with me. I'll get you a soda."

"I cannot join you," she said, her voice flat and dead. "No longer am I of your world."

"But your hummingbirds are, Millie... and your hummingbirds are killing people."

"Killing bad people!" Millie cried, the flames rising in her eyes. "Bad people who knew what was happening to me... and did nothing! Bad people who deserve to die!"

"John Galvin was a bad man, Millie. He deserved what he got. But the rest of them aren't bad, just weak. Most people are just weak, Millie. Afraid to do anything even when they know it is the right thing."

"The Germans were 'afraid to do anything' when Hitler was killing Jews! The Chinese were 'afraid to do anything' when Mao was killing his own people, and the Soviets were 'afraid to do anything' when Stalin was killing his own people! The U.N. was 'afraid to do anything' when the Hutus were killing the Tutsis and the Serbs were killing the Bosnians and Bashir was killing his own people in Sudan! They were all 'afraid to do anything'... and see what happened! Fear is no excuse!"

"Millie, I couldn't agree more. All of these things were terrible. What happened to you was terrible. But how much vengeance is enough?"

"Until everyone who was a part of it is gone."

"Even their children?"

"Their children are a part of them. Their children share their genes."

"But genes don't make people bad, Millie. Genes are a possibility, not a certainty. You were a child, and you were hurt, even killed. Is it right that you should kill other children, children who were too young to know what was going on? Children who weren't even born?"

"I do not kill them," Millie said. "The birds kill them."

"You control the birds, Millie. You are their queen, and they love you. If you tell them to stop, they will stop. Will you please tell them to stop?"

"My spirit is angry. It is not at peace."

"I know it isn't, Millie, and I don't blame it... or you. The adults deserve to be punished. Maybe they deserve to die. But the children? Will you at least stop them from killing the children, Millie?"

Millie gazed up at him. It surprised him to hear her sigh. The fire had left her eyes, though the darkness remained. Death had taken all the sweetness out of her, leaving a grim and calculating hardness in its place.

"Yes."

A warm rush of hope raced up his spine.

"I will trade their lives," she said, "even the lives of the adults. I will trade them all... for yours."

Cousey sprang awake, staring wide-eyed into the darkness, his T-shirt damp with sweat. It was 4:00 AM, early even for him, but when he couldn't get back to sleep, he got up and made coffee. He drank coffee and thought about the dream as the cool of early morning, the mist rising from the lake like wisps of spirit, gradually becoming tendrils of spun silver as the sun came up and another day eased into gear with all the sublime subtlety nature could muster.

The dreams gave him pause, the message they hammered home night after night increasingly clear. The evening of April 14th was especially momentous, with it the feeling of a last day. Because he suspected tomorrow would mark the most significant change of all, not for a lake that had resigned itself to business as usual, but for him. Something bothered him about tomorrow, and it wasn't so much the momentousness of the day as the notion it would end without the fulfillment of his mission. The notion that the best he could hope for was a martyrdom that, while perhaps enshrining his memory, benefitted no one.

At first, his mission appeared to be medicine. He envisioned joining Doctors Without Borders some day when the kids were old enough to embrace a Grand African Adventure. Then Theroux's *Mosquito Coast* came along and shot that idea all to hell. Such humanitarian ventures were great for an idealistic loner, not so great for a family man whose life hinged on responsibility. No, any mission he undertook would have to be here, which, when he thought about it, wasn't so unlikely. Mission was everywhere, and all you had to do was open your eyes and be willing to leave your comfort zone and involve yourself in other people's lives.

Then came the firecracker, and his mission was reduced to one of mere survival as he struggled for a reason to keep living. Not until Millie Fremont came to the lake and he became aware of her plight did his sense of mission return. And yet it seemed a red herring, his inability to do anything about it — especially after finding her body and pinning it on Galvin — causing his shoulders to sag beneath the weight of impotence. Until now. Once again, the possibility of achieving something meaningful dangled before his eyes like a jewel on a golden chain that was just out of reach, albeit at a grim price, and even then, who knew how it would all shake out? Nature's logic never danced with man's, the latter having left their communal dance floor years ago.

Sheila had gifted him with her recipe for shrimp fajitas, including the distinctive way she seasoned her charro-style beans and rice, and he made them tonight, pleased that his results should approximate hers.

Too bad I won't be able to tell her about it, he thought somberly.

There was a Last Supper feel to dinner tonight, preceded by a whole pitcher of margaritas on the stump at sunset. He hadn't gotten this trashed since that fateful night twenty-one years ago, and he was determined to reach a similar state of oblivion, however artificial and temporary, always with the next day to answer to. The sky was always pepper red in his dreams of Millie. Something unsettling about it being that color tonight, the 'red sky at night' part of the saying notwithstanding. He gazed at the sky, at the lake and its swimming platform — finally graced with new boards, courtesy of the scuba club (who else?) — and the dam and the trees behind it, the rustling already underway, a rustling that would grow to a deafening crescendo when they rose above the trees and embarked on their menacing swirl around the platform at 7:00 AM. He wondered what the lake would look like from out there, what their response would be if anyone dared encroach upon their shrine at that crucial time. How their wings and, soon enough, their beaks would feel as they closed in on him. He took in his surroundings with a pleasant sort of detachment, his mental meanderings well-cushioned by alcohol as Michael framed it all with the gentle, golden curve of his wings. Tequila was the femme fatale who lulled you to sleep only to become an ugly, ill-tempered bitch when she awakened you the next morning. Murderous hangover that awaited him or not, there was no pleasant way to face tomorrow. Tonight this condemned man would take whatever pleasures he could.

Including an after-dinner movie. He surfed the movie channels, not finding anything of interest until he stumbled upon an old friend he always seemed to stumble upon somewhere in the middle, to the point he doubted he had ever seen the whole thing. He smiled at the irony of coming across Hitchcock's *The Birds*, tonight of all nights.

Tippi Hedren was having a cigarette on a bench in the school playground as she waited for Suzanne Pleshette to finish her class. All the while, the birds were massing on the swing sets and monkey bars behind her as the children sang a bird-like song that perfectly echoed their movements, a scene that ended with Hedren reacting in horror when she found herself surrounded by thousands of birds.

A brilliant piece of editing! Cousey thought. *Up there with the shower scene in* Psycho*!*

The school was on the outskirts of town, and Cousey watched as Pleshette proceeded to evacuate the kids — on foot, no less — as the birds attacked them. He couldn't help but laugh in disbelief.

Brilliance juxtaposed with stupidity; two more disparate scenes could not have been written! They're in the comparative safety of the school, and the teacher violates every rule of common sense not only by bringing the kids outside, thus provoking birds that have yet to attack, but further attracting their attention by having the kids run to town! Holy "Plot flaw big enough to drive a truck through," Batman!

Be they in books or movies, plot flaws drove him nuts. The spell of his interest broken, he decided to call it a night. He was barely able to make it up the stairs, the runner writhing like an anaconda under his feet, singing "Tequila" as he cleaned up in the most perfunctory of ways — rinsing his mouth out; splashing his face; getting his shoes off but keeping his clothes on — and fell into a numbed sleep. A thread of method ran through the madness of this evening: alcohol to anesthetize him, spicy food to enliven his dreams and hopefully provide some insight into what lay ahead.

For four hours, he was dead as a floating log, his head in a Mexican vise when he got up to urinate. He threw back a couple of heavy-duty pain meds with extra water — complete rehydration would have to wait until morning, thus forgoing the need to piss every hour — then headed back to bed. This time the show began in earnest, unlike anything he had dreamed before:

He dreamed he was naked, echoing the spread-winged posture of the St. Michael statue he stood in front of. His skin was sticky, tasted sweet when he put his tongue to his forearm. The sun had just risen, and he shivered in the chill of early morning. His arms felt leaden, but he could not lower them, even though the insects were tickling his armpits. No one was on the lake, but it occurred to him that someone might be watching from his window, standing there buck naked for all the world to see like a misfit scarecrow.

The nakedness of an old man whose body had seen better years especially made him self-conscious. Soon it was displaced by fear as the rustling in the trees behind the dam became a flurry of activity, the birds rising into the air for their pregame ritual, commencing their raucous convergence of the swimming platform.

How could anything so frightening be so beautiful? he thought, likening the phenomenon to a fiery funnel cloud. Watching as their bodies teemed with all the colors of the rainbow in the morning sunshine.

Then, as if on cue — he wasn't wearing his watch, but it had to be seven-fifteen — the birds on the platform rose to meet the birds in the air in a massive, deafening coil of life. Rose and came at him like fear itself, tiny, cold eyes briefly meeting his before disappearing in his near vision, the thorns of their beaks taking out one eye, then the other.

"Ahhh! Ahhh!" he cried, but he knew it would happen… and it was better this way.

Better not to see what they were about to inflict on him, the onslaught of a thousand needles: not doing acupuncture, not inflicting the minor discomfort of a tattoo, but actively seeking to kill. Seeking out every soft spot, starting with the veins, moving to the neck and armpits, the tender skin in the crooks of the knees and fingers and elbows, the genitals. Occasionally they dug into something especially painful, and it was better not to see it, to merely endure a nebulous, preternatural torture that blurred the line between the real and the unreal, with it a blessed numbing of sensation as he finally crossed the barrier from one dimension to the next. He saw nothing, felt nothing as the pecking finally stopped and he found himself plunged into a dark, womblike void.

He cried out as he sprang awake, the darkness real enough. His head was pounding, adding to the disorientation of awakening in an unknown place at night. For a full minute, he sat up in bed, hugging his knees to his chest as if they were mooring him to the bed, trying to regain his composure. Gradually he realized where he was, letting out a sigh of relief. He checked the bedside clock: four-fifteen.

Three hours, he thought.

Everyone would be watching the clock this morning. Determined to be proactive in spite of his fear, he used the toilet, splashed his face with cold water, and threw back two more pain pills, this time with a lot of water. He popped the leftover beans, rice, and tortillas into the oven, added the leftover shrimp, onions, tomatoes, and peppers to half a dozen eggs — *cholesterol is one thing I don't have to worry about!* he thought — in a large skillet, and whipped himself up some huevos rancheros, Hombre de Cousey-style, with salsa on the side. There was something about eggs.

Any day that demands your best demands eggs, he thought, trying to lighten the mood by pretending he was doing a commercial. *I think it's called gallows humor,* he thought, carrying his breakfast with a pot of coffee to the deck.

As things tend to when you know you are seeing them for the last time, every detail took on an added significance this morning. The air had a slight piney smell as he opened the door and strode out onto the deck. There were few pines on the lake, his sense of smell being his least-developed, yet he could never remember smelling them before. The wooden deck had a slightly ringing, hollow sound as he walked across it, the chair he pulled out scraping against it like a jet at high altitude. A darkness that was never really black was morphing into ever-less-subtle gradations of midnight blue, interrupted only by the glimmer of a light, the pale side of a boat, in its gradual journey to daylight. Complete darkness was the stuff of tourist caves, one guide after another seizing upon the would-be novelty of turning off all the lights in an underground place that had no business being anything but dark.

As much as the growing daylight, its accompanying quiet made this his second favorite time of day. Even then, the quiet was relative, tinged with the dreamy murmur of night birds, the wind hushing through the trees, the passing of a faraway plane that seemed even farther away in a night that tended to push things away only to have them drawn back in by the day. Always the scratches on the record: a barking dog; an arriving or departing car; the throaty roar of a motorcycle or a diesel engine on a distant highway.

Kevin Cousey enjoyed the contrast between the cool, invigorating air that enveloped him and the hot, head-soothing food and drink he was taking in. It was like huddling around a campfire, and he meditated on the pleasantness of this dichotomy as the first hints of day arrived. The advent of day was both the gradual addition of light and the gradual dissolution of darkness, one natural phenomenon displacing another until the first pinkening of the horizon announced the sun's approach like the whistle of an oncoming train. Pink was followed by orange and then blue, tinged with purple, gray if there were clouds, and there were clouds this morning. A strange thing happened, and Cousey wasn't sure if his mind was playing tricks on him after the damage he'd inflicted on his gray matter last night: The entire sky froze, everything hovering in horizontal bands for what seemed a full ten minutes before going about its business. It reminded him of the sky in Munch's *The Scream*, and the appropriateness of that metaphor wasn't lost on him today. As the celestial show unfolded he found himself expecting the blood-red sky of his dreams, the red sky of sailors' warnings. Instead, it blossomed into the most beautiful sunrise he had ever seen, making him wish he'd taken his breakfast down to the stump for an unobstructed view.

A good day to die, he couldn't help but think.

He usually kept a neat — as opposed to fastidious — house, and he would leave it that way today.

Never be caught dead in dirty underwear, he thought, remembering the words that could have only come from a mother.

"Shit!" he said when the plate he was washing slipped from his hands and broke the handle off his favorite coffee cup, a heavy ceramic number he'd had forever.

What the hell difference does it make? he thought with a sad smile.

When it became clear what these dreams were pointing to, he'd gone to his attorney and gotten his affairs in order. Even in his relatively healthy sixties, it felt strange to be contemplating what he'd be leaving behind, and for whom. Stranger still when he could so well remember being in his forties: at or near the top of his profession, seemingly indestructible. Regardless of the happy memories, he was not sentimental about his family. His daughter, who still met him for lunch in St. Louis, still told him she loved him and he still believed her, would get half of his estate minus the house. He decided Paul Mahr, a local in every positive sense of the word, a man who loved a lake his daughter would never visit, would get the house. People like Mahr were good for the area, and he was afraid Mahr would get discouraged and leave. The house was a sneaky way to keep him here. His wife who bailed on him when The Dream became The Nightmare, who'd left him for dead when he needed her most, whose apathy since the divorce had settled the matter in his mind; his son whom he never saw or even heard from — they would get as good as they gave: nothing. The other half of his estate would go for scholarships to the juco nursing program, nurses being the forgotten foot soldiers of the medical world. In the end, he was satisfied.

Thinking of Mahr gave him an idea.

I wonder if he's up this early on a Saturday? I wonder if he has to work today? Screw it, I'm calling him! He won't be annoyed with me for very long! he thought.

***

Just as he finished mixing up a concoction that was equal parts sugar and water, pouring it through a funnel into an empty gallon jug, there was a knock on his door.

"Come in!" Cousey said, slopping some of the mixture over the brim of the funnel when he turned his head.

Another mess. Who the hell cares?

Paul Mahr stumbled in. Although he looked technically prepared — there was a camera around his neck and a camcorder tethered to his hand, an extra videocassette in one pocket of his cargo pants, and an extra microcassette and spare batteries in the other — Mahr looked anything but physically prepared. In fact, he looked as if he had just gotten up.

"Have you had breakfast?" Cousey asked.

"No."

"Have some; you'll need the energy. There's some leftover beans and rice and huevos rancheros on the stove, probably still warm. Sheila's recipe, and I think I came close to doing it justice. There's also some salsa and half of one of your avocados — good advice, by the way! — in the fridge. There's still some coffee in the cowboy pot; I reckon I'd opt for the stove over the microwave if'n you want to heat it up, pardner."

"Sounds good," Mahr said, helping himself as Cousey wiped the jug and screwed the cap on.

"So, tell me," he said as Cousey poured himself a cup and joined him at the kitchen table, "are you sure about this?"

"It's like this, Paul: I can't keep living like this, pretending life is good 364 days of the year when that 365th day is what it's all about. I told you about my dreams. I have a feeling about this. There's a chance my life can still serve a purpose, and if, perchance, it can help the lake while helping you-know-who pop start his career, hey, why not give it a go?"

Mahr eyed him steadily. "Because I'm going to miss you, Doc. I'm not so sure I can just stand there and maintain my 'professional distance' like some National Geo photographer, capturing it all on film while you're busy getting pecked to death."

"Don't disappoint me, Paul. Don't back out now. If I'm going to get pecked to death, the least you can do is capture it all on film and write a hell of a story to go with it. You know, immortalize me, if it helps you to frame it that way. Is your recorder on?"

"No, but I think I can remember what you've said. One nice thing about dead guys: They can't sue you for libel."

Cousey cracked a smile. "Are you with me on this, Paul?"

Mahr sighed. "Yes, Doc, I suppose I am. I've come too far not to be, although I'm sure what I'm about to see will haunt me for the rest of my life."

"Paul, do you think the deaths on this lake haven't haunted me, especially when you consider I haven't been able to do a damn thing about them? Do you think the family members, the next-door neighbors, the people on the lake who knew these people, aren't haunted by them?"

Mahr sighed. "Point well taken. I guess I'm as ready as I'll ever be."

"Good. Now let's get this place turned off and locked up and ourselves down to the boat. Damn, it's already six-thirty!"

"The boat?"

"I'll tell you on the way. Here, take the keys. This one's the house key."

"Can't I just fish them out of your pocket afterward?"

"Do you really want to? Besides, they might fall into the water. Besides, it's about to be your house, anyway."

"Say what?"

"I'm willing you my house."

Mahr smiled and rubbed his hands together in mock greed. "Gee, this might work out better than I thought!"

Cousey laughed, and it was just what they needed to cut the tension.

***

It was 6:45 by the time they reached the swimming platform, Cousey shedding his clothes in the chill morning air. For the sake of modesty and the threat of arrest for indecent exposure — *Just my luck to get busted before this all goes down*, he thought — all that remained were his boxers and a pair of shorts that looked as if they'd escaped a luau. He hoisted himself up the ladder and stepped onto the platform, immediately getting a splinter from one of the new planks.

"Damn!" he said, inspecting his big toe. "At least I don't have to worry about pulling it. Hand me the jug," he said to Mahr. "This is the part I'm not looking forward to. Strike that: the first part I'm not looking forward to. Shee-it!" he said, pouring the liquid over his head and letting it run down his body like syrup on a stack of pancakes. Making a face as he splashed his armpits.

"Yuck!" he said, handing the empty jug back to Mahr.

"OK, why the swimming platform?"

"A couple of reasons," Cousey said. "First, this is where they congregate before they attack. What time is it?"

"Six fifty-four."

"Is your watch accurate?"

"I just got a new battery, and I always set it by GMT."

"OK, in about six minutes they'll be heading this way. Six minutes... shit!"

Cousey shivered, and it was as much from anticipation as the morning chill. Physically or spiritually, he could never remember feeling more out of his element.

"Anyway, this is the one place where I know they'll come."

"And the second reason?"

"If I can head them off here before they all disperse at seven-fifteen, maybe they never get started. What time is it, Paul?"

"Three minutes."

"OK, time for you to pull back to a safe distance while still affording yourself a good vantage point."

Mahr eased the boat a hundred feet away.

Cousey called out to him. "You've got a telephoto lens, right?"

"Yes."

"Use it. Stay safe."

"Says the man walking to the lethal injection room. I'm sure going to enjoy that house."

Cousey laughed, and with that, the birds rose from the trees.

***

Kevin Cousey raised his arms, a strange feeling of calm settling over him as the birds descended onto the swimming platform. He had never witnessed anything so strangely beautiful as a tornado of birds seen from within — surpassing even the Northern Lights for its sheer novelty — forming a tube of colorful, frantic, deafening activity all around him. He could sense their confusion, unused to having their shrine occupied by an interloper at this, the unlikeliest of times. They wheeled around him in ever-growing numbers, pressing close but not touching. Somewhere in his racing thoughts Cousey suspected they were trying to shoo him into the water. Sticky and uncomfortable as he was, the thought of taking the plunge was tempting. Ultimately, the birds faced the conundrum of an untouchable in a touchable place. Still, it was never far from his mind that he was an obstacle, undeserving of death but needing to be circumvented like Fritz the Rottweiler or the Baxters. While they weren't killed, some of them were maimed, and that's where his thoughts were gravitating as the commotion ensued all around him.

The birds drew ever closer, the chirping of their collective voices and the roaring of their collective wings ringing in his ears. It was a sound he would never forget… if he survived to remember it. Feeling uneasy as he felt the feathery beat of their wings, his heartbeat quickening as he steeled himself for the impending attack. They were that close, close enough to cover him like the latter part of a tarring and feathering. They were getting uncomfortably close to his eyes, so close that he shut them instinctively, all the while bracing himself for that first stab through the eyelid.

Finally, the first real contact.

Something touched his skin, and it wasn't a wing or a beak. It was a light, fleeting sensation, and soon it was happening all over his body. Cautiously he opened an eye and slowly turned his head, incredulous at the sight of tiny tongues flicking everywhere. The hummingbirds were licking the nectar, from his body. He felt as if he were being tickled by a myriad of tiny feathers, a sensation that was almost unbearable. It was all he could do to stand there and take it, not bring his arms down on the maddening tickle in his armpits that might have killed some of them and broken the spell and possibly even gotten him killed. For a time that seemed endless but was actually thirty-two minutes and fourteen seconds on the timer of Mahr's video cam — realizing he couldn't do two things well at once, he'd opted for video over still shots — Cousey stood like a statue while the birds lapped the nectar off him, his body transformed into a giant feeder. By the time they were finished he was shaking with laughter, his movements dislodging some of them only to be replaced by others. Incredibly, they weren't alarmed. None of them pecked him. He watched the spectacle all around him with both eyes now, the smile on his face so big that his cheeks were cramping up with the rest of him.

A dark thought intruded upon his reverie.

They never eat on the day of an attack. Today they're gassing up on high-octane fuel. Could they be using me as a mother log for the mother of all attacks?

Instead, a pair of unlikely things occurred:

Girlish laughter — it had to be Millie's — echoing around the lake.

Reger's *Basso Ostinato in E Minor* forming the mental soundtrack for the spectacle that played out before him, the hummingbirds forming an inverted funnel broad as the lake, tapering into a teeming, swirling column of life as it plunged not outward, but upward.

And disappeared without dispatching the thirteen people for this year's quota. Sparing the lake for the first time in thirteen years.

Mahr's camera followed them all the way into the heavens before panning back down to Cousey. Easing the boat up to the swimming platform with one hand as he continued shooting with the other.

Oh my God, could she finally be at peace? the impossible thought played through Cousey's mind.

He was on his hands and knees when wave after wave of great, heaving sobs shook him. Mahr saw it — and understood. Before him was no less than the resolution of a war, one that had begun long before the hummingbirds, its opening salvo a small piece of dynamite that had forever changed a man's life. The ropy, slimy body before him was no less than an emaciated Atlas, the weight of the grief and emptiness and impotence he had carried for so long tumbling from his shoulders with an almost palpable splash into the lake, like a dreary procession of boxcars that had finally reached its destination.

Mahr broke the silence. "You said it yourself, Doc: 'They never feed on April 15th.'"

The look Cousey gave him was beyond exhaustion, yet somewhere in his eyes a glimmer remained.

"I know! I know! I know! — and you just saw them feed, from the funkiest bird feeder you'll ever see!" he said. "My, did they feed! Damn near tickled this old man to death! My biggest fear was to give in to the tickling and bring my arms down and crush some of them and, heaven forbid, maybe spoil it all!"

Mahr laughed. "I hear you! Better almost tickled to death than pecked to death, I suppose."

Cousey had the wide-eyed look of an idiot. "Paul, could it be? Could it really be?"

"Let's have a look-see," Mahr said, panning the lake, the sky above it, with his camera. "Nope, I detect not a single hummingbird."

"Oh, God!" Cousey said, loosing a fresh barrage of tears.

Mahr concentrated on filming, trying to capture the mood while mixing things up with a wide variety of pans and zoom-ins and zoom-outs. When the cassette ran out, he popped in another, the sound of it breaking the spell. Cousey emerged from his trance and spoke to Mahr, who kept the camera running. An impromptu interview emerged, one Mahr realized was crucial in telling the story.

I'm a local, he thought, *and proud of it!*

He couldn't help but beam at Cousey.

"Doc, this humble observer thinks you're the closest thing to St. Michael this lake has ever seen!"

"Nonsense!" Cousey said. "Have you seen my statue? Why, it looks a hell of a lot more like him than I do — if anyone really knows what he looks like. By the way, tell me you heard what I heard when the birds rose into the sky."

Mahr looked puzzled. "All I heard was the birds, Doc."

"Shit, I really have rounded the bend," Cousey said. "I heard a girl's laughter... I'm sure it was Millie's... echoing all around the lake."

Mahr smiled. "Maybe you're not crazy, Doc, just gifted; it's all about marketing, you know. Oh-oh, we just killed my second and last tape, but, miraculously, you live on. Does this mean I don't get the house?"

Cousey laughed. "It means you might have to wait a few years. I may be happy enough to hang around awhile."

"It never fails: The good ones die young while the ornery ones last forever. Sounds like it's time to plan an unfortunate, alcohol-related boating accident," Mahr said.

Cousey laughed in earnest. "Nothing far-fetched about that on this lake! Honestly, Paul, you'll love it here."

"I already do. I might not even wait for you to kick before I move here."

"It would be great to have you for a neighbor. Hey, get ready for some fast driving," Cousey said, "I just realized how goddamn sticky I am, and I don't want to track this shit into the boat; I can already see the ants! I'm about to take a dip and freeze my ever-lovin' ass off."

And with that, he came perilously close to a belly flop in the most awkward dive ever executed.

"Damn, that's cold!" he said, suddenly feeling ferociously vital in spite of his age.

Mahr laughed. "It's always something with you old-timers."

"Brrr! I don't think I'm going to renew my membership in the Polar Bear Club after all!"

Chapter XVIII

Seeing as how Cousey had overdone it the night before, they waited until the following night to celebrate at the Mexican restaurant in Harper. So lusty was their reveling that Cousey hired a taxi to take them home. There he offered Mahr the guest bedroom — with it the loan of some fresh socks and underwear — and a nice brunch before retrieving Cousey's pickup at the restaurant the next morning.

Mahr managed to smile at Cousey over coffee through their mutual hangovers.

"No church this morning?"

"I've already been to church," Cousey said. "Lord, have I been to church!"

"With your permission, Doc, I'd like to do something with the footage I shot."

"Have at it," Cousey said, "with one condition: Promise you won't turn me into a sex symbol."

Mahr laughed. "Gee, I don't know if it can be avoided, Doc. I'll do my best."

***

Mahr brought the cassettes to a friend in the city who did video editing.

"For a non-pro your voice is pretty good, Paul; I don't think we need to dub this," he said. "Built-in mikes are better than they used to be. I think the overall sound quality is good enough to air this puppy as-is, albeit with some editing. I'm assuming that's the goal."

Mahr smiled. "Why not? How much usable film do we have?"

"Damn near all of it, I'd say. You did a good job. Enough for a ninety-minute docu if we make it tight, 120 minutes if we stretch it a bit."

"How about we go the 120-minute route, retaining the option of paring it down to ninety minutes if we need to?"

Paul's friend regarded him with mock graveness. "OK, but it'll cost you."

"How much?"

"Dinner, restaurant of my choice."

"You've got it, pardner."

"Cool!" his friend said. "I've always wanted to check out the Russian Tea Room."

"In St. Louis, smarty-pants."

"OK, you win. Just don't forget us 'little people' when you make it big."

***

The finished product was better than he'd expected, utterly professional-looking with a title, credits, and captions. Mahr opted against music, figuring such an addition would only be cheesy, and that someone who knew how could always add some later on. Just as he was contemplating his marketing strategy, his phone rang. Word had gotten out about the tape, as far as the East Coast. Mahr listened to them all, ultimately deciding to retain the services of an attorney who specialized in intellectual property rights.

"The only hurdle I can see is the subject of this documentary objecting to the release of a film that pertains to him. I would need what is called a 'permission,'" the attorney said.

"Dr. Cousey has already given me his verbal permission," Mahr said.

"I need something in writing, at least an email."

"I should be able to get it to you by tomorrow."

Mahr did and went with National Geographic, where he ended up with photojournalism assignments in Australia, Antarctica, and Easter Island in a sequence of events that struck him as no less than surreal. Suddenly he was the next Sir David Attenborough, the darling of the documentary world.

***

Kevin Cousey wasn't immune from the film's impact, either. One evening he broached the subject with Mahr over beers at the lake.

"You'll never guess who called me today."

"The hospital, offering you your old job back with a substantial raise?"

"No."

"Um, my girlfriend, saying she prefers the grandfatherly type to the fatherly type?"

Cousey laughed. "Nope, not even that."

"Hmm, let me see now… The AMA saying that last ENT article you wrote led to a surprising cure for AIDS?"

Cousey laughed so hard the beer came out his nose. "Damn you, Paul! I haven't done that since high school!

"You were drinking beer in high school?"

"Actually, it was milk."

"Yuck! Gosh, if it isn't any of those, I don't know what it could be. OK, lay it on me."

"It was an invitation to appear on a late-night talk show in New York, followed by a morning news show." Cousey regarded Mahr with mock accusation. "Don't forget your promise."

"Please refresh my memory."

"That you wouldn't turn me into a sex symbol… and all this celebrity stuff is coming dangerously close! Too many armpit shots, I think."

Mahr laughed. "Hey, your arms were out and I was shooting from below; what was I supposed to do? At least you didn't follow your dream to the letter and lose the shorts and undies."

***

So impressed was he by Mahr's handling of a hummingbird story one major weekly news magazine called "the documentation of an event so singular that it stands alone," Charles Hastings did, indeed, offer him the editorship of the Countian, at twice his previous salary, the use of a three-bedroom house and a Lexus, and six weeks paid vacation per year. Resisting the urge to tell the man off outright — he decided his days of staring into a computer screen were over, and that some things were just too easy — he said he would "give it some thought" on his way back from Australia and never got back to him. In the meantime, he used monies from his burgeoning career as a documentarian to buy a two-bedroom house on the lake and a nice little boat to go with his new Honda S2000, further solidifying the affections of his deli cutie who already loved him for his wit and wavy hair. Within a year they were married, and within two they were expecting their first child, forcing him to trade in the S2000 for an Accord.

Kevin Cousey weathered the celebrity storm "abroad" only to find it waiting for him when he returned to the lake. To say "weathered" was apropos, because it wore on him. While he was glad Mahr had made the most of this opportunity, more and more he found himself wishing things could return to normal, which was difficult because he was central to the story.

Once again his thoughts turned to the *Bible: They have their reward.*

And yet he had never sought a reward, at least insofar as fame and fortune were concerned. It was enough to feel he'd accomplished something, to have the place where he had chosen to live finally be at peace. It all came to a head at the mandatory dinner the Board held in his honor at the Rod & Gun Club, one at which he was the keynote speaker and which was catered by the same French restaurant as before. Paul Mahr attended with his radiant young wife, and Doris Kath brought the equally radiant Sheila. Seeing them in the audience was a balm to his spirits as they exchanged conspiratorial smiles.

The chairman, big and red-faced and fat enough to give the impression he attended many such dinners, kicked off the proceedings with a broad smile.

"Ladies and gentlemen, Board members and their significant others, and our distinguished guests, I am pleased to welcome you to this dinner of the Lake Tanaka Board of Directors. Tonight we celebrate the accomplishments of a man who has always managed to be modest and down-to-earth in spite of his professional credentials. A man who has shunned the spotlight while overcoming the obstacles in his path. Problem is some accomplishments are too big to ignore, the light they produce too bright to hide under the proverbial bushel basket. What with his recent celebrity, the lake's own Dr. Kevin Cousey knows this all too well," he said, smiling over at Cousey at the head table.

Already on display, Cousey squirmed in his skin, his return smile more of a grimace.

"But there is no escaping greatness," the chairman continued. "If great people don't hold themselves up — and people who are truly great have neither the time nor the inclination for self-glorification — rest assured those of us who appreciate their contributions will! That is why, after conferring with my fellow Board members, tonight I am proposing the first-ever statue dedicated to a lake resident: a life-sized rendering of Dr. Kevin Cousey."

Applause swept through the room as Cousey sat there, mortified. Even as smiling faces gazed his way, his face fell, his body tensing with an emotion he struggled to hold in check; and hold it in check he must before he rose to speak. The last thing he wanted to do was alienate well-meaning people. At the same time, he needed to get his point across.

"We already have some money in our budget to get started with this, left over from road maintenance after another light winter. Depending on how much additional funds we can raise, the plan is for the statue to be made of either granite or, preferably, bronze. We already have several likenesses of Dr. Cousey; we're leaning toward something candid, not posed or hokey-looking. We've all seen too many statues like that, haven't we?"

General laughter.

"Anyway, Doc, if you have a picture of yourself you're especially fond of, we're open to suggestions."

Cousey regarded the chairman with a tight-lipped smile.

"Now, without further ado, may I present to you the man of the hour, Lake Tanaka's own Dr. Kevin Cousey!"

Raucous applause as Cousey rose to his feet, smiling self-consciously as he moved to the podium. The initial shock having worn off, he had regained control.

"Mister Chairman, Members of the Board, ladies and gentlemen, your kindness overwhelms me. Really, this lovely dinner would have been more than enough thanks for anything I might have done, which, frankly, amounted to nothing more than turning myself into the world's ugliest hummingbird feeder."

General laughter.

"I must say I'm embarrassed by how many of you have seen me with my shirt off."

More laughter.

"Please, folks," Cousey continued, "generous as this proposal is, statues are for dead people. If you want to honor me when I'm dead, I suppose there's nothing I can do about it. As it is, the last time I checked, I was still sucking air and pumping blood. With all due respect, I must put the kibosh on this idea. You see, I'm just not comfortable with all the attention. Sure, it was fun for a while. Going to New York and L.A. on someone else's dime… riding in limos… seeing myself on the same shows I see celebrities on. It was a nice change of pace, an adventure, even, but the problem is I've never seen myself as a celebrity, just a doctor. Sometimes this old doc feels even older than he is physically. Frankly, I'm ready for this all to go away, so I can go back to sitting by my stump and having a beer and watching the sunset."

Utter silence.

"If you wish to honor anyone with a statue, might I suggest the thirteen-year-old girl who has been forgotten in all the hoopla, the girl who was the original victim here? The girl who communicated with me in my dreams, heard my concerns about the lake and, in the end, told me how to stop the hummingbirds. I was certain I was headed to my death, but Millie wouldn't let them hurt me. She did more for me than any of us ever did for her, that's for sure. So please, if we honor anyone, let it be Millie Fremont. She is central to the lesson we must take away from all of this: that we must give a damn about our neighbors,"— with this he slapped the podium, hard enough to cause several people to jump — "even when it means leaving our comfort zone, just like the Good Samaritan who stopped to help someone the 'holy' types had passed by. That is all I have to say. Thank you for listening to this old fart prattle on, and for honoring me with this lovely dinner."

Polite applause as Cousey returned to his seat.

The chairman glanced over at his fellow Board members with raised eyebrows.

"There you have it, folks. The Board will take up Dr. Cousey's suggestion. If we're talking a life-sized statue, I think we could go ahead and make it bronze since the figure will be smaller. We'll let you know, especially if we need any photos of Millie from anyone who might have them. Thank you again, Dr. Cousey, for your candor. Now, if there are no further agenda items…" At this, one of the Board members leaned forward and said something, the chairman putting his hand over the mike and shaking his head, "I hereby adjourn the business part of this meeting to get on with my favorite part: dinner!"

***

For years Kevin Cousey had made repeated attempts to be reinstated at Harper Memorial only to be rebuffed on every occasion with galling, sympathetic smiles. Still, he kept his hand in as best he could, kept himself current on the goings-on of his field. He was ready for a comeback even if they weren't, using the platform of his newfound celebrity to make statements about ENT that, for the first time in a long time, were getting people's attention.

Maybe they'll rehire me this time, he thought, *even if it's only part-time.*

He was wrong.

Although he didn't see himself as compromised, they told him his patients would, and that meant doubt, losing referrals to the bigger hospitals in the city. It could even mean lawsuits as doubt morphed into accusations of malpractice, accusations he had never experienced in the entirety of his medical career. He smiled bitterly as he considered his transformation from Golden Boy to Liability, each of them capitalized.

It occurred to him there was no longer any reason not to look into the group he had long thought about joining. He was pleased to discover they were more interested in what he could do than what he couldn't, gratified when they said they did, indeed, want him. Wanted anyone willing to forsake the money and cushy lifestyle that were the perks of practicing medicine in the West for how he had always seen the profession — Medicine as Mission — practiced where there would always be a need for it: the African bush. By the time the first fall winds blew across the lake Dr. Kevin Cousey was prepared to relaunch his medical career with Doctors Without Borders in the Afram Plains region of Ghana, West Africa.

His departure looming in only a week, the Board scrambled to get the statue ready, having originally planned its dedication for April 15th. Intent on allowing him to see the fruition of his idea.

As things at Lake Tanaka tended to be, the unveiling of Millie Fremont's statue was inflated into an all-day event, always with various ways for people to make money. Cousey grimaced at the sight of many of the same vendors he recognized from the tent revival, the absence of a single, huge tent creating room for many more booths. This time you could even get corn dogs and caramel apples, and the carnival company was back with an assortment of kiddie rides operated by the same seedy-looking bunch. All of which seemed a sacrilege given what had happened here as recently as April. Given how grim the lake's prognosis was mere months ago.

The unveiling would take place at sunset. This alone pleased Cousey, for it was well known that it was his favorite time of day. Already the statue seemed larger and more important than the person it immortalized, covered with a pink tarp held in place by a silken rope. Although he hadn't seen the finished product, he had been privy to information from the early stages of its planning, and that a likeness based on a photo her biology teacher had taken of her at recess — one of the few photos of her known to exist — had been chosen, subject of course to the need to incorporate hummingbirds into the finished product.

Seeing as how the statue had been his idea, he felt obligated to stick around for the dedication and the Board-sponsored barbecue at the Rod & Gun Club afterward. While he planned to divide his time between the lake and Africa — the warm half of the year here, the cold half of the year there; he wasn't a fool—increasingly he felt the need to leave. Now. A feeling that was only reinforced when they unveiled the statue that, quite simply, was not Millie.

In spite of their assurances to the contrary, it was stiff and posed-looking, thoroughly hokey. In face and even in gesture it bore little resemblance to her, with the added insult of the pigtails Millie never had springing from her head with their oversized bows like a caricature of girlishness. A cross between Heidi and Pippy Longstocking. It was all Cousey could do to hide his displeasure.

At least they got a few things right, namely the setting — in the field by the lake — the realism of the hummingbirds perched on her hand and shoulder, the spelling of her name on a granite pedestal that looked better than the statue it supported, and the inscription beneath it:

"In commemoration of Millicent 'Millie' Fremont, Lake Tanaka's Patron Saint of Hummingbirds." His words, and he was grateful they got at least this right.

Give them credit for trying, he thought.

Still, it was far from a perfect memorial, his thoughts turning to the far more appropriate shrine the hummingbirds had erected in the woods. He thought about it as he climbed the hill to the barbecue, harkening back to the time he had climbed it with Galvin. How much had changed since then — and how little! Perhaps because he was unchallenged, but his steps felt heavier tonight, anger and its accompanying adrenalin giving way to the exhausting effects of idiocy. At the barbecue he ran into Buddy Maxwell and Paul Mahr, both of whom were game for what he had in mind the next morning.

***

It occurred to them that they hadn't been out there since before they'd busted Galvin. Now that it was fall, their walk in the woods was more satisfying, from the starbursts of red and yellow and orange leaves all around them, to the crunch of khaki-colored leaves under their feet, to the mintiness of air that carried the first hint of snow. As they walked, Cousey's curiosity grew. Very few hummingbirds had been seen on the lake since their mass exodus on April 15th, even as the number of feeders grew in homage to them. In what amounted to the ultimate irony, the lake missed its hummingbirds. Cousey was curious to see what they would find today. His question was answered as soon as they approached the last clearing and heard the distant roar of wings.

They arrived at the tree to find its crown whirring with hummingbirds. They had based themselves there, an honor guard for a shrine eighty feet above the forest floor.

"What I wouldn't give to go up there and have a look," Cousey said.

"Your wish is my command, Doc," Maxwell said. "You still got that fancy little phone camera?"

Cousey looked at him, surprised. "Yes. Buddy, are you sure?"

Maxwell smiled. "Sure, I'm sure. Hand it over and I'll fetch you some pics. The day this ol' country boy can't climb a frickin' tree is the day he packs it in."

"OK, if you're sure. But please be careful."

Maxwell laughed. "Sorry, Doc, but sometimes a fella just has a hankerin' to... you know... break his leg... or even his dadburned neck, especially if I touch somethin' I ain't supposed to, and them little suckers knock me outta the tree. Look out below!"

Maxwell grinned, and Cousey and Mahr couldn't help but laugh.

"Call it a goin' away present, Doc, from me to you."

"But I'll be back in six months."

"That's what you say. We're talkin' Africa, man."

More laughter.

With that, they gave him a boost to the lowest branch, his powerful arms taking over from there. It was like watching a gorilla in action. Before they knew it, he was at the nest.

"Ho-ly shit!" Maxwell said.

"What is it?" Cousey called up to him.

"Millie Fremont is up here, all right, and she looks... like an angel! Like she's asleep, is all! Why, I'm tempted to give her a little shake — just to see if I can wake her up."

"Please don't," Cousey said.

"Just messin' with you, Doc. These birds are already actin' kinda crazy."

"Take some pics and get the hell out of there," Mahr said.

"Don't worry; I will."

The birds left him alone as Maxwell chanced a dozen pics and clambered back down, and they stared at them with their mouths hanging open. Before them was the most beautiful girl any of them had ever seen. Not a bruise or a sign of death anywhere on her. She glowed, the look on a face with closed eyes with long lashes and fernlike eyebrows, soft, full lips, and a delightful little beak of a nose, one of perfect repose. Tiny purple flowers sprinkled her hair like pastel stars. Her long, slim fingers were curled around a bouquet of fresh flowers of astonishing color and variety, shaped like a hummingbird with a bird of paradise for its beak.

Where the hell did they get that? Cousey thought, mesmerized by a flower he had only seen in Southern California.

Likewise, the photos revealed what had happened to the body bag: cut into strips and placed all around the body like the aureole that frames a saint.

St. Milburg, Cousey thought, convinced, his eyes welling up with tears.

"Wow!" he said, wiping his eyes on his sleeve. "Thanks, Buddy," he said, giving Maxwell's arm a little squeeze.

"No problem, Doc."

"I think it's called 'closure,'" Mahr said.

Cousey smiled. "Once again you've nailed it, Paul. All of a sudden I feel good, damn good — for the first time since that day on the swimming platform. A day that seemed to change everything."

"It didn't change nothin' for me," Maxwell said.

"Maybe I should shoot a video of you," Mahr said.

"That's OK."

"I don't know about you guys, but I'm ready for a beer," Cousey said.

Maxwell grinned. "Just one?"

Cousey smiled. "Is it ever just one? One at a time, at least."

"OK, Doc, now is as good a time as any. What is your beef with charter schools?" Mahr asked.

Cousey laughed in disbelief. "Paul, you're irrepressible!"

"I was going to ask you before the birds attacked the tent revival, but somehow the timing... didn't seem quite right."

"OK, you asked for it: Charter schools are considered 'alternative education,' and to me it doesn't make sense to give them public monies when our kids in public schools already aren't getting the education they need. Case in point: A teacher friend of mine tells me kids get only two weeks of penmanship — two weeks! — in public school these days, the standard 'wisdom' being everyone texts and uses word processors, so it's no longer important to know how to physically write the language. I can remember the endless hours I used to spend writing the letters of the alphabet, both small and capital, print and cursive, with those cheap wooden pens that looked like pencils and smeared ink everywhere, on specially lined paper with big and small spaces between the lines. Of course, all that training went out the window when I became a doctor — doctors having their own written language, after all — but at least I had it down at one point."

Mahr laughed.

"Anyway, I must say I was shocked the time I helped her grade papers only to discover high schoolers writing like third graders! And these kids can be accepted by charter schools if they can't hack it in public schools, places that can hardly be accused of having the highest academic standards; all of which strikes me as diluting the whole purpose of giving our kids a basic education! I say let's invest more in our public schools before we divert money to schools that are basically private, make their own rules, and lack accountability. Let's make sure our kids have the Three 'R's down before we teach them organic gardening and kinetic sculpture, stuff they can learn in college or voc ed if they really want to."

"For a guy on the wrong side of the argument, you sure make a good point, Doc."

Cousey laughed. "I'm not quite sure how to take what I suspect was an example of doublespeak."

"Good," Mahr said with a chuckle, "let's leave it that way."

"Save for some paddlins I probably had a-comin', public school ain't never done me no harm," Maxwell said, the forest erupting with laughter.

Final

Not since his practice was purring along and he still had a family to come home to had Kevin Cousey felt so much at peace. Mahr and Maxwell, Kath and Sheila — four unlikely people who had become his closest friends — saw him off at Lambert Field. An indescribable sadness gripped him as they waved goodbye, he turning to put on his shoes after passing through Security while they returned to what already seemed a different world that would go on without him. Although he would only be gone for six months, he couldn't help but feel the sharp sort of pangs one feels when leaving something precious behind.

When you've really lived in a place it's only normal to feel sad when you leave, he thought.

The feeling abated somewhat by the time he took his window seat, distracting himself with the gas pumpers and the baggage handlers, the guy with flashlight cones directing the plane from its berth. Things always looked slightly unreal from the window of a plane — like a world seen through sunglasses — his thoughts drifting to what John Galvin's last minutes must have been like.

Nothing more unreal than being pecked to death by hummingbirds, he thought.

St. Louis to New York; New York to Frankfurt (nice, big airport; one he'd never seen before); Frankfurt to Lagos (just stay on the plane for an hour), then Lagos to Accra and the novelty of a runway fringed by palms. Summery smell of sunbaked asphalt as he walked across the tarmac to the shuttle bus — yet another novelty! — grateful to be met after the Trifecta of International Travel (Immigration, Baggage, and Customs) by a tall, smiling African holding a little sign with "Dr. Cozy" written on it.

"Dr. Cozy?" the man asked as Cousey approached.

Cousey smiled. "Dr. Kevin Cousey, at your service, but please, call me Kevin."

Already he felt at home, even though he had never been to Africa before.

Immediately registering the difference between spelling and pronunciation, a man accustomed to language grinned broadly as he puzzled at the sign.

"The Brits taught us that a 'cozy' is something one puts over a teapot to keep the tea warm. I think somebody has misspelled your name."

"No biggie," Cousey said. "I like the sound of it. Why, I even prefer it."

The man laughed. "That being said, how does one spell your last name, Kevin, in the event I must write it?"

"C-O-U-S-E-Y."

"Aha! Oh, I am Dr. Kwame Ambu — but you may call me Kwame."

Big smile, firm handshake, and dressed for church, with shoes that tapered to a lethal point at fifteen inches.

"After Kwame Nkruma?"

"Ah, someone has done his homework! No, because our first president and I both were born on a Saturday. On what day of the week, might I ask, were you born?"

"Monday," Cousey said.

"That would make you 'Kojo.'"

"'Kojo Cousey' — I like that! It has a nice… bounce to it!" Cousey said. "Do the women have similar names?"

"Yes, and you will know them all by the time you leave Ghana… not the women, just their names," Ambu said with a grin.

Cousey liked the man immediately.

Chaos outside the terminal, people lined up beyond the ropes, craning their necks as if awaiting the arrival of a celebrity. In Africa, every passenger was a celebrity, mugged by exuberant family members. Suspicious-looking guys in baggy print shirts grabbed hold of luggage unbidden, trying to direct passengers to their overpriced taxis.

"O bruni!" one of them cried when he saw Cousey.

As always, he was grateful to be met at the airport, as there was nothing more disorienting than arriving unmet in a strange city, all the more so if it was international.

"Our hotel is close by," Ambu said. "Let us freshen up and partake of a real Ghanaian lunch, fufu. Now, does that not make your mouth water? Afterward we can see the sights or, if you prefer, you can take a nap."

"I've never been a good napper; all I do is lie there with my eyes closed. Tell me, what are some good things to see?"

"Despite its size, in Accra there are not many after the Nkruma Memorial. The Aburi Gardens are nice, but they are a bit out of the way, and traffic is always problematic here. Then there is Labadi Beach, right in town."

"It's all the same to me, Kwame, never having seen any of it. Whatever you feel like showing me will be fine."

Ambu smiled. "I never tire of watching women stroll the beach in bikinis with a cold beer in my hand. Labadi is a tourist beach, but it can be fun if you are in the right mood."

"I'm in the right mood," Cousey said.

"It is decided, then. Today the beach, tomorrow we will travel to the Afram Plains to meet our colleagues."

"Say, what does 'o bruni' mean?" Cousey asked.

Ambu smiled. "O bruni is a Twi word you will hear so often that you will tire of hearing it. Originally it meant 'wicked white man,' though nowadays it just means 'white man,' or even someone who is not from Africa. Ghanaians even call black Westerners 'o bruni.' Some people take it personally, but try not to. Most people are not trying to insult you, just label you in a generic sort of way. If someone insists on calling you 'o bruni' when he knows your name, then you may consider it an insult."

***

Fufu was the strangest thing he had ever eaten, yet it was very tasty once he had gotten past this. He heard it being made even before he tasted it, the whump! whump! whump! of a huge, wooden mortar and pestle as two women mixed cassava and plantains, one woman doing the pounding while the other turned the mixture by hand in a perilous-looking exercise in timing. The finished product had the look and consistency of a ball of dough, the centerpiece of a spicy soup —

in this case, peanut, featuring vegetables, in this case, okra and garden egg, and meat: in this case tilapia. You ate it with your right hand, the left hand considered dirty because it was used for toileting, breaking off a bit of the dough to scoop up the rest.

They spent the afternoon drinking Stars and Gulders in twenty-one-ounce bottles, the standard size for a beer here— a standard-sized Western beer is called a 'baby,' Ambu explained, eating gizzard kebabs and watching women who were unusually curvaceous by Western standards saunter by with their good posture and a rhythmic swaying of their hips that captured their female essence, at once animal and fluid and sensual. Everything happened by that day at the beach, from the acrobatic troupes that worked the crowd for donations (invariably setting up shop in front of o brunis), to people going by on rented horses, to a group of college types building an elaborate sandcastle. Although they didn't swim, they rolled up their pant legs and walked in the surf a couple of times. Enhanced by the oxygenated air and expansive surroundings, their conversation ranged far beyond medicine. It was just the sort of day Kevin Cousey needed, a soothing transition to Ghana after the emotional fallout of departure and the ever-wearying bustle of travel. He turned in shortly after a dinner of chicken jollof rice served with palm wine, and slept for ten blessed hours.

***

Accra was a city of jarring incongruities, from the two five-star hotels fronting Labadi Beach — "Your president George Bush stayed at this one," Ambu said — to cinder block houses with zinc pan roofs in dirt yards running with chickens. The clinic in the Afram Plains was a nine-hour drive into the interior, necessitating an early start. After a Western-style buffet breakfast they headed out in the sort of vehicle that, to Cousey, epitomized Africa: a box-fendered old Range Rover, its original olive green faded to gray.

As they drove, Cousey was struck by a couple of things, one of them the contrast between gleaming new cars cruising an immaculate new highway through shabby villages where nursing mothers unabashedly exposed their breasts and small children ran around naked.

The other thing was the recklessness of the passing, or "overtaking," as they called it here. Drivers tailgated the car in front of them like dogs on a bitch in heat before passing it seemingly at will, at times forcing oncoming traffic to yield. Cousey whistled in disbelief when they were passed by a van that was simultaneously being passed by a bus on the opposite shoulder. The modus operandi here was simple but deadly: The space is yours if you get there first, especially if your vehicle is larger. It was a good thing the drivers were alert — or *usually alert,* he thought, noting the occasional burned-out vehicle on the roadside. It seemed everything about Africa was on a larger scale, including disaster.

Growing signs of urbanization as flatland gave way to hills.

"Kumasi, the second city, capital of Ashanti," Ambu said.

"How big?"

"Two million people."

"Big enough."

"Kumasi is the home of the *Sika 'dwa,* or Golden Stool, an object that is sacred to the Ashanti people," Ambu said, launching into an explanation of a stool that is said to have descended from the heavens into the lap of the first king. "The Golden Stool is believed to contain the souls of the entire Ashanti nation; thus the desire of the British to capture it during the Ashanti Wars. No one is allowed to sit on it, not even the Asantahene, or King of Ashanti, nor is it ever allowed to touch the ground. In 1900 the War of the Golden Stool was fought when the British governor demanded to sit on it, resulting in the annexation of Ashanti to the British Empire, and we remained a British colony until the slightly more famous Kwame, our first president, declared our country's independence in 1957."

Soon they were in the much smaller town of Mampong —"Home of the Silver Stool," the second most sacred stool, with its accompanying history — and, an hour later, in the still smaller town of Ejura, where they left the highway. They proceeded down the dirt road that wound its way through town, past the big mosque on the right as they negotiated a minefield of potholes that would have done the moon proud. Just outside of town they met up with a battered car with a flapping fender that looked as if it had once been a Peugeot, dust roiling from the like water from a speedboat.

Ambu smiled. "Bush taxi! Unless you have your own transport, it is the only way to reach remote villages. Two more hours and we are there!"

For the first time, Cousey understood the need for a Range Rover. At times the vehicle lurched to either side as they navigated the ruts, its windows splashed by the long troughs of water they were forced to pass through. In a couple of places the road was reduced to a single lane, its crumbling edges giving way to ten-foot drop-offs. At one point they crossed a bridge made from two flattened logs that demanded the driver's utter concentration.

Africa! Cousey couldn't help but think. *The real deal!*

As they traveled he became aware of a familiar sound. It grew to a roar as they approached a round mud hut with whitewashed walls and a thatched roof, a bao-bab with a trunk thick as the house looming behind it and swirling with birds: the African version of crows in their distinctive white tuxedos, forming a teeming wreath of activity around its crown, yellow weaver birds tending to the nests that drooped jug-like from its branches.

"A little girl lives in that house," Ambu said. "Some people say she is a witch, but she has never harmed anyone, so they let her live. She feeds the birds, and the birds love her. They are always around. Some people say they protect her. Some people say she even controls them."

Cousey was incredulous. "Can we stop and talk with her?"

Ambu raised his eyebrows. "My friend, it is getting late. We still have another hour to go. It gets dark by six o'clock, and I do not like traveling at night. At night, bandits cut down trees and stop your car and teef you. Besides, I do not know the family of the girl."

Cousey was insistent. "Please, five minutes? It's important."

Ambu eyed him evenly. "Very well."

They got out and approached the hut. Two men were seated at either end of a bench, playing a game — Ambu later told him it was called *oware* — that entailed putting seed pods into two rounded rows of depressions in a wooden board. The larger of the two men played aggressively, emphatically slamming the pods into their holes. He suspected the men, their strong, sinewy arms those of a farmer, had been drinking. Sure enough, a bowl made from half of a calabash gourd sat on the ground between them, one Ambu said contained either *pito* — homemade beer — or palm wine. Sensing Cousey's gaze, the larger man turned and glared at him.

Ambu spoke to the men, relaying their dialogue to Cousey. "The bigger man is saying he is the father of the girl. He says many o brunis want to see her. He says it will cost us five cedis apiece."

"OK," Cousey said, handing Ambu the money.

The man made a curving motion with his hand to indicate she was behind the hut.

"Not the most likable guy," Cousey said as they were walking away, a sudden image of John Galvin flashing through his mind.

As they circled the hut, the chirping and roaring of the birds were punctuated by a familiar whump! whump! whumping! sound. An old woman was doing the pounding, a young girl the turning.

Ambu smiled at Cousey. "The old woman is very strong. *Ete sen* (How are you)?" he asked as they approached.

"*Mehoye* (I am fine)," the woman said.

There was a fierceness to her smile. Her arms and legs as gnarly as tropical vines.

The girl looked up, Cousey's heart skipping a beat as he met her gaze. Her silky skin was the color of milk chocolate, with a willowy gracefulness to her limbs and her hair cropped close like a schoolgirl's. There was no mistaking the eyes, dark and luminous and penetrating as they gazed calmly into his, the sheer beauty of the face they were set in like diamonds in a ring. The power behind them was unmistakable, and in them he saw the potential to inspire fear should it ever turn to anger. As he beheld her eyes, he knew he had seen them before — and why not her? A chill of recognition coursed down Cousey's spine. Long accustomed to thinking beyond the black and white box of science, he was as sure as he'd ever been about anything. If Millie Fremont was the reincarnation of St. Milburg, why couldn't this African girl be the reincarnation of Millie Fremont... if only as a natural continuation of the life that had been denied her? If she could travel fourteen hundred years from one continent to another, why not to another continent just fourteen years later? Was anything impossible? The merest suggestion of breast buds prompted him to ask her age.

Ambu asked for him, the girl responding in a low, musical voice that seemed too old for her body.

"She is saying she is twelve. Kevin, we need to go."

"I know, I know. One more thing: Can you ask the girl if she has… anyone to look after her, especially at night?"

Ambu asked her. After first sharing a look with her grandmama, the girl answered.

"She is saying her mother looks after her on weekends when she is not working in the market at Ejura. Her father and grandmama watch her during the week."

"Her grandmama, too?"

Ambu spoke to the girl. "Yes, she is saying this is the house of her grandmama. This is where she stays."

Cousey smiled, relieved. "OK, good. Please, thank them for me."

Ambu thanked them, flashing Cousey a puzzled look. "Kevin, what is this all about?"

"I'll tell you in the car. One more thing: Can you ask the girl her name?"

Ambu asked her.

"Her name is Marla."

Cousey shuddered. *Too close.*

"Please, tell Grandmama that Marla is a very special girl. Tell her that she must be protected from boys and men at all times."

Ambu conveyed the message. Grandmama smiled and nodded, cackling like an old hen as she made a cutting motion with her hand.

Ambu laughed with her. "She is saying she knows this very well, and she will protect her. She says any man who touches Marla before her wedding night will lose his manhood. She will see to it personally!"

Cousey smiled broadly, bowing to them. "Goodbye, Marla. Goodbye, Grandmama."

***

Ambu frowned at the shadows slanting across the road when they were on their way again. The visit had burned up half an hour of precious daylight.

"Now we will not arrive until after dark," he said.

"I'm sorry," Cousey said. "I wouldn't have asked you to stop if it wasn't important."

For most of the next hour, he related the story of Millie Fremont.

"So, you are something of a celebrity," Ambu said when he was finished, impressed.

"Alas, it was never my intention."

"Westerners are skeptical of spiritual things. It is good to hear someone who sees things as we do. Kevin, I think you will do well here."

Cousey sighed. "I'm ready to do something well again. Marla is a beautiful little girl. I can only hope Grandmama protects her. I can only hope the same thing that happened at Lake Tanaka doesn't happen here."

Ambu glanced over at him and smiled. "*Gyedea*, Kevin. Faith. Let God do His work while we do ours: the mission you shall soon embrace."

Cousey smiled, allowing himself the rare luxury of relaxation as he gazed down a road fringed by palm trees, lined with people riding bikes or carrying things on their heads or machetes in their hands or babies wrapped in colorful cloths tied to their backs, everything softened by the golden light of early evening. A tattered sheet of clouds streamed across the heavens like an ice floe, the sky appearing like water through its cracks. Africa lay before him and above him and all around him, and he marveled as he passed through what amounted to an interactive documentary of a beauty so rich and exotic it had a presence about it, filmed in hi-def and surround-sound.

Whenever he saw a particularly burdened-looking party, Ambu stopped and picked him up, using the ropes he kept handy for securing cargo to the roof, the area in the back reserved for people and sometimes animals when seating ran out — two or three people and their animals cramped for space, but ever grateful for a lift — and soon the vehicle was packed with happy, babbling Africans and their animals.

"It is wrong not to stop on a bush road when people are walking and there is room," Ambu said.

"Is that the unwritten law… or your personal philosophy?"

"It is both… for some, at least. I am afraid Ghana is no different than your lake. People take care of themselves first, then their families, then their friends, then their tribe. After that, no one else matters, and this is what plagues Africa. Not colonialism. Even though it has not been a factor in most parts of Africa for over fifty years, colonialism is the scab Africans forever pick at, forever blaming the West for their troubles. They do not see that they are their own worst enemy, forever tearing down what the man before them has built — I suspect as much out of pride and jealousy as anything — and, as a result, nothing stays built. Altruism is the rarest bird here, the animal most in danger of extinction," Ambu said.

As they drove, Cousey felt the sort of rush he hadn't felt since he began his medical practice, so long ago as to seem like another life. It occurred to him that he, too, had been reincarnated, reborn in a guise that felt so right it gave him the chills. The people who shared this twilight ride, with them the pungency of bodies that worked the land for a living, the animated banter punctuated by laughter that was comfortingly human despite its strangeness, the protests of small, tired children that were universal, the occasional squawk that reminded you a chicken was under the seat with its legs tied together, might very well be the patients he'd be seeing tomorrow. As they got off one by one, thanking the driver with smiles marked by overbites and missing teeth, Cousey found himself overwhelmed by the sweetness of it all.

Tears filled his eyes as he remembered Ambu's words: the mission you will soon embrace.

How good it felt to hear the word "mission" again, uttered without nostalgia by someone other than himself!

Ambu smiled over at him as if reading his thoughts.

"Welcome home, my brother," he said, putting a hand on Cousey's shoulder as Africa unfolded before them.

– THE END –

HISTRIA BOOKS

Addison & Highsmith

Other fine works of fiction available from Addison & Highsmith Publishers:

For these and many other great books visit
HistriaBooks.com